The Man I Married

The Man I Married

Elena Wilkes

hera

First published in the United Kingdom in 2020 by Hera Books

This edition published in the United Kingdom in 2021 by

Hera Books
28b Cricketfield Road
London, E5 8NS
United Kingdom

A CIP catalogue record for this book is available from the British Library.

Print ISBN 978 1 80032 505 0
Ebook ISBN 978 1 912973 49 1

Look for more great books at www.herabooks.com

Printed and bound in Great Britain by Clays Ltd, Elcograf S.p.A.

I

To Ian

And to Amy, Susie-Sue, and Karen

Prologue

Blood has a smell.

I look around me. I'm sitting on a bench.

It comes again.

It's visceral, like meat.

I gaze down at my hands. I don't recognise them; they lie upturned and curled in my scarlet-stained lap. Every crease is dark with what looks like rust. My palms open like flowers and I feel the skin stretch and tighten. A cold breeze skims the wet patches on my dress. The wool sticks unpleasantly to my skin and a chill slides down my spine.

I close my eyes.

Behind the lids the dying winter sunlight zigzags in orange and purple flashes. Somewhere beyond the bushes I can hear the girls, giggling. I squint; I can't see them now, but I know they're there.

'You can't hide in here forever you know!'

There's a woman's voice. She's getting closer.

'I think it's time we should be going though, don't you? Come on!'

I squint. The viburnum bush trembles; its propeller-headed flowers nod and bounce in bright pink bells against the thicket of black. I imagine her reaction as she walks past. She'll see the state of me and I'll see her face: the shock at my matted hair and dishevelled clothes. She doesn't know who I am and I wouldn't want to scare her.

'You don't know me—' I'll say. She'll look at me wary and unsure.

'—But can I tell you what happened? I think you'll understand when I explain.' I'll hold out my hands and she'll see the state of them.

I know my story is also her story.

I've done this for her, for the children, for all of us.

I turn my face into the last rays of the sunlight and let it seep under my skin.

That's why he's dead.

Chapter One

Some men have a darkness in them.

But this wasn't a man, this was a boy.

I walked into the sparse grey office at HMP Ravensmoor one blustery afternoon in April. I hadn't been back to Yorkshire now for over a year. 'It's the weather,' I always joked. 'It puts me off.' That was true: partly.

A sudden gust of wind against the barred window sent weird flickering stripes of light across the table where he was sitting: there was an odd, sickly smell in the room, like cheap plastic. He might look like a boy but his presence filled the whole room.

'Ah we meet again! Lucy isn't it? I'm sure you remember me. I'm Simon.' He got up and held out his hand. The familiarity jarred. I was acutely aware of the dry, yet sticky coolness of his palm against my own.

'I'm sorry Mr Cartwright couldn't be here,' I replied, stiffly. 'He sends his apologies.'

I pulled away from the handshake, gesturing for him to sit, which he did, shoving his hands under his thighs and leaning forward the way small children do.

'No problem.' He twitched a shrug and smiled. 'I'd much prefer you as my probation officer. I asked for you specifically. Did your boss mention it?'

I ignored the question. Dropping my briefcase onto the desk, I heaved out a file and laptop and flipped open the lid. I could tell his eyes were raking over my every move, but when I looked up, he was staring intently at the edge of the desk, tapping his foot against the leg and making it judder.

I busied myself, pretending to study the screen as it loaded, but my eyes kept being drawn to this small, tight figure. His incongruity struck me yet again: the pale freckled complexion with a hint of outdoor ruddy tinge, the longish pretty-boy dark hair, his slim build, like some posh sixth-former. But the blue eyes had a deadness behind them that betrayed what he'd done.

He looked away suddenly. 'Oh! The door's closed. Does that bother you?' he went to get up with a false show of politeness.

I knew precisely what he was doing; he was hinting at how dangerous he was. If this was some kind of test then I wasn't going to fail it.

'It's okay, Simon, if it doesn't bother you then it doesn't bother me.' I looked down at my files as though I were searching for something, aware that his face had dropped. 'This is just a quick chat about your release tomorrow. Nothing too scary… I don't bite,' I added.

I was pleased to see he wasn't smiling now. He sat down again. He looked a bit sulky.

'So, you have your train ticket from York to King's Cross sorted?'

He nodded into his chest.

'I see your new address is on file, and you're quite clear about the sex offender registration process, yes?'

I saw the tiny flinch at the words but he managed another nod.

'Then I think everything is in order this end. Is there anything you want to talk to me about? Any questions?

Any concerns you've got?' I was pleased I had the upper hand.

He raised his head and regarded me carefully. I was reminded how blue his eyes were.

'People have been telling me you're clever.'

'Oh yes? Well, don't believe everything you hear.' I met his steady gaze.

'The guys on my wing have been saying stuff. Some of them have come up from the London nicks and a pretty girl like you attracts attention wherever she goes. Word gets round. It's amazing the things they talk about—' he flashed me a smile. His teeth were unpleasantly small, like a row of seed pearls.

'Really.' I didn't drop eye contact. I wasn't going to be drawn. I'd seen it all before: the vague sexual impropriety; the intimidation masquerading as flirtation.

He returned my stare. 'They say you're good with people. I can tell you're the kind of person who can suss people out, so we've got a bit in common already,' his smile spread to a grin. 'I'm hoping we'll be able to keep in touch once I get settled. It'll be nice to see a friendly face once in a while and have a catch up. You're based in London too, aren't you?' His look didn't waver. 'North London. Am I right?'

I felt a slight frisson of alarm. 'Dave Cartwright is your allocated probation officer,' I replied carefully. 'And the meetings and appointments we set up are to do with ensuring that you won't re-offend and to help you lead a positive and fulfilling life after your release, *not*—' I made the point firmly, '—to have a chat.'

Even as the pat words left my lips, I knew I didn't believe one iota of it with this individual. He had an obvious need to control and to dominate. It came off him like a stench.

He paused, quietly assessing me before he spoke. 'Do you think people out there hate me?'

'I think people hate the kind of offences you committed.' I didn't allow my gaze to waver.

'But do *you* hate me?'

The question caught me off-guard.

'I mean, I wouldn't blame you if you did. I took children – I bought *little* children, used them and sold them on, so I can see why you would.' He held out his hands as though he was explaining something perfectly commonplace. 'How could I have done that? It *is* revolting, I know, but then to me it was just a business transaction… You know, like selling on a second-hand car, or a collectable watch or a fancy bit of estate jewellery – it was all the same, just a different thing to me, just a different commodity.' He stopped speaking and I realised he was slightly out of breath. 'But now I see what I did. I can see it as wrong which is why I'm a different person now. I've changed. Things have changed me.'

Nothing had changed him.

I was amazed I was the only one who could see it. I hated this part of the job for exactly this reason: how easily these kinds of offenders pulled the wool over people's eyes. I knew he'd be out on the street again, scoping out the children's homes, sniffing round the runaway kids on the street, having a laugh, giving out the bits of dope and the sweets, making them feel wanted and special. I saw the bait going down and the ultimate snap of the trap. They'd been bought and sold and didn't even know there was a market – Such was the lure of wanting to be loved.

'You don't believe any of that for a second do you, Lucy?'

He'd caught me.

'It's not about what I believe. It's about what the evidence tells us, Simon,' I lied. 'Stuff from your risk assessment and the work you've done with your psychiatrist... Err... Dr Webb.' I flipped through the file. 'For example, your psych report says—'

'We both know those are just the men who control all this,' he waved airily. 'Expensive professionals producing expensive reports to justify their own existence. A little old probation officer can't challenge the might of a psychiatrist, can you Lucy? That's not your job. You *have* to buy into what they tell you, but I can see you don't. It's written all over your face.'

'As I said—'

'I didn't do these things because I've been damaged, or abused, or because I have a sickness, which is what Dr Webb wants me to believe. I did it because...' he leaned forward, holding his palms out as though he was offering me a gift.

'Because I enjoy it... Oh, sorry—' his gaze dropped and so did his smile. '—Past tense, I *enjoyed* it. But I won't anymore.'

'Really.' My voice was stony.

'No, I'm not going to do any of those things again.' He shook his head like some abhorrent parody of a five-year-old. 'And it's not the desperate egos of the psychobabblers and the shrinks who've made me stop. It's something far more...' he gazed up pretentiously, searching for the word, '...compelling.'

'Go on.' I wasn't sure I wanted to hear this.

'I'm being haunted.'

7

I didn't allow my gaze to falter.

'Have you ever been haunted, Lucy?'

'I don't know what you mean.'

'By the things you've done?' The corner of his mouth tipped into an odd smile. 'I suspect you are... But I'm haunted by the children.'

Something cold prickled, but I didn't look away.

'The children. They come here. They stand at the end of my bed at night, watching me. Just watching, nothing else.'

'And who do you think they are?' I pressed.

'I don't *think* anything, Lucy. I know who they are.'

The darkness behind his eyes moved like a quickening shadow.

'Of course they're not *real*—' the azure eyes flickered abruptly in amusement and I felt the ground shift; I could breathe again. 'Dr Webb says they're a manifestation of my guilt and show an aspect of my new self-awareness.'

'Right.' *God these men and their high-blown assessments.* I tried to keep my face open and neutral. Not a flinch.

'He says I should use them as a reminder of who I once was, someone I recognise and acknowledge but a person who I don't know very well anymore.'

If only that were true. 'Good,' was all the response I could muster. His smug self-regard irritated me.

'When you think about it, I'm so lucky, aren't I?' He brought his hand and laid it flat on his chest like some camp drama teacher. 'All these wonderful professional people who believe in me now. It's fabulous, don't you think? The psychiatric help I've received! The fantastic case workers who've supported me! I'm really, really blessed. It must be great for someone like you to see someone like me on the road to recovery.'

'It all sounds very positive, Simon.' The hint of sarcasm in my tone wasn't lost on him and he sighed appreciatively.

'I'm glad you think so, Lucy. I think so too.' His eyes went blank. 'What you think is *very* important to me.' He leaned forward a little. 'I want to show you. I want to show all of you that I've got better. All I'm asking for is a chance, Lucy, a second chance...' the blue of his eyes glittered earnestly. 'Even you must give me that, surely? I mean, come on, don't we all deserve one of those?'

I stood outside the prison and rang for a taxi. Then I dialled Emma, praying she'd pick up straightaway.

'You've finished then? Great! Me too.' I could hear the smile in her voice. 'I was just catching up on a bit of retail therapy. They've got some brill shops up here haven't they?' I felt my neck and shoulders relax. Suddenly things felt right. 'The two of us should wangle a trip up here again...' she paused. 'Erm... What's the matter?'

I shook my head in silent astonishment. Emma had this unfailing ability to intuit even the tiniest change in my mood.

'How *do* you do that? You're the only person I've ever met who can read me like a book without my saying a word.'

'Lucy,' she sighed. 'You're hardly a difficult book – *War and Peace* you are not. In fact, I'd say you'd struggle at being a two-page pamphlet.'

'Thanks, Em,' I grinned. 'You always make me feel so much better about myself.' And that was true; she actually did.

'More revolting offenders then, I take it?'

'More revolting offenders.' I nodded dully. 'A particularly grim one who's going to be released down in London so he'll be on my patch, unfortunately. A sex offender. Kids.'

'God! I don't know how you keep doing it. You're too good at all that stuff, that's your problem. You'll notice Viv doesn't give me all the shit cases because she doesn't trust me with them. She thinks we'll end up on the front page of the *Sun*.' She chuckled merrily. 'You need to give off an air of complete incompetence like I do, and she'll leave you alone. Anyway, given all that, I'm assuming you need vodka?'

I realised I could discern the chink and hubbub of chatter in the background and I felt my jaw drop. 'You're already in the pub?'

'Does the Pope stand on a balcony?'

'Not with you, I hope. You'd keep harassing him to try on his hat.'

Emma laughed. 'You're such a comedy cock-head, aren't you? Anyway, I'll text you the address so don't be long, I've got shed-loads to tell you.' She sounded excited.

'Oh God. Really?' I clocked the taxi coming around the corner. 'Right. The cab's coming. Get me a voddy. A double. Actually, if I'm going to listen to you, I shall probably need two.'

The taxi ticked up to the kerb and I slid into the back and gave the driver the name of the pub. It was strange being back in this part of the country; it all looked the same but very different. I was so thankful that this time tomorrow I'd be on my way back down south where no one's interested enough or cares enough to gossip about what you've done or who you're seeing. Your business is your business. Yorkshire was too full of knowing looks over the photocopier, the smirks and whispers – 'Is she the one who…?' In the end I'd become a joke. Moving was the only answer. It was the best thing I could've done and I had Emma to thank for that.

She and I had met six months before at some Personal Development for Probation Staff conference in a terrible Holiday Inn in Loughborough. The place was a dizzying expanse of static nylon carpets and tootling pan-pipes wherever you went. The chap running the course kept banging on about 'effective communication' but was using a dried-up marker pen and kept scrawling diagonally across his flipchart so that we had to peer at it sideways. Emma was sitting across the other side of the room and kept sighing and making me laugh, So when we were asked to 'find ourselves a partner' we made a bee-line for each other. Unfortunately, it was one of those psychometric personality test quiz things that we both knew was a complete bag of bollocks before we'd even started it.

'Oh Lord, a northerner. This'll be interesting,' she'd grinned. 'I'll speak slowly and you can see if you can manage to read my lips. Now… Are you ready? Eyes down… Okay… Agree or disagree on a scale of one to six…' She pored earnestly over the paper.

'Eh? You've lost me already.'

'Christ, a real clunker. I'll mime it if you like.'

We giggled non-stop like schoolkids, finally working out that her personality type was a 'caregiver': a people-pleaser, highly sensitive, looking for approval from others, with a tendency for self-absorption. By contrast, I was a 'duty fulfiller': well-organised, loyal, faithful and dependable with a need for security that tipped over into being controlling.

'So I'm a bit of a namby-pamby twat and you're a mind-numbingly boring fascist. Is that what it's telling us?' She pushed the sheet across the table.

'Seems like they've got half of it right, then.'

The course tutor gave us a warning look, so we had to shut up.

'So are you pining for your whippet and your chavvy jeggings then?' she said as we were packing our stuff away.

'You're such a snob and so behind the times,' I shook my head and laughed. 'Most of us have pit bulls and shop at Primark.'

'But you do put curry gravy on chips, don't you?' She looked genuinely concerned. 'Don't burst my bubble about that too!'

'Rest assured,' I patted her arm. 'You can sleep easy. We do.'

Meeting her in the bar later meant we laughed and got drunk together. Getting drunk meant I told her stuff that was happening back at work, only hinting at the 'Dan' situation, then weeping copiously but scrabbling to find a tissue. She'd gone off to the toilet and come back with a whole toilet roll and got a dirty look from the bar manager. I didn't tell her the whole sorry story, but I think she filled in the blanks.

As a result, it was Emma who persuaded me to put in for a transfer when a vacancy came up in her office; it was Emma who told me what to say in the interview and told Viv, the boss, she'd heard on the grapevine that I was brilliant. I don't think I mentioned whippets or fried potatoes or curry in that conversation, and I certainly don't think even Emma realised the extent of the favour she'd done me. She never knew how grateful I was that I was finally able to run away – even if it was mostly from myself.

–

The taxi dropped me outside the pub just as the first few spots of rain hit the pavement and I pushed through the doors. It was one of those wonderful old Yorkshire pubs with a wide bar and wood panelling, its big crackling fire roaring in an ornate black grate. I was greeted by a madly waving arm.

'You made it!' Emma's moony face grinned up at me as I squeezed into the table by the window. 'A log fire in April! Shit, you can tell we're in Yorkshire can't you? My meeting was great by the way!' She lifted up and rattled a posh-looking carrier bag. 'How was yours?'

'Don't ask a single thing.' I dropped my coat and brief-case onto a spare chair and exhaled heavily. 'I don't want to talk about it. Talk to me about stuff that's got nothing to do with work.'

She pushed a chinking vodka and tonic across the table at me. 'No probs. Get that one down you while I show you my latest purchases. Look at this—' she reached into the carrier and pulled out a black and shiny top to go with all the other black and shiny tops she'd got. 'Half price! I'm going to wear it when I meet Connor tonight...'

'Connor?' I looked at her in surprise. 'You mean *Connor* Connor?' I took a long swig of vodka and tonic as things began to fall into place. 'So he's up here too, then? Ah, that explains it – and there's me thinking you were desperate to come on a jolly with your lovely mate. I wondered why you were so keen to volunteer to come with me on a visit to sunny Yorkshire when you could've stayed basking in even sunnier Hackney. I might've guessed.' I took another swig. The cold drink slipped down deliciously.

'I did want to come up here with my lovely mate!' she protested. 'And you know how much I love the cold and rain! I just thought while I was up here with *you*, I might as well...' she waggled her head comically.

'What are you like?' I gave her an old-fashioned look and took another long slurp. A half-melted ice cube tinkled dully down the side of the glass. Connor was her latest. The latest in a long line of lying charmers who treated women like shit.

'Let me get you another of those,' she nodded pushing her chair back.

'Guilty conscience?' I grinned.

'No! He's up here with the Prison Inspectorate. He's been off doing his inspecting thing, and I did my obligatory prison visit and then I went shopping. Who could possibly find anything wrong with that?' She batted her eyelashes.

'His wife, maybe?'

'Ex-wife.'

'Ex-wife in the same house.' I picked up my glass and let the ice cube slither into my mouth, crunching it loudly.

She flapped her hand. 'Anyway, anyway... Guess what?' She paused for dramatic effect.

'I'm guessing you're not getting that other drink.'

'I'm being serious!'

I sighed. 'Go on then. Tell me.'

'He's moving out and moving in!'

I literally felt my mouth open. 'Moving out? What, you mean out from wifey's?'

She grinned wildly and nodded.

'And moving in? With you, you mean?'

She started babbling on, ten to the dozen, describing the row he'd had with 'that cow', what he'd said, what the cow had said, all the complications running in together as I desperately tried to unscramble the very convoluted story.

'Anyway, anyway, that's not all. Guess the other thing?'

'I really can't.'

'He's looking into emigrating to New Zealand. Their Corrections department is looking for people just like him!'

'And?' I felt a quiet tickle of apprehension.

'He wants me to go too.'

I shook my head slowly.

'Can you believe it?' she beamed.

'But you said no?'

'No... I mean, no, I said yes!'

'You can't do that—' the words came out in a kind of choke that shocked us both.

'Oh Lucy!' She put her hand on mine and I pulled it away. 'Don't look so upset! Luce!... Lucy!...'

I could hear her voice but it felt very far away. She went on about how it wasn't for another six months, and that they would need to sort his divorce out and the finances. There was his house to sell... And that would probably take forever... All I could think was that I was losing the one and only person in my life, really. There was no one else, no one I cared about... Not since...

'Anyway, haven't you got a relation in Australia or somewhere?'

I sniffed and nodded. 'Perth, yeah—'

'Well then!'

'Well then, what?'

I bit the inside of my lip, hard, and fiercely brushed the stinging tears away.

'It's so not like you!' She rummaged in her bag for a tissue as I struggled to collect myself.

'Ignore me, really.' I took it, dabbing my face and blowing my nose. 'Too many awful prisoners telling me too many awful things, that's all. A shitty day, that's all.'

'You never have shit days, Luce. Oh, apart from...' she reached forward and extracted a bit of tissue from my lip '...when you look like you've got snot on your face.' She made me laugh and almost set me off again. What *was* this all about? Why was I so upset? Was it just the thought of the months, probably years without her, or had Gould got to me more than I thought? A surge of emotions tumbled one after the other. I hated being up here again; I saw my old life spooling out behind me: old wounds, old shames that dogged me wherever I went.

I'd have to deal with it sooner or later.

Emma downed the rest of her drink and glanced at her watch, nodding at my glass. 'Are you ready for the other one now?'

'One?' I pulled myself together. 'Tell them I'll have the whole bottle.' I gave her a watery smile to show just how fine I was. 'Are we eating here?' I glanced round. 'It looks okay.'

'Christ Luce, I've just realised what an arse I am—Err... Like, I said I'd meet Connor,' she winced apologetically. 'I know I should've said... You probably assumed, quite rightly that—'

'Stop, Em.' I put my hand out and she paused. 'Honestly, you seeing Connor tonight is no problem. I'd say if it was – I really would.'

'Would you, though? You look a bit teary—'

'Well that was just the shock announcement of you moving to the other side of the world,' I felt my chin wobble again but managed to halt it and give her a crooked smile. 'You're right; it's months away yet, we've got loads of time, and absolutely, I should take the opportunity to visit and go and see my brother.'

'You sure?'

'More than,' I patted anxiously under my eyes. 'God, what a sight I must be. I bet I've gone all mottled.'

She tipped her head on one side and peered at me. 'Nah, only... Um... A bit corned beef-y.'

'Thanks for the frank assessment,' I laughed, grabbing my bag and looking for the loo. 'I'll go and re-grout the gaps. Watch that lot, will you?'

I left my briefcase and coat on the seat and headed for the Ladies', squeezing past a couple of guys in suits, muttering the usual *sorry, sorry,* hoping they wouldn't notice my wrecked face, and then got the weird feeling I was being watched.

There was a man leaning against the bar. He caught my eye and looked away shocked, as if he knew me. I instinctively paused: *lop-sided face, slanted mouth, long nose.* *Did* I know him? Then I realised, awkwardly, that I didn't. *How embarrassing!* I felt his darting gaze as I leaned into the door to make a swift exit.

Shunting the lock across, I sank down onto the toilet seat and rested my head against the paper dispenser. Its cool metal edge dug into my temple: hard and soothing. Why the hell was I so rattled? It wasn't just Emma, or Simon bloody Gould, it was being back in this town: this whole damn area. I'd watched all those names – Bramham, Tadcaster, Towton – on the road signs skimming by the taxi window, bringing back places I didn't want to remember, things I'd tried so hard to forget, but his place wasn't going to let me. It had to remind me of all the crosses I was supposed to bear, the weight of them dragging me down further and further, forcing me to see myself and the people I thought I'd left behind.

People like my mother.

The sadness of her face the day I left. The shame of my behaviour scouring my cheeks into red rawness. How could I have just gone like that? But I knew I had to for my own sanity. I made the telephone calls to home the same time every week: the duty ones, asking the right questions and carefully listening to the answers, offering up all the right noises, but giving nothing of myself. But now here I was – having to see her and face it all again.

And then there was Louise. Mustn't forget Louise. Only five years older but it always felt like fifty. My big sister with that look plastered on her face, the 'so-you-think-you-can-waltz-in-here-with-your-fancy-clothes-and-posh-accent-do-you?' expression. My big sister, who finely combed through every conversation for details to be brought up months or maybe even years later – looking for those deliberate intonations and slights to prove what a truly selfish, self-absorbed bitch of a daughter I really was.

What would I say to either of them? That *I'm sorry, Lou, for leaving you to deal with everything. And I'm sorry, Mam, for abandoning you, even though you haven't got a fucking clue who I am now and you were never really interested in me in the first place…*

I pushed the hair out of my eyes and sat up straight. None of it made one hoot of difference. I couldn't have stayed, anyway. There was no option. I had to leave Yorkshire. I had no choice.

Dan had seen to that.

Threading my way self-consciously back through the bar, I made my way back to my seat, glancing once to see if the bloke was still there. He wasn't. I was almost disappointed. No one had taken a second look at me in a very long time. Emma was sitting at the table trying to put her lipstick on using a chrome salt cellar as a mirror.

'Jesus, Em!'

'What?' She smacked her lips together decisively. 'Oh, you look brighter! Less corned beef, more ham on the bone.'

I poked my tongue out at her, snatching a quick look back at the bar as I sat down.

'Someone caught your eye?' she squinted playfully.

'No.' I flicked my hair back. 'I just went to the loo, that's all.' I picked up my drink and made a 'cheers' motion. 'To new beginnings, then?' I grinned and she chinked her glass against mine and grinned back.

'You could do with someone in your life again, you know.'

'Could I?' I took a sip, aware that she was studying me. 'I feel far too old for all that.'

'You're only thirty-bloody-four!' she barked a laugh like a seal. 'There's plenty of men about! They're a bit like shoes: you buy a pair, find they're a bit tight, or too loose, or go saggy after a while...'

I laughed. 'Yeah, alright! I get the picture, it's just a bit visual!'

'So you go and get more, don't you? Forget that last bloke, what was his name again... Dan, wasn't it? Dan, Dan, the complicated man.' She shook her head. 'We've all had one of those. They appear to be one kind of person but actually they're another.'

I nodded and gave a wan smile. Yep, that was him. This kind of man who asks loads of questions – who comes over like a sensitive kind of guy, *who really wants to get to know you,* you think. You're right; he does. And then he uses what he knows against you. 'Don't ever fall in love,' he joked with me once. 'It makes you too vulnerable.'

'You want someone who's nice, funny, caring, a bit mad...' Emma mused. 'Someone a bit like me.' She cocked an eyebrow suggestively.

'You're forgetting I've sat in your bathroom when you've been shaving your legs,' I pulled a face. 'Sorry. You've gone and spoiled the mystery now.'

'Ah. Shame.'

'Anyway. What time was your dinner date?'

'Bugger!' She leapt up and then glanced around, giggling. 'Oops! Was that a bit loud?'

'Go on,' I shook my head laughing. 'Have a lovely time.'

'But what about you?' She looked genuinely concerned.

'I am going to spoil myself, actually.' I gave her a snooty look. 'I'm going to go back to the hotel, have a long bath with bubbles and possibly a glass of wine, and then order the nicest room service meal that our meagre expenses allowance can stretch to. And then, finally, as an end to a perfect evening, I shall get into bed and watch reality shite on TV to make me feel better about my own shite reality. What could be nicer?'

She looked relieved. 'Sounds good. See you then.' She bent to kiss me goodbye.

'Have fun,' I grinned, watching her scurry happily towards the door, peering into the street for a second before pulling out her umbrella.

The smile fell from my face. I picked up my drink and drank the rest of it slowly. I watched the gay yellow and blue stripes of her brolly bob past the window and felt my heart contract. I wasn't going to do anything of the sort. I was probably going to go back to the hotel, type up the notes from my meeting with Simon Gould, and then send them to Viv. I was even going to say in the email that I thought Gould was 'over familiar' and I believed it would be more appropriate if a man dealt with him from now on. That would wipe the smirk off his face. It was just a shame I wouldn't get a chance to see it.

Gathering my things together, I picked up my briefcase and glanced up as the door pushed open. A man and a woman clattered in, all breathless and giggly, their coat shoulders darkened with rain. A memory of me and Dan caught in a rainstorm suddenly ached as a brilliant flash of lightening lit the doorway and a gust of wet whistled through the gap. I was going to get soaked but I didn't care. I stood, pulling on my coat and wondering if I had my umbrella. I stepped back.

'Arrgh!'

My heel trod heavily into someone as I barged awkwardly into the poor person standing behind me.

'Oh God! I'm so sorry!' I wheeled round. 'I didn't know you were—'

The man was pulling a tortured comic face, and I realised with a jolt of embarrassment who it was.

Mr Lopsided.

He smiled his funny smile. 'I was going to say, "don't worry, I've got another," but—' He gazed down at his shoes and my eyes followed his. There was a definite dented scuff mark on the toes of both.

I looked up, horrified. 'Oh hell, I'm so sorry!'

His eyes swivelled sideways and I realised he was holding out a half empty beer glass with a large brown stain seeping slowly into the cuff of his shirt.

'Oh God! Have I done that?' It was a ridiculous question and one I clearly knew the answer to.

'Please don't apologise. It was an accident—' he attempted to shake off the worst of it. It wasn't working. His eyes caught mine and he grinned. 'You caught me good and proper! I have to give you that.'

His laughing eyes were the colour of newly burned ash. I must have looked mortified, but he only shook his head. 'Seriously, it's not a huge problem, but would you do me a very big favour?'

'Of course, of course,' right now I would do anything he asked.

'Would you look after this…' he put what remained of his pint on the table. '… And this…' He peeled off his jacket and shook it out, peering at the wet sleeve suspiciously before laying it on the back of the chair. 'I think my shirt bore the worst of it. Please don't feel bad… It's honestly no big deal but if I could just rinse it now, maybe I won't have to smell like a brewery all evening?' He smirked and began to unbutton the soggy cuff.

'Yes! Absolutely!' I pulled off my coat and it came away with the sleeve inside out. 'No problem. Take as long as you like.' I sat awkwardly on the edge of the seat, not knowing where to look as he wandered off. I didn't know what to do with myself: putting my elbow on the table and then taking it off again – I didn't dare watch the door of the Gents in case that just looked weird too, so I pointedly stared at the floor. Eventually he appeared, clutching a wad of paper towel and dabbing at his wrist. I immediately stood up, far too hastily and then immediately thought that came over as rude.

'Are you heading off?' The wet stained cuff sagged horribly against his wrist. 'It still looks a bit dodgy out there—' he dipped his head and peered through the window.

'Yes… I mean no… I'm— Oh gosh, look… Umm… Could I offer the cost of the dry cleaning or something? It looks a bit—' I gestured weakly. 'Is it ruined?'

'No, no, it's perfectly fine – Absolutely no professional assistance required—' he wrinkled his nose as he sniffed at his sleeve. 'Mmm… I've gone from Black Sheep bitter to a very pungent grapefruit and pot pourri. Maybe I should have stuck with the beer…'

He saw the look on my face. 'Oh look, I'm joking! I'm joking! Please! Think no more of it… And seriously if you don't have to be anywhere important, you might think—' He nodded over. The rain was twisting in skeins down the glass, with an occasional gusting splatter that sounded like thrown gravel.

'So do you?'

'Sorry?'

'Have to be somewhere?' I realised he was smiling.

'No.'

'I'm Paul, by the way.' He held out his hand, 'Oh! Mind the sog.'

The heat of it was warm and welcoming and I managed a smile. 'And I'm Lucy.'

'I think I might just get another drink,' he eyed his dreg-filled glass ruefully.

'Oh yes!… No! Let me get that.' I fumbled for my bag and found my purse, 'It was Black Sheep, you said?'

'Sure was. You'll have one with me though, won't you?'

'Well, I shouldn't…'

There was a clatter as the barmaid collected a clutch of glasses from the next table. 'I wouldn't think about going out there if I were you. Brrrr! Orrible!' She grinned at both of us. 'I'd stay here in the warm.'

I paused. 'Okay then… Thanks.'

'What are you thanking me for, I thought you were buying?' He arched a look and his face went from unconventional to attractive, all in the space of a grin.

'I'll go and find a table a bit closer to the fire, shall I? There's a good one over there. I can hang myself over it and have a quiet steam,' he winked at me but I pretended I hadn't seen it as I made my way to the bar. Despite my embarrassment I felt a bit fuzzy and giggly. He was a nice guy actually: funny, I could tell he was comfortable taking the piss out of me and I liked that. I smiled as I chanced a look round. He'd found a seat in a corner nook and, with a shock, I realised why this place had made me think of Dan. I'd been in this pub before.

With him.

A squeeze of something sour churned in my stomach. I suddenly recognised the wooden settle and the sepia photographs of the aproned coopers, arms folded, flat caps staring unsmiling into the camera lens. I'd not only been here, I'd sat in that exact seat.

Oh God.

I took a breath.

You never say no to seeing me. I remembered that teasing lift at the corner of his mouth. I loved his mouth.

Why would I? I'd said. *I love seeing you… I love you, in fact.*

The words had left my lips without me wanting them to. I remembered the deep burn and thrill of having spoken them out loud.

That's all a bit full-on, isn't it Lucy? Don't spoil it. Things are good as they are, there's no need to mess it up.

The pain had twisted like a razor-sharp barb. I watched his beautiful mouth articulating each syllable. I learned to hate his mouth. I learned to hate what came out of it.

'Yes, love, what would you like?' The barmaid shocked me back.

I ordered the drinks and paid for them feeling acutely self-conscious. My heart was racing inexplicably, and I was aware that my jacket must be all crushed at the back and then wondering why the hell I was bothered. I carried the glasses over.

'So,' Paul went to take his pint. 'What were you doing at the nick?'

I nearly toppled both drinks. 'How the hell do you know that?'

'Ooops! You okay there?' He rescued his glass from my clutches and sucked the drips from his fingers. 'I was visiting and I thought I might've seen you leaving the wing. Have I got that all wrong?'

'You were visiting?'

He laughed. 'Ah, yes, sorry. No. I have to come up on occasions and supervise some of the clinical interviews. I even do one or two occasionally. I'm the senior psychologist now, although I used to work in prisons full-time.' He sipped his pint as things began to fall into place.

'Ahh!... The infamous Dr Webb!'

He blinked in surprise. 'Hell, am I famous?' he looked at me over the rim of his glass.

I shook my head and laughed. 'No... Well, maybe... In the right circles.' I resisted all impulse to mention the Simon Gould case. I didn't even want to think of it.

'And how about you?'

I picked up my glass. I shook my head while swallowing. 'Just a paltry Probation Officer. Your name crops up a lot in the reports I read – mostly prisoners in the London nicks though.'

'Ah,' he nodded. 'I'm based at Head Office, but I travel all over the country dealing with some of the interesting cases.'

Interesting. I felt a tiny itch of irritation.

'So tell me then, who did you say you were seeing in Ravensmoor?'

'I didn't.' I was suddenly aware that might sound abrupt, and blushed.

'Gould. Pre-release interview.'

'Ah yes, Gould. I've spent a lot of time with Gould. He's a fascinating case.'

'To some I suppose.' *Why the hell had I just said that?*

I detected a smile at the corner of his lips. I felt a hole begin to open up in front of me.

'But I see you don't.' He picked up a beer mat and ran a thumbnail down one edge.

I swallowed. Right now, I could not afford to start challenging a senior psychologist, particularly one I'd only just met. Even I knew that.

'No, not really.' The itch moved into my spine.

His grey eyes searched mine. 'I can see why. I would think Gould found you threatening. You'll have scared him a bit.'

He peeled a thin top layer of card. It lay curled on the table.

'He'd be aware that you had all the control, and he wouldn't like that. He would immediately want to find ways to undermine you. He's a very astute individual. But it's a feral intelligence. It's instinctive: like an animal. He can smell vulnerability. But of course—' the ruined mat landed on the table. 'I can tell he wouldn't have got anywhere with you,' He picked up his drink, sipping a little off the top.

'But you supported his release?' The words came out before I could stop them and he paused, clearly a little shocked.

'Me? Christ, no.'

'But I thought—?'

'Absolutely not.' He pressed his lips together. 'I've made it quite clear to Gould, to the parole board, and to anyone else that would listen that I still believe him to be a danger; that's why I've advised very stringent release conditions. I want him on a tight leash, and I can see by your face that you do too.'

I watched his face: so impassioned, so alive, so clear. I smiled and put my glass down.

'Let's not talk about work stuff anymore, shall we?'

'You know what, you're absolutely right!' He slapped his hands on the table. 'Did you want another?... Vodka, was it?'

'Sorry?' I glanced down to find my glass was empty. 'Oh!'

He had stood up and was moving towards the bar before I could answer. I realised that I hadn't had anything to eat since lunchtime and the alcohol was already going to my head. I took a surreptitious glance at him while he was waiting to be served. He was leaning on one elbow and his crumpled cuff had shunted back. It showed his watch and the breadth of his wrist. His hand briefly touched his neck. The fingers were beautiful: square and slightly tanned. I immediately looked away, scared in case he caught me staring.

He came back with the drinks, settled himself and then winced a bit sheepishly. 'Sorry about all that... Before...' He scratched his chin. 'I have a tendency to put people on the spot a bit. I'm a tad inquisitorial by nature...' He grinned ruefully. 'Just tell me when I'm doing it and I'll back off. So, come on then. Tell me all about you. Your accent for instance – where's that from?'

'Oh, round here – but I'm based in London now.'

'Whereabouts?'

'Highbury,' I smiled. 'But I work in Hackney.'

'Ah, Highbury, I know bits of it.' He smiled back. 'Nice. I'm in Belsize Park. Do you have family?'

'A mum and sister. Mam's ill. Dementia.'

'Oh, sorry to hear that.' He looked genuinely concerned. 'You know you said "Mam" not "Mum". It's nice.'

'So how about you?' I deftly changed the subject. 'Where are you from?'

He sat back a little and put down his glass. 'My family are from Hertfordshire originally, that's where I grew up. But they're all gone now, I'm afraid. I never had any siblings, and no cousins, even – None that I'm aware of anyway. I'm afraid I don't come from very long-lived stock... Oh! And talking of not living very long... Are you starving? I am. Do you fancy dinner or something? I wonder what they do here?' He squinted up at the board on the wall behind.

I could barely keep up with him.

I laughed and he looked back at me expectantly.

'I could eat a horse between two bread vans,' I drawled in broad Yorkshire.

'Ah, I do like a woman with a bit of class.' He pronounced it with the short 'a'.

'You're funny,' I thought I might be flirting, but after more vodkas than was good for me, I'd stopped caring.

'Am I?' He regarded me, his head tipped on one side.

'Funny ha-ha or funny peculiar, though?' I gave him a quizzical look. 'That's the important question.'

'Probably a bit of both,' he chuckled back. 'I hope so anyway.'

–

I can't remember what we ate, or even what we talked about. I was aware of the time passing, the massive logs on the fire turning black and jewel red, the heat pulsing as the jostling bodies around the bar swam by in shapes and colours. I wasn't paying proper attention, I knew that. I also knew that despite my previous reservation, I was enjoying myself. I really was. I was finding this unusual man attractive; he made me laugh, he was intelligent and considerate and attentive and I deserved a bit of care and attention. Emma had been right. Why the hell shouldn't I?

I said something cheeky and he laughed. The lights from the bar caught his face and his eyes sparkled. I was aware of how close we'd got: how our cramped elbows had slid across the table, making us tight in our own circle. I was drinking too much, I knew that too. I was letting loose, making things inevitable. There was his mouth, soft, moving in front of me like a pale crescent moon, laughing suddenly; his lips moving with underwater slow-ness, shaping words that I wasn't sure had any meaning, but it didn't seem to matter. I lifted my glass and saw an endless snowflake pattern of fingermarks, quite perfect, and his odd face, right there, and me not understanding why I had ever thought it odd and not strangely beautiful. I was aware of all my nerve-endings: they felt suddenly alive; every breath was light and new and felt clean and sharp.

He's probably done this before.

Don't be stupid; of course he has, the voice in my head said. He's confident and at ease. It's bloody obvious.

He laughed right into my eyes and I knew he was keen, and his keenness made me feel confident too. I knew the game, I wasn't daft. I looked smilingly into his face. If I stayed right where I was he might lean forward, tip his head and kiss me. I felt it. Caught. We gazed, bright and engaging, into each other's eyes: a direct stare that didn't need words to tell us what we were both thinking, and then suddenly he looked away. He concentrated on a little ring of water on the table and I immediately felt ridiculous, sitting there so rapt and eager. He half-smiled, casually drawing his finger through the circle. It made a little squealing sound. Someone dropped a glass behind the bar and I took a breath as the real world thumped back into place.

He glanced around. 'What time is it?' He looked down at his watch. 'Ten past nine. What do you think? It might've stopped raining. Should we make a run for it?'

'Yeah. Great. Good idea.'

I managed the words clumsily, pushing my chair back, licking and biting my lips to get the feeling back into them, leaning down to grab my bag. The table edge loomed horribly close. He stood and moved with me, guiding me towards the door. I felt a prickle of intimacy as the heat of his hand hovered around the small of my back, the sensation tickling my spine as we stepped out onto the pavement. Dark clouds were roiling in overhead and a fine rain was slanting through the streetlights, making the world look patchy and phosphorescent. We fell in step with that uncomfortable tension of not holding hands: a couple yet not a couple, but knowing we were only a hair's breadth away from being just that.

We walked side by side in silence for a few moments. I was concentrating on my feet and we bumped shoulders as he went to cross the road.

He chuckled. 'Hey, careful! Which way are you going?'

'Sorry, sorry,' I mumbled. 'I wasn't watching.'

He stopped and looked at me. 'No, I meant which way? Do you want a lift?' He nodded to a white Audi.

'But you've been drinking.' I felt the road moving slightly beneath my feet.

'Actually, *you've* been drinking, I stopped hours ago.'

'Oh! I didn't realise...' I stood there awkwardly, not knowing what to say, my mouth feeling sticky and clumsy with drink, my face a stiff mask with me sitting stupidly behind it.

'Let me take you to where you're staying at least?'

'No. Really. I'd rather you didn't.'

'A cab, then.' He looked round. 'You can't be out here, in—' He paused. I thought he was going to say 'this state,' and I felt a rush of annoyance. '— this weather,' he added.

I drew myself up and staggered slightly. 'I'll be perfectly fine, thank you.'

'Would you like to exchange numbers?' he looked amused and patted his pocket.

'Why not?'

The words didn't come out as I wanted them to; I knew I sounded off-hand and aloof. He was signalling that the evening was over; part of me wanted it to be, and then another part of me... I distracted myself by scrabbling in my bag for my phone and then fumbled as I tried to turn it on, but the screen only flashed and died.

'Oh shit! The battery's gone.'

'Don't worry.' He grabbed my hand and turned it over. 'Here.' He pulled a biro from his pocket and began to stroke black numbers onto my palm. The ink felt cold and tickled a sensation right through my belly. I felt myself sway a little, watching his face as he worked. *This isn't you*, that little voice inside me said. *You don't meet men in pubs and think what it would be like to... Be like to...* We were so close I could smell his skin. His lips twitched a little with concentration. He ended with an ostentatious full stop, smiling, but didn't let go of my hand.

'There.' He blinked up at me.

I hesitated. He didn't move. I knew what I was going to do. I leaned forward and kissed him: gently at first, but then with an urgency and a passion, letting go of my reserve, my fear, my self-consciousness. I kissed him until there was no breath left in either of us.

'Fuck...' he said.

I could feel his erection against my hip. I pulled back slightly and slipped my hand down his fly to squeeze it.

'Fuck.'

'Yes. Let's,' I laughed. This man didn't know me. I could be anyone I wanted to be. With him, I felt liberated. Desire flooded through me in a wave, buoying me up; the sheer thrill of it; I was in control. He pulled me to him again but I pushed him off. 'But not quite yet,' I said flirting outrageously now. 'Come on.' I offered him my hand. 'Let's go.'

'Where?'

I was surprised when he took it meekly like a child. I only smiled. 'Somewhere.'

'What do you mean, somewhere? Where's somewhere?'

But I didn't answer. I led him, a tad unsteadily, across the road. 'This one?' I gestured to the Audi.

He fumbled for the keys, the immobiliser flashing into the darkness. I stalked round to the passenger side and yanked the door open. He paused for a moment to pull his shirt out of his trousers to cover his embarrassment. The power rushed through me.

He looked across the roof at me. 'Are you sure you're feeling okay?'

'I'm *faa-bulous*,' my lips caught on my teeth. 'How 'bout you?'

'Okay. Fabulous, so where are we going?' He turned to look at me. I couldn't see his eyes.

'Just drive and I'll tell you.' I waved at the road.

He didn't argue, just started the engine and glanced in the mirror. I didn't look at him. The streets skimmed by. I was minutely aware of every movement he made, the length of his thigh, the turn of his cheek, the back of his hand on the steering wheel. I began to feel a little more sober. *What the hell was I doing?*

'Just follow the main road out of York and then the signs for Bilbrough.' My voice sounded almost normal. A small tickle of trepidation slid quickly into excitement. *I was doing this. I really was.*

He didn't ask me any more questions. The windscreen wipers squealed a little in protest on the half-dry glass, smearing the road-view, laying it out there in front of us, long and empty. We drove, silently. The sky overhead was dark, black almost, the roads lined with trees that were silvered into sentinels. He peered at the lit road signs. 'How far are we actually going?'

'Don't,' I said, already knowing this was completely barmy.

'Don't what?'

'Ask questions. Turn off here.' I remembered something.

'Here? You're sure about this?' He glanced at me.

We'd come here as kids. I knew this place almost as though I'd dreamt it.

The road straightened out with bleak fields on either side. His phone rang and he ignored it.

'I have no idea where we are.' He looked around, anxiously. 'What if you're one of those female serial killers?'

'Then you won't have to worry about finding your way home, will you?'

He roared with laughter. I could see he liked the fact I was off-beat and outrageous; *this was really me*, I told myself, *but where had this me come from?*

We passed signs for the town centre. The fields became scattered houses and barns and then a school and a pub and then the streets narrowed, with collapsing red-brick Georgian houses and shop fronts. The pale square tower of a Norman church rose up from behind the trees.

'Pull up over there.'

He squeezed in under a low overhang of branches just as his phone rang and he dragged it from his pocket and switched it off.

'Someone wants you.'

He didn't answer. 'Where now?'

I inched out of the passenger side and walked away up the path next to the church, knowing instinctively he would follow.

He looked round. 'Okay?'

'Keep going.'

We walked along the gravel path down through the churchyard, past the ragged black tombstones, picking our way over slides of mud and puddles. The wind picked up as we rounded the walls of the church.

'I can't do this.' He suddenly wheeled round, pushing me back abruptly into the stone, catching me completely off-guard. He pressed himself against me, his hands cupping the sides of my face. I stared back at him, chin raised and unflinching. He didn't kiss me, he just held his face so close that his eyes lost all focus.

'You're going to have to.' I breathed his breath, our lips tingling but not touching, his hips jammed against mine. I was in control of this and I knew it. The equal amounts of excitement and terror set my whole body trembling. I pushed him off and walked quickly up the path that ran alongside the river towards a copse of trees. The sounds of the water churning and splashing almost cancelled out the shouts up ahead. Teenagers by the sound of them, their voices whisking away into the rushing water as it tumbled over the weir.

'Here.' I led him further into the shadows as we turned, me tugging my skirt up and pulling at my tights and then grabbing his flies to unbutton them while he stood there, seemingly incapable, his hands hanging limply at his sides, his breath rasping a little as he leaned into me. His erection slapped into my stomach before he entered me in one shocked gasp, my leg hooked ungainly, my knickers awry. Our kiss was animal, clumsy, open-mouthed, our jaws and teeth and chins grinding into each other, our tongues not caring about the wet and the spit as he pushed himself into me over and over. Neither of us made a sound. I clung to him, feeling his shoulders powerful and sinewy under my hands as, through half-closed eyes, I watched the red jacket of a jogger flash past and heard the languid chatter of a dog-walker on a mobile phone.

They were so close – one sideways glance and they would have seen us – their proximity making things dangerous, urgent, and I came, shuddering and gasping, his breath was wet on my neck. I opened my eyes. His forehead was tucked under my jaw; he nuzzled in, burrowing like a small animal.

Somewhere, far off, a dog barked and the ghostly outline of the trees whispered and shifted overhead. Everything was different; I was different. The remaining fuzz of the alcohol lifted, leaving behind some strange, hollow clarity I'd never felt before: not like this. It was as though I *knew* him; like I really knew him.

My hands were still on his shoulders; his every movement was mine too. My whole body thrummed and responded with his. *This was the bit of me I'd been missing and he'd just found it again.*

'Christ,' he said thickly, half laughing, half in amazement. 'Where the hell did you come from?'

'I was sent,' I whispered smiling. 'I was sent to do terrible things to drive you insane.'

He lifted his face and laced his fingers into my hair, pulling my head back and kissed me again, his eyes wide open. I saw something there, right that moment: a split second of desire and want and attraction, and yet something else: something that looked like fear. He leaned in again and we kissed, very gently. I smiled at him softly. 'Come on.'

He helped me scramble out of the bushes and onto the path, but he didn't let go my fingers, only wound and linked them into his own.

'Why all the way out here?' he tugged playfully.

I grinned. 'I just wanted to see if you would.'

We walked for another minute or so without him saying anything. 'You're a funny mixture, you know that, don't you?'

'Am I? Is that your professional opinion?' I gave him a playful sideways look.

'No, that's an "I'm intrigued by you" statement of fact.'

He said it so seriously and calmly I couldn't think of how to reply.

'I'm not... Like... *this*... Usually.' I felt almost bashful. 'I feel a bit embarrassed now.' I concentrated on the movement of my feet.

'God, don't be!' He barked a laugh. His hand swung with mine. 'I think you're probably quite a complex person. I like that.'

A tiny thrill rippled: he thought I was different. He liked that. Then a sudden dampening thought that I was a bit of a fraud, that I really *wasn't* like this and that deep down there was just the same old me, waiting tediously in the wings.

'Would you come back to my hotel?' he said quietly.

I was scared, excited, slightly sick, happy and wary all at the same time. Good things don't happen to me. Good things don't happen to me, particularly in bloody Yorkshire. Was it possible that the bad spell could be broken – or did I have to live like this forever? Could I give myself a chance? Could I?

'Yes,' I said.

—

His room smelled of difference. His bag was on a chair, unzipped, the toe of a sock peeping disarmingly through the gap. The bathroom was in darkness, but the door was ajar. His washing stuff was sitting by the side of the basin: a toothbrush and toothpaste, deodorant and his razor. The homely intimacy of it pulled at my gut and I suddenly thought how much I wanted this: how much I'd missed it.

'You okay?' I realised he'd been watching me.

'Of course.'

'You don't look okay.' He came across and put his hands on my shoulders.

'Don't I?'

'No.' He continued to look at me, scrutinising my face as though trying to read something there, I didn't know what.

'It just feels a bit weird. Being here.'

'Uh-huh.'

'As though I shouldn't.'

'Well technically, you shouldn't.' He reached forward slowly and slipped his fingers around the nape of my neck. 'Both of us booking our single rooms, making those expense claims. We should really be considering financial accountability and professional standards...' Strands of my hair caught as he drew me into him. '...All those kinds of things.' The kiss was long and soft. The room tilted. My breath was knocked out of me and I found I was trembling.

38

'Are you cold?'

I shook my head.

'You're nervous.' He said it matter-of-factly.

'Not nervous, more, kind of...'

'Not comfortable.'

'Maybe.' My shyness returned a hundredfold.

'Don't over-think things.' His arm slid into the small of my back and I felt the pressure of his hips pushing me backwards. I instinctively wanted to look round, but he wasn't going to let me.

'Trust me,' he said. 'I won't let you fall.'

He guided me expertly to the edge of the bed, my knees buckling beneath me, and suddenly, there he was above me, gazing down. His expression was strange, troubled, as through trying to figure me out. 'You're still in charge; you're absolutely in control. I'm in your hands,' he whispered. I smiled, but he didn't smile back, concentrating instead on smoothing my hair, his fingers threading again and again, pulling painfully at the snags as he arranged it into a coronet around my head. I went to move.

'No don't,' he frowned. 'Don't. Stay like that. Look at your curls – they're beautiful.'

My eyes met his, questioningly. I watched his lips as they dipped towards me and I closed my eyes; I felt his breath skirting past my cheek and I opened them. His temple was pressed close to mine, his mouth in my hair, I could feel the wetness loud in my ear as he breathed me in. 'You smell so good,' he whispered. He looked into my eyes, and then kissed me again, letting his tongue gently tip its way against each lip.

'Don't build your walls up against me. I won't hurt you – not ever.'

My brain challenged every word, but my body responded.

'*Shhh*... Trust your instincts,' he whispered. 'They're right.'

My head raged in warning, but my heart responded like bathing in the warmth of the sun.

'*Shhh* now...'

–

The sky was dark, framed by the open curtains. I had no idea if it was late. The bedside light was making a faint buzzing sound. I shifted my ear and lay against his chest, listening to the quiet *thrub-thrub* of his heart.

'You haven't asked me.' His voice suddenly boomed into my ear. 'Sorry, were you asleep?'

'No, just drifting.' I stretched my toes into the cool patch at the bottom of the bed. 'What haven't I asked you?' Every joint, every muscle felt loose and unbound. My brain was a scrambled, pleasant wooliness.

'Anything.'

'What do you want me to know?'

'God, you're good.' I heard the smile in his voice. 'Very cool.'

I gave a tiny shrug against his side.

His chin rubbed against my hair. It made a rasping sound. 'I'm not married, or in a relationship, nor do I have any kids. I have my own flat, my own teeth and my own car. I am a nice, decent guy – and that's not a contradiction in terms.'

'Is that possible?' I let him hear the smile in my voice.

'Absolutely possible and absolutely true.'

'Well that's good, then.'

His chin flexed in amusement and then he yawned, widely. He pulled me closer to him. 'Is there anything else you need to know?'

'Not just this moment,' I nuzzled in closer.

'Like you say, that's good then...' His voice drifted lazily and then he went quiet. There was silence for a few moments more and I felt his arm jerk. I wondered if he'd fallen asleep. I peeped up, carefully. His eyes were closed and his breathing was quiet and regular. I lay there, luxuriating in his warmth, fighting off the tiny frissons of anxiety that kept running through me. *The last time I'd allowed myself to get close to someone... The last time I'd let my guard down... Dan.* The pain of it had been physical... Somewhere, deep inside, the ache was still there... I batted the thoughts away. This didn't have to be like that. Paul wasn't Dan and sabotaging myself had become like a muscle reflex: instant and automatic knee-jerk reaction. I snuggled in and shut my eyes. I wanted to enjoy this. It was nice... He was nice. He was so right: thinking, over-thinking, letting my imagination run amok. I just needed to let things happen.

–

I don't know what woke me. The side lamps were still on in the early morning light, giving the room an unpleasant grey glow.

I peered over the hump of Paul's shoulder at the clock. 05:17.

Carefully and very gently, I eased myself from the side of the bed and patted around for my clothes, pulling them on any old how, and then finding one boot had gone missing. Fishing blindly round, I found it, clunking it against the side of the bed. Paul's breathing changed and I paused, my own breath caught high in my throat. I waited. After a few seconds, he sighed deeply and turned over as a sudden flash on his side of the bed lit the room with a dim blue light. His phone flashed silently again and then went black. I knew I shouldn't look. I'm not entirely sure what made me, but craning over, I gently pressed the 'on' button, and there, in front of me, were a whole stream of missed messages and calls, all from the same number, but no name. It took a moment for my brain to register and then a squeeze of mortification caught in my throat. What had I been thinking? Was I completely stupid? *Of course.* A woman: a girlfriend; a wife, even. *Why had I ever thought it would be any different?* Closing my mind to the stark humiliation, I blindly fished round for the rest of my clothes, and grabbing my coat and briefcase, gingerly tiptoed to the door. It glided smoothly open without a sound and I glanced back. He hadn't moved. Slipping through into the corridor, I let the door click softly behind me.

The corridor lay in muffled stillness. I walked quickly, feeling exposed and vulnerable; my whole body tingling and burning with the shame of it. *Thank God I'd seen it when I did.* I was too old now to deal with all that kind of rubbish, too old and just too tired.

Stepping out onto the street and into the gauzy dawn, I made my way along the short route back to my hotel and up to my room. It was stark and silent, and within minutes I'd stripped off and was standing in the shower, letting the hot wash of water drum across my neck and shoulders, scalding my skin. How could he have lied like that? I tried to shake the image of him away. I'd embarrassed myself. *Jesus. I'd fallen for it all yet again, hadn't I?* The acute humiliation of it seared with the heat of the water. The only saving grace was no one knew. *But what if he tells people?* I didn't think I'd been seen though. I'd certainly make sure I never bumped into him again. If anyone said anything, I'd just deny it.

Pooling a large blob of shampoo onto my palm, I began to lather my hair, digging my fingers into my scalp until the skin tingled. I could almost make myself believe none of it had happened. *After all, it hadn't seemed like me, had it?* It would only take a small adjustment to make believe it had all happened to someone else. *Whoever that girl had been, whatever she'd felt…*

I let the stream of water gush over my face, rinsing my hair and scouring the images away. When I squinted my eyes open again, I knew all that was left was me: the old me: the one who had always been there. I almost felt sad.

I turned off the tap, and was just wrapping myself in various towels when the phone beside the bed begin to ring. Swearing and hopping over, I grabbed it.

'Where the hell have you been?' It was Emma.

'Oh! Hi!' I felt like a kid that had been caught. 'What time is it?' I noticed I was dripping on the carpet and looked around for the clock.

'Never mind the bloody time, I've been worried sick!'

I stopped dead.

'I've been up half the night. Jesus Christ, Luce! Why didn't you answer your phone? I knocked on your door, I even contacted Reception. Where the hell have you been?'

I was simultaneously annoyed and suddenly flustered that she was angry. 'Oh God, Em, I'm so sorry! The battery died on me… I didn't think… Shit…' I scrabbled about, looking for my phone and charger and plugged it in.

She paused and I could hear her irritation breathing down the line. 'You weren't deliberately ignoring me, were you? I mean, because you're angry at the thought of me going away?' her voice was flat.

She had some real front to be having a go at me.

'Emma, no! Of course I wasn't ignoring you! I wouldn't do that.'

This was the closest we'd ever come to having any kind of argument.

'So where've you been?'

I took a breath. *Seriously?*

'I met a bloke.'

'Wow!' She sounded stunned. 'What? Someone in that pub?'

'Uh-huh.'

There was a pause.

'Are you okay, Lucy?'

I heard it. I knew what she must be thinking. This wasn't the person she thought she knew. I contained a prickle of resentment. 'It was just a one-off. I won't be seeing him again.'

'Right.'

I couldn't tell from her tone what 'right' meant. She clearly wasn't going to ask why not? I'd had a one-night stand. So what? Was she the only one who could do such things?

I let the silence hang stubbornly between us.

How dare she? After all the hours I had sat listening while she went on and on about one latest shag or another? How many times had she put me off, and reorganised dates with me because some man had clicked his fingers? And where was she last night, for God's sake?

'Are you going down for breakfast?' she said, eventually.

'Yep.'

'Best you tell me all about it when we get there, then.' Her truculence wavered, but my irritation hadn't.

'Okay, but there's nothing to tell.'

'Mm, sounds like it,' she said trying to jolly me up but I wasn't prepared to be jollied. 'See you down there then? Quarter past seven?'

I was just about to say 'make it half past' in a vain attempt at a bit of control, but with a rattle of the receiver, she was gone. I put my end down slowly, suddenly catching sight of the faded ink numbers of Paul's number on my hand. If I was Emma, I wouldn't give a toss that he was married and playing away. If I was Emma, I'd be saying that was his problem and not mine.

But I *wasn't* Emma. I was tedious old me.

Picking up my mobile, I waited for the screen to burst into life and slowly keyed the numbers to send a message, all the time thinking about what I could say. In the end I just typed '*I'm sorry,*' and pressed 'send' before I could over-think it. Dragging the towel from my hair, I rubbed it vigorously into a mass of tangles as a clutch of what felt like grief turned my insides into a similar knot.

I've been used yet again.

I wasn't sure who I was most angry with – Paul, Emma, or maybe I was just furious with myself. I'd spent my life saying bloody sorry when I wasn't in the wrong. Paul wasn't sorry was he? He'd had his cake and eaten it. Emma – well, those two words wouldn't even figure in her vocabulary. She wasn't sorry, not for anything: not for endlessly dumping me as and when it suited, not for running around with other women's husbands, and not even for disappearing off to the other side of the world. No, she wasn't sorry, she never was.

I pulled out the comb from my bag and began to drag it through the knotted snag of curls. Little clumps broke off. I stared down at them. Bits of me; people always took bits of me and then left the rest. Why was there no one out there who wanted me, the whole me and nothing but me?

The truth was, no matter what I did for anyone, I never seemed to be enough.

Chapter Two

Breakfast had been awkward. Every time there was a lull in the conversation I had this terror she was going to start interrogating me and so I'd distract her with more toast and gallons of juice and topping up the tea with vats of hot water. I kept being deliberately vague about last night and asked endless questions about Connor instead. She had just been about to wheel the topic of conversation around to me again, when I nodded over at the queue of people that were looking for spare tables and suggested we make a move.

She'd upset me and I'd upset her; that was the long and short of it. We stood in the hotel reception area, both of us trying really hard to get past it all. I heard my phone ping with a message but studiously ignored it.

'You're very welcome to come shopping, you know.'

'Thanks for the offer but there's stuff I need to do.'

'"Stuff" concerning a bloke?' She cocked an eyebrow trying to manoeuvre me into spilling.

'"Stuff" concerning my mother.' I knew she'd feel slapped down by that remark but I didn't apologise. Not this time.

'I could come with you?' she offered. She was trying to make amends for being sharp with me earlier, I knew that, but part of me just didn't want to fall right back in to being a pushover. 'We could have lunch, and then get the train back to London straight after.'

I put my hand on my bag, suddenly desperate to look at my phone. 'No, honestly. That's sweet of you but it's going to be awful enough. I'll just see you at the station. Twenty past two isn't it?' I leaned forward and kissed her cheek and she gave me a little squeeze on the arm in return. 'See you later.'

I watched her retreating back as the lift doors closed behind her. I felt bad leaving it like this. I honestly did want to make it up with her. This was the first time in our friendship I hadn't been totally truthful. I bit my lip; this had all got out of hand. It was silly: I knew how much I loved her company, I valued her. It was stupid to shut her out. I made a decision: when I saw her again, I'd tell her everything. My hand went to my bag again. I guessed who the message would be from. I was right.

> Not even a note? What happened? Are
> you okay?

I snorted a laugh. *The gall of it!* Yet something in me was pleased he was bothered. A quiet anger stirred nevertheless. I wasn't going to give him any more of me: there would be no reply, no acknowledgement, no nothing. I'd turn my humiliation into silence. At least I'd have the dignity of that.

Checking the time, I did what I'd been putting off: dialling my sister's number, sighing as I listened to the phone ring out. *Maybe she wouldn't answer?*

'My God! It's really you?'

No such luck.

'I'm in York. I was thinking of coming over to see Mam.'

'Right.' I could tell by the way she said that one word, she clearly wasn't going to make it easy for me.

'Well, I suppose you'd better come then.'

'Fine.' I said, in the way only sisters can.

She put the phone down quicker than I could end the call. It was her little victory and we both knew it. *All I had to do was keep rolling over, bowing my head, giving her the victories and taking my punishment.* She was a past master at it: never saying what she really thought, never overtly confrontational, just the quiet drip-drip of pressure like a kind of nerve gas sucking the life out of you. That was my family's party piece. It could have been our motto: *It's never the things we actually say, it's always the things we don't.*

–

The cab journey to Clifton took me along roads that were scarily too familiar. Nothing had changed and yet everything looked different. It was like being in a strangely disturbing nightmare: images past and present, awkwardly superimposed themselves one over another. I was thirty-four and yet somehow still a child, the past, fresh and poised and freeze-framed, had been just waiting to run by me again like a flick-book cartoon.

'Actually, you can drop me here please.'

The last thing I wanted was to rock up in a taxi. Lou would definitely add that to her inventory of me being 'fancy'.

I paid the driver, included a generous tip, and looked around me. It all seemed different suddenly; the engine sounds faded into the harsh clatter of crows overhead.

They swooped from the power lines, appearing and disappearing like ragged black flags behind the roof lines. I walked up the street of terraced houses, my feet treading on pavement cracks and fissures; each one taking me straight back to being six years old, creating dot-to-dot pictures: the head of a wolf, the elephant with his raised trunk; all so familiar, my stomach clenching as all the other memories flooded back.

The higgledy-piggledy windows stared out at me accusingly, some incongruously plastic and modern now, some still with their original sashes, mostly nylon netted and blank, giving no idea of what might be behind them.

I looked up, knowing precisely what was behind the window of number 76 with the green front door, the sound of my heels announcing my arrival as I steeled myself.

The door was flung open.

'Come in if you're coming.' Lou stood there. She'd lost weight and her cardigan hung loosely around her thin shoulders. I suddenly saw how old she looked.

'How are you?' I smiled and leaned forward for a kiss.

'Okay, I suppose.' She returned it, stiffly.

'How's Mam?'

I heard the television booming away in the background. 'As ever,' she shrugged. She walked ahead down the narrow hallway of my childhood. The smell of it hadn't changed, or the pictures: the 1980s photographs, bleached into garish yellow. Me as a baby, leaning awkwardly against the far-flung arm of my six-year-old sister – clearly dumped there under protest. Nothing had changed.

'Hello Mam!' I said loudly before I'd even seen her.

I knew where she'd be: in that room with the fake swirling gas fire and the flock wallpaper. I saw the winged back of the chair pulled up close to an appallingly loud TV with some soap opera bawling out, a pouffe under her feet, and her arms wrapped tightly around herself as she leaned forward, peering unseeing at the screen.

'Hello Mam!' I said again, crouching into her sightline. I saw her blink at my voice.

'How are you?' I shouted.

She turned her face towards me and I felt the shock, as I always felt it; there was her face, my mother's face, a beautiful woman still, the nose, the mouth, the cheeks, the skin – *I always had beautiful skin* she told me. *Peaches and cream*. Still not old… Not really – but the eyes. The eyes had become not hers. The disease, this terrible disease had slowly robbed her of all her memories – Not only her own life, but ours too. The light in her eyes had gone and left a stranger in her place. My mother, with her impostor's eyes, just wasn't there anymore.

'Are you from the Social?' My mother didn't speak like that. Those weren't the kind of words she used.

'It's Lucy,' my sister interjected. 'Remember Lucy?' The theme tune to the soap opera blared over the question.

'I'm your daughter, Mam! You know me, don't you?'

'Is the news on next?' Her stranger's voice rasped harshly. She looked up quizzically at Louise.

'Yes, it's on in a minute, Mam.' She gave me a look and shook her head.

'See what you're missing not living up here?… Let's turn this down, I can't stand it.'

'That's someone's daughter, there, look.' Mam pointed a shaking finger. A picture of a little girl with blonde hair came up on the screen. 'I think that's Grant Mitchell's. He had a thing with that Liz McDonald in the Rover's Return.'

Lou and I both frowned at the mix-up and then caught each other's eye as we laughed. The tension between us lifted. 'That's the news, Mam,' Lou said patiently. 'That's real life... Although *EastEnders* and real life are getting more similar by the day,' she muttered under her breath. For a split second we were sisters again.

'Has she gone somewhere?' Mam looked round and past me as though I wasn't there. 'I think she's disappeared.'

I tried not to mind. I got up stiffly and patted her on the arm.

'Do you want to stay for a cup of tea?' Lou was trying now. 'We have one about this time.'

'Go on then.'

I was waiting for the veiled accusations I knew must be coming. The fact Lou was being nice made it even more unnerving.

Lou turned to walk out of the door and I was desperate to follow her – anything to not sit in this room with an old woman who wasn't my mother. It was purgatory, but something I had to endure. I sat, feeling totally alone, staring at the side of my mother's face, the slack hanging jowls, the mouth slightly open as she gazed sightlessly at the TV screen, praying my sister would hurry up and bring the kind of tea that I knew was coming. It would be one of those brown glass mugs with the too-small handle, the sight of which would take me back thirty years.

She appeared in the doorway carrying a tray and set it down on a small side table with a crocheted fancy cover I hadn't seen before.

'Is that new?'

She looked up at me quickly and then away again as she busied herself with the tea things. 'No. It was Nan's. I thought Mam would like it when I cleared the house.'

A whole raft of unspoken accusation lay in that simple statement. I hadn't come up for my grandmother's funeral; I'd made some excuse about work. I hadn't helped with the house clearance. I was the selfish cow who'd swanned off. But in reality it was too soon after Dan. I drank the scalding tea as fast as humanly possible, feeling the roof of my mouth blister. I deserved it.

We made pointless and ridiculous conversation for twenty minutes, me watching the clock.

'The traffic was terrible getting here,' I lied, putting the cup down. 'I have to catch my train. I daren't miss it.'

'Of course not.' Lou nodded. She wasn't fooled, I could see it in her face. I felt worse than I had before. 'I'll walk you to the door.'

I knew every thread of wear on the carpet. I knew the shape of each scuff mark on the walls: those years of us all brushing past, leaving our stain. I could feel that house clutching at me, trawling me back in, and I could sense the old me: the child inside, and the new me, colliding and unravelling.

I turned to Lou to say goodbye.

'You've changed,' she said, matter-of-factly.

The lump in my throat hardened. I couldn't answer her for a second, I could only nod.

'I'm sorry... I'll keep in touch more... I'll ring you,' I said finally. 'I promise.'

She bent forward from the step, her hands landing on my shoulders, and kissed me gently on the forehead. 'I don't blame you.' She pulled back and looked directly into my eyes. 'You got out. You were good at school. You managed it. Mark did too – he had to go to the other side of the world to get away from Dad, but we all knew it wasn't just Dad, it was her as much as him—' She gave a painful glance over her shoulder. 'So don't feel bad, Luce. Feel free. Go and live a life for both of us. Go and live the life I could never have.' She retreated back into that appalling hallway and I saw her face crumpling in the gap as she quickly closed the door.

I stood for a few moments staring at the bubbled and peeling paint, the layered colours of my childhood, one under the other, under the other – skimming like a stone of memory on the surface of a pond: back and back and back to being six again, standing right here, on this spot, terrified of going in. Terrified of him. Of her. Of the two of them together.

I turned around and walked, the shock of her words thudding with each step.

I wasn't really thinking about where I was going.

My sister. It could have so easily been the other way around: me living her life and she living mine. But instead, she'd stayed and I'd left the dreadfulness for her to deal with.

'He's such a lovely man, your Derek,' the neighbours always said to my mother. 'You've got a good one there.' She only ever smiled back at them and said nothing. The brooding silence of it. His moods we could never speak about: the darkness of them, the atmosphere as real and as solid as a thing breathing shallowly in the corner of the room. The acute awareness of his jawline flexing, the way he moved his feet, agitated, getting angry – over what? Something? Nothing? Was there a difference? The silence of unspoken violence that might erupt at any second. The silence of *her* who said nothing to stop him, either during or after. We were all children together: powerless and afraid. She said nothing, so we said nothing. We endured: sacrificing our self esteem, our self confidence, just wanting it to stop. And no one ever said one word about it, until now.

My sister. My sister Lou. The weight of the guilt pressed heavy on my shoulders; I was a fraud in every sense, and a selfish fraud at that. How could I leave her?

I pulled my phone from my bag and thought about ringing her now. 'Pack your bags,' I'd say to her. 'Come with me. We'll find somewhere for Mam. It's not too late. You can't live the rest of your life like this.' But knowing all the time what she would say – that 'it was too late,' and she'd 'made her choices.' But I had to try at least to persuade her, didn't I? The screen lit up.

'Lou?'

'Hello,' Paul said.

I couldn't speak.

'Are you still in York?'

'Yes.' I could hardly get the word out.

'Would you meet me please? I want to talk to you.'

I swallowed.

'Are you still there?'

'Uh huh.'

'You're upset. I can hear it. Can you tell me what you're upset about?'

The tears pricked painfully behind my eyes. I was scared at what my voice would do if I answered.

'Is it your mum?'

'Partly,' I managed.

'Is it me?'

'Partly... Definitely' My anger bubbled.

'Then let me come and get you.'

A whole raft of conflicting emotions ran right through me, one after the other, none of which were good.

'I know this seems too soon...' there was the quiet slick of him swallowing. 'I know this must feel mad, but...' *he actually sounded nervous.* 'I really felt some deep connection with you last night. I don't know what it was, and I don't know if you were aware of it too?'

I couldn't speak. *The gall of him. The absolute bloody front!*

'All I'm asking is that you talk to me. Would you do that? I've clearly upset you in some way, and that's the last thing I would ever want to do.'

My silence lay like a stone. *I should tell the bastard that I saw his phone. Confront him. Watch the look on his face.*

'So would you?'

'Okay. Why not?' I was suddenly in control. I glanced around and gave him a retail park landmark.

'I think I've seen that off the main road. Give me a shop to meet you outside and I'll be quarter of an hour, tops.'

–

I was hyperaware of him sitting silently in the driver's seat as he watched me get in.

'Hi,' he said. He had one elbow resting casually on the door and his hand on the steering wheel.

'You okay?' His eyes skimmed my face.

'Fine.'

'You're clearly really angry.' *Christ, psychologist speak.*

'Yep.'

'Where did you sneak off to then?'

'Back to my hotel.'

I was giving him nothing. He dipped his head to gaze through the windscreen, pretending that something had caught his eye. 'If you don't want to tell me the real reason, then that's fine.'

My hackles rose.

'It's probably none of my business anyway.' He stared intently out.

'So who were all the texts from?' I was surprised how matter-of-fact I sounded.

'Sorry?' he blinked round.

'The texts. Someone was blowing up your phone all night... Are you married or something?'

He blinked again, slower this time, and the corner of his mouth twitched. He paused, as though thinking. 'Oh,' he said. 'I see.'

We sat looking at each other for a few seconds before he leaned back abruptly in his seat and delved into the front pocket of his jeans.

'This phone?'

I nodded. Thumbing up the screen, he held it out to me. It was a mass of missed calls and unopened texts.

'You mean that lot.'

He scrolled quickly through them. 'This is my work phone. I have two: one work, one personal. One black, one white.' He reached into the inside pocket of his jacket and flashed the white one. 'These texts are from a patient of mine. This is a woman who is at the peak of a psychotic episode and has been hospitalised. Unfortunately, just like some of the staff who work in prisons—' he eyed me, 'some hospital staff are not so security-conscious and allow the patients access to phones all bloody night.' He shook his head. 'They are the bane of my life.' He proffered it. 'Do you want to check them? You're more than welcome.' He offered it again.

My stomach contracted a little. I felt a bit of a twit.

'Maybe I should apologise.' I couldn't meet his gaze.

'There is absolutely no need. What else were you supposed to think?'

'Well, I'd like to say it anyway. I'm sorry.'

'I think you already said that in your text, didn't you?' He took a look at my face and then prodded my leg playfully.

'Stop it.' I almost smiled.

'So can we be friends now?'

'I think so.'

'Right. Let's move on then. So when are you heading back to London?'

'Today. I've got to be at the station at about two-ish. Umm... How about you?' I was cringing inside.

'I've got a few bits to tidy up, but I should be back tomorrow sometime.' He glanced at the clock on the dashboard. 'How about an early lunch then? Fancy that?'

'God, are you sure? I just feel so—'

'I know a fabulous café-bar. It really buzzes at lunchtime and they do a fantastic range of wine. That do you?'

'That sounds perfect,' I smiled and then paused. 'Thank you for being so nice to me. I don't think I deserve it.'

'Everyone deserves to be happy.' He turned the engine over and glanced in the rear-view mirror. He laughed and slid me a sideways look. 'Even you.'

--

The place was buzzing. Coloured globe lights hung at intervals from the beams giving a warm but jazzy glow. A long wooden bar stretched the length of the room with a television high on the wall. A large group of people were gathered at the end, laughing and joking. He was right; it had a great atmosphere.

We were perched on stools around a high bar table where we could look out of the wide windows into the busy cobbled street. He had ordered a whole range of tapas-style dishes, each one interesting and unusual: tiny squares of toast with creamy goat's cheese, chopped broad beans and fresh mint and hot garlicky mushrooms speared with slices of Iberico ham – all utterly delicious. My big goblet of pinotage was rich and warm and slipped down far too easily.

Paul casually picked up the wine menu as he ate. 'So, come on. Tell me about being in love, then.'

I nearly choked on a bean. 'What?' I spluttered and managed to swallow. 'What a provocative question.' I arched an eyebrow.

'No, seriously. I'm interested. Provocative questions are always the best. Go on. I promise I won't tell anyone.' He pulled a comic face.

'I don't quite know what you mean.'

He put down his fork and took a slug of wine, smiling at me over the rim. 'Yeah, you do,' he pursed his lips. 'You're just being shy. By our age everyone's been in love I think… I hope…' He queried my look. 'Come on, there's always one. The one that changed your life.' The glass wavered 'Isn't there?'

'Um… I suppose,' I said warily.

'So what was his name?' He took a long mouthful and savoured it.

It was a question and a challenge I didn't know how to get out of without making it a bigger deal than it needed to be.

I licked my lips and then said the name.

'Dan.'

The clamour in the room rose and fell.

'Ah. So. You were in love with him, were you?'

I fussed with my food a little. I really didn't want to talk about this. 'No, not after I realised what he was.'

Not only did I not want to talk about it, I didn't want to think about it either.

'What he was?' he pressed.

I gave him a look and put my fork down with a sigh. 'I suppose I let myself get drawn in by him. He was very charming. *Very* plausible.' I shrugged. 'I had no reason to believe he was... Well... Already in a relationship... A *married* kind of relationship.' I pulled a wry face. 'Which is probably why I was so—' I shrugged.

Paul nodded, listlessly moving a very tasty-looking load of aubergine into a pile on his plate. It was almost as though he was thinking something but not saying it.

'So what's *your* love story?' I smiled.

There was the minutest pause. I watched as he sawed a piece in two with the edge of the tine.

'Of course there've been women, I've even lived with some for a little while but none ended up being very serious. I've had one relationship that I thought might be a marriage-job, but it turned out not to be.'

'This was when you were living in Hertfordshire, or when you were in London?' I picked up a piece of toast and bit into it, inadvertently getting goat's cheese on my nose. I felt myself instantly blush.

Paul laughed and leaned forward with the tip of his serviette. 'Here,' he caught the offending blob. 'Christ! You wouldn't catch me living in Hertfordshire!' he chuckled.

'I thought that was where you grew up?'

'*Nooo* – *Bed*fordshire. Bedford, in fact—' he winced playfully. 'Can you imagine what that kind of culturally impoverished childhood did to me?'

'So where did Hertfordshire fit in then?'

'It doesn't. It didn't. You must have misheard that bit.' He sat back suddenly, discarding his fork with a clatter. 'Shall we tick that topic off the list then?' He sighed agitatedly. 'I don't know why I brought it up… I mean, partners, people from the past. The past, that *past* that all these psychologists bang on about endlessly. Who cares? I'm not the same person I was three years ago, ten years ago, even.'

'So you're not one of "those" psychologists, then?' I teased.

'Bloody hell, no. Boring bastards most of them: dead from the neck up and the waist down. The past is so tedious. They don't live in the now. Which is the only thing I'm interested in, actually.' He paused, his hands on the table edge. 'You're a very "now" person, aren't you? Actually, you're a funny, quirky, prickly mixture of very attractive things.'

I was amused by the statement, but wary. 'Am I?'

'I think you know you are. I think that's why you keep people at a distance.'

'And you're quite…' I searched for the word. '… Challenging.'

'Am I?' He cocked his head quizzically, parroting me. 'I told you before, just tell me to back off. I won't be offended. Would you like me to back off?'

'No.' I smiled and looked down at the stem of my wine glass, twizzling it in my fingers.

I could feel his eyes resting on the side of my face. I was self-conscious and ridiculously flattered all at the same time.

'You present as someone who wants to be left alone, but I'm guessing the opposite is true.'

I picked up my glass. 'Thanks for that, Mr Psychology Man.'

'That'll be eighty-five pounds then, please.'

I nearly choked. 'Christ, you charge that an hour?'

'Minute. Please!'

I laughed and shook my head. He was a bit bonkers and very funny. I really liked him.

'I know you're going to keep testing me and pushing me away and pulling me in, I get that,' he continued; his gaze flitted from my mouth to my eyes and back again. 'But eventually you will work out that you and I are on the same side. I'm the kind of person who'll have your back. No one will ever be more loyal, more faithful, more true to you than I am.'

I didn't know where to look.

He smiled as he hopped off the stool. 'Just popping to the Gents.'

'Oh, okay.'

I surreptitiously watched him making his way through the crowd. I really did like this guy. I liked the way his jacket hunched a little across his shoulders as he walked, I liked the way the hair lay in the nape of his neck. I remembered what his naked skin felt like. *You're being played like a fiddle, Lucy*, my head warned me. So much of me was jeering at the idea I would fall for any of this. He was a psychologist, wasn't he? He knew what to say and when to say it, but his full-on attention was attractive: exciting

62

even. Why shouldn't I enjoy a tiny bit of madness? Look where being straight had got me.

The group in front of the bar had stopped talking and were all staring up. The picture of the little blonde child I'd seen earlier on Mum's TV flashed up. There was a tickertape news bulletin running across the bottom of the screen with 'Breaking news' but I was too far away to read it.

Paul came back and glanced across. 'Oh yeah, that's terrible. Someone's snatched a child, apparently.' He eased himself into the seat.

'Oh god... Really?'

'A three-year-old, Cassie Edwards. This morning. They thought she'd wandered off, but now they don't think so. She ran out down the path to get in the car, her mum was only minutes behind her with a baby. Somewhere in Halifax. A nice quiet street, a decent area. No one saw a thing and of course there were no cameras. One minute she was there by the car and the next minute she was gone.' He picked up his glass.

'Jesus.'

'I know. The police will be trawling through all the newly released paedophiles.'

My thoughts immediately sprang to Gould. I stared at Paul.

He stared right back. 'When was our friend getting out?' The glass stilled.

'This morning.'

He considered it for a moment and then dismissed the idea. 'It's unlikely that he would re-offend so soon. If he's going to do something like that he'd want to get settled first, suss out his hunting territory, start networking with his known associates.'

I knew all this but still the notion appalled me.

'And anyway,' he went on, 'he's being released to the London area isn't he?'

I nodded. 'True. He's unlikely to start re-offending round here. If he was thinking of it, he'd be better off where he could take a child and disappear easily. London makes it much easier. He'd know that. There's more risk up here.' I glanced at the TV. The news item had moved on to a giraffe being airlifted in a zoo somewhere.

I looked back at Paul.

'Jeeze! This bloody world,' he said laughing and shaking his head. 'Just be grateful we're on the right side of all that craziness.' He raised his glass. I was immediately aware of the word 'we'.

I tentatively raised my own and he chinked the rim. 'To us non-mad people,' he grinned. There was a pause: did I like it? Was I flattered? I thought I might be.

'To us,' I repeated, sipping as I watched him through the glass distortion. He put his drink down slowly and then gently touched the back of my hand with one finger. 'That was nice.'

'What was?'

'You used the term "us". It was a really lovely thing to say.'

—

I saw Emma before she clocked me. She was standing outside the railway station holding the handle of her travel case and looking off into the distance. She looked a little sad and lost and I had an immediate pang of guilt.

'That's her there.'

Paul pulled up and gave her a wave. She looked unsure for a moment, and then it dawned on her as I got out.

'Hello, Emma!' He leaned across the passenger seat and grinned up at her. 'Nice to meet you. I'm Paul.'

'Very nice to meet you too, Paul.' Emma shot me a look as I went round to the boot. 'Maybe we'll meet properly sometime,' she gave me a questioning look.

'I'm sure that can be arranged.'

I pulled out my case. There was a very awkward moment where I leaned back into the car and kissed him.

'Bye, then!' He looked from her to me as I swung the door shut.

'Bye.' I raised a hand. I was aware of the car pulling away and felt instantly and inexplicably bereft. I smiled for Emma's sake. 'Good time shopping?'

'Clearly not as good as seeing your mother.'

I heard the jibe but she only laughed as we trundled our cases into the station.

'So that's the one you're not seeing again, is it? And what were you telling me over breakfast? Psychologist, eh? I bet it's not just your mind he's been figuring out.'

I instantly bristled but refused to be drawn. I peered up instead, pretending to concentrate on the Departures board as Emma wittered on about jeans and boots and how much she'd spent. 'God, have you seen the news?' she suddenly said, nodding over at a chap on a bench. He was reading a newspaper with Cassie Edwards's photograph blazoned across the front page. She was smiling shyly; my heart contracted.

'I know, I saw it on a TV report. It won't be a good outcome, we know that... Come on, it'll be over there on platform 2.'

We started to climb the steps. 'These people are every-where you bloody go, aren't they? And then we have to go and work with them too...' She paused as she suddenly remembered her train of thought. 'Oh, and talking about work—'

'I wasn't.'

'Well, don't think you're going to sidetrack me off the 'new man' subject,' she cocked an eyebrow. 'First you hook up with some guy you insist is a one-off, then out of the blue you're in his car getting a lift to the station. Honestly Luce, you change your mind as often as I hope you change your knickers,' she grinned. 'I think you've got some explaining to do, don't you?'

'Well, it—'

But she interrupted. 'I have to say he's a weird-looking bloke.' We reached the other platform. 'He seems nice enough though… Good thing he's in London… Oh, and talking of men in London…' And that was it, she was off; my contrary love-life forgotten, it was all Connor, how lovely their short time together had been, how he'd appreciated the underwear she'd bought, then about the dinner he was supposed to take her to but they'd ended up just with room service… On and on. But I didn't mind. I smiled and frowned and 'Ooo'd' and 'Ahh'd' in all the right places. I had the beginnings of my own little love interest going on. I'd joined the club, become part of the world that she inhabited, and that world looked different, smelled different, *was* different. *I* was different, that was the thing. Her prattling on left my mind free to wander. I hadn't even *thought* about being with anyone for such a long time. Here was a man who was funny, attractive, attentive, caring… And *single.* What a plus point!… So what was my problem? I was interested and I was excited, all of which was brilliant, but at the same time I was really, really scared.

Chapter Three

'Did we agree Dave was going to see Gould today, or you?' Viv paused as she passed my desk. 'You said something in your email about it.' She tapped her pen on a pile of papers.

I looked up. 'We said Dave. Why?'

'Has he been in contact?'

'Who, Gould? No, not that I'm aware of. What's Dave said?'

She closed her eyes briefly and then gave me a look. 'Just ring Stoke Newington Police Station, would you? That's where he was supposed to register. He's still within his timeframe, but I think we should just check. If you do it Lucy, I know it's done.'

I picked up the phone and dialled the number, listening to the tone ringing out as I stared at my mobile lying on the desk. I had been waiting for Paul to ring and he hadn't. I'd said nothing to Emma even when she asked this morning if I had heard from 'The Love Machine' while guffawing heartily.

I gave her a withering look but she only grinned, wandering off singing some mad disco song and doing all the actions until Viv shouted at her to knock it off.

'Stoke Newington Police Station, how can I help?' a female voice said.

'Ah. This is Lucy Skinner from Hackney Probation. I'm ringing about a newly released sex offender, Simon Gould. He was released from HMP Ravensmoor the day before yesterday to an address in Dalston. Can you confirm that he's signed the sex offender register, please?'

'Hello you! How you doin' my lovely?'

'Kath!'

Kath and I had crossed paths several times. She definitely had no truck with offenders who messed around. There was a pause while she checked. 'No, he hasn't as yet. He's got another twenty-four hours, just about,' she added. 'Don't worry, lovely, He won't get past me.'

We chatted on a bit about life, being over-worked and how crap the spring weather had been, before I wandered over and gave Viv the information.

'Hmm – right.' She perused the ceiling for a moment. 'Look, I know what you said in your email, and I probably agree, but how strongly do you feel about it?'

I knew I was being softened up. I could guess what was coming.

'Like, would you consider seeing him as a one-off?' She squinted and put her head on one side coquettishly. 'It would be a massive help to me if you would.'

I rolled my eyes and sighed, grinning. 'Fine… As a one-off.'

'Deal,' she grinned. 'Dave had arranged to go this afternoon, but he really should be doing the prep work for this offender group he's running and you know what he's like: he'll use it as an excuse to do a half-arsed job on both.'

'No problem, I just didn't want Gould thinking he can choose who he gets to see.'

'Oh I think he knows you've got his number,' Viv grinned. 'Thanks, Lucy. Let me know if there are any problems.'

Seeing Gould was probably one of the last things I wanted to do, but I went back and sat at my desk again and checked my mobile for missed calls for what seemed like the twentieth time since yesterday afternoon.

Paul hadn't been in touch. I had hoped he might, I wasn't sure why. It nagged at me even though I knew I was being hyper-keen. *Should I phone him?*

No, I wasn't going to do that. He probably wasn't even back yet. What *was* I stressing about? Jesus.

I tried to carry on with the report I'd been writing. The tightly written words on the screen jumbled and blurred as I tried to concentrate. Idly clicking onto Google, I typed in 'Paul Webb psychology' and a whole stream of Paul Webb's came up: a Professor Paul Webb at the University of Manchester Political Science department; a Paul Webb who was a Joiner and Carpenter; a Paul Webb Youth Worker on LinkedIn, but no senior psychologist with the Home Office. I had another idea. There was an internal system: Home Office intranet, so I went through some of the old documents there: procedural information stuff, advice notices and so on – and then suddenly there he was: P. Webb, mentioned in an offender management briefing. His office address was listed, with a phone number. Avoiding Emma's eagle eye and keeping my voice down, I casually dialled the number.

The woman on the end of the line told me that 'Dr Webb was in a meeting and could she take a message?'

'Oh okay, thanks. I'll ring again later.' I glanced over at Emma but she was staring myopically at her computer screen. *He was back, then. Should I start to be concerned that he hadn't called me? Oh, for pity's sake, Lucy!* Butterflies tickled my belly as I typed the name into 192.com. I was only *looking!* What harm was in that? The NW3 postcode on the electoral roll told me I'd probably got the right P. Webb, but the address wasn't listed.

'Everything good?'

I snapped up.

'Sorry?' I stared up into Emma's smiling face, surreptitiously closing the page. She glanced behind her. 'Are you at home tonight?'

'Yes, why?' *I was behaving like a poxy teenager.*

She gave me a pointed look. 'Got stuff to tell you. I'll ring you later.' The excitable eyebrows and the breathlessness said it all.

'Oh right. Definitely. It's a date.' I winked conspiratorially and she wandered happily off. My grin fell. Connor. What else? Did I really want to hear the rollercoaster twists and turns?

Tapping my biro agitatedly on my desk, I chucked it down. I really wished I hadn't made that call to Paul's office. I had to stop all this. Seriously, stop and chill out, I told myself. *Think carefully about what you're doing. You don't actually work with the guy, but still… Things can get… Complicated. The memory of Dan stung for a moment. Just put the whole lot out of your mind.*

–

Once in the car, I sat in traffic down the Stoke Newington Road, singing along very loudly to Florence and the Machine. I sang louder, blocking out all thoughts that were trying to barge their way in, but noticing the wary glance in the mirror from the woman in the car in front.

I grinned and twinkled my fingers and she looked away. *There. See? It's easy. Concentrate on the things you can control, not the things you can't.*

After pulling up outside Gould's address, I sat staring out of the window for a few moments and steeling myself. Mums were pushing pushchairs, big kids tagging along beside as they made their way home from school. The slow grip of dread squeezed. I knew my eyes weren't the only eyes watching the little kids and their distracted naïve parents. They had no idea what was living right next door to them. Behind those innocuous curtains was their nightmare of nightmares just waiting to happen.

I checked the address again. It was one in a row of three grubby council flats, squeezed into a driveway, their entrances at an angle, making the doorways dark and full of shadows. I was aware that he might be looking down on me from an upstairs window and I was careful not to raise my eyes as I walked from the car to the doorway of Unit B. The doorway smelled strongly of urine and there was a black plastic sack that had split into a slurry of what looked like tomato and pizza box innards. I tried the bell and peered through the tiny frosted pane of glass. I couldn't detect any movement at all.

I went back to the car and rang Viv.

'Yes, number 2, Unit B is definitely the right address. And it was arranged for half past three, yes?' she queried.

'Yep.'

'So he's not at his registered address and he hasn't shown up at the police station… Hmm…' she pondered. 'Okay, that's concerning but we can't start jumping up and down just yet. Keep close tabs though, would you, Luce? Maybe ask the coppers at Stoke Newington to give you a ring if he turns up.'

71

'Will do.'

'Oh, and there's no need to come back into the office today. It's Friday. Take a flyer. You can write all this up from home, can't you? I'll see you Monday.'

'Oh brilliant! Thanks for that, Viv! No problem. Have a great weekend. See you Monday, then!'

I sat in the car and made the calls before starting the engine and turning the car towards home. The whole weekend spanned out in front of me and suddenly I got a wash of... What? Anxiety... Or sadness maybe? The next two days sat like a great sea of time that I had to fill. Normally I'd be elated at the thought; I had my own little routines: fresh croissants for breakfast from the deli down the road, freshly ground coffee, a newspaper: a real one with proper pages. And now... It was Paul, the bastard. He'd done this to me. He'd made this happen by giving me expectations. No – I'd *allowed* it to happen by giving *myself* expectations. Now all I had to do was un-allow it. Block all thoughts of him. Simple. I closed my eyes and concentrated on clearing my mind... But it wasn't so easy.

His face came to me and he grinned: all one-sided and lovely, the way he leaned across the table, his grey eyes catching mine.

But you're one of those women. Dan's voice whispered in my ear. *You're just a bit full-on.*

I opened my eyes. Well then, I wouldn't be full-on, in fact I'd back right off.

I drove, turning the music up. I certainly wasn't going to be played like last time. The image of his face above mine as he lovingly smoothed out my hair. The feel of his hands: their warmth, cupping my face sent a shiver down my neck, but I banished the image immediately. No.

Paul who?

See? Done.

But something deep down told me it wasn't.

-

Kicking off my shoes in the hallway and dropping my bag under the row of coats, I hooked my jacket onto the peg, listening to the rhythmic ticking of the wall clock pulsing into the silence.

I was home, I reminded myself. I was home: *my home*, I didn't need anyone or anything else. This was my nest.

Padding into the kitchen, I found some cheese crackers in the cupboard and a glass and poured out the remainder of a bottle of wine from the fridge. Glass in hand and munching on the crackers, I meandered into the bedroom, stripping off my work clothes and finding my wonderfully sloppy yoga pants and a far-too-baggy jumper.

The silence was all mine.

Everything around me was mine too. The space and the light were perfect. It was only about the third flat I'd looked at but it was absolutely what I had been looking for: only one bedroom, a galley kitchen, but when I walked into the lounge and saw the size of it, that was my heart gone – *Bang*. A big, square, sunny room, with an original fireplace, and the sunlight slanting in through sash windows, I was sold in an instant.

Cradling my glass, I went over and leaned against the frame to gaze out at the tiny green rectangle of Thornhill Gardens. Birds chattered in the trees, frantically fluttering from twig to branch. I'd learned to love this gentle solitude: no one asking anything of me, no demands. I was able to close my front door and give myself time to think and just *be*, quietly, inside my own head.

But now, somehow and for some mad reason, this man had got inside.

Glancing back at the coffee table, I checked where I had purposefully laid my phone. The screen sat there, black and silent. It hadn't pinged, and even if it had, I wasn't going to check it I told myself.

Gazing again out of the window, I watched a couple getting out of a car; they were clearly having an argument. A thought crept into my head: had he not rung because I'd been so hard, accusing him about being married? I'd never really given him a chance to defend himself, had I? Was that it? I stared at the screen. A slight nervousness grew. I might just send him a text: something bland yet friendly: something that wouldn't require a response and then I'd leave it.

Hi, my fingers paused and deleted the two letters. I re-typed them and stared for a second before deleting again. I stared at the little green phone symbol, debated, and then took the plunge. It rang with a hollow ringing sound, the hollowed out feeling inside me drilling with it.

'Hello?'

For a second I was convinced it was the answer machine.

'Hello?' he said again. It was that slightly exasperated tone that people use when you've interrupted something important.

'It's me, Lucy.'

'Lucy! Ah...' He sounded guarded. 'Ah, right, sorry. Sorry... Can I call you back? I've got someone on the other line.'

And suddenly he was gone. I was a bit taken aback. I sat staring at the screen. Of course it was totally reasonable and quite probable that he *could* have someone on the other line, but I couldn't help thinking... It was the way he'd said it: that dismissive, slightly irritated, not overly pleased to hear from me... And then the whole thing lit up and my heart shunted a gear.

Emma.

'How come you got to slide off so early?'

I swallowed, trying to quell my racing heart. 'Because I'm the good girl.'

'You seeing your man this evening?'

'Um... Don't think so.' I briefly closed my eyes.

'No, I'm not seeing Connor either.'

'Oh?'

'Wifey found my texts on his phone.'

'Oh no.' I was trying to sound sympathetic but I actually felt antsy. I sat down and then got up again and wandered to the window, trying to shut down the rising burn of annoyance. On and on, she went. The 'text-finding' was great news, apparently. It meant wifey would probably throw him out and he'd be practically free. This was yet another chapter in this never-ending saga which was all variations on a sad and sorry theme. Unsurprisingly, New Zealand was now a non-starter for the foreseeable. 'He needs to get her on-side, you see. So she won't make things really difficult.'

Yes of course he does. A tiny needle of we-could've-seen-all-this-coming pricked, but I said nothing.

She glossed over why his wife would be checking his phone in the first place if they'd really been separated like he said they were. I heard her take a breath to begin the next chapter instalment but then my phone bleeped with a call waiting, and I fumbled for it.

'Can I ring you back, Em?' I tried to get rid of her as casually as I could. 'There's a delivery driver just pulled up and he'll want a signature.'

'Oh Lord, what have you been buying now?' She laughed. 'Yep, give us a ring later and I'll give you part two.'

'Sure will. See you.'

'The next bit gets worse.'

'Sure. Yes. Fine. Bye then... Hello?' I tried not to sound eager.

'Hello, you.' His voice slid like syrup into my ear and my skin shivered.

He'd rung, that was all that mattered.

'How are you?'

'I'm fine, how are you?' A circle of my breath clouded the window.

'What can I do for you?'

He sounded so matter of fact that I couldn't think how to reply.

'Are you still there?'

'Yep. Still here.' I made a circle in the mist with my finger.

'You sound pissed off.'

'Nope.'

'Really?' I heard him take a breath. 'I wasn't totally sure you wanted me to contact you. You seemed a bit...' he paused. '...Unsure, I suppose.'

Did I?

'About us seeing each other. I got the impression that I might be pressurising you, so I thought I'd leave you alone.'

I swallowed. 'Okay.'

'What does "okay" mean?'

'It means okay, I understand your reasoning.'

'So where does that leave us?'

I stared into the empty street. It was darker now. There were cars coming home, lights going on in houses. Kids playing out before tea. I imagined families behind closed doors chatting over their plans for the weekend. And then there was me, here. Alone. A car door slammed.

'I'd really like to see you,' I said.

Another phone began to warble in the background. 'Look... Sorry again, I really need to get this. I'll come back to you, yeah?—'

And then I listened to the click of the call ending and then the silence, followed by the echo of a heartbeat. I bit my lip. I didn't really know how I'd come across. Getting drunk had been a *really* bad idea. I cringed at the memory. I *wouldn't blame him if he didn't ring back. I thought about* how I must have seemed: how judgemental I'd been over Gould, then off-the-wall, then scratchy and prickly coupled with my sudden dawn departure... What else was he supposed to think, really? No wonder he'd backed off.

I began to turn the conversation over in my mind, reading meaning into every syllable, every pause, filling the gaps, imagining what he must be thinking and knowing all the time that this was just me being too much in my own head.

I went and sat on the arm of the sofa, clutching my phone. I stared out of the window as the late afternoon sun stretched out into the herringbone clouds, reflecting gold onto the bank of windows across the street. I wondered if I should eat something, but I wasn't really hungry. I thought about drawing the curtains and putting the TV on but I couldn't be bothered. I watched the brick of the houses beginning to burn red, each one with its own fire as the sun closed like a fist behind the roofs.

I somehow knew he wasn't going to ring.

And then he did.

I snatched it up without looking.

'Hello?' I breathed.

There was a pause.

'You're not too busy now?' His voice was muffled.

'Sorry?'

'You haven't returned any of my calls.'

The voice wasn't Paul's.

'Who is this?'

'I've left messages at work. I need to see you.'

'Who is this, please?'

'It's Simon. Simon Gould.'

My heart zigzagged into high gear.

'Simon...' I heard myself falter. 'How did you get this number?' Endless warning sirens went off in my head.

'I did tell you prisoners can find out all sorts of things.' I heard the smile in his voice. 'There's always a way if people are determined enough.'

My lungs wouldn't work properly.

'Is it a problem?'

'Yes, Simon. It's a problem.' I tried not to let him hear that I was shaking.

'But you weren't at your desk.' There was a whine in his tone, like a petulant child.

'Right. Now. Listen to me. This is not okay. This is a reportable offence. It's also a breach of your licence conditions, do you understand?' I tried to keep my voice calm, when I actually wanted to scream *What the fuck do you think you're playing at?* 'You will delete my number and you won't contact me in this way again. Is that absolutely clear?'

'But you need to stay in contact with me, Lucy. You have to. It's the law.'

'Simon, I have been trying to see you. I came round today. You weren't there.'

'I'm doing everything I said I'd do, Lucy. I'm going to prove that I can be trusted.'

'That's good, but this isn't the way to do it.'

'I don't need courses and support and monitoring, I just need to *show* people. Then they'll see how I've changed.'

'As I said, that's good. But you can't do stuff like ri—'

'You've seen the news?'

A tiny drumbeat started in my chest.

'I can be around little children. I can be their friend. I don't have to do anything bad. You *understand that*, don't you Lucy? You get it. You trust people.'

'What are you telling me, Simon? What have you done?'

I thought he'd hung up, but then I heard him swallow. 'You already know.'

The line went dead. I stood for a moment, I couldn't move. I found that my fingers wouldn't work as I rang Emma.

'Something nice?'

'Sorry?'

'Your delivery.'

'No.' My brain stumbled and snagged and I couldn't formulate the words. 'I've just had a phone call.' I could feel my heartbeat in my throat. 'That prisoner who just got released... Gould. He's just phoned me.'

'Phoned you? Oh my god, Lucy, You need to ring Viv. I mean, right this minute.'

'I know. But Christ, Emma. I think he's done something.'

'What do you mean, done something?'

'He seemed to be... Hinting at stuff.'

'Like?'

'I don't know... And I hope to hell I'm wrong... But as soon as I saw that news report about Cassie Edwards, I thought of him.'

'My god, what the hell did he say?'

'That's the thing. He didn't say anything, exactly, he just asked if I'd seen the news. It's not *what* he said, it's – Oh Christ, I don't know Em, he didn't say what he'd done, and he could be bluffing... He's a narcissist and he's dangerous and so this could all be about getting my attention, but...'

'This is pretty heavy stuff, Luce. This guy is clearly playing some fucked-up game. Ring Viv, just tell her exactly what you've just told me.'

'I'll do it now.'

'Call me back if you need to. I'm here all night.'

I sat with the phone in my hand trying to marshal my thoughts. *Just present Viv with the facts. Keep a clear head. Don't get spooked.* I found her number and repeated what had happened as precisely as I could.

'Okay. Right. Is there anything else he said? Anything at all?' I could tell she'd gone completely into professional mode.

'No. That was all of it.'

'So you think he's got someone to hack your phone account, yes?'

'Looks that way.'

'Jesus. And there is absolutely no way you he could have got it from you? You didn't leave your phone lying around or anything like that?'

'No! No.' I shook my head emphatically. *Christ.*

'Get on to your phone company. Cancel everything to be on the safe side. I'll contact the police. You've got a spare old one somewhere, have you?'

'I think so, yes.'

'So turn yours off and use the old one. Bring it in on Monday morning just in case the police want to see it, and in the meantime if you could do a report stating exactly what transpired and send it over to me asap, that'd be brilliant. I'll pass it straight up. If it all checks out, we can have him re-arrested.'

'Yes, absolutely. I'll get onto it now while it's still fresh in my mind.'

'Good,' she breathed freely. 'Fine. We'll talk about this again after I've spoken to the multi-agency team.'

'Okay.'

'No problem. See you on Monday.'

'Right.'

'Oh – and Lucy?'

'Yes?'

'Don't spend the whole weekend thinking and worrying about all of this.' I heard the note of real care and concern. 'I know what you're like. Don't stress. We're in this together.'

I ended the call. I knew Viv had to ask questions about how he'd got hold of my number, but it didn't make it sting any less. Grabbing a notepad and pen, I scribbled the date, the time, and a list of the things he'd said, and what I'd said… And then I stopped. I glanced at the phone lying next to me feeling its presence like it was something toxic and filthy. I was supposed to turn it off, to deny Gould any further access but I really needed Paul to ring me back. I so needed to tell him, someone who knew Gould and what he was capable of. A tiny bit of reassurance, but it didn't look like it was coming.

Going into the bedroom, I pulled open the bedside drawer and fished about for my old phone and charger and then grabbed my laptop. I was angry, furious… *How dare he?* But I found my hands were shaking as I accessed my account, changed all the passwords and transferred the data. My bank details, thank god, appeared untouched, but I cancelled everything to be on the safe side and then sat back, leaning my head against the headboard feeling my heart banging unpleasantly. Finally, *finally*, I could breathe again.

If only Paul would ring.

I picked up the phone, feeling its difference in my hand, letting my thumb scroll down and find his number… My thumb stalled.

No, no and no.

Getting up, I went back into the kitchen and grabbed an unopened bottle of wine. I didn't care that I hadn't eaten and how late it was getting; I wasn't interested in how I would feel in the morning. I shivered and walked about the flat, putting the lamps on, not knowing what to do with myself: whether to stand, sit, watch TV… I did all of it, glancing at the phone, the clock moving from seven, to quarter past, half past… He did say he would come back to me, didn't he?

Sighing, I flicked through the channels curling my feet up under a fluffy blanket and reached for a cushion. There she was again: Cassie Edwards. I almost couldn't bear to watch her parents at the press conference. 'Divorced,' the commentary said unkindly, as though that was important. Never were two people more separate from each other yet at the same time so bound together in joint misery. They sat, all hunched and terrified, the lights and cameras blindly snapping into their frightened faces, the journalists honing in on their confusion in one jabbering, faceless, pack.

'We appeal to anyone who saw anything... Who might know something or someone who might've taken Cassie...'

I couldn't watch it. I turned it off and rang Emma.

'This number comes up as your old phone. Have you swapped?'

'Yep, it was Viv's suggestion. I'm to use this one and give the other to the police.'

'Sounds like a good plan. Switch it off. Put it away somewhere until Monday. You don't want the threat of him contacting you all weekend.'

'No.' My hand reached for the button. *But what if Paul tried to reach me?* I left it.

'So it all went well with Viv, I take it?'

'Oh, she was lovely. Really supportive.'

'Good. What did she say about Cassie Edwards?'

'It was obvious what he was hinting at, but you know what would happen if we start making connections without something more concrete. The powers that be will jump all over her. The sick bastard could be just posturing and grandstanding. *Jesus.* Can you imagine if her parents found out...?' I shook my head slowly, appalled at the thought and glanced from the dead TV screen to the window. The curtains were open to the evening sky, framing the blackened panes. My eye registered the thing before my brain did.

Something moved outside in the darkness.

A cold fear snaked down my spine.

'Luce?'

'Em—' The blanket fell to the floor. I darted a look at the window again as a burst of light flashed once, then twice across the glass.

'You there, hun?'

I stayed motionless, not even breathing, watching for it again.

'Lucy?'

'Could you stay by the phone, Em? I'll call you back in two seconds...'

I could still hear her frantic jabbering as I cast the phone aside and dropped to my knees. Keeping my eyes fixed on the window, I crawled on all fours to the sill. With my body tight to the frame, I peered cautiously out into the shadowed street. The road was empty. The sodium lights burned a sickly orange, revealing nothing but shapes and shadows of the shrubs and bushes. The hedge, shorn part-way, bucked and jerked, the unkempt fronds shivered and went still. I didn't dare breathe, as, above its outline, something crept, slowly. My heart lurched into a drumbeat of fear. Something black moved and stretched. My heart skidded as a long shadow detached itself, unfolding and lengthening as a figure stepped out and a slap of light sent me instantly to the floor.

'*Lucy.*'

I crouched, panting, my phone blaring into a discordant jangle. I scrabbled and dropped it, sending it sliding across the room. Swearing madly, I clawed away from the window on all fours.

'*Lucy!* It's me! Paul!' The light danced again and I nearly cried out with relief. Scrambling to the sill, I hauled myself up. He stood pathetically in amongst the bushes, his coat hunched up around his ears, looking like an embarrassed schoolboy with an arc of mobile phone light wavering about his feet.

I levered the window catch and wiggled the sash open. 'What the—?' I was nearly hysterical. 'What the *hell* are you doing?' I hissed.

'I was trying to see into your window. I didn't want to tap on it in case I'd got the wrong flat. I kept thinking "why does her phone keep going to voicemail?" Now I know. You were on the bloody thing.' He was tiptoeing from the muddy path onto the pavement, the light flashing madly again. 'I gave up in the end. I thought, *she's never going to ring me back so I shall have to see if I can find her address.* You're not an easy woman to track down, you know. Now look at me!' He lifted one foot at a time, trying to shake the dirt off.

I started almost laughing and crying in terror.

'But I wasn't on the phone until—'

'Oh – yeah. Right,' he made a duck quacking motion. 'Yak, yak, yak...'

'How the hell did you find out where I lived?'

He tapped his nose. 'You said Highbury, and I remember you said green and leafy. This was the greenest leafiest place I could find.' He gazed round. 'And besides,' he shrugged, 'you're on 192.com.'

I laughed. 'Christ Almighty, you could've given me heart failure, you silly arse! Hang on, I'll come and get the door.'

I ran along the hallway and flung it open.

'Steady on!' Paul staggered back, fiddling with the torchlight on his phone. 'You *are* pleased to see me, aren't you?' He slipped his arms around my waist and his breath skimmed my cheek. '*Are* you pleased?'

I grinned. 'Of course I'm bloody pleased… God!'

'Shhh!' he laughed. 'I'm sure all your neighbours need to hear.' He glanced behind him and I glanced out there too. It all looked different now that we were playing and being silly. It was ordinary, unthreatening, just houses with steps and gardens and shadows, nothing weird, no Simon Gould, nothing scary. I was being hyper. Crazy. My phone lit up again as I ushered Paul inside.

'Em!' I laughed. 'No, I'm fine. Sorry, it was just me being daft. Yes… It was Paul, scaring the bloody life out of me.' I glared at him. 'Mmm… I know… He's a tosser…' I shot a glance at him, laughing. 'Yes… Have a relaxing evening…' All the time I was talking to her I couldn't take my eyes off him as he bent to wrestle his shoes off. It was the way his shoulders worked, the muscles moving deftly, the sweet look of concentration on his face. I put my hands on his hips as I eased my way past him and went to close the door.

'Hey, you.' He caught my hand and kissed it, drawing me to him. We stood there, holding each other in the doorway, half in, half out, and I glanced into the street. The bushes still crouched in their huddled shadows, hiding their secrets, but it was nothing bad, I could see that now. It was part of the railing, a caught plastic bag, some stunted tree, that was all.

Giggling, we pushed the door closed, feeling the lock catch tight and I led him by the hand along the hallway, kissing him as we stepped over the threshold and again as we closed my front door, and then by the TV and the sofa, and then by the window as I went to close the curtains. I glanced out. The hunched blackness sat there by the entrance to the garden as the wind sent a scutter of leaves down the pavement. *It really isn't him*, I told myself. *It's really not*, I repeated, as the breeze bundled and gusted slowly and I saw the blackness lift its head.

Chapter Four

'Jesus.'

Paul sat on the sofa listening and frowning and nodding and asking all the right questions as I told him about Gould. In the end, he sat back, cradling his glass of wine and studying me thoughtfully.

'Have you eaten?'

I nearly laughed.

'Have I what?'

'I bet you haven't. I bet you've been too wound up. So show me your fridge and your cupboards.'

'Wow! I've never had an offer like that!'

He stood, holding out his hand to help me up.

'This is the thing. Gould gets his power from worming his way into your head.' He tapped his temple. 'Your job, *my* job, is to keep him out. Don't let him in. Is there anything else you want to tell me about that conversation?'

I shook my head.

'Then that's it. He's gone. He's out there. We're in here. This is now a completely safe space. There's just you, and me and—' he picked up my wine glass and handed it to me. '—a very nice bottle of St Emilion.'

'Oh... Err... I don't think I have a nice bottle of St Emilion. Sorry—'

'Ah, but I do.' He reached for his jacket. 'Taa-dahh!...'

'I didn't see that!' I laughed.

Paul pulled a mock serious face. 'That's the thing you'll find with me. I am definitely full of things you're not expecting.'

That Friday night turned into Saturday morning. Hours became an afternoon which became a night again. There was nothing but a tangled duvet, over-heated pillows and sticky skin. I loved it. Nothing I had ever experienced before even came close, I never wanted him to leave.

'But that's an ostrich!'

He was showing me how to make shadow puppets on the wall – first a rabbit and then a goat – while we ate Cadbury's Chocolate Fingers which he'd gone out especially for, because I said I hadn't had them in years.

'It's actually a camel.'

'Oh, you're bloody useless,' I laughed, slapping his hand. His fingers landed on my cheek and he let them linger gently there until it tickled.

'Tell me about your scar,' he traced the line on my cheek.

'Are we comparing defects now?' I pulled away slightly. 'What about this one?' My fingers ran lightly down a silvery long leaf-shape beneath his ribs.

'You first.'

'Rollerskating. A lamppost and I got close up and personal.'

'My brother. Messing about with a kitchen knife.'

'Wow!' I shook my head in horror. 'I thought you didn't have a brother?'

'I don't. Not anymore. It was a car accident. He'd been drinking.'

'My God.'

'He was what people, including my parents, referred to as "trouble". But "trouble" when you're his kid brother, means being daring and exciting—' he smiled sadly, remembering. 'And nicking stuff. *Christ*, he was always at it. I used to skive off school and he'd let me tag along when he went off on his "jollies" as he called them.' His smile clouded. 'That's how you get to be a psychologist: always trying to figure out how someone you love so much could ever leave you.'

My heart hurt for him.

He took a breath. 'Yep, the moral of the story is: never nick a powerful car when you're pissed, and don't mess about with sharp knives.'

He gave a little smile and kissed me, but I felt his grief and his sadness. I had no idea how to respond. We made love then, quietly, intimately, and afterwards, we lay facing each other, sharing sweetened breath. For a moment I thought he was going to tell me that he loved me. Our intimacy had deepened. Some barrier had broken down. He didn't say it, I didn't say it but I knew the words hung there between us. We were both acutely aware of it right that moment, but neither of us said a word.

–

On Sunday afternoon we lay in the bath together in my echoing bathroom, his head against my chest. I'd lit candles, and we lay back in the steaming water, breathing in the scents of lavender and sandalwood. The oil bloomed in tiny golden circles on the surface, clinging to our arms and legs, the water running off us like droplets of mercury. The shivery coldness of his hair pressed into my cheek, and I remembered what being in love felt like.

'Come on.' He sat up suddenly in a wash of water.

'Come on what?' I stared at his naked back as he hopped over the side.

'Let's go out.'

'Out? What do you mean, out?'

'You know, that weird place with sky and pavements and people.' He grabbed a towel and started sawing it across his shoulders. 'Here you go.' He pulled another off the rail. 'What's the matter? I thought you liked mad spontaneity.'

I half got up. 'Where are we going?'

'Umm… I dunno. How about Belsize Park?'

'Belsize Park?'

'Yeah. I want to show you where I live. Why don't you bring some stuff and stay the night? You can go to work from mine. It makes sense.'

Sense or not, I wasn't going to argue.

–

The moment we walked down Belsize Park Gardens I knew I was going to love it.

It was a wide, peaceful street. Each side was lined with white stucco-fronted houses, with Italianate stone steps and impressive double-fronted doors. He pointed up at a glossy red front door with a polished brass lion-head knocker.

'That's mine. Top floor.'

He mounted the steps two at a time and the door juddered opened to reveal a beautiful black and white tiled hallway. White glossy panelled doors on either side denoted other occupants, but our footsteps carried on echoing as we wound our way up the richly carved staircase. I discovered I was panting. I shifted my bag uncomfortably. 'Ever thought of having a lift put in?'

He gave me a withering look as he paused to unlock a door before pushing it wide and gesturing for me to go first.

The whole place was black and white: a wide expanse of stripped, pale wooden floors with two black leather couches in the centre, black and white leather rag rugs and an amazing ornate white marble mantelpiece and black arched grate. There was a glass topped dining table with scroll-backed chairs in front of a white granite breakfast bar with black and chrome stools. Everything sparkled and oozed quality.

'Wow! This is amazing!' I walked slowly into the room, gazing up. 'Look at that ceiling! Oh my god!' It was truly out of this world: great hanging swirls of plasterwork fruit and flowers garlanded the cornice and the centre rose was exactly that, a wreath of white flowers. 'It's original,' he looked up with me. 'I suspect there are very few people around who have the skill to do that kind of thing now.'

'And the fireplace! My god! I've never seen anything like that!' I went over and ran my finger down the stone columns of tiered acanthus leaves and scrolls.

'It's French, so I was told.' He nodded. 'Like the clock. It was here when I moved in. The couple who were selling the flat didn't want it, so it got to stay. I think the two go together, don't you?'

'Absolutely.'

Its impressive gold face mirrored my reflection as I peered to look closer. Its mercury pendulum, minutely etched and decorated, swung regally to and fro. Two white porcelain vases sat on either side of it containing rather sad-looking peacock feathers, and behind one of the vases was a whole slew of what looked like bills and tickets and bits of paper.

'Not mine either, before you say anything.'

'The bills?'

'No, smartarse, the vases. I needed somewhere to stick them and they never got moved.'

Incongruously, tucked at the back, was a kitsch glass ornament filled with stripes of coloured sand with 'Welcome to Colwyn Bay' across the bottom. I laughed and went to pick it up.

'Don't!'

I jumped a mile.

'Sorry...' He came forward and went to take my bag from my shoulder. 'It was something my brother gave me years ago, it's just a bit sentimental, that's all – Here, let's dump this in the bedroom, shall we? I'll find you somewhere to hang your work clothes in a minute.'

He manoeuvred his way through a half-open door. The room was huge too: floor-to-ceiling wardrobes filled one wall, with bedside tables, one on either side of the crisp white linen bed. He dropped the bag at its foot.

'Gosh! This room is lovely too!' I crouched to pull at the side zip pocket of the bag where it had come undone.

'What's so special in there?' he winked. 'Anything I'd like?'

'Doubt it,' I smiled. 'A laptop, a few papers. You know, the usual boring work stuff,' I patted, checking the phone I was going to give to Viv was safely tucked away.

'Work is totally banned, by the way.' He held out his hand. 'So. Come on, the guided tour isn't quite over yet. Let me show you the one overriding and *singular* reason why I bought this place.' He helped me up and led me back into the sitting area and over to the window where a long unusual-looking sash went from floor to ceiling.

'A win-door,' he explained, undoing the catch.

A gust of chilly air hit me as he smoothly slid the whole thing up and clambered through. 'It's quite safe. Here, see for yourself.' He extended his palm through the gap. 'Come on, come and have a look.'

I faltered. 'I'm not very keen on heights.'

'Don't worry, I won't let go of you.' His face was grey in the evening light.

I couldn't see his eyes.

'Come on.'

My chest tightened. 'It's really not my thing.'

'You're missing out on so much.' He let go of my hand and turned, gazing out into the skyline. His feet scuffed on the gritty roofing felt. 'You're not afraid of heights, you're afraid of not being in control.'

'Whatever, Mr-Bloody-Analyst. Would you come in now, please?' I tried to laugh it off, but he only looked back at me. He wasn't smiling.

'All I'm asking you to do is take my hand.'

'Paul.'

'*Trust* me. It's that easy.' He offered his hand again. My whole body trembled as I looked down at it.

'No. I don't think so, thanks.'

'Please. Just take it. That's all. I'll do the rest.'

Bizarrely, my fingers twitched and left the rigid comfort of my side. They hovered above his for a second and then our skin met. His grip was firm and solid.

'Right. See? Just one step up. Don't think, just do it.'

My foot lifted and suddenly I was out there, holding onto him. The pressure of his body was firm and constant.

I breathed, my terror and his warmth mingling in the darkness.

'Now lift up your head. Look out there!' He slipped his arm around my waist and I managed a glance up. There was the cityscape, backed by a sky of deep blue carbon and alive with lights and the blare of cars streaming below.

'Fabulous, isn't it?'

He held me close as I followed his gaze across the rooftops. Ornate ridge tiles and turreted chimney pots stood sentinel against the orange-lit sky. I shivered and his arm tightened around me. 'Just a tiny shuffle forwards. I'm still here.' Both hands moved to my waist. My own came up in horror. 'I've got you, Lucy. Just calm down.' He inched me to where the edge of the balustrade slipped giddily away into a ten-foot gap.

'No!' I flailed automatically clutching at nothing and then my hands grabbed his forearm. He laughed. 'Don't worry. You're not going anywhere.'

I didn't like it. I didn't like any of it. The panic thumped through me. My whole body wanted to dip and slide from his grasp, sink to my knees and cling to the roof felt, but that drop yawned beneath me. I froze, breathing hard and trying not to look.

'You don't trust me.' He released me a little and I shrank back. His tone was tinged with disappointment.

'It's not you—' My teeth were chattering. 'I don't trust myself. I could've dragged us both off… You don't know what I'm like…' I broke off.

'That's the thing,' he was still smiling. 'I know *exactly* what you're like. And while you're panicking about being out of control, and whether you should trust me or not, you forget to see things how they really are. You're so busy being consumed by your own fear, you forget to look around you and see how beautiful everything is.'

I couldn't think of a reply. I felt the weight of his hand in the small of my back, a soft breeze tumbling my hair from my forehead. I steeled the core of myself and swallowed. *He's disappointed in me. I'm disappointed in me. I could try, couldn't I? I could just…* Dragging the cool air deep into my lungs, I managed to lift my head, slowly. My spine tensed a little but his hand was firm and solid. Letting out my breath, oh so carefully, I looked out at the vastness of the relentless city below. There it was: Primrose Hill, Canary Wharf and St Paul's stretching out on the skyline.

'See? I was right, wasn't I?'

I didn't say anything, but I knew, bizarrely, that the shaking had quelled and my feet felt firmer. I breathed in the night air and exhaled, allowing some of those fears to flutter off into the darkness. I was so tired of holding back, utterly worn-out with continually having to protect myself. The truth was I was sick of feeling scared.

My hand reached down for his and found it, bringing it up and placing it to lie flat on my stomach: my palm firm against his knuckles. We stood together, quiet and unmoving, gazing out, drinking in the writhing red and white snakes of car lights.

'Well?' I could hear the smile in his voice. 'Aren't I?'

I didn't look round at his gaze. I kept my face turned away but let him see the grin that was threatening my cheeks. 'Actually, Mr Analyst,' I said archly. 'You might well be.'

—

The next morning came too fast. We lay there, my head on his chest, arguing amiably over who was going to get the tea. Paul was unusually quiet.

'I have a question for you.' The heat of his thigh against mine had adhered our skin. I didn't want to pull away.

'I really do think it's your turn,' I said. 'I made it last time.'

'What?'

'The tea.'

'No I didn't mean that.'

'Oh? What are you on about?'

'Can I ask you something?'

'Sure.'

'That first time, you know, in that wood you took me to.'

'Uh-huh.'

'Well, that wasn't the first time you'd done that, was it?'

I paused. 'What do you mean?'

'You were so precise, so insistent. You knew exactly where we were going and what we were going to do. Christ, you even knew the clump of trees!' He wheezed a laugh but I could tell he wasn't really laughing.

I frowned, blinking, staring at a crease in the duvet. 'No, that was the first time.'

'Bullshit.' His voice was soft but with an edge.

I knew if I looked up, I wouldn't like his expression. 'Honestly.'

'Don't say honestly when you're not being honest.'

'But I am!' I propped myself up to see his face. 'I *am* being honest. I mean, you're right, I've been there before, my parents took us there as kids, that's all... In fact—' I grinned. 'My dad told me that was the place he first kissed

97

my mam, so that's quite sweet, isn't it?' I nudged him. His face didn't change. 'But I haven't done that with anyone else. You were the first.' I nudged him again playfully, wanting him to join in the game.

He stayed staring blankly at the ceiling.

'It's just I hate being lied to. Even something inconsequential. I can't stand it.' He looked genuinely upset.

'I'm not lying. I'm absolutely *not* lying. That. Is. The. Truth.'

'I've got a thing about it.'

'Well that's good, because I've got a thing about you.' And I eased myself closer, sliding my hand down his chest feeling the heat of his belly as I moved onto the stickiness of his cock which responded almost immediately. He turned to me and we kissed, not passionately, and we began to make love gently and slowly, in that kind of exhausted way that you do when it's not about sex, it's about comfort, and saying sorry for being on the brink of something you might be really sorry for.

Afterwards, we dozed a little, knowing, with that awful pull, that it could only be for minutes. I allowed my eyes to drift and close. *But you had been there with Dan.* My eyes sprung open, staring into nothing. I swallowed. It hadn't been the truth exactly, but it was the truth as to how I felt about Paul. Dan didn't even come close. The intensity of his reaction had shocked me. What did he mean, he'd got a thing about it? Was it some traumatic past relationship that had made him so hyper-vigilant?

'I'll put the kettle on and jump in the shower while I'm waiting shall I, oh slothful-one?' He suddenly threw the covers back.

I yawned and stretched into the warmth of his side. 'I told you it was your turn.'

I waited, snuggling languidly into the pillow as though on the brink of going back to sleep, watching the dimples above his buttocks roll as he staggered a little around my mess of clothes on the floor before disappearing into the hallway.

So this possible relationship – was this the near 'marriage-job' he'd mentioned? I lay there for a moment, listening to the sound of the kettle being filled and the chink of mugs, feeling the thing I was about to do itch at me, waiting to hear that movement in the bathroom, the reassuring squeal of the tap and the drumming water telling me he was in the shower and it was safe. I so wanted to find out.

It was like a compulsion.

I knew it was wrong. Why didn't I just ask him like an adult, like an ordinary person would?

I don't know. Insecurity maybe? A lack of belief I could trust what he told me?

I'd seen the drawer in his bedside table. I knew, even as my hand reached forward, this could be the end of something.

It was the kind of drawer that holds all kinds of rubbish. He'd gone to push it closed last night, and I thought I'd caught a glimpse of a photograph.

I watched my fingers pulling gently on the wooden edge. It opened silently and then, there it was. A photograph of a girl.

It was one of those small, passport-style ones. It was standing up, wedged in beside a whole muddled mess of papers and old tickets and dried up biros. I looked at it feeling suddenly scared and slightly sick.

She was very young: twenty at the most, and very pretty.

Picking it up very carefully, I stared and stared at it, imprinting her face as though any moment the image might dissolve and disappear. She had curly dark hair, like me, and was smiling. It was clearly someone from a long time ago. I imagined him with her, their young love, puppy-like and happy. A pang of jealousy suddenly caught me. I was bothered, I realised: stupidly, ridiculously. It was years old.

Somewhere off in the background the splash and wash of water drummed and I knew I didn't have too much longer. Sliding it back into the gap in the joint, I shoved the papers and tickets and maps back on top. Then, scooping up a baggy T-shirt from the floor, I pulled it on, tiptoeing quickly into the bathroom where he was just about to turn the shower off.

'Did you finish making the tea?'

'Don't know where everything is,' I smiled disarmingly.

'Hardly difficult.' He rolled his eyes, pulling the towels from the rail, and slinging one low around his hips before starting to rub the other though his hair. He paused and touched my shoulder. His fringe stood up comically.

'Happy?' he queried.

'Very,' I smiled back.

'Sure?' He scrubbed a corner of the towel across his forehead so that I couldn't see his eyes.

'Yes, why?'

'Because you suddenly look… Hmm…' The scrubbing paused. 'I don't know. Different, somehow.'

'I was lying in bed, just thinking—'

'Dangerous. Always dangerous.' He flapped the towel out in front of him. His hair looked like Coco the Clown.

'You know what you were saying before?' I reached up and smoothed one of the ruffled bits over his ear.

'When before?' He moved away to the mirror.

'Like *before*, before – about that one girl, the serious relationship... The woman you went out with—'

He blinked, puzzled. 'I'm trying to think what I might've said.' He picked up a comb and started to rake his hair into thick furrows.

'You know, the almost-marriage-jobbie—'

'Me?' He looked at my reflection. 'Marriage? Are you sure?' He chuckled and started combing again.

'Yeah, you said you'd had a few, kind of serious living-together relationships but one almost-marriage.'

'Don't think so. Wrong bloke. You must be getting me confused with one of your other boyfriends... Are you getting in that shower? I would, while it's still warm.'

'Oh. Okay. Right.' Puzzled, I pulled the T-shirt over my head and stepped into the cubicle, twisting the tap and hopping out of the way of the sudden blast of cool water.

My phone jangled in the bedroom somewhere.

'I'll get that for you, shall I?' He darted out before I could answer. *He had said that though, hadn't he?* I tried to remember the conversation when I became aware of his voice in the hallway, querying whoever it was on the phone. I had this sudden and appalling realisation. *The ringing tone... It was my old phone.* A shot of adrenaline banged into my heart.

Simon.

The water went suddenly hot but a tingling chill crawled into my neck. *What if it was?... It doesn't have to be*, I told myself. *You're being paranoid, it could be anyone.*

I stood, straining to listen to the conversation over the torrent of splashing water as Paul reappeared in the doorway waving my phone.

'I picked it up and my thumb pressed the answer button by mistake. I didn't mean to. Sorry.'

'Uh-huh.' I pretended to be soaping my hair, half-heartedly rinsing it and reaching for the shampoo again. 'Who was it?'

'Some bloke. I thought I recognised the voice.'

The bottle slid from my fingers and crash into the shower tray. I bent to retrieve it, my thumbs and fingers fumbling.

'But not Gould?' My voice sounded weird as I straightened.

'No. I think I'd recognise Gould. The bloke said he wouldn't leave a number or a name. But he did ask me to say hello to you. Bit odd, don't you think?' He placed it precisely on the edge of the basin.

'My whole life is full of odd people.' I glanced over my shoulder. 'I shouldn't worry about it.'

'I wasn't worrying, but do you normally give out your number to random men?'

There was something in his tone. I turned to face him but he was looking in the mirror and running his fingers along his jawline, his chin tilted, his eyes lost.

'No I don't. As you say, very strange.' I kept my pitch bright and stupidly cheerful as I turned off the shower. The whole room went quiet. He seemed stiff and unfriendly suddenly.

'So, more importantly, would you like to meet for dinner tonight. Does that fit with your plans?' I opened the door and scouted for a towel.

But he only shrugged. 'I'm not sure. I might need to work.'

'I can rustle up something at mine as long as you're not too worried about food-poisoning.' I chuckled.

'I'll have to see.' He busied himself, not looking at me and then glanced at his watch next to the basin. 'I really need to get going.'

He wandered away into the kitchen. Something was wrong. The ground beneath me was shifting. Wrapping the towel around me and picking up the phone, I padded cautiously after him, aware that he was now opening and closing cupboards a little too loudly and clattering plates onto the granite. He didn't look up.

'You okay?'

'Yep. You want breakfast?'

'That would be nice. Are you sure you're okay?'

From here I could see the muscles in his temple working, wrestling and fighting under the skin. He looked up and his face suddenly smoothed. He smiled. 'You look lovely.'

My hand automatically came up and touched my unbrushed hair.

'Shame you have to tie it back.'

I hadn't thought about tying it back.

'Is toast and marmalade okay? I'm not sure what else I've got... Proper coffee too. Will that do you?' Whatever his mood was, it had now disappeared.

'It all sounds perfect.'

'You've got ten minutes then.'

He busied himself with the breakfast as I slid into the bedroom. Unhooking my work clothes from their hanger on the back of the door, I crouched down to find my clean underwear and realised something that hadn't dawned on me before: I hadn't taken this phone out of my bag. I purposefully had checked it, *hadn't I?* But now the zip of the side pocket was open.

I looked down at the black rectangle in my hand and opened the 'call log' screen. Seven minutes ago I had received a call from a 'withheld number' that had lasted for two minutes and twenty-four seconds. I couldn't think of anyone who would ring at seven in the morning and withhold their number. But then again I couldn't think why Paul would speak to a complete stranger for two minutes and twenty-four seconds either.

Unless it *had* been Simon Gould.

And if it was, why didn't he just say?

Chapter Five

'Lucy!' Viv called from her office as I went to take my coat off. 'Have you got a minute?'

Emma was walking out of the tearoom with a cup of coffee in her hand. She paused and gave me a wide-eyed warning look as I went in.

'Shut the door, would you?'

I was still breathless from the stairs and I could feel my heart pounding.

'Alright?' She smiled, but I knew there something was up. 'I'll cut straight to the chase. I've already been in contact with the multi-disciplinary team about Simon Gould, and I also managed to get Dave Cartwright to go and interview him.'

'Okay...' I said warily.

'He had signed the sex offender register, by the way. He did it the same day he got out.'

I looked at her uncomprehending. 'No he hadn't! I was told—'

Viv held up her hand. 'And he also says you gave him your private mobile number.'

'*What?* He said *what?*'

'He says that the officer at the prison had to remind you about personal safety.'

'Viv! *None* of that happened! Just ask the officer if you don't—'

She closed her eyes. 'You don't have to tell me, Lucy. I know the lad's a liar. And you don't have to point out how good you are at your job either. You are a very experienced, highly respected member of this team. Your integrity and professionalism are not in question here. Before we go any further, I want you to know that. You've got that mobile for me?'

I reached down and pulled it from my bag. I wasn't sure I liked the sound of 'before we go any further.'

'I think he called me this morning too, although I didn't answer it.' I slid it across her desk.

I watched her as she dropped the phone into her drawer and shut it. She blinked and licked her lips before looking up at me. My anxiety heightened.

'Look. Lucy. You've been working for almost two years straight with this type of offender. You've been immersed in it all, listening to horrible stuff, dealing with it without any proper, long-term break. I feel responsible because I've allowed you to do it. I shouldn't have. I should've taken more care of you.'

I let the words sink in.

'So what does "more care" mean?' I said warily.

'More care means you should take some time off. You deserve a break.'

'Uh-huh, but what you're really saying is, should Gould re-offend while he's on licence and under our supervision, you don't want any inference at the trial that one of your staff might've done something inappropriate because they were under stress from being over-worked. Is that about the gist of it?'

'Lucy,' she said patiently. 'That's your spin. That's not what I'm saying.'

'Not you, maybe.' I kept her gaze. 'But certainly those above you. Don't forget, I've been in the job a long time. I know how this works.'

'Yes, I know you do. And if you think about it logically, you'll see what I'm saying is right. Never mind them,' she jerked her chin upward. 'You've already identified that Gould can be a problem with women. Your first instinct, if you remember, was to give him to Dave Cartwright. Your instinct was right, mine was wrong. I shouldn't have ever sent you to see him. Gould is going to be attending Dave Cartwright's sex offender group anyway, so he can deal with him from now on. So you, Lucy...' she leaned forward for emphasis, '...You are one of my very best officers. I can't risk you getting burned out. I need to look after you a bit more, so I'm instructing you to take some time off.' She gave me a mock-serious frown. 'Let's say a month for starters – but take more if you want.'

'A month! Viv—'

'I'm not arguing with you, Lucy. You don't even have to book it as leave. Go somewhere nice.' She leaned back, waving. 'Get out of London, go and do something mad. Abroad maybe? Something off-the-wall. Try hang gliding in the Dolomites, or macramé in Moldova, I dunno!' She grinned. 'Just switch work off in that head of yours, would you?'

'But the thing is, I can't just—'

'Yes you can.' She searched on her desk for her glasses and then waved them at me as she looked at her computer screen. 'Now bugger off.'

Her being nice to me made it all even worse. Emma's eyes were like saucers as she watched me pick up the coat and bag I'd only just put down.

'Where are you off to now?' She looked to Viv's door and then back at me. 'I wanted to tell you stuff?'

I gave her a pointed look, eyeing Dave Cartwright's hunched back, knowing his jug-like ears would be swivelling. 'Later?' I mouthed and wiggled a phone sign. I tried to smile, but I knew that was pointless with Emma. She nodded, wide-eyed, as I clattered my way down the stairs and into the street.

It was Paul I really needed to talk to. It rang out for a while and then he answered.

'Hello. Paul Webb?'

'I need to see you.' I cut right to the point. 'There's things I want to talk to you about.'

He sounded guarded. 'Okay. When?'

I looked at my watch. 'You said you had an important meeting this morning?'

'I'll be near Camden. You can meet me there if you like. What time?'

'The sooner the better.'

'There's a pub in Primrose Hill. The Princess of Wales.'

'I think I know it.'

'I'll meet you there... Umm... Eleven?'

'Perfect.'

—

I leaned into the heavy door as a warm blast of lunchtime beer washed over me in one great swell.

Paul was perched at the bar. He already had a drink in front of him. He turned to look over his shoulder. 'So what are you having? Or is it too early? Or maybe too late?'

I was aware of his cryptic tone. 'Actually, I'll just have a tonic water, thanks.'

He turned to give the order to the barmaid. She had brown shiny hair and brown shiny eyes. The eyes skimmed across me but kept alighting on him, the pupils stretching and sparkling for his benefit. He counted out the money and she leaned across the bar and said something that I didn't quite catch. He laughed back at her.

A sudden suspicion sent a quiet tension through me. He handed me my drink, and I knew he saw my discomfort.

'Cheers.'

'Cheers.' I raised my glass to his. 'You know this place?'

He took the head off his pint and shrugged.

I touched the base of my glass and traced a drop of water. 'I meant, you seem to know the staff.' I kept my voice lowered so that the barmaid couldn't hear.

'Ah.' I heard the amusement.

'Ah what?' I took a sip of water.

'*Ah* meaning, no, she and I have never known each other in *any* respect.'

I flinched, embarrassed that I'd even mentioned it.

'So are you going to tell me about what happened this morning?' His directness caught me by surprise. He arched an eyebrow. 'I'm assuming that's why we're meeting?' His face tightened a little.

'This is all something to do with a bloke, an ex...' He tipped his head. '...Or a current boyfriend? Is that what's been bothering you?'

'Boyfriend? – Ex? No! Nothing like that!'

He only gave a wry smile into the rim of his glass.

'I won't be angry if you tell me the truth. As I said, the truth isn't a problem, we can deal with that. It's the lying I can't deal with.' His lips wrapped around the word.

'No, no, no. You've got the wrong end of the stick completely.' I took a breath. 'I should've told you this before. I don't know why I didn't, but...' I licked my lips nervously. 'As soon as my phone rang this morning, I had this thought it would be Gould. I told you on Friday that he'd got hold of my number somehow – well that wasn't totally the truth. He hinted he'd got someone to hack my account... I have no idea how.' My hands waved blindly. 'Which means that he could have all kinds of information...'

Paul blinked slowly. 'Christ.'

'Well anyway. My boss got someone to interview him and he's saying that I gave him my personal number. He's implying I was over-familiar with him.'

'What? And they believe him?'

'But you know what head office are like: they want a tidy case. It's far easier to deal with some naïve probation officer giving out her private details to the cons than it is bring in some very expensive IT people to go on some wild forensic goose chase. So basically, Viv has told me to take some time off.'

Paul shook his head slowly in disbelief.

'But you definitely didn't recognise his voice?'

He paused. 'I suppose it *could* have been.' He stopped to recollect. 'Whoever it was stayed silent a lot of the time. I knew they were there and I kept repeating "Hello?... Hello?..."'

He looked at me, his face softening. 'You should have *told* me, Lucy!'

'Hence the change of phone number and why I've been a bit jittery.'

'Jeeze, of course. I get all that! But why didn't you just say? Why couldn't you tell me?'

'Because...' I gathered myself. 'Because that's not quite the whole story.' I swallowed involuntarily. 'I did something... Something bad, years ago. Viv knows about it which is why she's trying to look after me...'

'Go on.'

'I was stupid.' I took a breath. 'I hadn't been qualified long. It was my first job in a prison. There was a prisoner called Jonathan Peters.'

The name still made my skin crawl.

'A prison officer came to me and told me that the prisoner's mother had died, and that his sister had attempted suicide. He was not coping and would I supervise a special visit with his brother?'

Paul's face didn't change.

'Peters was devastated: grief-stricken. I didn't know what to say to him. I was sitting in a room on my own with him waiting for his brother to turn up. I knew I was supposed to stay there the whole time, but I got distracted by someone at the door. I left him alone in the room with an outside phone line. Sounds such a small thing, doesn't it?' I glanced at Paul's face. 'I had no idea that Peters was a high-risk sex offender. No one had told me that.' I closed my eyes at my own stupidity.

Paul put his hand on my knee.

'I got hauled up by the Governor.' I kept my eyes lowered. 'I had to attend a hearing at head office... All that. Then the newspapers got hold of it. They had a field day with me.' I chewed my lip. 'Peters had contacted his "known associates". He told them about a little seven-year-old girl he'd spotted on visits. Of course, he'd also managed to find out the mother's address, and because the child came to the prison in her school uniform, he knew the school she attended. So when she went missing...' I stopped, feeling physically sick at the memory. 'All he'd needed was to use a telephone, and I'd given him his opportunity.'

Paul's hand squeezed in sympathy. 'You can't beat yourself up about that Lucy. He would have found another way eventually. You know as well as I do he could've paid to get the use of an illegal mobile phone. He could've found another prisoner to—'

'But he didn't need to though, did he?' I looked up and saw how kind his eyes looked. 'Because he had me: the mug, laying it out for him on a plate.' I sighed deeply. 'It was the usual accusations: that I was blundering, incompetent, woolly-headed – Naïve at best, and at worst, that I was somehow complicit and had been groomed by the prisoner. You know the score.'

There was a moment where neither of us spoke. Paul picked up his glass and drank a little, thoughtfully, and then put it down, squaring it with the edge of the beer mat. 'Is that it, then? The whole story?'

'That's the whole sorry tale.'

'And there's nothing else to confess? No other omissions or disclosures?'

I saw the girl in the photograph laughing up at me.

'Nothing,' I smiled. 'I promise.'

He looked at me and I looked straight back.

'So you're off today, then?'

'Looks that way.'

'Then we shouldn't waste it.'

'What do you mean?'

'I think I can afford an afternoon off too, don't you?'

–

We walked down the street and I took his arm, but he straightened it and my hand slipped into his. I felt the heat of his palm but it wasn't enough. I wanted the closeness of last night back. *Was that only last night?* It felt like months ago. We'd come so far in a matter of only hours: all that intimacy and togetherness, an almost quarrel, a confession, and now we were like some partners in crime. We'd opened up: shared our vulnerabilities, broken down barriers, been totally honest and open... *Honest... The woman that goes snooping? The fact he had no idea I'd broken his trust made it even worse.*

'Camden Market, then?' He playfully veered me across the road.

'Brilliant idea! I haven't been there for ages!'

Whatever had been undone, I'd undone it, but I wanted to find that connection again. I wanted to press myself into his side and meld my skin into his until neither of us knew who was who. I contented myself with tucking my hand into the crook of his elbow and he squeezed my fingers reassuringly.

'You cold?' He glanced at me concerned. 'Here have this.' He pulled a red patterned scarf from around his neck and wound it carefully around mine, tucking the ends in to make sure I was snug.

'There,' he smiled. For one moment we were back where we should be. I breathed. I would make it better. It was all going to be okay.

–

We walked down side streets, through the skeletal frames of unoccupied market stalls. A watery sun hung low in the late morning sky. The air was full of the promise of blustery April afternoons. There was a sweet scent on the breeze: a sharp orange tang from the broken fruit in the gutter. I leant my face briefly against his arm. His coat smelled sharply of fresh air and I savoured the moment. I lifted his hand and kissed it. It was cold from the strengthening wind yet his skin smelled of soft salt and sugar like he'd been out in the sunshine. I licked his scent from my lips. I didn't want him to have any past at all; I wanted to rub it out in the same way he'd rubbed out mine.

We meandered our way through the market, threading aimlessly along narrow passages where the main group of stalls were jammed in together. The flapping awnings showed a multitude of goods: fruit and veg, boots and shoes, clothes on rails, antiques, and junkshop bric-a-brac. We came across a bookstall set back slightly from the rest with strings of coloured bulbs jostled across the tented entrance. We stood just inside, huddled together out of the gusts, watching the tarpaulin roof bulge and creak against its guy ropes.

The books were neatly wedged into trays, yards of them. Paul picked up a miniature book of sepia prints. The cover was brown thick paper: porous like old skin. He held it in his hand, weighing it, gently turning the fine gilt-edged tissue paper as though he were touching some precious thing.

He looked up at the stallholder. 'How much do you want for this?'

The man shrugged. 'Forty quid?'

Paul smiled and shook his head, putting the tiny book back on the stand.

'They're all originals, mate. All them pictures are collectable. Nice little set, that.'

He smiled again. 'I'm sure they are.' He moved off to another pile, touching the book covers, turning them over, reading the spines. I stood slightly back, my hands deep in my pockets. I watched his fingers as they searched: touching, stroking, selecting. He was totally absorbed, unaware of my gaze. Somewhere, from the depths of his jacket, I heard his phone ring. He stiffened suddenly.

'You're not going to get that?'

He shrugged noncommittally. 'It'll be someone I don't want to talk to, I expect.' Without glancing at the number, he switched it off, and picked up another book but I noticed he wasn't really looking at it.

'Hey.' I reached for his arm.

He smiled. 'Hello you.' For a second we caught each other's eyes and whatever it was, lifted. I pulled him closer to me and rested my cheek on his arm, looking back into the melee of bodies milling around the stall. There were streams of people, all pushing their way past. It was cosy in here: just me and him. I knew it was really early days but this all felt so *real*. This wasn't a romance or a fling or just seeing someone; this was the beginning of something really special.

Simon.

My eyes flickered in alarm, seeing and not seeing the figure in the crowds moving past.

A jolt of panic hit me.

Simon. Simon Gould with a little girl.

He skirted past the stall, coming close and glancing in and away again. The collar-length hair, the greeny jacket and dark jeans... He moved past in a blur lasting only seconds, the tiny blonde head bobbing next to him. It was him, definitely. I almost cried out: I opened my mouth, my hands climbing up Paul's arm, my heart beating out of my chest.

'Did... Did you see him?'

'What?' Paul snapped round.

'Stay there,' I ordered as I turned and almost fell over the guy ropes in my rush to get out of there, blundering into the moving crowd, shoving people out of my way as I frantically searched the space where he'd been. My eyes scanned over faces and coats, one after another. I looked back to the stall. A woman was standing there, clearly waiting for someone, watching me curiously. Her eyes caught mine. There was something familiar about her, but I didn't know what. She looked away self-consciously, turning her head so that her dark hair feathered across the side of her face.

Paul was where I'd left him, looking for me anxiously. 'What is it?' His face was pinched with concern.

'Gould.' The name stuck on my tongue.

'Gould?'

But I'd already pulled out my mobile. 'Ring the police, would you? It was definitely him. He had a child with him... The kid that's missing... Cassie Edwards. Tell them—' I was dialling Viv and walking out of the tent, darting glances this way and that as Paul delved for his phone.

'Come on! Come on!' I muttered. The woman with dark hair had moved back a little into the awning of the children's clothes stall opposite. She looked across at me again.

'Viv!' I nearly collapsed with relief. 'It's Lucy. I've just seen Simon Gould. I'm in Camden Market. He's got a little girl with him. I am almost a hundred percent it's

Cassie Edwards, but we've lost him. He disappeared into the crowd—'

'Lucy? Oh my God! Hang on.' I could hear her talking to someone in the background.

'Viv? We've already got onto the police, we've told them—' I was aware of Paul finishing the call and nodding to me.

I glanced behind me. The thought that Simon was here sent a slide of horror into my hairline. He was here. I was here. He couldn't have known that, could he? There was no way.

'Lucy? Are you there?' Viv's voice dragged me back.

'What do you want me to do?' I looked back at the woman. She was talking to the stall holder.

Viv sounded distracted. '... Um... Can I ring you back, Luce?' I could hear the urgent chatter of voices in the background. She said something away from the phone and then she was gone.

Paul looked at me, his eyes huge. 'Well?'

'She's going to ring back. What did the police say?'

'They'll be here any minute.' Even as he said it there was the wail of sirens.

'My God, Paul...' I felt sick at the thought of Gould watching me, following my every move. My stomach went sour at the idea of how close he'd been; I hated the fact that he must've seen me with Paul... That he knew things about my private life... My phone suddenly jangled.

'Viv! The police are here. What do you want me to—?'

'Lucy.'

The edge in her voice made me stop.

'It can't have been him.'

Something odd cut into the silence.

'What?'

'It can't have been Simon Gould.'

'Viv. It was! It was!' I couldn't get my words out properly. 'He was here. I saw him! He had a child with him!'

'Gould has been with Dave Cartwright all morning. He's at the community sex offender group. He's still there now.'

'He can't be!'

'He is. Dave assures me he's not moved an inch.'

'Where is it?'

'Where's what?'

'The group. Where is it being held?'

'Arlington Road Centre, but—'

'That's only *minutes* from here!' I cut across her. 'You know what Dave's like, he—'

'Lucy stop. You made a mistake, that's all. Just leave it. Please.'

I could only stand there, breathless. I *knew* beyond any doubt. I *knew* it.

'Excuse me – Miss?' A police officer appeared, her radio jabbering loudly. I looked round for Paul. He was in the entrance to the tent looking uncomfortable as two officers made their way purposefully towards him. People had stopped to stare and whisper. It was as though I was watching it happen to someone else.

'Could you just go through again what and who you saw?' The officer jogged me back to the present. She was smiling encouragingly and I glanced over again at Paul who was gesticulating and pointing into the distance. I saw that a little crowd had gathered now, their whispers more inquisitive: *what had we done?* and then, again, I suddenly saw the woman moving quickly through the people on the fringes. Our eyes locked, her face suddenly withdrew, and she turned.

'Miss?' the officer looked at me enquiringly.

What could I say?

I could feel the absolute humiliation scorching my skin. I was aware of the looks of the other police officers as they spoke quietly to Paul. I didn't want to hear the conversation.

I had no defence. I had no case to argue. I was wasting their time; they didn't say it, but I knew that's what everyone thought.

'Let's get out of here, shall we?' Paul led me by the elbow away from the milling bodies and towards a pub on the corner. 'How about a drink?'

I could see the police cars beginning to pull away and the groups of people dispersing.

My shame stood with us, uncomfortably, in the gloomy bar. A thin man in a tweed jacket peered at us over the top of his spectacles. He smoothed out the newspaper in front of him and tapped his biro, leaving dots of blue ink in the margin. Behind his head a television on the wall flashed in garish colour.

My whole body chafed and squirmed. 'I can't tell you how bad I feel Paul. God, I feel so stupid.'

'It could easily have been him, though.' He ordered vodka for me without asking. 'We both thought it as soon as we saw that girl had gone missing. Have you seen the latest?' He nodded up to the TV screen, which was showing a reconstruction of the child's disappearance: a semi-detached Victorian yellow-brick house, a car on a street, a mother with her baby. I thought of the real mother watching this nightmare playing out yet again, literally morning, noon, and night, and my heart contracted with grief.

'Can we not talk about it?' I didn't think I could stand anymore. 'But thank you for trying to be nice.'

'I'm not just being nice.' Paul handed over the money and waited for the change.

'Yes you are. But I appreciate it,' I added.

'You don't get it, do you?'

'What don't I get?'

He leaned in closer, making me look straight at him. 'I care about you very, very much. I'm on your side, no matter what happens.'

My grief almost choked into tears.

'Don't you believe me?'

I didn't dare speak.

'Do you want me to tell people how much I think of you?' He raised his voice slightly and the barmaid and the newspaper man glanced round. 'Maybe shout it? Shall I? Shall I shout it—' he got louder. 'Is that what you want?'

'No. Please.' I grabbed at his hand. 'Shhh!'

'Say you believe me, then.' He shouldered down right against me and put his face close to mine.

'Or shall I shout it again?'

'Okay, okay – I believe you!' I twitched a glance round and he nearly laughed.

'Best you forget all about this morning and concentrate on me and us and being happy,' He nuzzled my neck, breathing heavily, and then paused. 'Unless you feel differently?' he pulled back.

'No! I don't! I mean I do… Don't… Feel differently, that is…' I petered off and he laughed.

'I think you should show me then.' He kissed behind my ear, wetting my hair. 'If you want to. Finish that drink and come home with me, and show me just how much.'

'Say that again.'

'What?'

'Where we're going.'

He licked my neck; the skin tingled with the warmth. 'Home,' he whispered.

We slid off the stools, leaving what was left of all that awful afternoon sitting there as we bundled along the streets, being all daft and giggling. I was inexplicably happy: light almost: the pavements rolling away beneath my feet, the weight of his arm slung about my shoulder, the solidity of him there right next to me. He made me realise with him by my side it was okay to give myself a break sometimes. I didn't have to think about Gould, or the girl, or Viv, or the police – I could let it go for a while. I felt better. *He* had made me feel better.

I looked away into the shadows of houses and shops, the cold sunlight sparking intermittently from the windows. We went to cross the road. Paul's hand tightened, pulling me to dodge between the passing cars and I had to look away from the darkness. I blinked painfully – the red and orange glowing shape of him bobbing and darting, moving blindly in front of my eyes. I had no choice but to follow, my hand in his, strong and decisive, and for a second I couldn't see anything else.

Chapter Six

We didn't mention the episode again. I picked up some stuff from my flat and then stayed at his. I didn't say it, but I was actually too nervous to go back. I didn't read the daily newsfeed on my phone, and when anything looked like there might be an article about Cassie on the TV we turned to another channel.

I was scared of what they might be saying about me at work. I sent Emma 'funnies' so that it looked as though I was keeping in regular contact, when in truth, I was keeping her at a distance. On the few occasions we spoke, it was stilted and uncomfortable as though we were passing acquaintances rather than best friends.

'How are you feeling?'

'Mm… Okay.'

'Just okay?'

The elephant in the room sat between us. I stalled, she stalled.

I heard her take a breath. 'Enjoy your time off, yeah? Don't even think about work stuff, okay?'

'I'll try not to.'

'You've probably let it all get to you.'

Meaning?

'Probably.'

'We all know it happens to people.'

I knew what they must be saying. I knew how they thought. These conversations always depressed me. Even to Emma I had become one of those 'people.' The ones who take the job too seriously. The ones you had to be 'careful' with and who were spoken about in whispers. Was Emma whispering with them?

'I haven't heard you mention your mate at work recently. You haven't fallen out, have you?' Paul looked away from the TV programme we were watching. The question came completely out of the blue.

'No, we haven't fallen out exactly. We've kind of...' I shrugged, not really knowing what had happened.

'You would have thought it would be the perfect time for her to keep in contact and make sure you're okay, wouldn't you?'

'It's probably me as much as her,' I looked back at the screen.

'You shouldn't defend her, you know. It's you that needs support. Does she know you're staying here now?'

I sighed. 'I don't think she does, no.'

'Speaking of which, you probably need these to make your life easier.' He reached down beside the cushion and threw something with a yellow ribbon tied to it. It landed with a dull rattle at my feet. It was a set of keys.

I looked across at him, a bit shocked. 'Oh! Are you sure about this?'

'Perfectly.' He carried on watching TV.

I picked them up, quietly thrilled.

They looked like the keys to a whole new life.

I was given a space to hang my clothes in the wardrobe and a drawer of my own. I had part of the shelf in the bathroom and my shower stuff sat primly on the rack in the shower. It was a very easy place to live. Paul worked from home a lot of the time and I got myself into a little routine: making breakfast for us both and then me pottering round the shops in the village, or up into Hampstead or across to Chalk Farm, finding great places to drink coffee and read a book. I cooked most evenings, while Paul took over on Friday nights, usually the same thing: steak or lamb and some delicious salad-y thing. I'd watch him, his shirtsleeves flapping over a wooden chopping block as he wielded the blade a little too recklessly, dicing cucumber and tomatoes, oiling slippery slabs of meat before sliding them into a hot frying pan. I loved that time, standing, nursing a glass of wine, observing the whole theatre of the performance. He'd glance up at me, suddenly aware of my presence, and I'd smile happily back. I felt utterly complete in those moments. Nothing could get between us. I wouldn't let it.

I made a promise to myself that I wouldn't go snooping again. I kept my word. Days and weeks passed. I was acutely aware of the drawer and its contents but I studiously ignored it, walking past it time and time again until it became ordinary. In the end, I felt nothing but a mild and fleeting curiosity about the girl and who she might have been to him – no more than that. I was nicely ensconced here and part of his future. She was tucked away in there and part of his past.

Or so I believed.

Until the morning Paul picked up his work phone.

I was getting dressed when it rang on the bedside table. He scooted past me and picked it up.

'Hello. Paul Webb,' he said breathlessly.

I carried on buttoning up my shirt as he turned away from me and began to pace answering questions abruptly with 'yes' and 'no' answers.

'Right... Right... Yes... Hang on—' He waved to attract my attention. 'Pen?' he mouthed squiggling in the air. I looked about and shrugged. He pointed down at the drawer. 'Yes... Absolutely... One moment, just let me grab a—'

I tried to make my actions appear natural: putting my hand inside, lifting the bits of paper and maps again, going right to the back and picking out a stray pen – when I saw it: the miniature book from the market. In those few seconds, my eyes immediately scanned the gap in the wood. The book had appeared and the photograph had gone. I handed the pen over.

'Thanks.' He gave me a brief smile as I was forced to slowly push the drawer closed again. 'Won't be a sec—' I looked up to find him holding the phone away. 'I've left some papers in the car.' He nodded towards the door and disappeared, carrying on the conversation, his voice trailing away as he went down the stairs.

It took me seconds.

Lifting all the contents out, I went through the lot as quickly and as carefully as I could, even shaking out the papers in case it had got lodged. There was no photograph. Puzzled, I picked up the tiny book. It was exquisite, real quality: hand painted illustrated plates and clearly worth the forty pounds the guy wanted. *Had he gone back and bought it?* I was there the whole time though, he couldn't have done. Had he moved the photograph? The query hung over me as I put it all back, all in the right muddle.

When Paul came back from the car, I was sitting at the breakfast bar.

'Okay?'

I'd put out some cereal for us both and I took a mouthful and waved my spoon to show just how okay I was. He detected nothing as far as I could tell, gathering together his papers and sorting his stuff out for work. I watched him as I chewed, thinking I was making too much of it, wondering if it had got lost, or thrown, or picked up deliberately.

But untruths sit heavily, their indigestibility means they have to come back up sometime.

And they surely did.

–

It was a Saturday morning. We were sitting companionably reading on the floor in the lounge, cups of coffee by our sides with the win-door wide open. From here I could see the tips of the chimney pots sitting up against a blue backdrop of sky. I had been thinking about the photograph a lot. It was really bugging me. I wanted to hint; I wanted to give him a chance to just tell me. A warm May breeze picked up the edges of magazines and newspapers distracting me from saying the thing I knew was coming.

'I've been meaning to ask you.' Someone else's voice uttered the words. I kept my eyes lowered. 'I found a book… Like… By accident. In your bedside drawer.'

'Mmm?… What book?'.

'The book you were looking at in the market. Did you go back and get it?'

I watched the corners of his mouth pull down. He twitched a shrug. 'I don't remember looking at any book. You'll have to show me sometime.' He carried on reading.

'Paul,' I chewed my bottom lip.

'Hmm?'

'Remember you told me about that relationship you had, years ago?'

'Not really... Which one?' He licked the tip of one finger and went to turn the page.

'You said she was someone you could've married.' I stared at the edge of the paper, not managing the forty-five degrees it would take to lift my head. From the corner of my eye I watched him slowly lift his own.

'You're becoming obsessive, you know that?'

I ventured a glance up. He was regarding me steadily.

'You did say that, though, didn't you?'

'Fucking hell, Lucy!' He snapped the paper in front of him. 'What is all this?'

'I was just—'

'Well don't "just".' He shook his head irritably.

I watched the muscles in his lips purse and relax, debating. Eventually he took a breath.

'Her name was Caitlin. We went out for quite a while but it was never a marriage job. Does that tell you what you want to know?'

The sound of her name knifed through me. *Caitlin.* There she was. All of a sudden, whole and three-dimensional.

'Was she important to you?'

'Important to me?' His whole body went still.

Leave this now. Leave this, leave this.

'I just want to know what she was like.'

'No you don't—' his eyes were steely. 'No one ever wants to know what ex's are really like. They don't want the boring reality. They want to torture themselves with the fantasy of them: imagining the drama, picking over the ghosts of a romance that probably never even existed.'

He snapped the paper as an end to the conversation and pretended to read.

I shut up. The newspaper lowered. Abruptly, he eased one leg out from under him and kneeled up to stretch. He looked past me to the open sky as though I wasn't there, his shirt riding up in two curtains, showing that delectable patch of stomach that made me want to lean forward and nuzzle it. I reached out.

'I'm bored,' he yawned widely, shifting out of my reach. 'I might pop out for a while.'

'Oh.'

'I won't be long.'

'I could come with you if you like?'

'Depends how long you're going to be getting ready.'

'Seconds... Not even that.'

I cast around for my trainers but he was already up and pulling his jacket on, scuffing his feet into shoes.

'Come on if you're coming.'

He clattered down the stairs in front of me while I was still pulling the front door closed and trying to wrestle with my coat and bag. The soles of his shoes squeaked smartly across the tiles and I had to trot to keep up. He reached for the catch on the front door, but halted so suddenly that I nearly crashed into him.

'What's the matter?'

He stared down.

'What—?' I said peering over his shoulder. But didn't get to finish. At his feet was a rose, a single perfect flower: brilliant red.

He stooped to pick it up.

'What is it?' It wasn't the question I was really asking. A dull feeling of disquiet rippled through me.

I watched him as he bent the stem in two, crushing the petals, and walked ahead of me down the steps. The feeling wouldn't go away. All I could think was there was something acutely wrong with this; he knew it, I knew it. His phone began to ring.

'Aren't you going to answer that?'

'Nope.' He kept his back to me, as he stalked straight to the dustbin behind the front wall and dropped the flower inside. 'There.' He dusted his hands off and turned to walk briskly down the path.

'Paul,' I put one hand on his arm. 'You don't think that could be anything to do with Simon Gould, do you? I mean, I know he saw me with you. If he could hack my account then maybe I should mention it to—'

'Jesus Christ!' He spun round, his jaw tight with anger.

'Why not?' I stared at him. 'Clearly he's got a thing about me, so I thought…?'

'Gould?'

'Yes, Gould, he's—' but he cut me dead.

'Are you being serious?' He gave me a furious look of disbelief and then strode quickly away down the street.

'Paul!' I hurried after him. 'It's possible! Look, what's wrong for god's sake?'

'If you don't know, then I'm fucked if I'm going to tell you.'

'Jesus! All I said was—'

He wheeled round, almost barging into me. 'You really don't get it, do you?' His eyes were marbled with anger.

'No I don't.' I really didn't.

He shook his head slowly. 'Can you actually *hear* yourself Lucy? Someone accidentally drops a flower on the step and you think you're going to ring Viv, or the *police*… Do you know how completely mad that sounds? Jesus Christ.

You honestly want to drag me through that all over again, do you?'

I was so stunned at the ferocity of the attack I couldn't answer.

'I mean, have you thought about what happened at that market?' He jabbed the air. 'Have you actually considered what it was like for me, *me*, in my position, ringing the police with some bloody cock-and-bull story about seeing a bloke who's not really there? Have you thought about that? Have you?' He paused, breathing heavily. 'Well I can give you the answer right now. *No. You. Haven't.*'

My mouth wouldn't work. I suddenly thought I might cry.

'Christ. I'm sorry. I'm *sorry*.' My breath came out in gulps.

'Yeah, you seem to spend an awful lot of time being sorry.' He went to cross the road and then halted as a car whizzed past.

I had no idea where all this had come from.

He glanced over my head to check the traffic. 'I really can't do this.'

'Paul!'

He was scaring me now. 'Look, I said I was sorry. It was only a thought! I didn't mean anything by it, it was just a—'

But he'd gone, striding off across the road, leaving me jaywalking down the white line, waiting for the traffic to pass. I glanced at an oncoming car that slowed. The driver was a woman. As she passed, she turned slowly to face me and I felt an instant jolt of recognition. She was wearing the same green jacket as before, and her dark hair was clipped up at the sides, but it was her, the woman I had seen in the market.

'Paul!' I shouted.

He had his head down and was marching off ahead.

I shot a look at the car. Its indicator winked, signalling she was pulling in.

She parked, killing the engine, and reached down to pull on the handbrake. Her eyes never left me; they followed me intently as I hurried past.

I glanced back. *Did* I know her? There was no acknowledgement or smile, but then suddenly with a punch to my heart, I realised why she'd seemed so familiar.

The woman from the market.

The girl in the photograph.

It was *her*. Older, but not so changed that I couldn't tell. I looked again, longer this time, and she stared straight back.

'*Paul!*' I had no choice but to run after him. There was no way he was going to stop. '*Paul!*' I caught up and grabbed his arm. He went to swing me off but then checked himself. He was breathing heavily.

'What's going on?' I didn't let go of his arm. He didn't speak, only stared away into the middle distance. I shook him; I wasn't giving up.

'None of this feels right. What is going on?'

He paused for a moment. 'I shouldn't have said those things.' He gazed over my head, his face stony. 'It wasn't fair.'

'I'm not talking about that.'

He glanced at me.

'I want to know about the girl... That woman.' I tried to sound assertive. 'I know something's off. Please just tell me.' My anxiety level thumped inside my ribcage. I was dreading what he might say.

His eyes narrowed. 'What girl? What woman? What are you talking about?'

I knew how dangerous this was. I was going to have to tell him about the photograph.

'If I said Caitlin, would you know then?' I watched his face. 'There's a woman in the car back there. It's the girl in the photograph in your drawer—'

'Photograph? I have no idea what you're going on about!' I heard the aggression but I saw his eyes flicker warily.

'I shouldn't have looked, but—' I took another breath. 'In your drawer. I found a photograph of a girl, an old one. But I've seen her. Once at the market and now she's back there – In a car.' I pointed over my shoulder. 'I just want to know what the hell is going on?'

He stood for a moment staring at me and then I saw him swallow. 'Really, honestly, you're barely making sense.'

'She's there, outside your flat, sitting in a car. She just pulled up. Come and see if you don't believe me...' I was emboldened with anger. 'Come on! I'll show you!' I stalked off, suddenly aware that he wasn't following. I didn't care. I was going to prove my point if it killed me. I hurried along the line of parked cars, peering into each empty driver's seat until I'd gone further than I meant to. I turned, puzzled. He was following slowly behind.

'She was here. Right here,' I gestured. 'I think it was a red car, but I can't see it now. I didn't see her drive past—' I looked off up the road and back again.

'Well she's clearly not here now.' He sighed, irritated.

'Oh, *come on*!' I walked back along the line of cars again, and then glanced up and around as though she would appear out of nowhere. 'She wouldn't just turn up by accident, would she?'

'Lucy. What are you saying?' He sounded quite calm now. 'What are you suggesting?'

I wheeled round to face him. 'What the hell do you think I'm suggesting?'

He glanced at the houses to see if anyone could hear, but that infuriated me even more.

'You've fucked up, haven't you? Letting me stay at your flat. Is that what all this aggression is about? Have you had to make excuses as to why she couldn't come round? Is that what's happened? Has she come to check up on you?... Have I just sussed what's really going on?' I spat the words.

He only stared at me, saying nothing.

'The past is *so tedious*, isn't it?' I mimicked him. 'Too right. We don't want to dwell on past relationships, do we Paul? That's because they're not past, they're in the present.'

The words left my mouth and I heard them like an echo coming back. I had no idea where the fury had come from. I sounded like someone else, the emotion tight and high in my throat.

Paul said nothing for a moment. 'You know what I said before?' He looked away. 'About seeing stuff that isn't there? About making stuff up?'

My anger faltered a little.

He looked away and briefly closed his eyes. 'Well I suppose the good thing is, now I know.'

'Know what?' Something drained inside me.

'I've done nothing but try and look after you.' He stared at me blankly. 'I've supported you when other people would've let you sink. I've treated you like a princess

133

and what do you do? You invade my privacy. You think it's okay to go *fucking prying*.' He blinked rapidly. 'And you want to know about that book, do you?' He tipped his head questioningly. 'Well that book was a gift. A surprise… For *you*.'

I flinched.

'Knowing what I know now, I suspect there was no woman driving past in any car.'

'She wasn't driving, she had parked—' I knew I sounded ridiculous.

'Oh for God's sake!'

I stood, mute and completely spent.

'Think about it, Lucy. If there *was* a woman, why would you immediately assume it's something to do with a girlfriend of mine from nearly twenty-bloody-years ago? Are you off your head? How likely is it, do you think, that I have been seeing someone for twenty years?'

My brain tumbled.

'Go on. How likely?'

'Not likely.'

'A bit louder.'

'Not likely.'

He studied me for a few seconds and then his eyes darted back to the flat. He licked his lips slowly.

'I'm sorry, I shouldn't have—' I started.

'No.'

'I was being absurd. I saw something and made a connection that was just barmy.'

'Yes.'

'Will you forgive me?'

He paused and surveyed me coolly.

'What does that look mean?' I could hear the whine.

'It means, how about you go back to your own flat for a while?'

My heart shrank.

'So we both get a bit of time to think.'

Think?

'So may I have my keys back?' He stood there with his hand out and waited. My fingers fumbled for the keyring in my bag and I tried to detach it. They wouldn't budge. He sighed, annoyed, as the ring split painfully under my nail and I yelped. He made no offer to help but took them and turned to cross the road.

'Paul—' My hand came up but he didn't even hesitate. I watched him walk up the path to the flat, jangling my keys in his fingers and pushing his way inside. I stood on the pavement feeling bereft and utterly, utterly stupid.

I considered all kinds of things: running after him, begging, ringing him, staying right here outside until he was forced to come out and talk to me, but I knew none of it would work.

I walked, not caring where I might be walking to. I had done this. I had made this happen. I had behaved like a stupid teenager; I had shown how immature and pathetic I truly was, and now I was paying the price.

–

I sat on the tube, dully watching each station name roll in and then roll out again: Chalk Farm, Camden Town, and then we shunted slowly into Mornington Crescent. The engine ticked and whirred to itself, and with it, my own tiny heartbeat drummed softly as some vague old anxiety pattered beneath my ribs. *You spoil things Lucy. You can't help yourself. Things are fine, it's just you*, Dan's voice murmured quietly. *Things could be great, but you have to throw a spanner in the works. Do you have a problem with men or something?* I glanced up and realised I was being casually observed. A thin man sitting opposite occasionally allowed his gaze to bat over my hair and face, and I was suddenly conscious of how I must look. Swollen paunchy face from crying, hair like a knotted nest. I had no makeup, no hairbrush, no nothing.

I looked away, catching my reflection in the glass. I was right: I was a state. I saw the dark mass of hair, the heart-shape of my face, the deep-set shadows of my eyes, and in the strange distortion, the photograph of that girl reflecting oddly back.

Did I look like her?

I straightened my neck and tilted my head. *Possibly.*

I tried to think rationally. Twenty years ago he'd liked a girl, and I looked a little like her. Maybe he just liked a 'type' and I fitted? *Was that so terrible?*

I realised I'd let crazy thoughts run amok in my head. In reality, Paul had been pretty straight with me. He hadn't tried to play games – I had just been so scared of what happened with Dan happening again…

I glanced up at the tube map and guessed we were coming to Euston. I wasn't going to do as he said. I wasn't going to walk away. He wasn't Dan. Paul wasn't a mistake. *I* had messed this up. I had. No one else. So now I had to try and put it right.

–

The road was quiet and I looked up. Each massive bay window mirrored only clouds. I wondered if he was up there looking down at me right this minute, relieved and thankful that I'd come straight back.

I walked steadily up the steps. I heard a slam some-where deep inside. Suddenly the door was flung open and a young bloke went to push past me.

'Sorry!' he panted and ran down the path. I glanced at the slowly closing gap and placed my hand in it. I looked back once and then stepped over the threshold.

The hallway was silent. I stood at the foot of the stairs and peered up. I had no idea what I was going to say. I made my way up, feeling silly and ill-prepared now, listening to my footsteps, slow and steady, as I wound my way up to the top. His door was slightly open as though he'd popped out.

'Paul,' I said softly, but there was only silence in return. 'Paul?' I touched the door with one finger. It swayed slightly and then the gap yawned and a tiny sound escaped from the back of my throat. The room was in complete disarray: the leather seat cushions were slashed and hanging from the couch, great rips in the back of the sofa showed the poor pale wooden skeleton beneath. There were violent splatters of brown coffee across the floor and up the walls and the kitchen cupboard doors were wrenched from their hinges. Shards of smashed porcelain and glass littered the floor.

I took a tentative step forward as a sound sent me wheeling round.

'Good, isn't it?'

Paul was standing in the doorway to the bedroom. He stared at the scene as though not really comprehending what he was seeing. He leaned against the frame and rested his head wearily. 'It could only have taken them a matter of minutes to do this. They must've seen us leave.'

'Who? Who did this?' I stared at him.

He shrugged as though he couldn't have cared less. 'I have no idea. Maybe you were right. Maybe it *was* Gould. Who knows? It could be anyone: some opportunist druggie looking for cash, or kids, maybe?' He raised his hands helplessly and let them fall. 'The police probably won't know either. They say they'll be here in a minute, but I doubt that too.'

'Has anything been taken?' I looked round, horrified.

Paul only shrugged wearily. 'Nothing as far as I can tell, which, I suppose, points to Gould doesn't it? The most valuable thing was that.' He waved at the mess of glass on the floor and I suddenly realised where the spray of glass had come from.

'Oh no! Your clock!' I crouched to look. The dented face lay on the hearth. Its bald and exposed inner workings lay bruised and bent amongst the scatter of broken porcelain.

Paul only gazed mutely at the chaos.

'If you mention Gould's name they'll have stuff on file though, won't they?' I looked quickly up. 'About that day in Camden.'

'Which is why I'm not going to mention your name.'

'You won't?'

He regarded me steadily. 'I'm not involving you. Because despite the fact that you think I'm a cheating, despicable, manipulative, lying no-good piece of shit, I also happen to care about you more than anyone else ever has or ever will. Protecting you is my first, last, and only thought.'

A sudden tide of emotion rushed through me.

Paul sighed and gathered himself. 'If this *is* Simon Gould's doing then he's just put his own head in a noose. His DNA will be all over this stuff and the police will easily find him. It also means that he's transferred his attention from you to me... Which is great for us.' He pulled a wry face.

Us. There it was.

'So then.' He tilted his eyes. 'Let me ask the obvious question. What are you doing back here?'

In that second I couldn't tell if he was annoyed or pleased. I took my chance and shrugged non-committally. 'Well, it looks as though I'm here to rescue you.' I waved at the broken furniture. 'My place was never quite as posh as yours, but it's a damn sight posher now.' He didn't respond. 'But it's completely up to you of course. You can stay at mine as long as you need to – Or at least until you can get the professionals in to sort this lot out. The offer's there.'

I tried not to show I was nervous. He didn't move for a second. I couldn't tell what he was thinking, if he was still angry or not, would agree or not – but then he turned and went into the bedroom. I could hear him dragging cases out. I was flummoxed and taken aback. I went and stood in the doorway. He had the suitcase open on the bed and was pulling things off their hangers. I was amazed.

'You sure you're okay?'

I realised the room hadn't been touched. Odd.

I watched the side of his face. I couldn't tell what he was thinking or feeling.

'Yeah, yeah. Fine. Just give me a few minutes on my own, would you? I need to get my head round this before the police get here.'

'Sure. Of course.'

I went back into the lounge and stood amongst the wreckage. It was like a nightmare. I thought about telling Viv – I still hadn't heard from her about the phone I'd handed in. But now this. *Jesus*. My hands came up to my face as I looked at it all – then something really odd struck me. The jacket that Paul had been wearing was hung neatly on the back of the dining chair. My brain accepted yet questioned the ordinariness all at the same time. It appeared such an odd thing to do – the notion that he'd walked into a wrecked flat, taken his jacket off and bothered to hang it up seemed strange? There was something else... My eyes glanced over at the mantelpiece. I'd noticed it but not properly registered. The marble was completely bare – swept of everything as though a giant arm had just ploughed through the whole lot, yet... The sand-filled souvenir stood up like a little lone sentinel, a little glass lighthouse in all its muted pastel layers, welcoming me to Colwyn Bay. A solitary survivor in all that devastation. Impossible, yet there it was.

Chapter Seven

I made myself scarce when the police eventually turned up, but Paul said the guy in charge was barely interested anyway. He got the paperwork for the insurance sorted, and a team of people came in to begin clearing up the damage. He went online and ordered new furniture: exact copies of the old stuff, even from the same shop. He didn't seem at all concerned that the clock was irreparable. I was more upset about it than he was. He appeared to accept the break-in almost as though it was just 'one of those things.' We picked up our relationship exactly where we had left off.

The last week in May had produced several sudden hot days that had taken us by surprise. My flat felt small and stuffy and he decided he would work from the office in town 'to give us both more air', he'd grinned. It made it so much easier. I thought I'd be territorial, but I wasn't. He fitted right in as though he'd always been there. The weekends were ours: going out to dinner or the cinema. Drinking wine and talking. This was the life I'd been waiting for. I just prayed it didn't end.

–

'I'm back at work next Monday.' I grimaced.

We were lying naked on the top of the bed, our heads where our feet should be, our heels on the windowsill side by side, waggling our toes. The sky was pink and pale blue like the inside of a seashell.

'Not looking forward to it?'

'No.' I gazed up at his chin, studying the tiny commas of black hairs, each in its own pocket, watching how the muscle ticked and moved as he spoke, the tiny flinches at the corner of his eyes as the light changed.

'I just want to stay here and do this all day.'

'It's funny, y'know, lying here like this. I'd forgotten what it felt like.' He laughed a little and spread his toes in the breeze.

'What do you mean?'

'Lying on a bed the wrong way round.' He scratched his chin and the stubble made an unpleasant sound. He cast an eye at me. 'It's a weird thing to do, isn't it?'

'So this is something you've done quite often then?'

'Eh?' He looked at me, puzzled.

'You said you'd forgotten, implying you've done it before.' I was grinning at him, but I knew, deep down, I could feel a soft prickle of insecurity.

'Are you being arsey?' He pulled his head back to look at me, smiling.

'No,' I chuckled. 'I was just pulling your leg.'

'Don't do that.' He looked away, his lips formed a thin, hard line.

'Do what?'

'Lie about your feelings.'

I stared, slapped down, at the rectangle of summer sky, concentrating hard so that his words wouldn't hurt me.

'Look, I understand... I get it. I totally understand how you feel, but you're too—'

My body steeled itself, waiting for the blow, telling me I was too insecure, or over-sensitive. I closed my eyes.

'—beautiful to ever be worried about stuff like that.'

They dropped open.

'Which is why I want to marry you.'

I wasn't sure if I was still breathing.

'That's the only way I can show you – to make a lifetime commitment. Otherwise you'll say I never said it, or mishear me, or some other nonsense.'

'Are you seriously being serious?' I propped myself up to look at him.

'Perfectly seriously serious. So what do you say?'

My chin rested on his chest, and I looked into his eyes, disbelieving.

'Is that it?' He lay back, grinning. 'Is this your silent response to such a massively life-changing question?'

I searched his wonky, beautiful face, to see if he was having me on.

'You can't marry someone after just weeks!'

'Why not?'

'You just can't!'

'Is there a rule book somewhere?' He raised himself up and patted all around the mattress. 'You'll have to show it to me when you find it...' His hand flopped. 'Come on Lucy... Two weeks, twenty, a year, ten years. What difference would it make? It won't make any difference to me... Are you saying it might to you?'

I was so stunned I couldn't speak.

'That's a possibility then?' He shifted his head quickly. 'You might change your mind?'

'No... I mean... I don't know. How can I know?'

'Precisely.' He waved a hand. 'How can anyone know? I'm forty-three. You're... How old?'

'See? You don't even know how old I am! I'm thirty-four.'

'What's important is that we're both of an age where we know our own minds. Some arbitrary, socially acceptable time period for *dating*...' he rolled his eyes, '...has absolutely no meaning for me. I love you. I want to spend the rest of my life with you...'

He held up a warning finger. 'Possibly not in an apartment that cooks us every night at two hundred degrees Celsius, but I do want to be with you forever. It's *that* simple.'

I laughed, then stopped, then laughed again. I couldn't get my head around it. 'I don't know what to say.'

'Try yes or no.'

I leaned up and kissed him.

'God, you're complicated!' He pulled away and laughed. 'Is that a yes, then?'

I kissed him again feeling the room tilt and dissolve into nothing.

He cupped my chin in his fingers and gently searched my face. 'I could do with an answer, you know.'

I took his hand and slid it slowly down until neither of us were asking questions anymore.

—

The wedding was going to be in the registry office in Camden. I'd rung Lou, who sounded both stunned and oddly delighted.

'Oh my life! Congratulations!' she laughed.

'So why don't you come?'

Part of me wanted her to and part really didn't. I cringed at the thought of Paul meeting my sister. There was an anxious pause on the end of the line.

'I'd love to, but—'

The instant feeling of relief in the pit of my stomach was quickly followed by one of absolute guilt.

'—But I can't really. It wouldn't be possible, not with Mam as she is. I couldn't leave her with anyone.'

The statement made me squirm. 'We'll come up then, afterwards.' I kept my voice cheerful and positive. 'Maybe we could all go out for afternoon tea somewhere?' The thought of Paul sitting in the room with the swirling gas fire made me die with embarrassment. 'Betty's tea room in The Square, maybe? Mam'd like that.'

'What a nice thought!'

I could tell Lou was trying to go along with my happy little make-believe, both of us knowing that nothing would ever come of it.

And then there was the terror of telling Emma.

'I keep thinking,' I said to Paul one morning. 'I'm back at work on Monday. I can't keep getting married a secret for ever and then I'll feel awful that I never even mentioned it to anyone.'

'You mean Emma?' he frowned. 'Were you thinking of inviting her then?' I could tell he didn't want to. 'Don't you think it would be fantastic if it was just the two of us? We can please ourselves what we do. We don't have to explain anything to anyone. It would mean more – To me that is.' He put his hand on his heart. 'You must say if you feel differently.'

So that's how it got to be just me and him. Paul was right. It was truly romantic.

We stood in the solemn room at three p.m., the sunshine pouring through the long sash windows, me in impossible heels and a flowery dress I'd bought last year and never worn and Paul in a leather jacket that creaked as he reached for the ring. The ladies from the back office acted as witnesses. They stood placidly like quiet cows in the background, their wide eyes taking us in. The ring felt big and heavy on my finger and I couldn't stop fiddling my thumbnail under the edge. Paul said he wouldn't wear a ring and I said I didn't mind. I didn't mind anything right that moment. It was as though we'd been together for years. I took that as a sign that I was doing the right thing. How giddy I felt. How mad this all was. How wonderful.

He thanked the registrar and took the envelope with our certificate in it. I had been stupidly pleased seeing the box on the form that said 'bachelor' and below it, 'spinster.' Neither of us had a proper past and here was confirmation, official confirmation, that this was the case. Now it was just us, all brand new.

We sat across the table from each other in the gorgeous boutique hotel in Hampstead overlooking the heath. It had once been a coaching inn, complete with mahogany staircase and thick carpets with brass stair rods. The maitre d led us into the conservatory, all hushed and elegant: a sea of white damask tables and muted gold mirrors. Old money opulence. We caught each other's eye as the waiter pulled out my chair and fussed around for what seemed like forever, asking questions that I let Paul answer. I was so happy. The champagne arrived, the glasses got filled and the ice bucket clanked reassuringly under its napkin. Finally, he clicked his heels together with a stiff nod to each of us and trotted off. We smirked, conspiratorially and I rested my hand on the table. Paul couldn't stop touching the finger where my wedding ring sat.

'Doesn't seem real,' he whispered. 'Can't quite get my head around it.'

'I know. Too weird.' I picked up my glass and we both gazed out at the view.

The Victorian glass roof and ornate iron windows looked out over the magnificent heath on all sides. We gazed out, appreciatively catching the looks of the other guests who smiled benevolently, guessing, I think, that we were newly married.

The food was amazing. My dress hadn't been tight, but it certainly felt it by the end of the meal.

'Wow!' I licked my lips appreciatively. 'That was absolutely divine. How was yours?'

'Really, really delicious. Faultless from beginning to end.' He put down his knife and fork. I laid my napkin to one side and he reached for my hand. The sun disappeared behind a cloud for an instant and then broke through, sending shafts of light to shift into pearlised geometrics across the floor. The champagne bottle listed lazily in its cooler. Paul squeezed my fingers and I looked back at him, totally content. I was feeling more than a little tipsy. The waiter approached and busied himself clearing the plates.

'Can I interest you in dessert?' He inclined his head graciously.

Paul darted a look at me. 'I think we'll have a break for a few minutes, what do you think?'

'I think we'd better.' I smiled.

The waiter moved silently away and Paul squeezed my hand again. I felt blurry and blissfully relaxed. Paul glanced to make sure the waiter had gone and leaned forward as though he were about to say something.

'Go on,' I smiled.

His thumb chafed my knuckle. He stared down at my hand. 'You're right, it's totally surreal. How have we got here? It's like magic.'

'Magical and wonderful,' I smiled.

He didn't say anything. His tongue traced his lip, and he kept a tight hold of my hand. I detected an almost imperceptible change.

He stared at the tablecloth for what seemed like forever. 'This is going to seem like a really big deal to you.' He shifted in his seat.

'What is?' My smile caught on my lips.

'But it's not really. I just think that today of all days, I should be completely and totally honest.'

'Honest?'

Please don't spoil this. Please don't.

I scanned his face, trying desperately to second-guess and failing.

'I haven't lied to you...' He shot a look into my eyes. 'Nothing I've told you about me has been untrue.'

I sensed something awful. 'Go on.' *Please no.*

He steadied himself. 'You know... You know I mentioned... Umm... Caitlin?'

Something inside me contracted.

'Well... What I told you was all true... Only...' He shifted again and took a better grip. 'It wasn't that simple...' My hand jerked involuntarily.

'Because...?'

'Caitlin and I—'

The choice of words sent a shot of pain straight into my heart.

'We lived together.'

'Right.' I slowly took it in. 'Right. She was one of the women you lived with. You lived together.' I tried out the words. 'How long for?'

'Quite a while. Years. I met her when I was at Uni in Birmingham. We lived together there and afterwards.'

I went cold. 'But you said—'

'I know. I know, I don't know why I said different.'

I shook my head and nearly smiled, wondering if this was some kind of bizarre wind-up. His face didn't alter.

'Actually… I do. It's because when we split up—' he shifted. 'Caitlin was pregnant.'

His words punched me back in the seat.

'But that's it. The lot.' His hands came up to placate me. 'That's the big secret. All my cards are on the table now.'

'She had the baby?' My voice didn't sound as though it belonged to me.

His eyes flitted. 'I have no idea. I have not seen her from that day to this.'

My face must have betrayed my thoughts.

'Honestly,' he went to grab my hand but I wouldn't let him. 'I haven't seen her for years. No contact, nothing.' He was speaking very quickly. 'The child, if it was born—'

'*If* it was born?'

'Well I don't know, do I? Whichever and whatever happened, it would be practically grown up now. Caitlin probably went back to her family in Ireland. I tried all the contact numbers I had for them, but they'd moved…' He managed to grab my little finger and he hung on tight.

I struggled to make sense of it all. His relationship with Caitlin, the one I'd built in my head, this short-lived thing… I saw her again: the dark tumbling hair, the green eyes, the girl-next-door but sexy look. My absolute rival.

'It's our wedding day.' The words fell from my mouth.

'I know, I know.' He leaned across the table earnestly. 'I should've mentioned it before, I should've said something, but the thing is… The *thing* is… It was so long ago, and so…' He sat back. The diners around me flooded back in a wave of soft chatter, the chink and scrape of glass and cutlery. 'It was another life Lucy… It's not now. It's gone… She's gone. It's the past. I know you hate me saying that, but it's true. It means nothing to me. Absolutely nothing.'

It means nothing. He could have a child out there somewhere and it means absolutely nothing to him?

I was numb. He let go of my hand and I snatched it to my lap. I looked up to find the waiter standing there smiling down at us, one to the other.

'Sir? Madam? May I get you some dessert?'

'Ah yes!' Paul cleared his throat. 'Yes, what a great idea!' He leaned back expansively, picking up the menu and studying it. 'I think we'll have the chocolate and raspberry assiette to share. Is that okay?' He looked across at me with theatrically wide eyes and I was stunned into a reply.

'Yes… Yes, great… Thank you.'

The waiter wandered off, leaving me sitting there staring at a small pale yellow spill of champagne on the tablecloth and wondering what the hell had just happened.

'Nothing's changed, you know.'

I looked up at him in disbelief.

'Nothing's any different than it was this morning, or last week, or last month. I'm still the same person.'

Apart from the fact that he had a life, a proper life, that could reappear at any moment. A grown up child with a beautiful woman called Caitlin.

I registered his face, taking the parts in slowly, piece by piece. It was true; he looked the same as he had an hour ago, he was identical to the man who stood opposite me and exchanged vows. Identical, but fundamentally not the same.

'How can a child be nothing?'

He pulled back. 'I didn't say that. You're twisting my words as usual. Look, I don't know how to explain this so that you'll understand... I would be lying if I said I never think of it because I do, but it's not often, and it's like a... A video of something that happened to someone else. Someone else's life. Not mine.' He leaned in and grabbed my wrist under the table, drawing me to him. 'My life is here with you, right this moment.' He gave me a little shake. I wrenched my arm away.

'So it was her? That day in the car, was that her?'

There. I'd said it. I'd laid it out squarely on the table between us.

His face coloured with anger. 'Lucy...' He could barely articulate my name.

I glared back. But I wasn't giving in. I'd been made to crawl and apologise and now I was having the truth. 'Well? Was it?' I hissed. I scoured his face. I was aware of the other diners in the restaurant but I didn't care.

'I'm going to tell you something now,' he said carefully. He was staring grimly at the table edge as though his gaze might bore right through it. 'I'm going to tell you this because you've pushed me. I wasn't going to, but now I am. I'm going to tell you the whole sad and very sorry story.'

A crawl of fear inched its way into the nape of my neck. I felt dread and desperation in equal amounts. His gaze didn't alter but his voice wavered.

'Yes, Caitlin was "the one",' he said haltingly. 'She was the love of my life and all those other appalling clichés.'

Hot tears pricked the backs of my eyes but I blinked them away. *This was supposed to be our day.*

'But that was all before I was old enough to know better.' He paused. I didn't speak. I didn't know if I still could.

'We were young enough and stupid enough to think that having a baby was the obvious step. We were not only stupid, but immature and poor. We found a house in Shropshire; it was really cheap, we could afford it and I thought I'd be able to get work. I don't know what the fantasy was, but reality set in soon enough. Living away from everyone you know, and me on short-term contracts, travelling all over the place, was a recipe for pure stress. We hardly saw each other and her pregnancy forced us to acknowledge that neither of us could cope, either financially or emotionally. I suggested an abortion before it was too late – an insensitive and cruel thing to suggest, I admit – but I was a kid and was panicking. Of course that ended up in more massive, vicious rows. Caitlin struggled, I struggled. She became the kind of girl I couldn't stand. She went from this funny, relaxed, confident person, to this… This…' his hands sprang apart, '…anxiety-ridden, panicky, obsessive, jealous… Nut-case, really. It became more and more extreme. She had wild ideas and was madly possessive. I had to give up several contracts because she didn't like the fact that young women worked there, I even had to get rid of my dog…'

'Your dog?'

'Yes, she was even jealous of a little animal.' There was pain in his eyes. 'I tried to help her, I really did. I begged her to talk to someone…' He stopped speaking, and I saw the extent of his desperation. I felt sick.

He laughed bitterly. 'And there's the irony. She *did* talk to someone – she went and found herself a sympathetic ear in the shape of another bloke—' he swallowed, 'her friend's husband, to be precise.' I watched as he gathered himself. 'I don't think you can imagine how appalling that whole situation was.'

'No.'

I didn't know what to imagine anymore.

The waiter appeared at my side and, with a flourish, deposited a long slim plate, beautifully decorated with flower petals and chocolate shavings adorning tiny cakes, mousses and miniature tarts, all dripping with raspberry coulis and fresh fruits.

'Wow!' said Paul. 'Look at this!'

I attempted to look appreciative for the waiter's sake.

'Please, enjoy,' he bowed his head slightly. 'And, on behalf of all the staff here, may I offer our sincere congratulations on your marriage!' He looked smilingly at both of us. 'And to honour the occasion, we would like to offer you complimentary coffee, liqueurs and petit fours which you are more than welcome to take here or in the lounge, whichever you prefer.'

'Thank you, you're very kind.' I beamed but I couldn't stop my face from falling as he moved away.

Paul held out a long spoon. 'Come on. Please—'

But I couldn't bring myself to take it.

He dropped it with a clatter and sighed. 'So she up and left; she just disappeared.' He blinked in disbelief. 'She told me I'd never find her, so I can only assume...' He sighed, 'I didn't have much choice, I put the house on the market and I moved out before it was even sold. I just wanted out.'

'How far pregnant was she?'

He pulled a face. 'Six months, seven, maybe?'

'She *left*, that far pregnant with no money and nowhere to go?' I could only sit there staring.

He caught my look. 'Don't judge me, Lucy. Please. Just *don't.*'

A couple of the other diners glanced round at us and I smiled quickly, pretending that he'd just made some kind of private joke.

'What's funny?' He glared round.

'Nothing!' I whispered. 'Nothing's funny. People are looking over, that's all.'

He rocked the plate with a bang. 'Do you want any of this?'

I shook my head.

'Christ, I feel like getting pissed.' He straightened his shoulders, easing his neck. 'Isn't that what you're supposed to do on your wedding day?'

There was the hint of something mean. He pushed his chair back and stood, stiffly, holding out his hand to me. I automatically took it. I was aware there were whispers in our direction and I was desperate not to let them see anything was amiss. I forced a broad grin as the waiter bustled over.

'Ah, this way, *Mr and Mrs Webb.*' He gestured. 'Let me show you the lounge area, it's just through here.' And he ushered us into a small, very ornate drawing room. The lights were low behind the palm plants in the corner, sending soft fingers of shadow across the walls. Somewhere in the background was the tinkling of a classical piano. We were led over to a low table in the window flanked by high-back comfy chairs. On the table was a silver tray bearing coffee cups and next to them was a plate of tiny delicate chocolates, petit fours, and miniature cookies.

'May I?' He indicated to the coffee pot on his tray.

'Actually, I think we'd quite like to have another bottle of wine.' Paul slumped down heavily into the nearest seat. I sat opposite, saying nothing.

If the waiter thought anything he did a very good job of not showing it. 'Of course, sir. Would you like the same as the previous bottle, or something a little different?'

'What do you think, darling wife?' Paul looked at me, challengingly. 'More of the same?'

I let the silence tick between us and the waiter inclined his head and moved away.

I was furious. 'You're acting as though I'm the one who's in the wrong here!'

'Am I?' He raised a sardonic eyebrow.

'Firstly, you lied about not having a relationship and secondly, you lied about the woman in the car. Now there's the possibility you've got a child, for God's sake! What the hell do you expect?'

He only stared insolently back.

'Oh Jesus, I've had enough of this!' I went to get up but he grabbed my arm with such force that my knees buckled. He kept hold of me, sitting on the edge of his seat. His knuckles around my arm were white.

'*Okay*... Okay... You want the truth, do you? Well here it is!' A tiny pulse began to throb in the tips of my fingers.

'There was no woman in a car, do you get that? There isn't and never was any photograph in any drawer. I mean, how ridiculous can you get? What do you take me for — some thirteen-year-old kid?'

I stared at him defiantly. 'You've moved it.'

'What?' He gave a bark of laughter. 'What? I moved what?'

'The photograph. From the drawer in your bedside table.'

He opened his mouth as though to speak and then stopped. 'You know how bizarre that sounds Lucy, don't you?'

I did. I knew exactly.

'So let's work through this. We have no photograph of any woman in any drawer, but you're convinced it's Caitlin. Caitlin who would be twenty years older than the photograph but who you amazingly recognise outside my flat? Have I got that about right?'

'I saw her, Paul. She was—'

'You didn't. You know you didn't. There's a tiny bit of you that knows you're wrong but you won't admit it.'

I wasn't sitting listening to this for one second longer. I jerked my arm away and stood up, head swimming, lurching clumsily back through the restaurant, past the surprised diners towards the French windows and the terrace. I pushed through the doors, the wisps of tulle curtain clinging to my shoulders as I floundered out onto the terrace.

The shock of the evening air hit me, but suddenly I was able to breathe. My fingers skimmed the mossy balustrade as I ran down the first two flights, hearing the sound of Paul's footsteps close behind me.

'Lucy.'

I wheeled round at the bottom and nearly fell. 'Lucy.' He caught my waist and saved me.

'Can you let go please?' I stared resolutely into the darkness.

He loosened his hold. 'For Christ's sake, Lucy; you made a mistake, that's all. What are you getting so uptight about?'

'I didn't make any mistake.'

'You know you did.' He let go completely. 'I can see it in your face, but if you want to walk away, then walk away. I won't stop you.'

I stared off into the night. I could've run down those steps if I'd wanted to. I could've run into the hotel reception and got a cab and been out of there. I took another two steps: one foot in front of the other, moving away from him.

'Is this it then?' he called after me. 'You're going to throw it all away before it's even started? Is that what you want to do?'

My feet were moving but my heart wasn't letting me go that easily. I slowed, realising he was following.

I drew to a halt. 'What do you want Paul?'

'Will you do something for me?'

I watched his imploring face.

'Will you?'

I wasn't sure I wanted to do anything right now.

'Will you tell someone – I don't know, Viv maybe, Emma. Someone you trust – will you tell them all the weird things that you think have been happening: about the rose on the step, the photograph, this woman in the car, the one at the market... Will you tell them the whole story and then ask them what they think?'

I smarted. I knew what he was trying to do. He purposefully hadn't mentioned Gould's name. He didn't need to. I went to turn and walk away.

'Lucy, will you just listen for one second!' He held up his hands. 'I'm not saying you're mad, I'm just pointing out the bloody obvious. We both know you're tough and you're switched on and you're clever, but you do that God-awful job.' He moved closer. 'You've been doing that job day after day, no let up, and then out of the blue you're shoved in front of this highly manipulative, highly sophisticated sex offender who has fixated on you... That's real, *real* stress, and then he's got you in his grasp. Suddenly he's ringing you, you think he's hanging about outside, he might even have got one of his mates to do my flat over, he *could* have left that rose, we don't know, do we?... But what we do know is he's playing with your head and you're caught – *bam!*' His face was pleading. 'He's definitely got you off-balance. And when you're *under* threat, you *see* threat. It's a perfectly normal response to a totally abnormal situation.'

I tried to gauge his face.

'Is any of what I've just said remotely possible?'

I swallowed.

'Is it *possible*?' He tried again. 'Think about it. Is it possible you could have got any of it wrong?'

'It's *possible*, but—' I started.

He held up his hands. 'See? Possible. That's all I'm asking you to consider.'

Hugging my arms across my body against the growing chill of the evening, I suddenly became aware of the clatter and conversation coming from the restaurant.

'You're cold.' He went to put his arm round me, but I shrugged him off.

'I think you're being a bit unfair now,' he said quietly.

'Me?' I snatched a look at him.

'Yes. I've tried to confide in you this evening. Lay myself open to you. Tell you stuff that's really very, very painful.'

I looked away. His voice became even softer. 'Shall I tell you what I think is even more unfair?' He reached forward, gently turning my face so that I was forced to meet his eyes. 'The reality is, my relationship with Caitlin was a terrible, terrible time in my life. I thought I was in love and I was betrayed. I lost the child she was carrying. I lost my house. I had to beg for my job back. I had no family to call on, and all the friends I knew at Uni went their separate ways. I had nothing. I had to re-invent myself, start from scratch, drag myself out of a hole and begin my life again. I didn't trust anyone. I didn't want anyone. Sure I had a few flings, but no one got close. And we both know what that's like.' He stopped and looked directly into my eyes. 'I *thought* that was how it would be forever. And then I met you.' He stopped and took a small step back. 'And when I met you, I was hoping that I could start again, you know... Have a new life. Leave all that shit behind. I don't want to keep raking it up every five minutes; I don't want to keep having to go over and over it, re-living it all the time.' He rubbed his hands together as though they were cold; the palms stuttered and then he turned them over and studied them. He stared up at me. 'I'm asking you to start afresh with me. I'm asking you to start again where everything is clean and right and good with the world. I'm asking you to be by my side through all the crap and all the fabulously muddled, wonderful mess that two human beings create when they love each other...' He stopped, slightly out of breath. 'Would you be prepared to do that?'

I looked into his eyes. In the muted lights from the restaurant, the gold glinted on the grey irises like sunlight.

'Will you... I mean, *can* you forgive me, and do that? I mean, not right now, but eventually... Would you even *consider* forgiving me?' He turned his palms upward, pleading.

Something shifted inside: I'd learned lies and I'd learned truths. My insides were numb. I didn't know what I could do.

'That's all I'm asking. Just to consider it.' He sighed. 'I'm sorry. I should've told you but I was so, so scared. I know how it all sounds. But I love you so much.' A wash of tears blurred the grey.

'I hate you,' I said. I put my hand in his.

'I don't care as long as you're with me,' he whispered, pulling me to him, holding my forehead against his own. There was a wave of sadness, of anger, of confusion, and hurt — Hurt for both of us — And questions, questions... More questions... But throughout it all was a deep, deep feeling of weariness.

I just didn't want to fight anymore.

'Just say you'll stay with me. Work through it. See where we go. Will you do that?'

For a moment I couldn't answer.

'Will you?'

I found my head moving slowly against his.

'Is that a yes?' He shook me a little.

I nodded.

'Thank God. Thank God.' He kissed my hairline over and over as my heart cleaved wide and he walked right back in.

Chapter Eight

'Morning!' I popped my head round Viv's door and grinned. 'It's me!'

'God! Lucy!' Viv got up from her desk and enveloped me in a great bear hug. 'Welcome back!' She pushed me back by the shoulders and studied my face. 'I am so, so pleased I gave you that extra time off. It looks like the break has done you good. How are you feeling?' She gave me a look. 'Honestly now.'

'I'm raring to go,' I smiled back.

'Well, you've certainly got some colour in your cheeks. Emma says you've disappeared off the planet. What have you been up to?'

'Oh this and that,' I laughed.

'And a bit of the other?' She squinted teasingly. 'Go and get yourself settled in and catch up in your own time. There's no rush. Dave appears to have it all under control.'

I wasn't sure I wanted to hear how fabulous Dave was. I glanced over at his moody shoulders.

'Morning, Dave!' I called out cheerily. 'I'll just grab a coffee and I'll be straight over!'

Dave grunted a reply as I went into the tea room to put the kettle on. He was the least of my worries. I glanced at my watch. Emma would be in any minute, and that would be a whole different story. Emma, with her inquisitive eyes and unerring nose. She was the one person I couldn't bullshit and the one person I'd seriously let down. I was on the hook and I was definitely wriggling. I couldn't risk her hearing about me and Paul from anyone else. There was only one thing I could do.

I strode over to her before she even had a chance to take her coat off.

'Lunch?' I said breezily. 'My shout. I've got stuff to tell you. All I want you to do is listen.'

She looked shocked, but I knew there was no way she was going to say no.

Ten minutes to twelve, I went across to the bakery café over the road, found a quiet table and sat and waited. I'd already thought about all the things I was and wasn't going to tell her. I certainly wasn't going to tell her how I'd lain awake on my wedding night watching dark shapes shifting on the ceiling, listening to Paul drifting in and out of a restless sleep.

Caitlin's face kept coming back to me: the young and smiling woman in the photograph, the dull stare of the woman in the car. There *had been* a photograph though: I *knew*, I'd seen it. Could it have got caught up in the bits of paper in there and got thrown out? Was I even sure that was Caitlin? And how sure was I that it was the same person in the car? Twenty years is a long time.

I was sure of one thing though: I loved Paul. I wanted to believe what he'd told me. None of it painted him in a great light, so maybe it *was* the truth?... My mind tumbled over and over... I was comforted by the fact that at least I had *some* answers. The ground, in every respect, had slipped and skewed. The one thing I could cling on to was that, in every respect, I now knew the worst.

'Married? Shut the *f*—' Her teaspoon was paused, mid-stir, and she stared at me, utterly gobsmacked. I think she thought this was one of my more peculiar jokes, or had I completely lost it now? Either way she dissolved into a loud squawk of surprise.

'Married! I *mean*... My God... F'fuck's sake, Luce. How can you be? Did anyone else know about it?'

I shook my head, laughing.

'You conniving sly old tart! Why didn't you say anything?'

'Because I'm a conniving sly old tart.'

Emma hooted. 'My God. My God, I knew it!' She narrowed her eyes at me.

'I *knew* you were up to something. You were so quiet and off the radar I thought you—'

'You thought I'd gone off my trolley?'

She had the good grace to blush. 'I was going to say "were really upset with me".' She looked sheepish, but then collected herself. 'Well, bugger me with a bargepole. Married, eh?... Hang on, hang on... There aren't any other surprises, are there? I mean, you're not—'

I paused and then suddenly worked out what she meant. 'Oh hell no!'

I looked aghast. 'No, I'm not. Definitely not!'

'So when am I going to come round and get to know this delicious lump properly, then?' She pouted. 'The man who's stolen my bezzie. I need to make sure his intentions are honourable.'

The thought of her coming round made me uneasy, but I grinned anyway. 'He hasn't stolen me.'

'So when then?'

'Soon.'

'How soon?'

'They're doing a bit of work in the flat downstairs at the moment,' I lied. 'So as soon as the drilling and dust

clouds die down, we'll have to sort out a date for lunch.'
I knew what Emma would do. It would be a version of
a Jeremy Kyle interrogation, and right now, I didn't have
the mental strength.

'Hang on, so you're not at your flat then? Hell, he must
be worth it!'

'It's just easier… And cooler,' I added with a laugh. 'He
lives in Belsize Park.'

'Ooo nice!' She widened her eyes appreciatively. 'So
you'll sell yours then?' It was a sensitive question: she knew
exactly how I'd feel and I knew her antennae would be
twitching. *Sell my flat?* It hadn't crossed my mind.

'Or maybe you don't need to. Maybe you're so minted
now.' She let me off the hook, smirking mischievously
over her coffee cup. 'But I'll want an up-to-date progress
report on the building work then. Hour by hour if neces-
sary.'

'I'll get on to the project manager,' I smirked back,
picking up my own cup to hide my thoughts.

'*I told you it would be amazing.*'

I remembered Paul's words from this morning as we
left the flat.

'What's that?' I looked at him in surprise. 'The joy of
the first day back? You are joking aren't you?'

'No, idiot. Having the wedding with just the two of
us. Why would we have ever wanted anyone there? Every
moment was perfect.'

We made our way down the stairs. I tried really hard to
keep all the other not so perfect moments from flooding
back.

'And now it's just us. I can't tell you the sheer bliss at the
thought of coming home tonight and closing the door and
shutting the world out. You know, I'd be perfectly happy

never having to socialise again. God. How wonderful would that be, eh?' He reached forward and tucked a stray strand of my hair back. 'You'll need to sort that when you get into work by the way.' My hand instinctively came up and he watched as I struggled to tuck it back into the hairband. We stepped out onto the pavement and walked towards the car. He caught my arm.

'Look, can we make a promise that at least we'll have a honeymoon period with just us – Like no friends or family or work people?'

I knew by that he meant Emma.

'Where we just stay at home and see no one – at least just until after we've had a real honeymoon a bit later on in the year?… Can we say that? Please… Can we promise?'

I'd agreed. Why did I do that? But all the time I was wondering how I'd feel once I'd seen Emma again… And right this minute, I realised just how much I'd missed her.

'You know I'll be chomping at the bit, don't you?' Her squawk jolted me back to the present.

'I've actually missed you, you old bat.' I deflected, making a sad face as her own lit up into a brilliant beaming smile.

'Oh, I've been hoping you'd say that! Let's make it soon then, shall we?'

'Absolutely we will. Just give me a week or so and I'll sort it.'

I hid my face in the cup again and pretended to drink the last of my tea. Thankfully she was distracted by a good-looking guy who had just strolled over to the counter. He gave her a look and I had to laugh at her googly-eyed excitement. She prattled on about Conner and then moved on to some other bloke she fancied, but I found I didn't mind. We'd had a hiccup in our friendship and now we could rebuild things, but I knew this wasn't going to be easy.

'We could do Sunday lunch or something!'

I hadn't really been listening.

'When I come round,' she went on. 'We could make it a Sunday?'

'I'll definitely check the calendar with Paul and let you know,' I laughed.

'I can't wait to meet him properly!'

'He wants to meet you too!'

It was wonderful – and I was excited at the thought of being close friends again, yet somehow a bit sad and uncomfortable, because it meant I'd founded this new beginning on a lie.

–

That evening I was sitting at the breakfast bar, thoughtfully nursing a cup of tea.

'How was your first day back, then?' He put his hand on my shoulder, making me jump.

'Oh! Good thanks! Great. No problem. I went out for lunch with Emma, actually.' I hadn't realised my tea had gone cold.

'Oh yeah.' He hopped onto the stool next to me, reaching out and flipping over a menu flyer for a Chinese takeaway. 'How was she?' He flipped it back again.

'Good. She was good.' I could feel him watching me, waiting for me to reveal more. I couldn't broach the subject of her coming round.

'She asked me if I was pregnant.'

'Christ!' he laughed. 'Bit random wasn't it?... Or is that why she thought we'd got married? How sweet and old-fashioned.' He chuckled, shaking his head. 'What an awful thought.'

'What? Having kids? Is that so awful?'

He heaved himself off the stool and went to walk off.

My eyes followed him. 'That's not something you'd want, then?'

He paused, and then went around to the kitchen.

'It's pretty important, so I think we should at least discuss it. Can we discuss it?'

'Lucy,' he frowned. 'We've only been married five minutes.'

'I know. I know. I don't mean *now*,' I shrugged. 'I'm talking about the future. I know it's a huge deal given what happened... Before—' I broke off, suddenly realising he might not want to talk about it.

He stared off into the distance for a moment and then his gaze landed blankly on me.

'Can't we just enjoy our time together?' He sounded irritated. 'It's like we always have to be working to some kind of event-planner.'

'I only meant—'

'Can we drop it?' He slid the flyer back across the table. 'Do you fancy something from here? Save us cooking. Celebrate your return to real life.'

I looked down.

'I was thinking about beef in black bean sauce with a combination fried rice. How about you?'

I bit my lip. I would've liked him to ask about my thoughts, my feelings.

'You like that fish stuff, don't you? Which I don't mind, so we could have both and share...' He raised his eyes. 'Oh hell, don't sulk!'

'I'm not sulking, I just—'

He grabbed the menu up and waved it in my face. 'Now stop all that, and listen: I've got something exciting to tell you! So while you've been earning an honest crust, what do you think I've been doing?'

'I'm sure I'm going to find out.'

'Are you? Well, you'll need to get out of this strop first. You see, while you've been getting wound up about nothing, I've arranged a surprise.'

'What kind of surprise?'

'Ah, ah!' He waved an admonishing finger. 'Now you're interested! Are you still stroppy?'

'No.'

'Go on then. Ask me.'

I sighed. 'What's the surprise?'

'I've found us a house.'

'Sorry?'

'Well, we can't spend the whole of our married life holed up in my tiny flat or yours, can we? So I've spent the last week looking.'

I couldn't quite get my head around it. 'While you were at work? You can't just "find a house", Paul. It doesn't work like that.' I stared at him, flabbergasted, as his mobile tootled into life and he pulled it from his pocket. He didn't answer. He just held it, watching it ring.

'Someone you don't want to speak to?'

'An estate agent who's been chasing me. I'm trying to push them into lowering the price. I've told them I'm a cash buyer. If they think I might walk away, they'll shift their position, I expect.' He clicked it off.

'There were an awful lot of "I's" in that sentence, Paul. I think you're going to have to rethink this.'

He leant back and folded his arms. 'Okay, You're right. Of course you're right, but I challenge you not to love it when you see it. Seriously. I know I shouldn't have gone about it this way, and if you look at it and hate it, then that's that. You absolutely have the right of veto.'

'You're more than generous and fair,' I inclined my head sarcastically. 'And so, you have the money to pay for this?' I was scared even at the thought.

'With a careful bit of juggling. Look, we'll pool our resources. We sell yours and this and we'll start afresh. A new life. That's what marriage is supposed to be, isn't it?'

My gut turned over. *Just as Emma predicted.* 'Sell my flat? Sell? Wow.' I tried not to let him see my expression.

He got up and came over to put his arms around me. 'There's no "my" and "I" anymore,' he grinned. 'Or so I was informed very recently.'

'You're funny,' I said straight-faced, but finally forced to twitch into a smile.

'Think about it. You're the one who was just on about kids.' He swept a hand about the room. 'There's no way you could have kids in a place like this, is there? It's lovely but even you hate the stairs, so—'

'So you're saying—?'

'So I'm saying one step at a time Luce. I'm saying create a future with enough room to grow so that all our options are open. That's what I'm saying.'

I couldn't argue, how could I argue? We still hadn't talked about children, and yet we had sort of... In a way. A whole unsteady sea of change washed over me – one that I thought I was ready for, but now I wasn't so sure. I was being asked to let go of my lovely apartment: the one thing I had clung onto that was mine, that thing that no one could take away. But now...? Now I'd got married, I'd bound my life with his, I'd made a new commitment. The past had to be the past.

Paul came round and kissed the side of my head. 'You won't believe what I'm going to show you,' he laughed. 'Get ready to fall in love.'

–

Oh my god.

Love.

Yes, absolute love.

We had driven through Palmers Green into Winchmore Hill, past newsagents with their plaques outside still shouting Cassie Edwards's name in big black and white letters. I turned away; I couldn't look. Viv had deliberately kept me away from all that, and I was grateful.

We drove through streets of 1930s houses and then turned into a quiet cul-de-sac with big houses on either side. It was like another world. Pulling up outside, I looked out of the window – and I knew as soon as I saw it. The house stood on a corner plot with an amazing copper beech tree, its heavy purple branches hanging right over the front stone wall that curved around the garden, protecting it from view. I got out of the car slowly, savouring the moment: each step, each glance. I knew I was walking into something magical.

The place had been empty for over a year so the estate agent had given Paul the key and told us to take as long as we wanted. On the right was a space for cars, and on the left a pathway that was ramshackle and cottagey. It was full of weeds and tall grass, totally overgrown, but none of that mattered. The thick branches above us shushed in the breeze as we carefully picked our way around the back to a wild, untouched garden, busy with summer bees, the mass of green tangled with splashes of acid yellow and soft pinks, and then the soft brown of rust on an old lawnmower poking its handles out of a hedge.

'This garden will have colour all year you know. Look at that massive viburnum! That'll flower even in winter.'

We pushed our way through, our hands trailing, taking it all in. There was at least twenty years of planting that had gone on here – Someone had clearly loved it and taken great care. We found mounds of white-trumpeted bindweed that we realised was hiding a load of rusty iron-work seats.

'Wow! Could we clean those do you think?'

'Of course we could. Come on. Let me show you inside.'

He took my hand. Two small stone steps led us up to a dirty stained-glass door, that, with a bit of a shove and a lot of protestation, creaked open. The light caught the glass and I saw, with amazement, the astonishing beauty of it. A trail of red roses, garlanded by leaves and birds. Exquisitely painted, the colours like muted jewels.

'My God, have you really looked at this?' I breathed.

'I know. Wait till you see the rest.'

As soon as I stepped over the threshold, it was as though I'd lived there before. It was so mine – from the grimed Victorian tiled entranceway to the echoing high-ceilinged rooms with their fly-dirt bay windows. I knew I'd come back and haunt the place. It was so perfect. I loved it all.

Paul walked purposefully about, tapping walls, turning the taps on and off as though he knew what he was doing, while I wandered into the bedrooms. There were three: a large spacious one at the front that was clearly earmarked for us, a middle one with a very pretty art deco fireplace and then a smaller one at the back overlooking the rear garden. It was bright and sunny, and I knew where my thoughts were going.

I played with them, carelessly. I envisioned the cot and the comfy rocking chair near the radiator, and me, my socked feet resting on the top, looking down at a child, suckling, heavy-lidded, breath as soft as moth wings against my skin.

I saw all that as the future I'd never allowed myself to think about.

I shivered as though someone had walked over my grave.

'Come and look at this!'

I went out onto the landing. He was pointing up to an arch of ornate plaster moulding.

'What do you think of that, then?'

'Absolutely stunning. It really is.'

'Well don't keep wandering off, we're supposed to be enjoying this together.'

'Yes, you're right. Show me all the things you're in love with.'

'You, for starters.' He kissed my ear noisily. 'Look at this!' He ran his fingers over the rich warm mahogany of the wooden banister. I touched where he touched, running my fingers over the dust and dismissing all negative thoughts. I was too excited, too thrilled, too head-over-heels with the whole idea of it all. Maybe this was where everything turned around. I saw my single life going into cardboard boxes, my flat being viewed through an estate agent's eyes. I saw all that, and somehow it didn't matter, because here I was in a house that was talking to me, telling me our pasts were behind us and this was our future. This was more than just bricks and mortar and plaster and glass, I knew this place; it was in my bones. I'd come home.

—

'I've got a buyer,' I told Emma. 'So I'm officially putting you on hold until the housewarming.'

We were having lunch together. We did that most days now. It was a strange 'new beginning'. There were things I would have told her six months ago and now found that I couldn't. It seemed disloyal. We kept the conversation chatty rather than intimate, which suited me fine as I got to talk endlessly about the new house until I knew she was sick of hearing it.

'Christ that was quick! And the offer has been accepted on the new place?'

I nodded, a thrill of excitement turning my stomach upside down. 'The logistics are a bit of a nightmare, so all my stuff has gone into storage. What we need now is for Paul to get around to sorting all his gear out. Honestly, you've never seen so much crap — cupboards full of the stuff! It's unbelievable.'

'Lucy, are you totally sure about all this?' She gave me a look.

'What do you mean?'

'I mean everything seems to be happening so fast. You haven't had time to process everything, surely? With all the things that are happening.'

I could detect where this was going and I wasn't sure I liked it.

'You know, after the break-in he's never felt the same way about the flat. It'll be good to leave it all behind.'

'I was meaning you, not him.' She leaned forward. 'We all worry about you, you know.' She saw the look on my face and checked herself. 'But if you're sure, I'm not going to put a dampener on it. Wow! A summer housewarming! How fabulous is that?'

'It'll be a bloody Christmas party at this rate!' I laughed. 'So don't hold your breath!'

But I didn't really feel like laughing. 'We all worry' had been enough to make me step right back. She'd moved away from me and gone to 'them'. I knew then that Emma had been whispering.

–

June became July and we waited. Every day we checked for emails back from the solicitor or the surveyors, every day we eagerly searched the pile of letters on the mat as the process ground interminably on, until suddenly we were taken by surprise and it all happened in a matter of days: packing up, removers, bills to settle, new utility accounts, keys to collect, and no time to do it.

Paul stood with his hands on his hips peering into the jumbled gloom of his storage cupboard.

'It'll take me ages to clear out this lot. I really should've done it before.' He gazed at the piles of books and boxes of paperwork.

'No! Really?'

He ignored the sarcasm, kneeling to drag out a huge plastic bin and begin leafing through the contents. I looked around. He'd made a start at least; there were empty suitcases, packing boxes, cardboard files and black plastic sacks lying in readiness – just nothing in them. I could tell by the way he was approaching the task that it was going to be a very long-drawn-out process.

'Okay, I'll leave you to it.'

I didn't think he was listening. He was busily trying to pull something from the back of the cupboard that was obviously completely jammed, and he wasn't being very successful.

'Do you want a hand?'

'No,' he said sharply, and then sat back on his heels. 'Thanks, but I'll manage.' He gave me a preoccupied smile and waited for me to get out of the way.

I walked into the kitchen and listlessly wandered about, opening and closing cupboard doors, wondering what I could start on, and, in desperation, peered into the half-empty fridge, to see what needed doing there – when a flashing green light on the worktop caught my eye. Paul's work phone was blinking silently and I leaned over to look. There were several missed calls.

I went and stood in the doorway, dangling the phone between my fingers.

'You gave the storage people your number and they might be trying to get hold of you.'

He stopped. He'd pulled a battered-looking briefcase out and pushed it into a black rubbish sack.

'You're throwing that away?'

'Yeah, it's just paperwork and rubbish. Years old. School stuff mostly.'

'If you're sure?'

He gave me a withering look, reaching over to take the phone from my hand. 'Trying to interfere won't make it happen any quicker you know. All you need to do is leave it all to me. Seriously.'

'So you'll ring the storage people back?'

'Yes. It'll be fine, don't stress. It's all in hand.' He waved me away. I skirted around all the gear in the lounge and went to the window, running a finger across the sill. A spider scurried on impossibly thin legs into the corner of the frame. Opening the sash, I attempted to help it out. The blast of air brought with it a zoom of cars and whirling voices and I quickly pulled it closed. This was a normal Saturday morning: people going places, car boots open in readiness, the shouts from kids running backwards and forwards, and across the road a lanky teenager of indeterminate sex scuffing the toe of their trainer on the pavement edge. Ordinary lives. Ordinary people. Going back to work had made me realise how sick I was of dull tired offices and casework files and the endless depressive chaos of offenders. I wanted to do something clean and positive and creative. I imagined myself stripping floor-boards and painting skirting boards in that little bedroom at the back of the house and I smiled.

There was a family walking past, two women, and a little girl of about three running ahead with her dog, a little terrier thing. The dog was barking excitedly as the pair of them ran past a woman in a green coat. The woman stopped briefly and looked up towards me. My heart and throat met.

Caitlin.

She turned and walked back on the other side of the road.

It was her, I knew it. She was standing quite still and I could tell by the way she was looking that she was searching the windows. I glanced over to where Paul was kneeling, engrossed in tearing up papers, and when I looked back, she was crossing the road. There was a sound behind me and I whirled round.

'We need to organise curtains for the new house.' Paul was staring into the street. He'd sounded strange and distracted.

'You saw, didn't you?'

'Saw what?'

I looked back and she'd gone. Something inside me folded a little. I wasn't going to say her name. He turned and shifted a box with his foot. 'We need curtains. Unless you fancy doing the northern version of interior design and putting blankets up at the windows?' He laughed and then noticed my expression. 'What's the matter?'

That whole argument wavered in front of us and I just couldn't go there again.

'Nothing, nothing. You're right, we need curtains. Something cheap to tide us over.' I scrabbled about, searching for the car keys and found them on the top of a roll of bubble wrap. 'Okay,' I shot him a look. 'See you later.' I squeezed past. He was bending, picking up a pile of papers and shoving them into a briefcase. If he'd seen her then he was being really calm about it.

'Yep, great. See you later, then.' He didn't pause to look up.

I went down the stairs, my hands shaking as I attempted to press the exit button. *He must have seen her, surely?* I had visions of her standing on the other side of the door, waiting. *Would I challenge her? What would I say?*

Hardly daring to glance round, I made a beeline for my car, blipping it unlocked and sliding clumsily into the driver's seat. The mirrors revealed nothing. Where had she gone? There was just a guy getting out of his car and an older woman loading her boot with bags. What did she want? The old grind of insecurity started up again in my gut. Part of me wanted desperately to confront her but the other part…

Shaking the dread away, I managed to start the engine and find reverse. Checking the rear-view mirror, I looked out across the bonnet and there she was. My heart lurched. She was on the phone, strolling between the parked cars, frowning and checking the screen, redialling, and trying again. She looked round quickly and suddenly our eyes met in the mirror. I couldn't look away. Her hand holding the phone dropped and she began to walk towards me. I panicked; my legs shook as I jerked the car into gear, almost stalling the engine. I was aware of her steady gaze as I pulled forward out of the parking space.

I shot a look again, terrified that she was going to walk right over and knock on the window and force me to speak. But she just stood there on the pavement watching me, unmoving and impassive – a terrifying blankness in her gaze.

No, no. Please, no. I saw my life unravelling as I almost skidded out onto the main road and drove, my brain scrambling and a thumping pain tightening horribly in the back of my throat. *I'm such a coward, why didn't I speak to her?* I willed myself not to cry. I wasn't going to become hysterical; I would talk to Paul about it, rationally and calmly. I would ask him. I would ask the questions and make him confess to what was going on. *If I know, then I can handle it, if I know, then I can deal with it.*

I had no idea where I was going. I found myself sitting in the car on a street in Camden with no clue as to what I was doing there. I got out, walked blindly a little way along the street and turned around again. A newsagent had a board outside blaring the headline: *New Leads in Cassie Edwards Case*, but even that couldn't distract me. I imagined her in the flat right now. In there. With Paul. I felt sick at the thought. Why had I driven away? What I really needed was to speak to him. I needed the reassurance of his voice telling me that I'd got this all wrong and there was no affair after all.

He'd lied about the photograph because he'd been scared and he'd panicked. He thought I'd walk out on him. This woman was mad. This woman was crazy. I should feel sorry for her, not threatened.

I sat in the car looking at the pad of speed-dial contacts with his name right at the top. My fingers found the number but the connection dropped into silence. I tried again. There was a long pause of emptiness, and then the automated message telling me that Paul's phone was switched off but I was very welcome to leave a message. Not even his voice. Why had he changed the voicemail? I tried again. And then again.

I started the engine and drove slowly back to the flat, terrified of what I would find, trying him over and over on speakerphone, listening to some automated faceless woman telling me things that I really didn't want to hear.

–

I stood in the centre of the lounge which was now topsy-turvy with packing stuff. The carpet was covered in foot-prints and bits of dirt. Empty boxes sat waiting to be filled. All the cases and black sacks had gone. Paul had gone. I walked into the kitchen and peered out of the open window. So had his car. I listened to the birds clamouring on the roof as I tried his phone over and over and still no answer. All I got was that depressing message that left me feeling irritated and angry and with a deep nagging sensation that something was seriously wrong.

And then my phone pinged. I pulled it from my pocket, glancing down. There was a video message from an unknown number. In the corner of the screen, a smiley face bobbed and waved. I clicked on it. The newspaper photograph of Cassie Edwards zoomed and blurred into view. My stomach somersaulted and the world around me went silent.

There was a pause and then a voice message icon popped up.

'Now where have you been all this time Lucy?' Simon Gould's boyish voice giggled. 'I told you I wanted to prove how good I am now, and then you go and disappear on me. This could all have been over much sooner if you hadn't run away.'

There was a high-pitched cry off the microphone somewhere and I froze.

'Just a minute, darling, I won't be a minute.' There was a shuffling rustle.

'No one ever listens, do they, Lucy? Especially people like you with your treatment programmes and your leaflets and your challenging offending behaviour courses, busily patting each other on the back and talking about how successful you are at changing people like me—'

The phone shook wildly in my hand.

'Simon? Simon…' I whispered. 'What the hell have you done?'

I heard him let out an astonished whistle and he chuckled. 'They thought they could change me. Of course, that's just arrogance talking.'

I heard the child say something. I could hear my own heartbeat. I closed my eyes.

'I do what I do, not because I've been abused, or I have a mental illness, or some kind of addiction. I do what I do because I *enjoy* it.' His voice slid inside my head and the message ended.

I opened my eyes as it hit me: *He couldn't have this number, could he? It was a different phone. There was no way.* Cassie Edwards's smiling face froze on the screen for a second and then a box popped up. 'This message has been deleted,' it said.

My mouth fell open.

He was gone.

—

'Viv?'

'Oh! Luce—'

'Viv, Gould has just sent me a message: a voice message. He has that little girl.'

'Lucy...'

'Viv. You know what kind of person I am. I don't make stuff like this up. Gould is clever. He's covered his tracks. As soon as I played it, it—'

'But I'm standing here looking at him, Lucy.'

'What?'

'I'm doing a filmed supervision of Dave Cartwright running the weekend sex offender group. Gould is sitting right on the other side of this window. I only left the room and answered because I saw it was you.'

'No, that's not possible Viv... No. It must've been a timed sending or something... Look, interrogate my phone; you'll see it on the call log. I'm not wrong Viv, he has that little girl!' I suddenly realised I'd raised my voice. She went quiet for a few seconds.

'Go to the police, report it, get it on file, and when you've done that—'

I found I was breathing hard.

'You need to talk to someone, Lucy,' she said gently. 'I want to see you first thing on Monday morning.'

'It *was* Gould, Viv. It was him. It was him again.'

'Lucy, I haven't said anything before because... Well, I didn't want to freak you out. But the police said they weren't able to connect Gould with any of the calls that were made to your phone. Now I know what you're going to say, but you just need to—'

I didn't care about what I needed to do. I wasn't listening.

'He has the little girl.'

'Lucy?'

Her voice seemed very far away. 'Lucy? Can you hear me? Are you still there?'

–

You are totally alone. No one believes you.

If I couldn't go to the police, where else could I go? I couldn't phone Emma; I knew she'd run to Viv, so there was no one. No one.

The only person – the *only* person who would know what to do was Paul. *But Paul, the man who I was supposed to trust, who I was supposed to depend on, was where? And with who?* I had this sudden, agonising thought that he would take her to the house. I drove there slowly. His car wasn't in the drive. I pulled into the empty space, not knowing what else to do or where else to go.

The house looked blankly down, offering no answers. I switched off the engine, listening to the twittering tumble of birds fighting in the bushes. A black cat slunk warily across the garden and disappeared into a hedge as a diesel engine roared and a white removal van lurched round the corner. Paul's car was following. He pulled up behind me and leapt out.

'Christ, it's been completely mental on the roads this morning!' He came up to my door and stood there, expectantly. 'Why didn't you answer your phone? I've been ringing you. I've still got bits back at the flat but I needed to let these guys in. I didn't know you were coming.'

'Paul—'

He glanced up at the slam of the removal van doors opening. 'Your stuff is here too. So I take it no curtains then?' he laughed. 'What are you like?' He began to walk away. 'It'll have to be blankets. If we leave the washing machine outside as well the neighbours will think we've been re-housed by the council... Anything you want me to do?' He called out to one of the removal guys.

'Paul!'

'What?' He turned, smiling.

'I need to talk to you about what's happened this morning.'

I watched the smile fall. I tried to assemble my thoughts. A whole raft of things went through my head: *you know what he's going to say, you know he'll be angry. Do you really want to do this?*

'Simon Gould contacted me. He has Cassie Edwards. He just sent me a voice message. I heard her.'

The relief of not mentioning Caitlin flooded through me.

'What the—?' He glanced back at the removers unloading the van and then to me. 'Show me.'

'I can't.' I was feeble and shaky.

'What do you mean, you can't? What did he say?'

I shook my head, terrified that I'd start to cry. 'The message deleted.' I pulled the phone from my pocket and showed him the unknown number. 'See? I phoned Viv.

Viv said it couldn't be Gould because he was sitting right there in front of her...' I stared off, blinking the tears away. I wasn't going to tell him what the police had said to her. 'I think I'm going mad—'

The thoughts of Caitlin and Simon Gould and a little blonde girl lurched through my mind.

'Lucy,' Paul cut across me. He touched the side of my face; his fingers were firm. 'Look at me. This is Simon Gould we're talking about. This is mega serious. We're taking this to the police. It doesn't matter what Viv says or doesn't say. It's not her call.'

'But what proof have I got?' I was frantic. 'I need someone to examine this phone and without Viv's support...' I stared up at him. 'We've been here before. I'm just some crazy cow. They'll never believe me, will they?'

I looked up into the grey softness of his eyes as they assessed my face. He threaded his fingers into a curl of my hair.

'I've told you, *we* will go to the police. *We* will report exactly what happened and we'll hand it over to them. You're going to do exactly what you did before, only this time we're doing it together. You and me. We're a team now, right?'

I nodded dully, opening my mouth, fearful, wanting to say the name 'Caitlin' but suddenly found I couldn't. I closed it.

I stared at him; his eyes were piercingly clear and utterly truthful.

'So we'll go inside. We'll make that telephone call, then we'll put this out of our heads and we'll enjoy the rest of today. Is that a deal?' He took my hand.

My eyes were puffy and sore and I felt totally worn out. He drew me close, putting his arms around me. 'Is that a deal?'

I nodded.

'There is only you and me and today, and today is special. We'll never get this time back. Look.' He gestured to the beautiful grand old house. 'This is us and this is ours. Our furniture is here, all your stuff. We've got loads to do. Now forget everything else. Aren't you excited?' He kissed me and I said I was. 'Nothing bad can happen here. Only good things. Just look at it all. See?'

I looked at the house and I believed him. I so wanted to believe him.

—

We telephoned the police. I recounted the content of the message as accurately and precisely as I could.

I didn't mention the last incident when Gould contacted me. I could tell by the officer's tone that he already knew all about it. I ploughed on regardless, trying to stop my voice quavering, trying to present the facts and nothing else.

I ended the call to find Paul looking at me.

'Is that done now?'

'It's done.'

'You'll go back into work on Monday. You'll have a conversation with Viv, knowing in your own mind that you've followed protocol and it's all logged and recorded. Now it's down to you. I suggest we put all that behind us and enjoy the next few hours. Okay?'

'Okay.'

Paul was at his funny and affectionate best. We went from room to room with the removal guys, him with an arm thrown round my shoulders, hugging me to him, willing me to forget what had happened and jolly me into feeling better.

'Your furniture looks great in here, far better than mine will look… Yeah, brilliant! Let's try that sofa just there… What do you think?' His mood was infectious; I let his enthusiasm seep under my skin. One of the removal guys started to laugh and joke with me and I managed to join in. This morning hadn't happened. I didn't have to dwell on it. All I had to do was shut stuff out and open boxes. How difficult was that?

'I'm betting you don't hear from your friend for a while now.'

I looked up from a box I'd delved into. 'Who, Emma?'

'Yep. I think you'll discover she'll be a bit jealous. She won't like the fact you've suddenly got all this—' he cast a hand around. 'I suspect that's why she's distanced herself from you in the last few weeks.'

I didn't reply. I hadn't told him about going out for lunch with her every day. I wasn't sure why.

'Actually, it's probably me that's been a bit distant.'

I could see by his face he was pleased.

That wasn't a lie. We didn't talk like we used to, that's all. *Of course I trusted her* – just not quite as much.

'Look what I've found!' I pulled off a load of wrapping paper to reveal the little sand-filled souvenir. He took it carefully and put it on the fireplace.

'Its new home,' he grinned and started to whistle. He was happy, we'd moved on from the subject so why spoil it by explaining? What did telling him about lunch with Emma matter, really? It was only a little thing after all.

That night we lay in bed surrounded by the tall figures of still unpacked boxes looming around us like godmothers at a christening. The moonlight stretched in unfamiliar patches on the walls. It was quiet here. Far quieter than we were used to and I was too wound up to sleep. I couldn't stop the thoughts about that little girl, about Gould, about Caitlin, from whirling round and round in my head.

'We should get a dog,' Paul said suddenly.

'A what?'

'A dog – as a housewarming present to ourselves. The garden's got a wall around it. It'd be perfect.'

'I thought you wouldn't want one after...' I remembered what he'd told me.

'After what?' His head shifted on the pillow.

'Well, you had a dog before didn't you?'

'When I was a kid, yes. A Jack Russell my parents had. It was a horrible smelly thing.'

'No, I meant... *before*, before...'

His head rustled against the pillow and he rested his cheek against my temple. 'No. I always worked long hours so it never seemed fair. It's not right to leave a young dog all day.'

I frowned a little and stared up at the ceiling. A car headlight stuttered through the tree branches and then melted into a corner.

'Unless you were thinking of giving up work for any reason.' I heard the smile in his voice. I turned slightly to face him.

'What do you mean?'

He pulled me onto my side and lay with one arm crooked under his head and the other draped across my hips. His erection pressed into my thigh.

'What d'you think I mean?'

'I thought—?'

'Maybe that's the problem. Too much thinking.'

'But—'

He put a finger to my lips. 'I hate the thought of being on some kind of life route-march. Why don't we just let go? Let fate decide. See what happens. If it does it does, if it doesn't, well—'

I stood at a crossroads. My future, the possibility of my future, lay one way: the house, the husband, the children – the dog leaping around that magical secret garden. And the other path? The other was full of darkness and uncertainty. The foundations of my old life were cracking and shifting under my feet: my lovely flat, my friend, even my job had drifted away and now I was out and floating in an endless sea of suspicion, questioning everyone and everything – But the overwhelming terror this all brought, was the feeling of never, ever, being at peace.

We kissed deeply. Everything else around me disappeared. There was only us, set adrift, the soft rhythm of our movement, me, him, him, me, I didn't need to think about anything, there was nothing to think about, only us.

—

'What time is Viv in?' I dropped my bag onto the seat of my chair.

It was Monday morning. Emma looked as though she might have had a hard weekend. She briefly swivelled her eyes from her screen. 'About ten, I think. There's some kind of meeting this morning.'

'Oh. Right.'

I heard the slight squeal of wheels as she shunted her chair over towards me.

'Hang on... Why?' Her nose was clearly telling her something was up.

I looked round to see who could hear. 'She wants to see me.'

'Ah.' She glanced about her. 'Have you got a second?'

She cocked her head towards the door of the Ladies' and I got the gist. The door closed behind us with a soft *whump*. She leaned against the basin and folded her arms. 'You look awful.'

'Ever the flatterer.' I smiled wanly. 'You don't look so swish yourself.'

'No, honestly, Luce. Have you looked at yourself recently?' She pulled me round to look at my reflection in the mirror. 'I mean, look how pale you are? You feeling okay?'

'We're both knackered. The house is definitely a work in progress. A lot of work and not much progress,' I sighed.

'And you're not worrying about the Gould thing? I mean the phone stuff. The police?'

The mention of his name made my stomach turn over and with irritation too. 'God, the jungle drums are fast round here, aren't they? How do you know about all that?'

'You know you can always talk to me, don't you?' She searched my face. 'I know I've been replaced and you've gone up in the world now, but—'

'Oh don't talk daft!' I laughed, but Paul's words came back to me. 'You could never be replaced. Talking of which, how's the complicated love-life with Connor? You booked your plane tickets yet?'

She wrinkled her nose and sighed. 'Connor's been well and truly relegated to the back-burner. He's being a bit of

189

a cock, actually. And "complicated" is bloody spot on. There's always some drama or other to deal with.'

She began to give me snippets of the latest ruck he'd had with his wife. I watched the shadows moving over her lovely face, wondering how I didn't know all this and why the hell our friendship had got in this state.

'Anyway,' she shook herself. 'Enough of all that. I still haven't been invited over to this amazing work in progress to meet this spectacular bloke who managed to crack your defences.'

'You leave my cracks out of it,' I grinned. 'You're a wonderful woman, Emma Roberts. Look, let's sort something, shall we?' I immediately thought about Paul but dismissed it. I'd talk to him. He'd be fine. 'Come over, see the house and have a lovely meal at the same time. I promise I won't cook.'

'Sounds perfect.' She stepped forward and gave me a massive hug. 'Just say when… Oh—' she cocked an ear, listening. 'I think those are Viv's dulcet tones I can hear. Weren't you supposed to be meeting her?'

A wash of dread turned my guts to water. 'I am, but I really wish I wasn't.'

'It'll be fine,' Emma kissed me on the cheek. 'You'll see.'

—

She was wrong. I saw that as soon as I walked in.

'Ah Lucy! Have a seat.' Viv got up from behind her desk and gestured to the comfy chairs around the coffee table. Michelle from H.R. was already sitting there, a folder on her lap and her H.R. smile at the ready. There was a cheerfully decorated pottery bowl on the table next to a strategically placed box of tissues.

'I'm hoping both of those are for decorative purposes only,' I joked. I sat awkwardly. I knew the blow was coming.

'Now. Lucy. Thanks so much for agreeing to this meeting…'

That was how it started, but it wasn't the way it ended. The words that I'd been dreading *Indefinite leave due to work-related stress* with a 'care plan' in place, was the conclusion. I was 'advised' to make an appointment to see my G.P., then I'd be seen by occupational health, with a weekly follow-up phone call from Viv to monitor my progress and address any 'worries' that I might have.

No one wanted to hear my side of the story, not really. Viv said that they had to be careful not to be seen to be 'harassing' Simon Gould, who was meeting all of his post-release requirements, was perfectly co-operative with all interventions and wasn't posing any threat to the community 'as far as anyone was aware'.

It was clear to me that Simon Gould was a pat-on-the-back rehabilitation success story, whereas for me, the plot and I had parted company some time ago.

'Give yourself some time to breathe and then let's look at where we are in six weeks time,' Viv said. I left her office smiling and thanking her, a performance designed for Emma and Dave and anyone else who might be watching. 'Time to breathe,' they'd framed it as. That was just about all I could do.

Emma was nowhere to be seen as I walked blindly out into the fresh air. I was aware my feet were moving but it was as though a pane of toughened glass was sitting between me and the real world. I just wanted to be at home.

'Sweetheart, let me have your phone.' Paul held his hand out across the heap of empty packing boxes in the kitchen. 'That place and those people are toxic. I'm not saying it's deliberate or they're even aware of it. It's the system; it's the way these places work. Don't see anyone from there, don't even think about it. Concentrate on making this old place shine – You know you want to.'

And so I threw myself into the house renovations with blind and frenzied enthusiasm: pulling up ancient stuck-to-the-floor carpets, hacking at the worn lino, pulling down filthy blinds and piling the whole lot into skips and watching it trundle away. The physicality of it calmed me. Paul calmed me. I thought I'd panic with no contact with the outside world, but the opposite was true: it was a blessed relief. Simon Gould and Caitlin were like something from a terrible recurring dream that now I'd woken up from. Cassie Edwards became a name of a little girl lost along with all the other little girls I'd dealt with in my past life. I was determined this new life would be my future.

We peeled the walls back to brick, and we sealed over all the cracks. We mended and we restored. The house smelled of new beginnings: the tang of wet plaster and drying paint. So far, we had a bathroom and half a kitchen – Its solidity grew, with me secure and solid inside it.

The tension in my neck and shoulders turned into the physical ache of hard work, but it was a good ache. My shoulders strengthened and loosened, my back muscles tightened and eased; the tendons and ligatures learned to remember how strong they were, as strong as the person I used to be.

–

Paul became the man I'd always dreamed of. I watched him when he wasn't aware of it: wrestling with some pipe or fixing – an intent look of concentration on his face. I felt a huge rush of something intensely powerful then, more than anything I'd ever felt before. All thoughts of Dan were gone – replaced by a new and all-consuming sense of belonging. Something bound me to Paul so tightly I knew I would never be able to break free, even if I'd wanted to.

Doctor's appointments came and went; I made excuses for some, others I accepted their prescriptions that went along with it. 'These are very mild,' they always said. I assumed 'mild' was just like them: wishy-washy and point-less. The prescriptions lay in the drawer, uncashed. Viv rang me as she'd promised, and we exchanged pleasantries and then I handed the phone calmly back to Paul. I didn't want to listen.

'Good girl,' he said. 'Right decision.'

I thought about Emma and I thought about mentioning something about seeing her but each time I put it off. We were too knackered, I told myself. It would be too much hassle. I didn't want to hear about work. All of that was true, and yet wasn't but I dismissed it. We were happy, weren't we?

Each night I lay listening to the reassuring steadiness of his breathing, luxuriating on the brink of sleep, my fingers creeping over the flat plains of my stomach, and allowing myself to imagine the unimaginable. *Could I be pregnant?* It was possible, after all. I thought about what might be happening deep in there – would it be this month, or the next, or the next? It was a supremely weird idea that this time next year I could have a baby. The thought didn't frighten me as I thought it would; I had this feeling of quiet and calm contentment. My body had turned away from the outside world to the possibility of an inner life. For the first time in my life I was centred and sure. It was a sensation I wasn't used to: I'd become me.

—

We'd begun tackling the garden; the rusting lawnmower we unearthed was joined by an upright vacuum cleaner and an abandoned garden hoe, only held together by a mass of beetles and wandering roses. It was hot and dusty and my hands were sticky with sap, but I was in heaven.

'So here are those iron seats then.' Paul dragged a load of bindweed into a pile so I could see what he was talking about. 'And look what was with them.' He pulled away another load. There sat a stunning stone carved bench, green and grey with lichen and moss.

'Oh my God!' I went over, running my fingers across its pitted surface. 'How beautiful is that?'

'We'll shift it round by the French doors. What do you think?'

'I think it's absolutely perfect.'

We rubbed the ironwork down and bought some paint. Then I remembered I'd seen a motley collection of old cushions in a junk shop in Southgate. So the next day I went and bought them, along with some gorgeous velvety material I'd spied which I painstakingly cut and hand sewed it into cushion covers. I was incredibly proud of my achievements and took them out to show Paul. He was busily tying back the massive viburnum.

'Hey, what do you think?' Each chair was now adorned with my beautiful cushion creations. I stood back to appreciate my work.

'They look great, don't they?' Paul came up behind me and put his hands on my hips.

'Thank you.' I leaned my head back against his shoulder and he absent-mindedly pulled his fingers through my hair.

'Doesn't all this hard work make you want to show it off?'

'Mmm?' I didn't really get what he was talking about.

'Do you think it might be time to come out of hibernation now?' His fingers twisted into the hair in the nape of my neck and it pulled a little. 'I mean, start mixing with people again? It's not good to live completely like a hermit, you know.'

'No?' I tipped my chin quizzically, not quite believing.

'Why not? While the weather's holding. We could eat out here.' He untangled his fingers and in so doing, yanked strands of my hair.

'Ow!' I squawked.

'You should cut it.' He lifted an end and tickled my nose.

'Sorry?' It itched where he had pulled and I rubbed the spot.

'You should have your hair shorter. You always clip it up nowadays anyway. It looks good off your face. Quite sexy, actually.'

I unwound myself from his clutches, giving him a warning look but he only grinned and gave a little shrug. 'Just my opinion.'

'The great thing about opinions is that they're yours and yours alone.' I collected up my paintbrush and tin. 'I'm going to ring Emma, okay?'

'See if she's free tomorrow for Sunday lunch!' he called after me, reaching for the garden rake.

I looked back in surprise.

'While everything is looking so fantastic. Why not?'

—

'My God! Is it really you?' She sounded like she'd been running. 'Where've you been! Where've you been! It's like forever since we've spoken! Literally!'

'It really is. I'm back from the dead.'

'I've been asking you to call me. I've been really worried!'

I frowned, puzzled. 'Because I didn't know you'd called.'

'Your man Paul said he'd tell you. Anyway, what was he doing answering your phone?'

'Probably looking after my mental welfare,' I said sardonically.

I was a bit surprised he hadn't mentioned it. 'Anyway. What are you doing for Sunday lunch?'

'What, like tomorrow Sunday lunch? Err... Coming round to you by the sounds of it. Are you cooking?'

'Paul will be, don't worry,' I laughed. 'Will Connor be joining you?'

'Connor?' she said, all mock puzzlement. 'Ah, you must mean *Harry*. Do you ever get names right?'

'Oh Lord!' I laughed. 'Do I take it New Zealand is off the cards then?'

'No New Zealand, thank god,' she chuckled. 'My best friend is here, why would I want to go there?'

'At last! She realises! Right. Harry, is it? Must remember that.'

'Actually, talking of friends, I've just realised I've got some friends, Jess and Luke, staying with me at the mo.

Is it okay if I bring them too? Can you stretch to four of us?'

I mentally calculated if the table would be big enough and if we'd have enough chairs.

'If you don't mind sitting on the recycling bin,' I laughed. 'It's no problem at all.'

'Why not?' she sighed theatrically. 'You can put me and the empties out first thing on Monday.'

'I don't think we'd want you recycled would we, Emma? You're bad enough in your current form. We don't want you coming back as something else.'

'Ooh! Look who's feeling better then?' she retorted.

And she was right. I was.

–

Pushing the trolley round the supermarket, I mulled over the menu we'd planned. I'd got the salad stuff so far, and then thought it might be nice to make some little canapes, and wondered what I should get.

Rounding the cosmetics aisle, I happened to catch sight of my reflection. My hair was off my shoulders and my neck looked long and sleek. I paused, pretending I was reading a lipstick advert and turned my face to the side. Maybe Paul was right. Why not have it cut short? I never had, so why not give it a whirl?

Whizzing round the aisles and picking up loads of delicious bits, I chucked it all in the car and called my hairdresser. I'd been going to her for ages and I knew if she could fit me in, she would.

'You're dead lucky,' she shouted over the noise of the driers in the background. 'My five o'clock has just cancelled so I'm all yours.'

I rang Paul and made some excuse about why I'd be back later than planned. He didn't sound particularly pleased, but I was ridiculously excited. I loved the smell and the bustle of the hairdressers. Late afternoon was a great time to go. It was a completely different atmosphere; there were only a couple of other clients being finished off and it was cosy and unhurried. The dark blue sky filled the huge windows and the passers-by were getting fewer. Bex, my stylist, was going out for a birthday drinks later and had bought in a few bottles of prosecco which I was invited to share. It was girly, fun and chatty, and I found I was really enjoying myself.

'Married, eh?' She grinned at me in the mirror as I watched curls of wet hair falling in shards down the front of my gown. 'You're a dark horse, aren't you?' she laughed. 'You never mentioned it. I love a good wedding, me. Big party, was it?'

'Oh it was back up in my home town and it was all a bit of a whirlwind,' I said and changed the subject. I'd started to feel more than a little nervous at the amount of hair in my lap. I chatted on, more to distract myself than anything, but I shouldn't have worried. Bex finished blow-drying and moved away from the mirror and I saw myself for the first time. The dark wildness had been tamed to a choppy bob, the fringe framing my eyes making them look huge and even greener. Caitlin came into my head but I immediately dismissed the thought.

'I love it,' I said. 'I really, really love it.'

–

As I pushed open the front door, I could hear Paul clattering about in the kitchen. Smiling, I dumped the bags, slipped off my coat and went and stood in the doorway. He didn't look round.

'Do we need to get more beers, do you think?' I waited, amused.

'Is that an actual question?' His tone wasn't pleasant.

I took a few steps into the kitchen. 'What's the matter?'

He ignored me, starting to wipe down a work surface that clearly didn't need wiping.

'Paul?'

The cloth stopped, mid-arc. 'Would you like to tell me about this?' He turned and grabbed something but suddenly froze, paralysed for a moment, with a look of absolute horror in his eyes. 'What the hell have you done?'

I stepped back, steadying myself against the door frame.

He couldn't take his eyes off me. One hand instinctively came up to my neck. 'I've had my hair cut.' I knew I sounded lame.

'Why would you do such a thing?' He looked appalled.

'I fancied a change,' I tried to shrug it off. 'And anyway, I thought you said I'd look good with shorter hair.'

'I said I don't like short hair, I never have.'

'What?' I pulled back. 'This morning. You said—'

'Sorry, I was under the impression that what I say doesn't matter. Only now strangely, it suddenly does.' He opened his fist and my little strip of silver contraceptive pills fell out.

I looked down, not fully comprehending.

'Is this yet another example of my irrelevance?'

'I don't get what—'

'Don't you?' His hand came down on the worktop with such force I thought it might crack. He stood there leaning heavily with his head down, his jaw jutting in fury. 'No. Clearly, you really don't, do you?'

I stared at him.

'This packet.'

'Yes,' I looked down at it, not comprehending.

'It's full.'

'Yes, I haven't been taking them since we talked about it—' My breath staggered high up into my chest.

'*Jesus!*' He gave a sudden bark of laughter. 'Seriously? *We talked about it*,' he mimicked angrily, his mouth crumpling into a sneer. 'We talked about what?'

I opened my mouth but his fury wouldn't let me speak.

'Let me ask you something and I'm *really* hoping you're going to give me a truthful answer.'

I could only stand there, dumb with shock.

'Is this what you did with that *Dan* bloke?'

My lips could barely form the word. 'What?'

'You heard. Did you think I wouldn't find out about your grubby past?'

My cheeks burned. I turned my face away. 'I told you about that.'

He gave a snort of derision. 'No, you didn't. Unfortunately I've had to find out from so-called colleagues. Strangers really. People who clearly enjoyed the fact that I had no fucking idea.' He leaned forward, his face was ugly.

'What do you want to know?'

'Try the truth.'

Dan's face came to mind. '*Your choice*,' he had said. '*I want to be with you Lucy, but not with a kid. I'm just being honest.*'

'I got pregnant.' The humiliation of it burned.

'I know. It feels as though everyone in probation and psychology in the north of England knew too. But you didn't think to mention it to me. And? What else?'

I felt sick at the memory. 'I had an abortion. It was a dreadful, dreadful time. I didn't want to talk about it; I didn't want to remember. It was over, done, gone...'

'So, I'll ask the question that everybody's been hinting at. Did you get pregnant on purpose to get him to leave his wife and then the plan backfired?'

'Jesus, no! For God's sake! No, of course I didn't!'

'And were you planning on getting pregnant without me knowing either?'

'What? No! We talked about it! You said—'

'No.' He held up a finger. 'Lie number one, we've *never* talked about it.'

'Yes we did! You said—'

'Go on, what did I say?' He cocked an ear towards me.

'We talked about getting a dog, and—'

'A dog. And what did I say about that?'

'You said, we should get a dog because—'

'Ah. Right. And from that sole comment you deduced that I meant for us to have a kid.' He paused with mock solemnity. 'Tell me, Lucy. What the fuck is going on in your head?'

The anger, the frustration, the hurt, the *horror* of the last few months spilled over and I dissolved into a rush of choking and sobbing, the kind of blind crying where I couldn't get my breath, and I suddenly found his arms enveloping me, rocking and comforting. 'Oh god I'm so sorry Lucy! Shhhh... Forgive me! Shhhh,' he kept saying. 'Shhh now, it's okay, it's okay. Look, I'm sorry. I shouldn't have said that. I went over the top, I'm sorry—'

I gulped for air, spluttering and hiccoughing.

'I was just so angry when I found your pills. It was me being stupid. I overreacted.' He held me away so that he could look right into my eyes. But I wouldn't lift my face.

'Lucy, look at me... Please, look at me. It's nothing to do with Dan. Nothing, do you hear me? That was before we were together. It's...' He searched for the words. 'It's not you either, it's about me. About her. Caitlin. All this talk about kids has brought back a—' He stopped. 'I just can't do it right now. Please tell me you understand. Please. Just say you get it... I can't even think about... I mean. What happened before was so—' He pulled me to him, kissing my forehead, my cheeks. I could feel his arms trembling against my back.

'Of course I understand, of course I do.' *The relief, the relief that whatever awfulness there had been, was suddenly over.*

'I mean, I'm not saying not ever. I'm not saying that.' I heard the slight panic that he'd really upset me, that he'd gone too far.

I understood; of course I understood. I could hear his heart pounding away in his chest as he breathed his heat into my hair. 'I know,' I said. 'You don't have to explain.' I sensed the fragility of him: something child-like and scared and vulnerable, and how he was showing me all of that because he loved me.

'What I'm saying is, I don't know about the future or how I'll feel in three, four, five years' time.'

Five years as a timespan hammered into my brain. I'd be nearly forty. I paled. I thought about never having a child. I looked up at him.

'Do you think you could be okay with that?' His eyes were full of remorse and pain.

I nodded silently. What else could I say?

'Are you sure?'

'Of course,' I whispered. There was an instability beneath my feet: things crumbled and swayed a little. He put his head on one side and surveyed me with a tiny comic pout. 'And you know I love your hair, whatever you do to it. You know that, don't you?'

I didn't know what I knew or what I didn't. I saw this house: our house, all the possibilities whispering to me from the walls. I saw a version of myself walking away from him and up the stairs to where that little back bedroom waited for me. There was no baby, no crib, just me standing in the centre of a vacant room, my arms hugging myself, listening to the emptiness of my future – and then, suddenly, I looked down, and in the crook was a tiny newborn. It mewled, a tiny sound, as a delicate milk bubble blew and popped, just like my dreams.

'I know I'm here and you're here,' I said. 'And neither of us are going anywhere.'

But even as I said it, I knew that in reality we had just moved one step closer to each other while inching one step further apart.

–

I tried to put it all out of my head. The last thing I wanted was Emma sensing something wasn't right. We spent that Sunday morning being acutely mindful of each other, tiptoeing carefully, as though some great black hole had appeared between us that was too deep and dangerous to contemplate.

In a quiet moment I had gone upstairs and sat on the side of the bed, staring down at the little strip of contraceptive pills in my hand. *Of course I understood, of course I did.* I pushed one out of the blister pack and held it in the palm of my hand. Such a small thing – that changed everything.

The day brought warm breezes and beautiful sunshine. The house shone, showing itself off at its best: the staircase looked glorious and the hallway tiles were colourful and inviting. I banished all thoughts and misgivings and concentrated only on seeing Emma again. She would never guess anything was amiss; I'd make sure of that.

Paul was in the kitchen finishing off the salad and I was taking a tray of wine glasses and nibbles outside onto the table, when I heard a car draw up. Peering around to the front garden, I could just make out figures through the beech tree branches and hear the chatter of voices. I saw Emma first, her hand on the gate as it squealed open. She hadn't seen me. She glanced solicitously over her shoulder to the person behind and I followed her gaze. The sight paralysed me for a second. The woman had a baby in her arms.

I made my way down the path, a big smile plastered on my face.

'Ohhhhh!' breathed Emma as she hugged me. 'Oh Luce! Your hair!... Wow!' She stroked the ends gently. 'It looks fab! You look amazing!... And where did you get that top? You're going to have to be careful I don't mug you.'

'Oh! Thanks!' It had been so long since I'd seen her, didn't know how to react.

'And *this*. Oh. My. God!' She gazed up in admiration at the house. 'It's absolutely stunning!'

'Hello! Hello!' I bustled them all inside. 'Welcome! ...and who's this, then?'

I peered into the bundle of blankets.

'Oh yes, this is my friend Jess, and this is little Hope.'

I touched a tiny finger that was curled around the edge of the blanket; the nail was like a miniature pearl. Emma touched my arm to distract me. 'And this is Harry,' she flashed me a pointed look. 'And this is Jess's husband, Luke.'

I looked up, momentarily distracted, and smiled. Harry was huge, possibly some kind of rugby player, and Luke was one of those good-looking scruffy men with an easy grin.

Luke placed a hand on Jess's back. 'D'you want me to take her so you can relax?'

We all stood watching as Jess carefully manoeuvred the sleeping baby and placed her into Luke's arms.

'There.' Emma beamed and suddenly glanced round. Paul was standing in the kitchen doorway, one hand resting on the frame. He had a strange look on his face: one I couldn't decipher. I felt a warning shiver without knowing why.

'Oh hello!' Emma enthused, striding over. 'Paul! Lovely to see you again!' She kissed him firmly on the cheek and took his hand to introduce him to people. 'This is my man of the moment, Harry, and this is Jess... Luke... And Hope.'

Paul nodded a shy hello around the group. I was surprised: I had never seen him anything but self-confident and easy in his own skin. He looked totally ill at ease. There was a pause that was slightly too long and I immediately filled the silence.

'Right, come in, come in! Let's go this way through the dining room, you get to see a bit of the house that way.'

They all dutifully followed me through the rather ramshackle dining room where Paul's modern elegant dining table sat alongside one of my old, fat, pillowy couches. The French doors stood open, the filmy white voile curtains just catching the late morning breeze.

'Oh my god! I love it! I love it all!' Emma fell on every-thing, exclaiming over my old mismatched candlesticks on Paul's posh table as though this was a new kind of chic.

'You've seen a lot of it before, Em,' I laughed. 'But come out here.' I gathered back the floating curtain to reveal the weathered table set out with gaily coloured rush mats and a bowl full of peony heads from the garden.

'Please everyone – sit wherever you like.'

Emma couldn't get over it: she cooed over the cush-ions, exclaiming what a genius I was at renovation, touching the table and the chairs, holding the jazzy cutlery up with a gasp as people admired and nodded and finally sat down. I took a moment to stand back with Paul as we watched them, smiling. I slipped my hand into his, squeezing his little finger.

'I want all this in my place,' Emma pronounced deci-sively. 'I absolutely love every bit.'

'You can have it,' I laughed. 'Most of it's junk shop tat.'

Paul shook my hand away. 'So what can I get you all to drink?'

'Red please!' called Emma, and everyone laughed.

'Harry? What'll you have…? And how about you Luke? Who's driving here?' There was the sudden chill of his absence. He walked away, chummily joking with the guests. He was instantly back to his old ebullient self.

'He's not as weird-looking as I remember, Luce,' Emma came over and whispered making me snort a laugh. 'I can see why you haven't been parading him around. And this house!… My God! I've got to have a tour… This must've cost a bomb!'

Paul shot me an unpleasant look as I heard him begin to tell a story about sanding window frames and pulling up dirty carpets as he went round pouring the wine.

Emma hadn't noticed. 'You know, Luce,' she shook her head. 'I had no idea you had such an eye for nest-building. You'll be having babies next!'

My antenna flared in warning as I steered her away to point out the views of the garden, front and back and what we planned to do with it all. I saw Paul making his way over with a huge goblet of red wine for Emma and nothing for me. He was being the perfect host, smiling and genial, but wouldn't catch my eye. I dismissed it, concentrating on pouring myself a glass of white and handing round the canapes. Everyone seemed to be settling in to enjoy themselves. Paul wandered back and forth from the kitchen, bringing bits and pieces to nibble on, each time studiously avoiding looking in my direction.

I drank and chatted happily along with the others, suddenly becoming aware that I was gabbling on about something to do with bathroom renovations and that no one else was speaking. Paul stood in the doorway watching me stonily and then disappeared indoors, and Emma chipped in.

'C'mon. Show me this appalling pipework then. Y'can bore me with all your push-fit flange stories, or whatever.' She got up a little unsteadily.

'I think you're mixing your plumbing metaphors there, gal,' Harry laughed.

'Oh shut it!' said Emma good-naturedly. 'Who cares! She's obsessed with 'U' bends and 'S' fixings, so I'm off to salivate over her "P" trap.' There was a crow of laughter and she linked arms with me and we tottered out of the room.

The hallway was cool in comparison. The kitchen window must have been on the latch and a pleasant breeze skimmed past us, bringing with it a heavenly cooking smell.

'There's the living room where we're camping out a bit, so it's really messy. Let's start up top and then we'll work our way down. We've made more changes up here, but there's still tons to do.'

'This is stunning, Luce. Seriously, a complete dream.' Emma looked up admiringly at the ornate cornicing as we went up the stairs. 'Look at this,' she ran her fingers over the barley twist stair struts. 'Wow! How on earth did you manage it all?'

'It was already there. Paul found it.' I shrugged. 'He pulled off some boarding and—'

'No, I meant how have you managed it all in such a short space of time?'

We reached the landing and stopped.

'A few months ago you were definitely single and feisty and showing us all up at work. Now you've gone all soft and homely.'

I noticed she left out the incidents in between. She was really trying.

She leaned in conspiratorially. 'It was so sweet, he was telling me earlier how much he adores you.'

'He was?' I was shocked, I hadn't seen them talking.

'He said you've blown him away.'

I thrilled at her words. I was warm and happy suddenly as we walked down the passageway to the bedroom. 'This is ours.' I pushed open the door.

'Wow!' Emma gazed round appreciatively and I suddenly saw the room afresh through her eyes: the sanded floor, the Chobi rug which fitted the space perfectly, the French carved bed-head and huge wardrobe that we'd found at a second-hand place on the Holloway Road. I'd struggled to put up the proper curtains only yesterday and I smiled at the memory of myself standing on a stool with a swathe of material balanced on my head.

'He said he'd never lived with anyone before, but as soon as he met you he knew.'

My smile wavered a little. 'Is that what he said?'

Emma laughed at my expression. 'God Luce, I think that's supposed to be a compliment!'

'Well it is, it's just that—'

'Oi! You two!' Paul's voice echoed up the stairwell. 'We're all starving down here! Could you leave the grand tour till later?'

Emma caught my eye and laughed. 'Actually, he's right. I'm starving too. Shall we?'

We were met by Paul's grinning face peering up the stairs. 'Impressed?' he said.

'Incredibly.' She tapped him on the chest as she wafted past. 'And not just with your interior design.' Her heels clip-clopped their way back down the stairs as she called out to the others that they really should come and have a tour. I followed behind. Paul stood at the bottom watching us, smiling.

I smiled back, relieved. 'Everything under control?' I whispered as I passed. 'How are we doing for wine?'

But his grin fell into a thin, hard, line. 'Everything is great apart from you. Do you have to wear clothes that show everything off when you lean forward? It's embarrassing for all of us.' He turned on his heel and walked down to the kitchen, leaving me standing there stunned and bewildered. I stared down at what I was wearing. It was a pretty scoop-neck top with lace panels. I couldn't see anything wrong but now I felt uncomfortable. I went upstairs and put a camisole underneath. *It's nothing*, I told myself. *Just sort it out and forget all about it. It's such a little thing. Get over it.*

—

Paul was standing by the French doors as I walked back into the dining room.

'So how do we like our steaks?' I heard him say. 'By the way, if anyone's a veggie, there's an aubergine and tomato bake too.' There was a chorus of approval as they chirped up with their orders amidst a chattering scrape of chairs as Paul handed Harry a bottle of wine and a corkscrew. 'And Emma, could you just give me a hand?'

She bobbed her tongue out to me as they passed, laughing about something he'd just said and disappeared together into the kitchen. I fixed a smile on my face, distracting myself with fussing pointlessly with the serving spoons on the table until Paul and Emma processed in, plates and dishes all piled high. Paul had outdone himself. He'd cooked his fabulous steak dish and had managed to get each one exactly as each guest liked it, which they all declared was a miracle and never possible, even in restaurants.

He kept the food and drink flowing; he was funny and jolly and fielded all questions about his work, cleverly turning every query round to the person who'd asked it and getting them to talk about themselves instead.

It was going brilliantly. Harry had just told a very long-winded joke and had got the punch line wrong, and Emma was drunkenly trying to re-tell it with disastrous results. Paul excused himself from the table to check on the pudding and I left it a few moments and then slipped inside after him.

The hall was instantly quiet. I crept cautiously along the hallway, but then stopped.

He was talking to someone. It took me a few seconds to register that he was on the phone. He was keeping his voice very low, but was clearly very angry, clipping each monosyllable in spitting temper.

I didn't move but stood at the door, ears straining, trying to work out who the hell he could be talking to. I heard the beep of the call ending and waited a minute before going in. He was stooped over the oven.

'Everything okay?' I put my hand on his shoulder.

'Yep, fine. You?' He moved deftly away to the sink to pick up a knife.

'Anything wrong?'

'Should there be?'

I hesitated. 'I thought I heard you talking to someone?'

He looked round theatrically at the empty space. 'Now who would I be talking to?'

'Someone on the phone?' I said cautiously.

'Ahhh… Eavesdropping to add to your snooping skill-set. Right.'

'I wasn't, I just heard…'

'It was someone from work. A colleague.' He opened the oven door and slid the knife into the pudding he was cooking. 'Or are you going to get paranoid about that as well?' He dropped it onto the side with a clatter as footsteps scuffed in the hallway and we both looked round. Luke was standing there holding the baby over one shoulder and a large floppy bag over the other. 'Sorry – is there somewhere I can change her?'

Paul took the opportunity to extract himself. 'Yeah, mate sure!' he said brightly. 'Let me show you where it is,' he gestured through. 'Be careful of the basin taps though, they're still a bit wobbly.' They laughed together and I heard the tread of their feet up the stairs. There was the creak of the floorboards across the landing and then the bathroom door opened and the patter of amiable exchange.

I stood in the kitchen, fighting that same disembodied feeling I had earlier. *Did I even know this man?* I listened to the rise and fall of voices from the dining room and the gentle hum of the oven. Then I saw his work phone. It sat, black and small on the table where he'd left it. I picked it up. The last message sat there on the screen, its first few words visible:

> I came to your flat and saw your new girl.

I flicked the screen and the rest of the message scrolled up.

> Did you think once I'd found you I was ever going to let you go?

The phone fell back onto the table as if it were alive and I snapped a look up. I could hear Paul moving about and I wasn't going to take a chance of getting caught. Creeping back into the hallway, I glanced up the stairs.

He was sitting on the landing gazing down at the baby in his arms. There was such a look of rapt concentration on his face, such absorption, that the shock of it sent a jolt of pure physical pain through my chest. I heard the toilet flush and then the sound of running water before the bolt on the bathroom door shunted back.

'Thanks, mate.' Luke bent to take the baby, and I followed Paul's eyes, utterly enthralled, taking in the trail of blankets. I turned quickly, almost crashing into the doorframe and stumbled through the dining room and out into the fresh air. Emma was still laughing when she looked round and saw me. She got up quickly, leaving them to it.

'You alright, hon?' The warmth of her touch sent a hot prickle of tears to the backs of my eyes.

'Oh, yes, yes. Fine.' I blinked and squinted tearfully into the sunshine. 'I've got a bit of hayfever I think.' I fumbled in my pocket for a tissue that I knew wasn't there.

Luke appeared with the baby. 'You alright?' He frowned at me, concerned. 'Hayfever,' said Emma.

'Hold on—' he handed the baby back to Jess. 'I use them sometimes. I think I might have some tablets in the bottom of this bag.' He rummaged around at the bottom. 'Here.' He held them up triumphantly. 'These'll do the trick.'

I took one, wavering a bleary smile just as Paul appeared, carrying a huge fruit and jam-filled sponge. There was a whoop of admiration from the table. He gave me a look and then beamed round.

'Pudding, anyone?' Then he cast about, concerned. 'Oh Emma, would you grab the tub of ice cream, please? I've left it on the side, the serving spoon's with it.'

I pretended that it was perfectly normal that Emma would be asked yet again to help, but I went and sat anyway, smiling and pretending, watching them serve up the pudding together.

I found I had no appetite, but cooed with the rest of them at how delicious it was, pushing spoonfuls of it around my dish. In reality it was as though I was sitting watching the world from somewhere very far away. I could hear the diffused laughter; I could see the vibrant colours of the mats and the tablecloth; I saw someone pick up the baby and begin to feed her. Paul must've gone inside and put music on: some discordant jazz began moaning away in the background. The flies hummed, zig-zagging in a net of black above their heads. The reflected scene tipped and began to shimmer as if on molten steel. I sat at the centre of it, in the eye of it all, feeling utterly empty and very much alone.

–

The front door closed and the gale of goodbye chatter with it. The hallway was sullen with silence.

I knew he was standing at the end of the hall watching me, his shoulders cutting out the light. A squeeze of anxiety gripped my stomach. Somewhere outside, the birds twittered in the haze of early evening. I turned round. He was drying his hands on a tea towel. There was a minute before he spoke.

'That went well, then.'

'Yes, it did.' I knew something was coming but I didn't know what form it would take. I thought about the phone message. I couldn't cope.

'They're a friendly lot, aren't they?' I deflected.

'Well *you* were certainly very friendly, so I'm not surprised they reciprocated.' He turned and went back into the kitchen. I considered going upstairs and getting changed out of the offending clothes, but I didn't want to draw any more of his attention.

I walked carefully down the hall, aware of the bruising strike of my heels on the tiles.

'You'll ruin that floor.' He spoke with his back to me as he started the washing up. I held onto the doorframe and slipped my sandals off. The floor was freezing.

'Did my clothes bother you that much?'

'No.' He carried on scrubbing at a plate.

'That's not the truth though, is it?'

Let's get this over and done with.

He paused, resting the heels of his hands on the sink edge.

'I'm disappointed, actually.'

My insides tightened to a knot. 'Because of the baby?'

I watched his shoulders stiffen. His eyes lifted and he stared blankly out of the window. 'What madness have you dreamt up now?'

'I saw you with the baby... I thought...'

The head moved slowly from side to side. 'I'm talking about you. I'm talking about the way you behave when there are men around. I'm talking about the way you dress. I'm talking about the kind of friends you choose to have: the silly women spouting rubbish, prancing about and putting themselves out there for any man who wants to take them.'

'What?' I was stunned. 'You mean Emma?'

He swung round and a spray of suds from the glass plate he was holding spattered across the floor. 'Oh come on! Please don't insult my fucking intelligence! Is that why you felt the need to lie about going for lunch with her all the time you were at work?'

I blanched.

'Don't bother making more lies up. She's already told me. You and her, handing it all out on a plate.'

'I really, honestly, have no idea...'

'Course you don't.' His eyes narrowed. 'The day we moved in here you were flirting with the removal men. If you could've only seen yourself!' He laughed bitterly. 'You spend your time tarting yourself up in clothes suited to someone ten years younger... I mean, what do you think you look like?' He broke off, shaking his head like a bull elephant. '... Seriously?' His eyes were blazing. 'I suppose you have no idea about how you were draping yourself over that Luke bloke, have you? Desperate to get his attention... *Aww! What a beautiful baby Luke... Aww! I've got hayfever!* Didn't you get that he wasn't interested?' The whites of his eyes were marbled and wild. 'That poor wife of his had to watch you showing yourself up and saying nothing. They've just had a *kid* together for Christ's sake!' He waved his hand. '*Ohh!* But of course, you'd know nothing about that, would you? You'd know nothing about *that* kind of bond.'

His words sliced like a blade. He went to slam the plate into the rack, but it slipped from his hand and shattered into shards at my feet. I stared down at the pieces, shocked and stunned and utterly appalled. I looked back at him. He was breathing heavily and swaying a little. I wondered how much he'd had to drink. I felt for the wall behind me, my fingers inching round the edge for safety.

'Oh for fuck's sake!' He pushed past me in the doorway, knocking me back against the frame. I went to grab his arm.

'Paul!'

He swung me off, fist lifted, shoving me backwards. I took a step, and felt a sickening crackle of something underfoot. A violent pain shot from the ball of my foot to the top of my skull. '*Jesus!*' I gasped, grabbing onto the door for support. Paul was there in an instant.

'Lucy? *Lucy!*... Oh my God, Lucy!'

He picked me up and carried me straight into the living room. I buried my face in his neck, unable to think, just aware of the searing pain that was burning up through my calf. He set me down gently on the sofa and dragged a stool over. 'Don't move,' he muttered. 'Don't move an inch. I'll be right back in one second.'

I lay with my head against the seat, my back arched with the pain, staring at the ceiling. I couldn't bear to look down; I thought I might throw up at just the thought of it. He appeared again at my side, with a bundle of tea towels, a basin, and some antiseptic. He touched my leg and I jumped a mile.

'Hold still, hold still, just let me have a look.' There was the immediate pressure of his hand as he lifted my calf to examine the bottom of my foot. He took a sharp intake of breath. 'No, no, this is pointless. We're going to have to go somewhere with this. You've got a big piece of glass still in the wound, it's sticking out, don't move—'

'Oh Jesus!' The thought of it made my head swim.

'Don't worry, we'll get you sorted. Don't panic. I'll go and bring the car round.'

A wave of sickness hit me as soon as he'd gone and a spring of sweat slicked through my hairline. I was trembling so much he had to carry me into the car, but we got to A&E with me in the front seat with the heel of my foot resting in a mixing bowl full of tea towels. The whole lot had turned bright red by the time we got there. We saw a very sympathetic nurse and then a doctor who gave me a tetanus injection and something to kill the pain.

'How did you manage to do this?'

I listened to the minute buzzing of the strip light as I lay on the trolley. I could feel him digging around in the sole of my foot and I closed my eyes. I tried really hard to think of something else. I squeezed Paul's hand.

'It was my fault,' I heard him say. 'I dropped a glass plate and hadn't cleared up all the bits properly.'

I opened my eyes and stared at the light. The doctor's words blurred and re-focussed. '...maybe she shouldn't drink wine and then walk around with bare feet.' Paul gave a little laugh.

'Now, I'm just going to put a few stitches in here.'

I heard the percussive clatter of instruments dropping into a metal bowl and took in the strong smell of something like peroxide. Something cold touched my skin and I instinctively jumped.

'Two more minutes.' Paul squeezed my fingers and smiled down at me. His face was full of love and worry. 'Hold on in there. Brave girl. Soon be over.'

I breathed in slowly through my nose and counted down from a hundred.

'Don't think, don't think about it.' He turned my chin to face him. 'Concentrate on me, only me. You're fine Luce. You're fine, you're fine.'

–

His mood, whatever it had been, had lifted. All the way home in the car he was like a different person, chatting on about how brilliant the staff had been and how wonderful the NHS was. I could only listen. I was in too much pain to hold a conversation. I clutched the bag of tablets I'd been given and said nothing. I think I was in shock. Shock at his words and his face and his fist...

The argument stuck and burned into my brain.

'*You'd know nothing about* that *type of bond, would you?*'

But maybe Caitlin would. Was there a child?

'*Did you think once I'd found you, I was ever going to let you go?*'

It was all suddenly becoming very clear. The words buzzed through my brain. Caitlin. This was proof. It was

Caitlin: the woman I wasn't. His anger, his fury, the accusations, would all make sense if he felt so bad and wanted rid of me now. His guilt over her and the baby: the need to drive me away: to punish me and punish himself at the same time. Yes, of course.

I rested my head, keeping my mouth rigid-lipped and eyes tightly closed, unable to bring myself to utter any words or ask any questions, because I really, really didn't want to hear the answers.

He'd been seeing someone else; I didn't know how long, or if it was over between them or if he was still seeing her, but that's what had been happening. Nothing I could say or do right now would change that. I should have been screaming, I should have been shouting and demanding and walking out. I should have been. Other women would, I knew. But I kept remembering the other moments: I remember watching him sleep, naked on the bed, the patterning dawn light from the curtain giving his skin an eerie underwater glow. The way he lay curled in on himself, like a little child, the fan of his eyelashes against his cheek, his eyes suddenly dropping open and looking at me as though he was looking right through, and into, some part of me that had been buried for years.

'You're mine,' he whispered. And on some bizarre, strange and profound level, I knew that to be true. He had me, all of me, and he knew it. I knew it too.

–

He fussed around endlessly, getting me drinks and cushions, settling me in a chair in the living room with my foot up on a stool; then he and set to work cleaning the blood from the carpet.

'I don't know how this got here or whether this is going to come out.' He had a mixture of baking soda and detergent and cold water and was kneeling, scrubbing it into the stain.

'I'll have a look when I feel up to it.' I watched him as he worked: his shoulder blades moving easily under his shirt, the slimness of his hips as he crouched, the muscles in his haunches flexing. He was lithe and beautiful and sexy. I could've burst into tears right then at just the sight of him. I didn't want to love him as much as I did. *Hating him would have made things so much easier. So why couldn't I?*

'God, what an end to a perfectly brilliant day!' He grinned round at me and I smiled hesitantly back. The Luke thing was clearly forgotten. I eased my leg, feeling a slow drift of pain from my foot creeping into the back of my knee. I squirmed uncomfortably in the seat.

'You okay?' He was at my side in an instant, leaning on the chair arm, his face a mask of concern.

'Yeah, yeah, fine. Honestly. Stop worrying.'

'It's my job to worry.' He kissed my forehead tenderly. 'I'll get you up to bed in a minute when I've finished this.'

'Thanks.'

He stood up and smiled, collecting his cleaning stuff together. I rested my head back; the cushion cradled it as my spine tightened horribly and then relaxed. A slow heartbeat of pain began to thrum the length of my body. I glanced into the hallway. There, on those perfect tiles, was a thin shard of glass, glinting in the soft light, my own blood running along one edge as though it'd been painted with a very fine brush. Quite beautiful. I closed my eyes. The pulses between the pain grew a little longer as the tablets began to kick in and the quiet draw of sleep dragged me down to somewhere I really wanted to go. *Thrub, thrub, thrub, the pain said.*

Blood. So much of it, I mused, half in sleep and half awake, feeling the irony that the one thing I hadn't seen this month was blood, and now here it was, lots of it, but a different kind.

Chapter Nine

Then my sister Louise rang.

'So is your foot worse? You sound worse.'

'Oh I'm getting there. It's better than it was. How are you? How's Mam?'

'Did you ever get my housewarming present? I thought you'd always find use for a bottle of bubbly.'

'I sent you a card to say thank you ages ago. You've not got it?'

'Mam might've picked it up and hidden it. She does that these days. Hides things.'

Don't we all.

'Anyway, I was asking how you were.'

'I'm okay.'

We both stopped.

'You're not alright though, are you Luce?'

It was the softness of her voice that did it. 'No.' I managed eventually.

'And it's not just your foot.'

'No.'

'Can you talk about it? Is he there?'

We'd never spoken like this, Lou and I. This wasn't what we did. It felt unfamiliar and disloyal and oddly comforting all at the same time.

'He's gone into work. I don't think I know him, Lou.'

'No, well. Mam always said that about Dad, didn't she?'

'Did she?'

I realised Paul had left his phone on charge on the arm of the chair.

'You're not having second thoughts about getting married, are you?'

'I don't know, Lou. It's all so bloody hard, there are so many things—' I trailed off. Where would I start?

'Have you spoken to him about it?'

'Tried to.'

'Yeah, well, Mam said you never know any man until you threaten to leave him.'

I smiled. 'Is that what she said?'

Easing myself forward, I hobbled over to pick the phone up. There was no password.

'It's when you try to leave them, then all their true colours come out.'

The message from Caitlin still sat there. I checked the number against the one that had rung him last Sunday. They matched. My stomach turned over.

'But you're only just married, Luce! You can't be thinking like that! Not all men are like Dad! It'll work itself out, you'll see. It's bound to be a bit of a learning curve for both of you. Not that I'd know a thing about any of that!' The chuckle trailed off wistfully but then she paused. 'If only you lived a bit closer—'

A sudden lump caught again in the back of my throat.

'So my advice is, don't lose your friends. They're the people who'll celebrate with you in the good times and be there for you in the bad times – and if you ever *really* need them...' she paused and I heard her swallow. 'Dad wouldn't let Mam have friends; did you realise that? And he chased away any that I might've had. So don't let go of them Luce... Trust me, I know when you allow that to happen...' She suddenly sounded sad. 'You find you're in it on your own.'

—

'Emma?'

I had this urge to tell her.

'Oh hello you! I was going to ring you later. How is it? Is it still really painful?'

If only she knew.

'Aw, ouch!' she sympathised. 'Never mind, Paul's picking up those stronger painkillers at lunchtime so they'll maybe work better.'

'Stronger painkillers?' I had absolutely no memory of discussing that.

'Yeah, he mentioned it last night.'

'He rang you last night?'

'No—' There was the slightest hesitation. 'He came round on his way back from the office. He just popped in to let me know how you were getting on.'

'Oh.'

In those seconds I mentally configured Emma's flat and Paul's office. They were in opposite directions.

'He's a lovely guy, isn't he? So easy and nice to talk to when it's just one on one. I think it's because he's so comfortable around women.'

Harry wasn't there.

'That'll teach you to wash up in bare feet.'

'I didn't,' I said, but I don't think she registered the comment.

Paul hadn't said anything about seeing Emma. He'd said he was late because he'd put petrol in the car and picked up some milk.

I tried really hard to listen to what she was saying.

'...Hold on! Someone's just come to see me, Luce, I'll ring you later... Oh, will you be in?' I heard the smirk.

'Oh such a comedian! Bye.'

Hopping into the kitchen, I dropped a teabag into a cup and flicked on the kettle. Hitching over to the fridge, I pulled open the door and dipped inside, looking for the milk he said he'd bought, but knowing I wasn't going to find any. I made the tea, poured the dregs of the old carton into the cup and limped my way through into the living room and then I stopped. Something: a sound, or a sixth sense, I don't know, but something made me look at the window. My stomach somersaulted.

She was standing at the end of the driveway next to the copper beech tree, the colour of her linen jacket and the colour of the tree in perfect contrast. Her face was pale against the dark hair; her jacket was open and flapped slightly in the wind. She took a step forward as if considering coming up to the house but then changed her mind.

Somewhere, out in the kitchen, my phone started to ring, its insistence shrilling into the quiet. If I moved, I knew she'd see me. I looked back; it was too late, she was walking cautiously up the path.

The thought of her knocking on the door terrified me: it meant I could speak to her. I could open the door and invite her in and I would know everything: but now it was here in front of me, I couldn't do it.

Within seconds, I managed to get into the shadow of the wall. From here I could see the hallway and the front door. Her outline weaved menacingly on the other side of the glass; the darkness danced for a moment, and then slid away. There was the crunch of stones and I realised to my horror she was making her way round to the back of the house. *Was the back door locked?* I panicked: I wasn't strong; I was vulnerable and wounded. She'd got me; I couldn't get away.

Dropping to my knees, I half-shuffled, half-crawled into the hallway, pulling myself into a stooped crouch so that the kitchen window was in full view. She was there, cautiously peering in. I absorbed every detail of her: the wide forehead, the weird maddened eyes, dark cropped curly hair, white shirt collar, green jacket. She looked odd, desperate. It was Caitlin, there, right in front of me. Real. Not imagined. Caitlin.

I watched in horror as the kitchen door handle began to move, slowly, slowly down and then stop. *Locked.* My heartbeat thudded in my ears. Her eyes glossed over the walls above my head for a moment and then she dipped away. The breath I'd been holding left me and I let myself sink to the floor, feeling the grinding ache in my foot ease. I leant my head back. *She wants to see me. She wants to talk to me. I'm going to have to face her…*

The phone's sudden jangling smashed into the silence. Heart pounding, I saw it flashing on the worktop as I half-fell, half-hopped to grab for it.

Paul.

'Hello you, how's it all going?'

I tried to keep my breathing level and my voice steady. 'I'm okay. I'm okay.'

'Sure?' he sounded doubtful. 'Are you resting enough?'

I was too scared to think or speak – especially to Paul. I glanced out of the window I couldn't see her. 'I'm fine.'

'Look, I don't know what time I'll get back. It won't be this afternoon. I'm sorry. I'm stuck on a bloody train trying to get to a meeting in Kent and it hasn't moved for ten minutes. Thank God you've got Emma coming round tonight.'

'Emma? Emma's coming?'

'I'm glad you're meeting up.'

'Are you?' I couldn't imagine what had changed his opinion about her. 'Did you ask her, then?'

'Me? No, you did.'

'I did?'

I suddenly saw a movement. She was standing facing the house, leaning against the copper beech tree.

Paul sighed audibly. 'I was there at her flat when you rang, don't you remember?'

I was distracted by her watchful gaze as she checked up and down the street as though looking for someone.

'The junk shop stuff?' he sounded irritable. 'You asked me to drop off some old candlesticks and rubbish that she forgot to take with her on Sunday... No? No recollection?' I heard the sarcasm as a loud tannoy announcement blared in the background. 'Look, there's no point going over all this, I'll just see if Emma can come earlier and I'll ring you back—'

He disappeared, my anxiety rocketing as I peered out of the window again. None of that mattered. *This can't carry on. I won't let this carry on. She wasn't doing this. Not anymore.*

I limped to the front door. She had walked onto my territory. She wanted to speak to me? *Well, come on then.* I flung open the door. She turned her head.

'Aren't you coming in then, Caitlin?' I shouted, my voice sending a clatter of birds skyward. 'This is what you want, isn't it? You want me to know you're in our life?' I gestured angrily. 'Well I know now, don't I? Come on, then. Come right in!... What's the matter? Not scared, are you?'

A woman walking past with a child in a pushchair glanced round at me warily and then looked away. Caitlin looked startled, glancing back before scurrying off across the road to where a car was parked. She got in, hurriedly slamming the door and driving off.

I stood breathing heavily as pulses of pain fired again and again into my calf. I was close to tears, close to being defeated, and very close to just collapsing right there on the step.

Who was this man I'd married?

Birds fought wildly in the guttering above me and the sound of car horns blared somewhere far away, but everything else remained oddly flat and still. The pain throbbed persistently, bringing me back to myself. I was sick of feeling afraid. I was sick of not knowing. I was right; this couldn't carry on. I wouldn't let it. No more phone calls, no more texts, no more of this. I was done.

Emma was the answer.

Lou was right. She was the only possible answer. No matter what had gone on before with Gould, I knew if I talked to her she'd help me... Emma had been my constant, my immovable, my rock. But how the hell would I begin to tell her?

Closing the door, I texted her there and then. 'What time are you coming?'

The reply came straight back.

> Afternoon appoint just arrived. Be there
> soon as poss

The pain in my foot was becoming sharp and insistent, shooting its way up through my groin. Picking up the tiny vial of painkillers from the coffee table, I unscrewed the top. The label caught my eye. My name, my married name, shocked me: Lucy Webb. I didn't know her. She was like some blank page of a person, ready to be written on, and Paul had made up her story. She was a character, performing a part in some terrifying drama without knowing where it was going or how it would end. Paul and Caitlin were the real main players. Whatever my role was, whatever the function, I wasn't playing anymore.

The pain in my groin pulsed again and I shook a tiny white pill into my palm as the pulse in my belly throbbed and grew stronger. But this time I recognised the pain: it was that same monthly grinding ebb and flow, internal and secret and one that I didn't want to blunt this time. I savoured every cramp and twinge as I dropped the tablet and limped my way to the bathroom.

Blood. And with it came a raft of emotions, but mostly a terrific sense of relief. A baby would have chained me to Paul forever, and yet somewhere in the background was the memory and grief of Dan and that other time, and with it came a terrible feeling of emptiness.

My little secret wasn't a secret, and it never had been. It was just messy, and ordinary, and gut-churningly sad.

–

'God you look awful.' She bustled past me into the hallway.

I attempted a weak grin. 'I think your record's stuck.'

'No, I don't mean awful, awful. I mean you just look like death warmed-up. Here.' She grabbed me under one arm and helped me back to my chair.

'Oh well, that's okay then.' I wiggled my bottom back and raised my leg stiffly onto the stool.

'How is it?' She nodded at my foot. 'I can't believe you severed a tendon.'

'Better than it was.'

'Has Paul been a ministering angel?' She dumped her bag down and gazed around. 'This room's very cosy isn't it? I thought you said it was a mess? You should see my place. I'll make my own tea, shall I? You want one? I'm starving actually. Have you eaten?' Her voice trailed off as she headed down the hall to the kitchen. 'Oh, are there any biscuits?' I heard the kettle boiling and the chink of cups.

I took a breath. 'Emma—'

She appeared in the doorway. 'I see that ministering angels don't do milk. Hey, no one's perfect... For God's sake, Lucy, sit back and relax! Have you got a lemon then?' She disappeared again.

'Emma—'

'What?' She called from the kitchen. 'Hang on, be there in a sec!'

She came in carrying a tray with two mugs of tea that she shoved onto a side table. 'My God, Luce, seriously, let's get you upstairs and into the shower. I'll go and get a plastic bag for that foot. You'll feel miles better once you've washed and dried your hair. Trust me.' She pattered off into the kitchen and came back with a battered plastic stool and an old Tesco bag. 'As you look like Worzel Gummidge's girlfriend, I thought it'd be very fitting!' She grinned. 'I'll go and stick these in the shower and once you've drunk your tea we'll manhandle you up there.'

'Emma, stop. I need to tell you som—'

But all I could hear was the sound of her bounding up the stairs. What would I tell her, though? I didn't know where to begin.

'Right!' she appeared breathlessly back in the doorway. 'What were you saying?'

'There's this woman…'

'Uh-huh.'

I tried to gather my thoughts but my brain was sluggish and fogged. I started again. 'There's this…'

'I suspect you need those stronger painkillers. Paul will bring them later.'

'No these make me feel bad enough.' My mouth felt dry and sticky. I couldn't formulate my words. I had to tell her before Paul got back.

'Hmm… You do look a bit out of it,' she chuckled. 'Come on anyway. Let's be having you… I'll cook us something decent while you're abluting,' she grinned. 'Sorry, washing, I forgot you were a northerner.'

I'll tell her over dinner, I promised myself. She heaved me up and bodily managed me up the stairs. I did everything she said and found myself ensconced in the shower cubicle, perched on the stool with my foot out of the door and lathering my hair. She was right: it was wonderful. With Emma in the house, suddenly everything came right in the world.

'Alright in there?' Her voice boomed from the other side of the door.

'Emma?'

'What?'

'Thanks.'

'You haven't tasted my cooking yet. Don't get too grateful.'

Ten minutes later, I turned off the shower and, holding on to the cubicle door, tentatively tried my foot on the floor. Actually, it didn't feel that bad at all and my head had cleared a bit. I'd tell Emma everything. She'd know exactly what to do and what to say. It was going to be okay.

Wrapping my hair in a towel, I dried myself off and then pulled on some clean clothes. Examining my face in the mirror, I understood what she meant. I looked pale and drawn, but I also saw a determination back in my eyes that had been missing for a while. I grimaced a smile; the old me was definitely still in there somewhere.

Clicking the bathroom door open, I was just stepping out onto the landing when I heard voices. I recognised Paul's straight away and gingerly managed the first three stairs. I could just see the sleeve of his coat. He was standing in the living room with his jacket on as though he wasn't staying. They were talking: it sounded serious.

'Of course I will,' I heard Emma say.

There was the jangle of keys and Emma asked a question, but I couldn't make out exactly what she was asking. I cleared my throat and they both stopped talking instantly. Emma came out into the hallway, wide-eyed. 'Oh heck, that was quick! Let me give you a hand—'

Paul stood at the bottom of the stairs watching me.

'I thought you were stuck on a train?'

'Mike's rung in sick.' He avoided the question. 'He's supposed to be at a conference in Hull so they've asked me to go in his place,' he shrugged. 'I told them I couldn't because you weren't well but they're putting real pressure on me. I would have to get up there tonight so I was wondering if Emma could stay with you. It would really put my mind at rest.'

'You don't even have to ask, you know that.' Emma helped me down the bottom step.

I knew what he was doing. The hurt formed a hard stone in my chest. Caitlin. Who else?

'Here,' Paul came towards me and bent to scoop me up. 'Let's get you off that foot.' I caught the smell of his jacket as he pulled me to him and my heart lurched: he smelled of road fumes and sweet soap. Hers?

My stomach rebelled. As he lowered me into the armchair I looked into his eyes.

He was smiling appreciatively over my head at Emma, but to me they only looked hard and dead, like a grey winter sea. 'This is so good of you, I really appreciate it.'

'I'll think of a way you can reciprocate.' She smiled coquettishly and for a moment I saw what he meant about her flirting. 'You can invite me round again to sample your cuisine!'

'I'll go and pack my overnight bag, then.' Paul leaned down and kissed my cheek. 'Won't be a minute.'

I saw the look that passed between them as they parted in the hallway and things became clear to me. He'd gone round to her flat to get her 'on side' and Emma, being Emma, had fallen for it. The only person I could trust, helping my husband meet his lover... Disgust, then anger burned as the room blurred. Once Emma knew... Once I told her... I busied myself with my head down searching for a tissue up my sleeve and blew my nose to cover the tears that were streaming down my face. Neither of them noticed.

–

We stood on the front step watching Paul get into the waiting taxi and I shivered even though the evening was warm. As the door slammed, he waved cheerily. I raised a hand but couldn't bring myself to smile. Emma did.

'Let's get inside. I'll go and put the pasta on.'

I limped slowly after her into the kitchen and leaned against the door post as she set the kettle on to boil. '*C'est ou?*' she queried. I gave her an odd look.

'That's "Where is it?" in French. Are you impressed?'

I pointed to the cupboard in the corner.

'Did I tell you? We're off to the South of France in ten days' time, so I've been practising.' She pulled out a packet of spaghetti and ripped the top with her teeth. 'A whole month away. I can't wait. Harry says—'

'Emma, what do you think of Paul?'

She stopped mid-pour and gave a little shrug. 'Seems nice, seems to care... Still a bit frog-like in some lights,' she giggled. 'Why, what's up?'

'I think he's seeing someone. We had a fight. My injury wasn't a complete accident.'

She swung round and nearly dropped the whole lot on the floor.

She stood there open-mouthed, her eyes wide and frightened. 'Oh my God, Lucy. What's been going on?'

'There was a message on his phone.'

'What kind of message?'

'It said something about *once she'd found him she wasn't letting him go.*'

Emma frowned. 'What? Say that again.'

'It's this woman. She's started hanging around. I've seen her. Paul disappears. I have no idea where he goes. He has calls on his phone that he won't answer in front of me, and then these texts that—'

'Hang on, hang on.' Emma had turned to face me. 'I'm not following, just—'

'Her name's Caitlin.'

'You know her name?' She stood there, astounded.

'They had a relationship, years ago. He told you he'd never lived with anyone, but that was a lie, he had. He lived with this girl: this woman. She was pregnant and they split up. Now she keeps turning up. She even came here.'

'Pregnant?... What?...' She couldn't get her head around it. 'Here? Hang on. You spoke to her?'

'No, she came to the front door and then stood watching the house.'

It did actually sound weird articulating it.

Emma frowned. 'So they've got a kid together?'

'He says he doesn't know.'

'Could that be true?'

'Could be. He says she disappeared and he hasn't had any contact with her for donkey's years. He says he has no idea what I'm on about and this is just some random person...' I took a deep breath in. 'There was a flower too...'

'A flower?'

'A rose on the doorstep at his old flat. I thought it was Simon Gould, you know, that prisoner—'

Emma's look hesitated.

'So there's messages and then she turns up and then he tells me he has to go away overnight...'

She held up a palm. 'Just stop a minute. Rewind. Why would you think that Simon Gould was leaving you roses?'

'Because he was ringing me up, harassing me—'

'But I thought—' She didn't finish the sentence. I knew what she thought. I knew what everyone thought.

'So you don't believe me, then?' I thought I might cry.

'Of course I believe you!' She chucked the packet of spaghetti onto the side and came over, putting her arms round me. 'God, Luce, what do you take me for?... Look, come on, talk to me about this. Lead me through it, step by step, okay?'

I nodded dumbly.

'Okay. Let's look at this. Firstly, there's a message from a woman on his phone. Did it sound... You know, sexual...?'

I swallowed. 'I don't know. It was a text.'

'And it couldn't be from a bloke?'

I sighed, exasperated. 'What kind of bloke leaves messages like that?'

'Threatening blokes? The I-know-where-you-live type of blokes?... Erm... Like the ones he deals with all day?' She looked at me. 'So presumably he's deleted it?'

'No.'

'What do the others say?'

'There's just one.' I sniffed.

'One? But lover wouldn't just leave one message, would she?'

I didn't know how to respond.

'And if he's deleted all the others, why wouldn't he have deleted that one?'

I didn't know. I didn't know anything anymore.

'And you're thinking this is the same person he used to go out with?'

I nodded.

'How long ago?'

I shrugged. 'Eighteen, twenty years maybe. Dunno.'

I could see the look on her face.

'So she comes to the door and goes away again...' She frowned. 'That makes no sense. If she's involved in some kind of illicit liaison with Paul, why isn't she off illicitly liaising with him while she's got the chance?'

'I think she wants to talk to me.'

'Christ.' Grabbing the kettle, she poured the boiling water into a saucepan and I watched her as she extracted a handful of pasta from the packet and dropped it into the pan. 'I was like that with Connor.' She reached for a spoon, stirring the meaty ragu sauce bubbling on the hob. 'I wanted to force the situation. I wanted to tell his wife what was going on. I understand that madness.' She shook her head, slowly.

'He's kept a photograph of her. From when she was a lot younger. Why would he keep something like that?'

She chucked the spoon to one side. My eyes followed her as she went to the fridge and yanked it open. 'Jesus, I need a glass of something... I don't suppose you're allowed one?'

'And the thing with my foot—' I so wanted her to believe me. 'It wasn't really an accident.'

Her back stiffened and she looked at me.

'Well, it *was* but... We were in the middle of a fight and I grabbed him and he pushed—'

I saw her eyes flicker.

'You don't sound appalled or shocked by anything I've told you.' My eyes tracked her as she reached in to retrieve a bottle.

'Well firstly, hand on heart, I've had some fights with blokes where I've been the one doing a bit of pushing and shoving. Once you start grabbing people though—'

The way she was saying it made me start to doubt myself.

'I know exactly what it's like Luce. I know because I'm as guilty as the next person.' She put her hand on her chest. 'Things happen and you make them fit a particular story. It's so easy to make things add up when they really don't. So. A photograph, you say? Well, it's a *photograph*, Luce. If you went through all the boxes in my loft I suspect you'd find a photograph of some old boyfriend somewhere — Possibly even more than one.' She raised an eyebrow. 'And is it remotely possible this woman is a client?'

I sighed distractedly. 'Well he did tell me, early on, there was a patient suffering from psychosis who was blowing up his phone, but—'

'Don't you think that's more of a likely explanation then?' Emma held up a hand. 'Look. Luce. I've watched Paul, I've seen the way he looks at you.' She found a wineglass. 'I've listened to the way he talks. It's all about you. That doesn't sound like a man who's having an affair. Plus, did you notice he brought milk when he came in? Men who are off shagging don't think about picking up milk.' She gave me a wry sideways look and her eyes became gentle. I thought I might cry again. 'You really, really love him, don't you?'

'Yep.' I sniffed. 'I thought I did. But I just can't live like this.'

'You definitely can't, but when you really, really love someone it makes you unbelievably vulnerable. Then you start over-thinking things and getting stuff out of perspective.' She saw the hurt on my face. 'I know exactly how it is. I had all that crap with Connor, remember? You end up so you can't think straight.'

I went to blow my nose. 'That's what Paul says.'

'So you've told him how you feel?' She topped up her glass. 'So he's clearly not taking the piss out of you for being a silly old tart. He *is* trying to understand. Give him credit for that, at least.'

I shifted against the post trying to ease the pain in my foot. 'Caitlin cheated on him, but I didn't know any of this until our wedding day.'

'Great timing, Paul.' Emma did a little 'cheers' motion. 'Him being an insensitive coward at times does not mean he's off shagging – and anyway you don't think he'd go back with her after that, do you?'

'But he tells me *lies*.' I spat the words in tearful frustration. 'You really don't understand Em, he doesn't tell me the whole truth.'

She paused to take a slug of wine and swallowed slowly. 'Yes, I know.'

'What?' I stared at her.

'I know. He told me.'

I couldn't believe what I was hearing.

'We had a little bit of a heart to heart when he came round. He admitted he'd handled some things really badly from the very beginning because he was scared of losing you.'

He'd *said* that?

'You must admit you two got married so bloody fast there wasn't the time to do all that finding out that couples normally do, was there? I bet there are things that you've not told him, too.'

I shifted again uncomfortably and not just because of the pain in my foot. Thoughts of Dan surfaced and I batted them away.

Paul had confided in Emma?

'I bet there are, Lucy. Everyone has things in their past that they'd rather their partner didn't know too much about. Even you… I mean, did you tell him everything about Dan?'

What had he told her?

'Emma,' I flinched. 'That's not the way—'

'I'm honestly on your side here, Luce.' She put her glass down to open a cupboard. 'But so's Paul. He worships you. We aren't the enemy. There is no enemy. He's a bloke; that's all. They're all knobs, trust me, but I think he's a trustworthy knob.' She grinned and fished out a colander. 'Now let's leave this. Let's chat about rubbish like we normally do. So – how hungry are you?'

And so the conversation ended. She turned and picked up the saucepan from the hob, straining the spaghetti and starting to talk about a chap she quite fancied in her French class and how Harry was beginning to get on her nerves. The mention of Dan's name had effectively shut me up. I couldn't tell what she was thinking, or whose side she was on, I could only stand, listening and nodding in all the right places.

We ate the delicious pasta, and afterwards she dried my hair and straightened it while my facemask dried, and then we watched television, her drinking three quarters of a new bottle of white and me on the tonic water. I decided to let it go. I needed her right now, arguing with her was pointless. Paul rang several times, but the signal kept cutting out each time I answered. I smiled and shrugged and she smiled back indulgently, her smile disappearing into a massive yawn. 'Yarrggghh! Well, I might have to leave you two to smooch down the phone without me. I'm totally done in and a bit pissed actually… Plus, there's work in the morning… Shall I give you a hand with the stairs?'

'Oh hell, I've just remembered!'

'What's the matter?'

'I've just realised the spare duvet is still packed in a box in the loft.'

'Oh God,' she yawned again and stretched. 'Do you have a loft ladder or do I have to start waking up the neighbourhood trying to find your steps?'

'No there's a ladder, it's just the hassle of getting up there.'

'You tell me which box it's in and I'll sort it. No worries.'

She managed to haul down the ladder and clamber her way up. It creaked and groaned alarmingly as she hoisted herself into the space. I watched her lumbering shadow above me, listening to her muttering and grumbling about 'if I was so bloody organised, then why couldn't she see it?' I got a sudden memory of this was how we used to be, alongside a massive rush of sadness that we just weren't in that place anymore.

'*Whereabouts* am I looking?' she tutted.

'It's a big and white bundle in a see-through bag. Look! Hold your hand out… Now left a bit… Left a bit more…'

It was then that I saw it. Paul's briefcase, the one he told me he'd thrown away, sitting there just inside the opening. Curiosity tingled.

'Oh that big white bundle! Why didn't you say in the first place!… Ow! Hang on a minute. Let me get this thing out of the way.' She shifted the briefcase.

'Actually, just chuck that down, I don't know what it's doing up there anyway.'

The black rectangle appeared at the gap and slid down the edge of the ladder.

It was light – much lighter than I'd expected.

There was a clump and a heave as the duvet appeared in the hatch. I stood back as it tumbled to the floor.

'Is that everything?'

'Yep. The spare pillows and the sheets and stuff are in the cupboard in your room.' I quickly slid the case inside my bedroom door and shut it.

The ladder juddered as Emma made her way down.

'Brilliant places, lofts.' She clapped her hands together to dust them off. 'You can chuck stuff up there and forget all about it, can't you?'

She shunted the rungs back up again and clicked the trap door shut. '...Oi! Leave that!' Emma saw what I was doing and grabbed the duvet from my hands.

'You don't need to get involved. I can manage perfectly. Now off to bed with you.'

'Nighty-night then. See you in the morning. Sleep well.' I kissed her lightly on the cheek and watched her toddle off to bed.

Her bedroom door clicked shut and I stayed standing on the quiet landing for a moment, listening to the house settle. How I wished it could go back to how it was between me and Em: the two of us messing about, doing girly stuff. We'd had glimpses tonight, but that old 'us' seemed very far away.

I glanced through the open bedroom door, seeing the case sitting there, innocuous and ordinary: a scruffy old thing that should have gone out with the trash. But it hadn't. It had been taken out of its plastic sack and had been put up in the loft. '*School stuff*' he'd said. Well school stuff might mean University stuff which might mean Caitlin.

The leather felt warm under my hand. This was Pandora's Box. Once this thing was opened, I didn't know what I would discover, but I knew whatever it was, could never be hidden again.

—

Of course it was locked.

I sat on the edge of the bed staring at the combination tumblers for a moment and then attempted a few guesses – his birthday, mine, our wedding date – as though, stupidly, I believed those things held any significance for him. I ran my fingers around the edges of the case, testing its give, and then I noticed the hinges had tiny screws. My stomach thrilled.

If I did this, there was no going back: he would know I'd been snooping again.

How much did I want to do this?

It was a pointless question.

Finding a pair of nail scissors, I carefully managed to twist each one in turn, but the metal hinge dug tight into the leather so that even a fingernail wouldn't release it. Using the tip of the scissors, I managed to prise up one edge of the plate, feeling the sticky give, and ease a corner free. See-sawing a little, I was able to lever the metal up. *Jesus.* I was really doing this.

I prayed there would be papers inside – old bills, tax returns, certificates. But it was nothing like that. Nothing like that at all. It was full of photographs.

My whole body shook. A rush of something: adrenaline, shock, fear, coursed through me. The pictures blurred. I couldn't see them properly.

And then I could.

There were loads of them, all crammed in a jumbled mess. I picked up two at random, gripping them so hard that the ball of my thumb pressed a crease into the shiny paper.

My eyes wouldn't focus.

Babies. Caitlin.

Something inside me plummeted. She laughed up at me, holding two little ones in her arms.

It was Caitlin with children. Not pregnant. Not gone. Not one baby, but two. Babies that weren't mine. The woman who wasn't me. A whole case full of lies. A whole case full of truth.

In one, Caitlin was young, rosy-cheeked and shining in all her heavily pregnant sharp focus. Full of happiness. Full of baby happiness. I flipped over the next and the next, and there it was: pink blanketed and newly born, all hospital-swaddled, with Caitlin about to plant a kiss on her dark squiggle of hair. Something terrible lurched inside me. Then a picture of a baby in a plastic bath: that same dark hair, all chipmunk podgy faced and a blob of soap on her nose. She was smiling and looking up at the camera: Paul's eyes. My gut and my heart collided. In the next she was sitting on a mat on the floor holding a yellow toy dinosaur. There was a hand holding her arm making sure she didn't fall. Paul's hand.

The pain in my heart was physical. I was looking right into a moment of their life: a window into their past. There it all was: one after another, after another... The ache rose gradually into something sour that burned my throat and I struggled to breathe.

His knees, his hands, *his baby*. She must've been there, taking the photo. Another newborn on a mat and the little girl, older now, playing on a bedroom floor in front of a white chest of drawers. Was he there? Was she? I imagined her holding the camera, saying something funny, making him laugh, the two of them sharing these perfect moments.

I looked away into the blank empty wall of my own bedroom, the lamplight making a canopy of shadows across the ceiling. I put my hand on my stomach: the cramps tightened and released in a slow drumbeat of real pain. The house was in silence. I thought of that little back bedroom, blank and empty too, my arms empty, my insides empty, in my empty half-life. I thought of lying in that bed in the clinic, all those years ago, watching the shape of Dan's shoulders as he walked out of the door. I thought of the guilt and the grief. I thought of my mother and my sister. This wasn't about jealousy: this was far, far more than jealousy. This was all the things I'd given up to have this life and now look at me. This was deceit, this was absolute betrayal.

The bruising hard ache behind my breastbone burned. I wanted to cry but crying wasn't deep enough, I was too furious for that. I imagined him going up there into the loft, sitting in semi darkness, poring over her and their children, thinking about the shared intimacies, yearning for them. Was that what happened? Did he go searching to find her, or did she find him?

I stared down again into her face, Caitlin's face, laughing up into the lens, her hair whipped by the breeze and tied up with a red scarf so pretty against the dark brown. 'Caitlin.' There... I whispered her name out loud: '*Caitlin.*' The pure joy of her, the tumbling curls caught in a fluttering patterned scarf... My hand stilled along with my gut.

I'd seen that before. I knew that scarf. It was here. Flinging the wardrobe door open, I pawed through his things on the shelf... *Camden Market. The one he lent me the day we went to Camden Market*. My stomach sickened as I searched and searched. It wasn't here.

A wave of bitterness swamped me. He'd kept it all these years. A token. A remembrance of the woman he was in love with. So what was I then? The also-ran, the fill-in until he could persuade her to come back? My brain whirled... So what was the plan? To shove me out, to dump me: to begin real life again with her and leave me with nothing? Well that wasn't happening. He'd have to find me first.

Cramming all the photographs back into the case, I pushed them away, curling up on my side and dragging the duvet up to my chin. The bitterness hardened around my heart, becoming a solid, gnawing weight. My phone rang, rang off, rang again and then stopped. I reached for it and typed in a message to Paul.

Tired. Foot hurting. Gone to bed.

I pressed the 'Send' button and then buried my face in the softness of the pillow as I bit down hard, the pain in my chest finally loosening and breaking and the bedroom disappearing in a muffled howl of weeping.

−

I'm not sure I slept much. When I did my dreams were ragged and fitful. At one stage I was standing on a cliff edge. There was the keening moan of the wind around me, but, gazing down, I realised it was the sound of children, crying. Their eyes were huge and pleading, and their mouths opened and closed like baby birds, begging as I crouched, floundering desperately, reaching out. The edge began to crumble; I felt the tickle of their clothes as everything gave way around me and we plunged, hurtling into the black. I woke gasping.

The room was full of pearly dawn light. I was exhausted. I lay there mute: a dried-up rag staring into nothing as the phone rang.

'Mummy?'

There was a rattle in the background and then a tiny voice.

'Mummy?'

My heart stopped.

'Come on, say "hello Lucy",' Simon cajoled. 'Say, "please come and find me".'

And then the line went dead.

I let the phone drop from my ear. A band of pain tightened and I was shaking so hard I could hear it in my teeth. My head was screaming to tell someone – anyone. But no one was listening, no one cared. This child was just another lost soul in amongst all the other souls: a statistic, a number, a case file, an everyday unsolved tragedy. Well, I wasn't waiting for anyone anymore. I was going to find her myself.

Chapter Ten

I stood with the kitchen door open watching the water pouring out of the guttering, chuckling and gurgling as it swirled down the storm drain. I loved this time of year, when September has those few October days: that thick, musty tang of turned soil and sodden leaves as the rain pounded down. I breathed in, filling my lungs with the sharp, cool air. Things smelled of endless possibilities – all dormant and hiding right now, but ready and full of promise.

Emma scuffed into the kitchen wearing one of my old dressing gowns. Her hair was standing on end.

'Gawd, it's chilly with that open!' She banged about a bit, all disgruntled. 'Sleep well?' She clattered a cup from the cupboard and poured tea from the pot. I shifted from the step and quietly closed the door and she stopped suddenly. 'Oh! You're dressed.'

'I am.' I winced, easing myself down onto a chair.

'Are you going out?'

I shook my head slowly, 'Nope.'

'Are you okay?' She peered closely into my face. 'You look a bit—'

'I'm fine. It's probably those new tablets.'

'Okay. Right. Well just take it easy today, yeah?' She sloshed some milk into the cup. 'Look, I'm going to have to get going or I'll catch all the traffic in this weather.'

She peered out into the patchy storm-laden sky. 'Dunno what time Paul's due back, do you?' I didn't answer. 'I'll pop round at lunchtime anyway and say hello. Oh, and I don't want to find out you've been doing anything stupid with that foot or I shall get very cross.' She slurped her tea deliberately noisily. 'Do you hear me?'

'I hear you.'

'Right. I'll go and sort myself out. And you, girlie, need to stop worrying yourself stupid with – Hang on—'

I smiled up at her encouragingly.

'—How come your top's all damp? ...and your hair?' She reached out and touched the ends. 'And you've got your shoes on...' She frowned. 'Have you been out some-where?'

'Me?' I looked at her, wide-eyed.

'That's what I'm asking.' She scanned my face.

'Where on earth would I have been at this time?'

–

I had asked the taxi driver to wait. His yellow hazards flashed a warning into the darkness as I walked up to Simon's door. I glanced around, watching the needles of rain slanting through the headlights and listening to the thump of music from one of the flats. I rang the top bell. There was silence for what seemed like an age, and then there was the thud of a door, and a lone figure stood in the gap.

I couldn't tell if it was male or female; its wraith-like shaved head bobbed cautiously in the shadows.

'Yeah?'

'I'm looking for Simon Gould. He lives in the flat upstairs. I need to speak to him.'

'He's not here.' The eyes peered at me blankly.

'Have you seen him recently? Did he have a little girl with him?'

The head swayed loosely from side to side. 'Dunno. The Old Bill came and got him about an hour ago. Try the nick.'

Something like ice water ran down my spine. 'Thanks… Thank you,' I stammered. 'Thank you very much.'

I don't remember getting back into the taxi, or the pain, or the movement of the cab. I was locked in my own pounding terror as we pulled up outside Stoke Newington police station. I asked the driver to wait and made my way to the front desk to find Kath, the officer I knew, standing there.

'Oh! Hello, lovely!' She glanced up at the clock. 'Blimey, you're keen aren't you? I'm assuming you're here because… Hey, are you okay? Someone told me you'd been poorly.'

'You've got Gould. What's happened?' My words gulped and choked.

'You're not, are you?' She went to move round the desk.

'Just tell me, Kath.'

She gave me a look. 'Well, officially, he's breached his licence conditions,' she kept her voice low and glanced at the other officers who appeared to be busy doing paperwork. 'But unofficially, we got a tip-off he'd been seen with a kiddie.'

I swayed and had to hold onto the counter.

'You sure you're alright, lovely?' She made a grab for me.

'Honestly, I'm fine, I'm fine——' I held up a hand. 'I just need to know——'

But a booming male voice interrupted us as two officers appeared from a back office.

'Physically, the doc says the kid's unharmed,' the tall one said. 'But it just depends now if Gould will spill. He's a weird one alright. The duty solicitor is on his way, so——' he stopped and looked at me. 'Can I help you?'

'We're all sorted here I think, thanks,' Kath butted in. 'She's just here to get some information.'

The officer nodded abruptly and they both stalked off. Kath shot me a look. 'Well thank God we got him, eh Luce?' She smiled but the weariness and sadness of it all shadowed her face.

'Can I have just two minutes with him?'

'You want to talk to him? I don't think that's——'

'Please Kath,' I pleaded. 'Please. It's really important.'

She looked at the door again and then at me. 'I can't unlock him, so you'll have to speak to him through the flap. Remember if the brief turns up and you're still there I'm seriously dead.'

'One minute and I'll be out of your hair. I promise. Just one minute.'

She gave a quick nod and gestured to the corridor housing the cells. 'Third one down on the left.'

—

The studded door sat there in its line of identical doors: scuffed and dirty, with its peeling yellow paint. Behind it, I knew, was the horror of a boy I didn't even recognise as being human.

I reached up and slid the catch. The weight of the metal flap leaned against my fingers and I let it drop. He was sitting there quietly, hands linked loosely in his lap, looking straight at me.

'I knew you'd come,' he smiled.

'Did you,' I said levelly.

He smiled softly. 'See Lucy? I proved it didn't I? Did you hear what that officer said? "Unharmed." Did you hear that? You and your colleagues will be able to put me down as a rehabilitation success story. But you're all so stupid I even managed to do it right under your noses. Good though, eh?'

My venom rose instantly.

'You're one sick bastard, do you know that, Simon?'

'Is that a professional assessment?' he smirked.

My anger began to burn: hot and vicious. 'I'll tell you what my assessment is, shall I? I'll make sure every report from every department will keep you behind bars for the rest of your life – I'll make it my personal mission.'

Simon only giggled, shaking his head, and then frowned as he licked his lips. 'Well firstly—' he held up one finger. 'We both know that I get everything I want from being in prison. For a start-off I'm practically a celebrity!' He chuckled. 'And secondly—' the second finger rose. 'They got a tip off, didn't they? So where do you think that mysterious tip-off came from?' He looked up at me. 'I gave myself up – that's all.' His hands lifted. 'Which will all go in my favour in court, as you know.' He smiled his appalling smile. 'The thing is, Lucy,' he sighed, 'I just wanted to see if I could get you to jump if I pulled enough strings?... And look!...' His palms sprang apart. 'Abracadabra... Here you are.'

I became aware of my fingers clutching the metal door flap.

'Oh, and while you're here, Lucy. I meant to say to you. Maybe you should enrol on those offender rehabilitation courses that Doctor Webb runs in the prisons. *Honestly* if you want to learn about manipulation, you should sit in on one. *Anything* you want to know about coercion… That's the place to learn it… So if you run into him anytime, do thank him for me, won't you?'

I felt the metal plate bite into my fingers. There was a sour sick taste on my tongue. I couldn't listen anymore. I took a step back, slamming the hatch back into its housing, the echo reverberating with his voice as it echoed down the corridor behind me.

'Didn't you ever wonder why it was you, Lucy!' he shouted. 'Didn't you ever wonder why I specifically asked for you?'

The voices of the police officers at the front desk grew louder. All I wanted was to get away from the voice – to walk over that threshold, to breathe clean air.

'You were like Cassie Edwards, Lucy,' his voice rang out. 'You were ripe for plucking.'

My lungs fought as I stumbled through the doorway and almost fell into Kath's waiting arms. 'My God!' she panted. 'Are you okay? What happened?'

'I just need to get out of here.' The air dragged painfully into my lungs. 'Please. There's a cab waiting. Please.'

A bald-headed man in a suit carrying a briefcase was coming through the door and was met by the tall officer. He was speaking but I was having difficulty catching the words. All I could feel were Kath's arms supporting me as we slewed awkwardly towards the exit.

'As Mr Gould's solicitor, I shall be advising him accordingly, but I don't believe, on this first charge, you're able prove any kind of premeditation, or indeed, any intent to do physical harm.' The words jagged through my head. We had nearly reached the door and Kath grabbed for the handle.

'You're having a laugh, aren't you?' the officer spluttered angrily. 'Have you seen her? That child's completely traumatised!'

My head swung round to look at Kath but she blocked my view. 'Go home Lucy. Just go home.'

She bundled me though the door towards the taxi that was sat ticking at the kerb.

'Kath—? She is okay? You would tell me, wouldn't you?'

But Kath only shook her head. 'You don't need all this Lucy, you really don't.'

She got me into the backseat, fussing a little, pulling the seatbelt for me, and I suddenly grabbed her hand. 'Kath—' the power of my grip shocked both of us: her eyes snapped up into mine. 'How do we stop these people?'

She gave a humourless little laugh. 'Stop them? We can't stop them. You heard that solicitor back there, minimising and defending him,' she tipped her chin towards the police station. 'Then he'll get to court and they'll believe he needs some kind of treatment programme: the psychologists, the psychiatrists, the case workers will all put their five pennyworth in, while people like Gould are laughing their bloody socks off while they line up their next three year old. I don't have to tell you that.'

'So what's the answer, Kath?' I let go a little and she patted my hand.

'We're not allowed to put him down, are we?' She wrinkled her nose. 'So the next best thing is to put ourselves as far away from those kinds of people as we possibly can.' She smiled. 'Keep the filth of them out of our lives: mentally *and* physically.'

–

It was raining much harder when I got home. I looked up at the closed curtains as I slid my key quietly into the lock. I knew Emma would be getting up for work soon. Tiptoeing into the living room, I looked at the time: 06:13. Pulling a throw from the sofa, and wrapping it round my shoulders, I switched on the TV.

Cassie Edwards's father stared back at me; it was breaking news on every station. I pressed the mute button, I just couldn't listen to anymore. The footage, again, was of the candles and the teddy bears outside the house. Then Cassie's smiling face: cheeky-eyed and grinning with no clue as to the horror that was about to befall her. I stared at the screen for a moment, my thoughts churning and distilling as I got up and crept up the stairs. The briefcase lay where I had left it. Gathering all the photographs together, I went back downstairs and tipped them out onto the carpet. Kneeling to the task, I began to lay out the photographs one by one, sorting and grouping them so that they began to tell a story... Paul, his babies, Caitlin... Would I ever know the truth?

My phone bleeped to say there was a message and I glanced at it. It was Viv. I didn't even want to listen; I didn't care what she had to say. The TV was still flickering in the background; a newsreader's face flashed up like a ventriloquist's dummy. He was mouthing things that made no sense. Simon Gould. Cassie Edwards... The truth, the lies... Who knew? Maybe it was all just a good story, just like Paul's, to lure the punters in. I concentrated hard on the image, watching the newsreader's muted lips moving, trying to read what he was saying, as a talisman to keep the heartbreak of my thoughts at bay.

—

I knew I wasn't going to tell anyone that I was leaving. I was alone in the house. My case lay unzipped and still only half-full on the bed as I checked the time. I'd have about three hours before Emma reappeared.

I knew there'd be tons of reasoning, and explanations offered, all designed to talk me round, to tell me I'd got it all wrong and that Paul was really a great guy.

I threw a T-shirt angrily into the case. There was more trauma, less certainty, less clarity every which way I turned. There was no one to rely on.

Screwing up some underwear I rammed it down the sides. If I could, I'd have gone back to Lou and holed up there for a while, but I knew that would be the first place that he would look. Then I thought about Broad-stairs... Or Whitstable... Somewhere with no connec-tions... Somewhere along that coast...

I listened to the rain beating incessantly across the roof tiles. I imagined this weather and the rolling sea, the stoney beach, and being alone and extremely happy.

'What do you think you're doing?'

I wheeled round. Paul's bulk stepped through the doorway.

My legs nearly gave way at the sight of him.

He barged past, filling the room, the shoulders of his jacket darkened with rain.

'What the hell is going on?'

I was aware of his breath coming out hard and laboured as though he'd been running.

He glared at me, his eyes red and bloodshot.

'Go on, then, tell me!' He swung his arm angrily. 'Go on. You've normally got so much to say.'

'I'm going away for a while. I need to think—' I went to move towards the door, but his arm shot out and grabbed me.

'Oh no you don't!' He blocked my way, one hand on the doorframe. 'You think you're going to treat me like some kind of mug, do you?'

I winced.

'*What?*' He put his face very close to mine. I got the sudden sour blast of booze.

I felt a fleck of spittle hit me on the corner of my mouth. I involuntarily licked my lips and was instantly repulsed.

'Where is he?'

The question stunned me. 'Where's who?'

He stood there panting like an animal unsure of its territory. His hair was plastered with damp; the sound of his breath whistled angrily, but there was something panicked there behind his eyes.

'This bloke who you're going off with.' His voice was whispered and hoarse. 'Where is he?' He narrowed his eyes. 'Or do I have to drag it out of you?'

'Bloke? Jesus, Paul, there is no bloke! Is that all you can think of, after all that's happened? Get out of my way.' Grabbing up my case and fumbling with the catch, I pushed past him, and to my amazement, he let me.

'So you're just leaving me, then.' His voice rang out behind me as I ran down the stairs. It wasn't a question. I was desperate to get into the living room where the briefcase was sitting waiting for me. He lumbered into the room after me, dragging his weight in heavy strides, arms flailing, before he collapsed on the sofa. His eyes were glassy. He hadn't seen the briefcase.

'I'm leaving because you're a liar.' I stood between it and him, hearing the calm surety of my voice, its strength, its dignity. 'You've lied to me. Probably from the first day I met you. The man I fell in love with doesn't exist. It has all been a fabrication. All this,' – my hand spanned the room – 'us, our relationship, is built on lies. Dirty filthy lies.' I felt my mouth trembling, but I was not going to stop now. 'Go on then, Paul. Tell me. Tell me about the children.'

I waited for his face to register the shock, the surprise, but it didn't come. He sat there, blinking up at me, his breathing audible, and then leaned forward suddenly, dropping his head, elbows on knees, his hands hanging like gloves in front of him. He hunched heavily, stupid with effort.

'Did you think you could hide it forever?' I glanced at the case.

'And how did you find out?' he mumbled dully.

'These?' I turned and crouched, flipping the catch and pulling one out. The baby sat laughing up in the bath, the suds sparkling on her nose.

I watched him flinch. He closed his eyes and looked away. 'Ah...' he rocked a little. 'So you've seen the ones of Caitlin too.'

A knife drove its way straight to my heart. 'What, this one?' I threw the one of Caitlin wearing the scarf at his feet. 'Yes, I've seen it all. The children, the two of them, and you and her. You kept the scarf and then let me wear it – My God—' I looked away.

His head bounced up. 'Scarf?'

'Oh don't! This...' I toed it angrily. 'This... Christ. The perfect family.' I heard the hurt and the pain and the disgust.

His head bobbed. 'Yes, *the* children, *the* family; you're exactly right to make the distinction. Not *my* children or *my* family.'

I stared at the crown of his head. 'What are you saying?'

He sighed, the breath catching in his throat. 'The kids. They weren't mine.'

He waved a hand wearily. 'Oh yeah, they were passed off as mine all the time I was providing a house and a car and an income, but once the father, the real father, finally decided he wanted her, then she told me the truth in the four words that no one wants to hear. *They are not yours.*'

I tried and failed and tried again to process what he was saying.

'The problem with our relationship was...' his fists clenched and released, squeezing the words out. 'The whole crux of it was... I loved her more than she loved me. She was the most beautiful woman I'd ever seen.' His voice broke and he dropped his head further. 'I couldn't believe that someone like her had looked twice at someone like me.'

The wound in my heart tore wide in the face of this unguarded, drunken, simple truth, and I bled, internally, profusely. I stood looking down at him with a hard hurt of pain in the back of my throat. I was terribly tired all of a sudden, as though I could've dropped to the floor right there at his feet, curled up and shut my eyes and just stopped the world from ever touching me again.

'Jesus. *Jesus.*' His voice trembled. 'You're right, I couldn't stand the humiliation, the indignity of explaining all that, so you're absolutely right – I lied.' He nodded slowly. 'And now I'm going to pay the price for that, because you're going to leave me too. *Fuck...*' He almost laughed. 'The irony of it. The things you've been accusing me of... Seeing Caitlin?' He shook his head in disbelief. 'If you had any idea. The truth is, I wouldn't touch her if she was the last woman on earth. I mean, can you imagine?' He lifted his head. His eyes were full of pain. 'After what she did? What kind of mug would I be, eh?' He laughed again. 'You've got it though, you've sussed me. I am the kind of mug that would lose you – the one woman who has healed that massive hole in my heart. The one woman I would actually consider having my own family with... But what do I do?... I balls it up because I'm a coward... Brilliant. Perfect.' His eyes bored into mine for a second and then his head sagged. 'I'm sorry,' he mumbled. 'Really sorry, about everything. The only good thing is...' he shook his head sadly. 'It really can't get any worse. For either of us.' He reached out and touched my hand. I didn't pull away.

I couldn't find the words for the questions I needed to ask.

'You know, as soon as I got to the train station yesterday I thought about you, here, unwell, and I thought *what am I doing?* Seriously? I've got my priorities wrong, I'm there, on the piss with the blokes, doing what men do when they go on conferences, and all the time I just kept thinking of you...' His voice cracked. 'And now it's all too late—'

'I'll make some tea.' It seemed such a ridiculous thing to say.

His leather jacket creaked obtrusively as he tried to take it off. His face, crumpled with concentration, frowned and then brightened. 'Let me. You're not well... You shouldn't be even on that foot—'

I didn't answer. I watched as he struggled to remove the jacket, his clumsy fingers attempting the zip but not managing as they closed precisely and slowly around empty air. The tea could wait. I went and stood by him patiently, watching the crown of his head tip and judder, his hair lank with wet and grease, flopping forward in the struggle. He pushed it back with unsteady fingers.

'I was so pleased to be coming home – And then when I saw the back door was open and I couldn't see you, I thought... I thought you'd gone... *Poof*...' his hands bounced and exploded apart.

I pulled his jacket from his shoulders and started on his shoes. He let me push him backwards on to the sofa, and I pulled the rug up over his shoulders. He turned over onto his side. 'Nice,' he said. 'Nice. Warm.' He looked up at me for the first time. His grey eyes looked huge in his face. 'Thanks for doing this. I don't expect anything from you. I know you're just being a decent person. So, just... Thanks.' His eyes batted lazily for a second and then opened and looked at me.

'By the way. There is no scarf.' He slurred a little. 'Check my bag, check ev'where.' His hand waved. 'Why would I do that? There is. No. Scarf.'

A whole wash of hurt and affection and concern and some other emotion I couldn't name came over me. I sat next to him on the sofa, tea forgotten, watching the drifting paralysis of alcohol take him, the hypnotic flakes stroking his face, drawing him down. I was helpless to control any of this; I had no part to play. The drink in him flexed and twitched, running through his veins, keeping him falling. His body relaxed into a smooth gentleness that made me want to kiss him. Another tremor passed quickly

through his shoulders and he sunk down into another
level.

'Paul?' I waited. 'Are you awake?'

But there was only the soft slur of his breathing. I got
up very gently, bending to pick up his jacket, aware of the
weight of something in the pocket banging against my
shin. Putting my hand inside, my fingers closed around
the hard rectangle of his phone. I scanned his face for a
moment and then slipped quietly into the hallway. I had
almost got to the kitchen door when the vibration nearly
made me drop the thing. The screen flashed white.

> We had to meet. U've always known we
> would.
> You and me. Bound 2gether for life.
> Neither of us can ever 4get
> Caitlin

Then it locked.

My heart stopped. The words imprinted themselves
into my eyes as I slid the phone back into his pocket.

There he was, his mouth slightly open, the cheeks
sagging with the booze and I saw him for the flawed,
selfish, plausible liar he was.

I'd believed what I'd wanted to believe; what it had
suited me to believe. The truth had been in front of me the
whole time. My gut had told me I was right all along and
I'd continually questioned it. But there were no questions
now. I knew.

–

I was suddenly very calm. He knew. I knew. I would wait for Paul to wake up. I'd make tea for us both, sit down and I would tell him, carefully and perfectly calmly, that I needed to go away for a while. There would be no histrionics, no screaming, no blame or accusations. I would explain and he would have to let me go.

I went up and packed the rest of my things before going to stand in the shower, eyes closed against the heat, feeling the gush of the water. Steam billowed in great clouds and condensed across the ceiling. It felt so good.

I'd rung Emma and given her a sanitized version of events, telling her that Paul had come back a bit the worse for wear. 'Still hung-over from the night before then?' she tutted, chuckling. I hadn't said anything about the photographs or the text messages, or his furious drunken accusations. I didn't mention leaving – Once I was settled in a new place, I'd tell her what had really happened, the whole story. Part of me wondered if she'd believe me.

I heard the click of the door handle and felt a vague surprise. Through the heavy steam I saw Paul's outline dipping and lumbering on the other side of the glass. I wiped a hand across the shower screen but it immediately fogged back up.

'What are you doing?' He swayed a little.

'Nothing. I'll talk to you in a minute.'

'Why are you showering?' He moved on the other side of the glass, I saw him bend unsteadily and turn.

I didn't answer, twisting round on one leg to turn off the tap.

'Why... Are you... Showering?' He laboured over the words.

I reached for the wall. 'For God's sake, Paul! Could you just—'

The door to the shower shunted open and I half spun in alarm as he stepped in naked beside me. He pulled the door shut. There was no way past him.

'What the hell are you doing?'

He looked at me. There was something dead behind his eyes.

'I want the truth.'

'What are you talking about?'

'There's massage oil downstairs, all kinds of stuff. You'd forgotten to hide it.'

'Hide? Hide what?'

'You know exactly what I'm talking about. I know, you see.' He leaned in, tapping his nose. 'When people are lying. I can tell. Soon as I walked into the house, I could smell it on you. There was something odd going on, something that you were hiding.' Lurching slightly, he grabbed at my face. 'I knew you were trying cover something up.' He tipped my chin back and stared into my eyes. 'I could see it.' I tried to snatch away. 'See?'

I tried to push his hands off. 'I don't know what the hell you're on about! The oil is Emma's, we were—'

He gave a short bark of laughter. 'Emma? For fuck's sake! She's probably in on the whole fucking thing! You expect me to fall for that one?' His mouth twisted horribly, his fingers dug hard into my cheeks.

'Get off me!' I tried to sound forceful, but the fear ramped up wildly as I attempted to fight him off. He had me caught.

'And now you're showering. Showering off the stink of him, are you?' his teeth bared in a weird grimace.

'For Christ's – Paul! *Stop! I*—' But my throat wouldn't let the words out. I struggled in terror as his hands raked all over me. He breathed me in, burying his face in my neck, snuffling wetly as his fingers looped around my wrist.

'Tell me what you're hiding Lucy. Go on, tell me.'

I was pressed up against the back wall of the shower, his knee forcing its way between my thighs.

'*Go on,*' he whispered.

I made a little strangled cry, elbowing and floundering madly at his face and he released me suddenly, staring wide-eyed into my face as though he'd just woken.

'What the—?'

I found I couldn't get my breath in the oppressive heat, the gagging humidity, the water blinding me as it streamed down my face. Hands flailing, I tumbled shaking out onto the floor.

'Jesus, Lucy! What is it?' He grappled with the shower control as I crawled around the floor shivering, casting frantically about for the towel.

'Lucy, please! For God's sake! What's the matter?' He crouched, reaching for me, his face full of concern.

'You know what the matter is!' I instinctively shied away from his touch. 'Get off me! Get off!' I shrieked.

'What? *What?*' He straightened, stepping back in alarm, his hands raised in surrender. 'Talk to me! What's going on?' He appeared instantly sober. 'I thought—'

I pulled a bath sheet from the cupboard and wrapped it tightly around me. 'I'm warning you,' I said slowly. 'Don't you *dare* come anywhere near me.'

His hands waved in mid-air. 'I promise I won't, I promise… Look, I'm keeping right over here… But could I please get a towel?' He grinned lamely and slowly reached for a towel from the rack, looping it around his waist. 'There… Look. See?… It's just me. Same old me.'

I backed out of the bathroom. 'Stay in there,' I ordered. 'Don't you dare move.'

'I'm not moving, I'm not moving!' He stood there, wide-eyed.

Grabbing clothes from anywhere, I desperately pulled them on, itching to feel covered, desperate to feel safe. Paul stood on the landing watching me, a strange enquiring look on his face.

'Lucy, what just happened? Are you okay? One minute we were—' his head swung slowly in amazement.

I couldn't answer him. Pulling on my shoes, I winced as the wound in my foot stabbed and throbbed. 'I don't know what is going on with you, but I want... I want you to keep the fuck away. I want you gone... *Gone!* D'you hear me? Out of my life, you... You understand me? Yeah?' The words stuttered from between my lips. My heart was juddering, my legs were shaking. It was anger and aggression and terror, all rolled into one. My things were downstairs; I had this acute over-riding panic he was going to try and stop me.

But he only stood, looking in amazement. 'You mean you're really leaving? You're not serious? Luce? I thought... I thought after we spoke, you... That is, we were—' He went to step forward but I turned and ran, hobbling as quickly as I could down the stairs. Grabbing my bags, I stumbled out of the front door as great gulping sobs racked my whole body. I was shaking uncontrollably, glancing round, terrified that he could be right behind me as the rain pelted and soaked into my clothes.

I floundered, fishing for my car keys and fell into the driver's seat. The pain seared, arcing through my foot as I revved the engine into life and accelerated hard. The wheels slipped and spun, churning up the wet gravel.

266

I glanced back once. He was standing calmly in the doorway, framed like a mannequin, his hands hanging at his sides. My whole body was rigid with fear, screaming to get out of there as I dragged the wheel round and backed off the drive.

'Lucy!' His voice called out. I snapped a look round. He had raised one hand as if waving a guest goodbye. He was standing absolutely still: a mute staring statue, just letting me go.

I drove, way too fast, my foot throbbing – the pain helping me to focus as the streets and houses, trees and hedges ribboned out on either side, the distance furrowing backwards farther and farther, taking me away.

I didn't know where I was heading. Which way was Kent? I'd looked on my phone but now I couldn't remember. None of the road signs were making any sense, I couldn't get my bearings... Southgate? No... No. This must be wrong. Where was I going? What should I do? I have nowhere sorted, nothing. Jesus, Jesus... Reaching into my bag to find my phone, I dialled the only person I could think of to call and started jabbering even as she answered.

'*Lucy?* Is that you?...' I could hear the alarm. 'Lucy? ...Lucy? Can you hear me? Christ! What's happened? What's the matter?'

I was making sounds, but not words, the sobs drowning everything out.

'Take a breath... Breathe, Lucy, for God's sake... What the hell's happened?'

'Paul... It's... It's Paul...'

'Oh my God! Is he okay?'

'He... He's—'

'Oh my God! Has there been an accident? Is he alright?'

I was picking up speed and realised I'd turned left and was heading onto the North Circular when suddenly the sky opened up with a flash of white.

'No, not him, me... I'm not okay. I'm in the car... He... Please, Em, I have to talk to someone. It's something awful... He's... I've...'

'What do you mean? What's happened? What is it?'

Cars drummed past, tyres whining on the planes of water. The world looked ashy green, boiling with mist and rain. The water illuminated for a second, toiling against the wipers.

'Lucy?'

'I just wanted him to stop...'

There was a junction. I knew there were lights. I saw them without really seeing. The change from one colour to another didn't register.

'Lucy?'

There was a terrible noise, a blaring high-pitched wail, as the road lights throbbed orange and red, streaming out on either side. I watched as a tunnel of brilliant light bore down suddenly in front and the car rocked and slipped. There was a terrifying screaming sound. Somewhere was the sound of Emma's voice. I think I said her name as a force took over the wheel. The car slewed hard into a kaleidoscope of whirling colours: traffic lights, tail-lights, searing headlights – a sickening sound of screeching metal on concrete convulsed through the car and then suddenly a wall of brick reared up. I was twisting and turning, the belt tearing against my shoulder and then I was grabbed by my hair – out into a cold blank sky. In those seconds there was a moment, an indescribable moment when I was overcome with the numbly falling assumption that I was going to die, and this was how, and this was when – and then out of the whiteness came a blackness.

And then there was nothing.

–

I opened my eyes into a bright tableau of blue lights flashing and a road scarred and scattered with things not meant to be there. Kind hands and a blur of faces lifted me from one world into the next, a place of stretchers and strip lights and screens and blankets that smelled strange.

The world outside was still thundering with rain and police cars: radios, tinny voices and sharp white headlamps, illuminating what was out there in that other place.

'Did I die?'

'Look at me,' someone said. 'Concentrate on me.'

I turned my face to the voice and the lights became brighter, shriller, and there was a stink of something caustic that burned my throat and stung my eyes into crying so that I couldn't see a thing.

'You're fine, you're fine,' the voice said from far away. 'It'll be okay. Don't cry. The ambulance is here.' I was aware of the outline of the person looking up and away from me, talking to someone over their shoulder. There was a police radio, flashes of acid yellow.

'*Is there any ID?*' someone said. Then: '… Lucy? You're alright, love. Just bear with us… *Do you want to go with her?*'

I gazed up into the face hanging over me.

'No.' I stared up in horror.

'Shush now. It's okay.'

'No, you don't understand.' I struggled to get up and the world fizzed around me.

'Shush. Lie still,' the mouth said. And then the world went dark.

—

What woke me was the lack of noise.

I was in a room – too bright. There was a terrible pain in the back of my head and I couldn't feel my right hand. I shifted my head. Emma was smiling across at me. I blinked painfully.

'Hello, you.' She wrinkled her nose and I saw her eyes were full of tears.

I stared at her face. All kinds of images floated in front of me, but I didn't know if any of them were real.

'How long have I—?' I lifted my hand.

'God!' she sniffed. 'You've been in and out of consciousness for ages. Christ, Lucy, we've been so scared...' Her eyes glistened and a single tear tracked down her face.

'I can't remember...' And then it came to me. *Paul. The shower.*

'You called me,' she scrubbed the tear away. 'You told me you weren't feeling well, do you remember that?'

'No,' I shifted and the tubes and wires shifted with me. My head hurt like hell. 'Emma, it was Paul.'

She looked at me patiently. 'You were in the car by yourself, Luce. Paul wasn't with you.'

'No, I don't mean... I mean Paul tried to—' I stopped to find the words.

'I thought he was going to rape me.' I knew by her look the words sounded over-dramatic and odd. I lifted my hand, and realised it was bandaged so thickly I could barely move it. 'I thought he was going to *rape* me, Emma...' My voice came out in a whispered husk. 'He *threatened* me, he came back drunk, accused me—'

'*Rape?* No. No... Shhhh... Lie back, sweetie. It's okay, it's okay. They've given you all kinds of stuff.'

'You have to believe—'

'You told me you'd done something and you needed to talk to me. I'm here now Luce. You can tell me anything, you know that.'

'Not me. Paul, Emma.' I struggled to pull myself up. 'He came home, raging drunk, he—'

Emma frowned a little. 'But we spoke, Luce, do you remember what you said? You said he'd come home a bit worse for wear. Remember that?'

'I wasn't telling the truth, Emma,' I rasped. 'That's not what happened.'

'Isn't it?'

'No, I couldn't tell you; he was there. I was going to leave him. I wanted to tell you, but—'

'You need to sleep,' she said gently. 'I've been speaking to Paul. You—' She broke off and I saw the pity in her face. Pity.

'Paul. You've talked to Paul.' I lay back on the pillow and closed my eyes, feeling the tears leak from under the lids. A nurse came in, bustling round. She touched my arm and the sticky tape pulled painfully.

'I think she's very tired.' I heard her say. 'Maybe you should come back another time?'

I opened my eyes. Emma was pushing the chair back. 'Of course. You're absolutely right. I'll be back when you're feeling brighter, Luce. Take care.' She bent to pick up her things and put her face close to mine. 'I'll ring him and tell you you're awake.' She kissed my forehead.

'She just needs to sleep,' said the nurse, turning down the light. She stepped forward to guide Emma awkwardly out of the door.

'How long have I—?'

My head swam. *Paul. Simon. Emma. Caitlin. Simon. Paul. Caitlin. Emma.*

Their faces whirled.

The nurse chuckled. 'Quite a while. A little brain bleed does that to you. Things get muddled. You'll be a bit confused for a few days, but try not to worry. I'll leave you alone and you can get some sleep.'

I heard the shunt of the door closing and I lay back on the pillows, my body flinching with memories I couldn't make sense of. I was out of control; time was out of control: *Paul. Emma. Caitlin. Simon.* Images came to me, weird snapshots laced with the whine of tyres travelling too fast, the gusts of rain on the windshield between odd windscreen wipers swiping back and forth, each swipe revealing the faces of two laughing children. I could hear them: their squealing and shrieking.

'Look at me,' said a voice. 'Concentrate on me.' I saw again the flash of police lights and the wail of an ambulance siren, and my eyes fell open with a shock. 'Lie still.' It was *her*. I saw her staring down at me. My eyes widened. She'd been there. *Caitlin*. The face was Caitlin's.

Chapter Eleven

'Oh, you're awake! Good, your husband's here to see you.'

My stomach turned over. I squinted painfully. The nurse, Clare, bustled round the bed. I'd got used to her coming and going. She was someone I instinctively liked with her comforting wide hips and curly blonde hair. She clattered something into a tray. *Please don't leave me.*

'He's been in a right two and eight!' she laughed. 'Mind you, he's managed to find some old friends here. What a coincidence!'

I licked my sore lips.

'Mr McAndrew was at university with him, apparently. What are the chances? Small world, eh?'

I heard Paul's laughter in the corridor outside and another man's voice, then the door clicked open.

'There she is!' His face registered absolute delight as he dragged a chair over and grasped my good hand. Every inch of me shrank from his touch, the drugs buzzed wildly in my ears, and I froze.

'Lucy, this is John McAndrew, a really good friend of mine from years back. John, this is Lucy.' I realised there was a man standing in the doorway. Paul looked up at the nurse and then round at him, smiling. I tried to pull my hand away; Paul grasped it tighter.

I looked at the man, his spiky blond hair, his pressed shirt, his tie. It didn't immediately sink in.

'John has a brilliant team here.' Paul smiled. 'You don't have to worry about a thing.'

John stepped forward in a waft of aftershave. He had a freckled, sandy complexion. He smiled broadly. 'We can have a chat, Lucy, when you're feeling a bit stronger. I've got a really lovely colleague called Diane I'll introduce you to. She's very easy to talk to. I think you'll get on with her splendidly.'

I blinked, not comprehending, the fog lifting a little as my eyes tracked down to John's name badge. 'Psychiatric Consultant.' My body jerked. I know Paul felt it.

'I've been explaining how you haven't been feeling well recently. Things have got on top of you a bit. Even your friends couldn't help.'

Emma.

'God, I feel so responsible.' He looked up at John. 'I mean, I should've taken more care.'

John put a reassuring hand on his shoulder. 'Don't worry. I'll come and see Lucy tomorrow and I'll bring Diane, too. We can have a chat and see where we go from there.'

I'd become a case. A series of chartable functions: of pulses and pressures and levels. A non-person. A thing to be managed, and moved, and manoeuvred. I knew cases: I dealt with them. I knew how it worked – only now I was on the wrong side.

–

The next day arrived and brought McAndrew and Diane along with it.

'Nothing like a bit of sunshine to cheer us all up, is there?' He stood at the side of my bed, rocking uncomfortably on his heels. Diane's crepe soles creaked softly somewhere behind his elbow. I looked down at the jigsaw puzzle someone had left on the table in front of me, staring at two pieces of sky that should go together, but didn't.

'Nothing at all.' My voice didn't sound like my own.

'So... Is this a good time?' His sickly scent wafted in waves. He raised his eyebrows as though he was actually asking a question. 'I hear you had a good night, anyway.'

'Yes thank you.'

'So I just thought it might help to have a bit of a chat.'

I smiled and nodded at them both. Diane's shoe made a sound like a dying animal.

'I was thinking it would be good to try and make sense of what happened and see if we can't get you home.' The carrot was dangling: I knew it and so did they.

'It appears you can't remember much... About the accident, I mean.' He sat chummily on the side of the bed. I saw the carrot jiggle. He ran his fingers down the length of his tie.

'Yes, that's right.'

'Do you remember how you were feeling when you got into the car?'

I watched his face. I knew I had to be careful.

'I know you'd spoken to your friend Emma on the phone that morning and you'd had an ordinary pleasant chat. Is that right?'

'Yes,' I nodded slowly.

'You were happy, then. Happy that Paul had come home.'

'Yes.' I lied.

'So something must've happened to change that?' I was aware of him studying my face. 'I understand when you made a second call to your friend you were in the car and were very upset about something.'

I swallowed. He saw it.

'So there must have been some trigger that really upset you and made you feel...' He chose the words carefully. 'Not yourself.'

'Yes I think there was.' My instinct told me I had to offer up something. 'I was in the shower. Paul got in with me.' I paused. 'We had a fight.'

'Paul says that he was in the shower and that you got in and became enraged. You attacked him.' The carrot began to move away, slowly.

I opened my mouth.

'You believed he'd been seeing someone. That's what your friend Emma said. Is that right? And you argued over that? You became violent. He has the marks.'

I understood immediately where this was going.

'You'd been on medication for an injury to your foot, hadn't you?' He nodded sympathetically. 'The second lot of pills were pretty strong. I'm wondering how many you took before you got in the car?'

I blinked. 'Only... Only what I was told to take.'

'Right.' McAndrew sat back in the chair. 'I'm sorry.' He licked his lips slowly. 'Forgive me for asking this question in this way but when you got in the car did you have any *intention* of hurting yourself?'

'Hurting myself?' My face fell. 'No! Absolutely not! It was an accident!'

His hand rested briefly on my arm. 'We need to be clear and truthful, Lucy. I'm on your side, I'm not the enemy, but I can't help you if I don't know what was in your mind at that precise moment.'

Emma's words came back to me: *neither of us are the enemy. There is no enemy.*

'You see, you say it was an accident, but you asked the paramedics if you were still alive... As though maybe you didn't want to be.'

I stared, horrified.

'Do you remember saying that, Lucy?'

Caitlin's face came back to me. Did I dream her? My head felt as though it was on a stalk. I must have dreamt her.

'Maybe you feel very differently now, and that's great, but it's just that given the level of drugs in your system and the nature of the collision, the police are at liberty to talk to you about endangering life by dangerous driving. Are you aware of that?'

I shook my head vehemently as he sat back, linking his fingers loosely in his lap. 'They were concerned, obviously, that you were out in your car, driving erratically and under the influence of drugs. They could have pressed for various charges, but we've persuaded them that we'd look at a care plan for you. Paul, of course, is resisting their attempts to get him to give evidence.' My brain faltered, not fully comprehending. 'And they know it's not in the interests of the justice system to take this matter further if you are released into our care and remain at home. I also understand Paul has been granted compassionate leave to look after you.' I heard the words as though he was talking about someone else.

'Plus with regular meetings with Diane on an outpatient basis, I think we should be able to get you back on your feet.' He smiled and his eyes twinkled bright blue.

I found myself gulping at dry air over and over.

'How does that all sound?'

'*We.*' '*Our.*' '*Us.*'

'There we are, then!' He slapped his knees decisively and went to stand. 'All sorted. Great! Now, I'll have to see if I can find that husband of yours and arrange some time to properly catch up! How brilliant after all these years!' He grinned. 'I lost touch with him after that bad business.' He shook his head and then smiled. 'Never mind, we're back in contact now!'

—

I was trapped and I knew it.

Two weeks passed. I had no idea what 'bad business' McAndrew had been referring to and with crappy hospital wifi, I couldn't spend hours finding out.

Some days he came with Emma. They sat, one on either side of the bed, laughing over stuff and chatting. *Who are you?* I wanted to ask him, but couldn't. I watched Emma's animated face as she laughed at his jokes. I didn't know her either. How much could I even trust *her*?

'Can you keep a secret?'

She arrived early one afternoon, but I knew Paul wouldn't be far behind. She looked around her, theatrically. 'Paul's bought you a new car!' she whispered bringing a finger to her lips. 'But act surprised when he tells you!'

If I was going anywhere, I knew I had to act all kinds of things. Paul might be the jailor, but Emma, I had realised, held a whole bunch of keys.

'That's exciting, but a bit scary too.' I picked at the sheet, knowing I'd got her attention.

'Oh yeah – sorry, I wasn't thinking!'

'No, it's fine. I've been wanting to say to you… About the accident.' I glanced at the door. 'That day. Do you remember what I said on the phone?… You know. What I said about Paul – What he did to me.'

Her face froze.

'I realise now it was some kind of madness.'

Her face crumpled with relief. 'Oh my God, Lucy! You don't know what that means for me to hear you say that!'

'I don't know what I was thinking…' I mused, 'what I *imagined* had happened. I can't believe I said it. Any of it.'

Emma was visibly heartened. 'God. What you've been through though, Luce. What you've *both* been through.'

I carried on meeting her gaze, forcing my lips to stretch into a smile of agreement as I nodded and made the right noises. Thank God for all the professionals who'd helped me get to this point. Thank God I'd now seen the light. I stared down at my hand, still bandaged, the fingers peeping out of the end. They didn't look like my own, they looked like they belonged to someone else. It was as though I was living someone else's life. My real life was out there somewhere, waiting for me. I just had to find a way to get back to it.

–

'I know it hurts, but we need to make sure you're properly mobile before you go home tomorrow.' Clare helped me out of bed for the umpteenth time. 'The more often you get out and have a little walk, the easier it will get. You've done so well in the last three weeks, don't let yourself slip back now.'

My legs still felt feeble as I put my bare feet to the floor, the soles numb and tingling. She helped me dress into tracksuit bottoms, a T-shirt, some socks and slippers.

'Take it steady now,' she smiled. 'Remember, don't go too far, just up to the end of the ward and back, that's all. We're not aiming to do a marathon just yet.'

She watched me as I started out along the corridor. I kept close to the wall, my hand gently touching the rail for comfort. I knew I was getting stronger and it felt good: really good. Even my injured foot had healed and it was great to be on my feet again.

The double doors at the end swung open and a white-coated registrar flapped past. I lifted my head and sniffed the air. He smelled of something other than hospitals: he smelled of outside, of cars and shops and people and I realised how much I was yearning to get out there again.

Carefully following the green line on the floor, I headed towards the signs for 'Exit'. My whole being thrilled. I stood back as the next set of doors swished open and a group of women bundled through, hooting with laughter. The doors stayed open, beckoning me, and I took the challenge and walked though them. Even the car park looked amazing. The early October weather had slipped into a real Indian summer: the soft morning sunshine warming my slippered feet. I watched the comings and goings: all the hospital staff beginning and ending their shifts. The parking spaces were laid out like some strange board game, intermittently filling up with moving counters. It looked like a whole new world.

I scanned the lines. There was a car there that was the same make and colour as my old one and I thought about what it would be like to get back behind the wheel again. Could I do that? An equal amount of anxiety and excitement tickled through me and then the excitement slowly died: Paul's car was sitting in a bay. I didn't know he was here. My eyes cast about nervously. I almost expected him to come strolling round the corner any second. I glanced back and suddenly understood the reality of what my life would be like once I left this place and all my protection was gone. This would be it: living with him, alone, always jumping and wondering and scared of what he would do next.

I turned into the safety of the foyer, the automatic door shunting open with a soft clatter, and with it, my stomach folded.

Caitlin.

I reeled with the impact, letting the doors close. This time she wasn't a dream. She was standing checking the signs above her head and then looked down at the guide on the floor. Her head turned sharply as though someone had called her and suddenly, there was Paul. They spoke for a few moments. He looked shifty and tense, glancing about to see who might be watching before they walked together down the corridor. It was like some terrible, terrible premonition coming true in front of my eyes.

'God, you'll get me shot!'

I jumped as Clare cupped my elbow.

'I said to the end of the ward, I didn't suggest you take yourself off to town!' she laughed. 'Now come on—'

But I pulled back.

'Paul's here. My husband's here.'

'Bit early for him, isn't it?' she smiled. 'The staff are only just coming on duty.'

'But his car's over there—' I looked back into the car park. It had filled up considerably. I looked for his car, but the newly parked vehicles obscured the view.

'You'll never spot it in that lot!' she laughed. 'Now please, if I don't get you back I'm going to be in *real* trouble.' Her grip tightened and she steered me firmly in the direction of the ward. I couldn't help myself: every person coming towards us, every voice at every turn had me snapping round in case it was him. But Paul didn't appear. And neither did Caitlin.

–

I didn't dare take my eyes off my bedside window. By the end of the morning I was exhausted. The afternoon rumbled into the early evening and still I couldn't relax. What were they doing here together? What was their plan? I envisaged some terrible moment of them walking in here together and telling me Caitlin had moved into my house and they were about to begin their new life together.

'You've been asking about your husband?' I started in alarm as Clare put her head around the door.

'He says he's been trying to get through to you but you're not answering. He wanted me to tell you he can't make it today. He'll be here tomorrow when you're discharged.'

I nodded, wide-eyed, as she disappeared away up the corridor. How I longed to just get dressed and run away, somewhere where they'd never find me. But I wasn't free to do that, was I? I'd got McAndrew and Diane and the weight of case notes on my shoulders weighing me down.

I closed my eyes. Free. I remembered what that was like. Living in my apartment with the windows wide open, a glass of wine in my hand, listening to the birds in the gardens outside.

A tray crashed somewhere and my eyes snapped open.

Caitlin was standing on the other side of the window staring straight in. Her eyes bored steadily into mine. She looked quickly to her right and left and then back at me. She raised a finger to her lips.

I couldn't move. I was aware of the jag of tension in my neck but I couldn't take my eyes from her. She moved quickly, slipping through the door and closing it softly behind her.

'Hello, Lucy.'

It was barely a whisper. I found I was pinned to the pillow. I tried to shift myself back but my arms shook like a frightened kitten.

'Please don't be scared. I only want to talk, that's all.'

'I'm not scared.' My own voice boomed into the quiet.

She looked back at the door as she pulled a chair closer. 'Do you mind?'

I couldn't speak.

'There are things you need to know.'

She was more beautiful than I'd realised: the paleness of her skin, the intensity of her green eyes. She blinked and the dark lashes fanned delicately against her cheek.

'I can guess what those things are.' My voice was a little shaky but it was a direct challenge.

Her eyes widened. 'Can you?' I heard the soft lilt of her accent.

'Yes, yes, it's okay. Don't worry, I already know,' I said stonily. 'I've spared myself that humiliation.'

She frowned. 'What's he told you?'

'He hasn't told me anything. I found out.'

'And you confronted him with it?' She sounded breathless. 'Is that why—' Her hand fluttered. 'Is that how you've ended up here?' She snatched a glance at the door again.

'Well it all makes life simpler for you, doesn't it?' I let my anger rise; it felt so good to let it go. 'You've got what you wanted. Well done, you.' My mouth worked horribly and I hoped I wasn't going to cry. I swallowed and refused to let my eyelids release their tears.

'I've got nothing I want.'

I nearly choked on the bitter laugh. 'Really? Well, you've got Paul. I hope he makes you very happy. I have to say, you deserve each other.' I shook my head. 'Those poor little kids.'

She gasped as though I'd physically struck her. I stared at her face. I couldn't decipher what I saw there: pain, puzzlement, anger, defeat. She didn't speak for a moment. The silence ticked for seconds.

'I don't know what he's told you. I don't know what you think...' Her mouth trembled.

'I think you're shagging my husband.' I felt bold. I was outraged that she'd come here – For what? To explain? To gloat? I leaned painfully forward. 'But think about this, Caitlin: there were reasons why you dumped him in the first place. Think about those.'

She made a small strangled sound as though she was laughing. I glared at her. She only shook her head over and over. 'No, no, no, no,' she kept repeating.

'I don't know why you've bothered,' I said. 'I really can't be—'

'I'm not *Caitlin*, Lucy. I'm Moire, her sister.'

My arms wouldn't hold me. The pillows caught me as my eyes dragged in the sight of her. I couldn't bring the photographs to mind; I couldn't see them. I found I was holding my breath so no sound could come out.

'He hasn't told you, has he?'

My head wouldn't stop shaking.

'About my sister and the babies...' Her eyes blinked away the pain.

'What about them? Where are they?'

'That's why I won't leave him alone, you see.' She gazed blankly at a place on the bedcovers and then looked at me sharply. 'He thinks I'll let go but I won't. I'm the thing that haunts him. I want him to pay. I want him to suffer for what he did.' She leaned forward and I saw the ferocity of hatred in her face. 'I know what he's doing to you; I've seen it before... This is just the start. I'm not going to stand by and watch him do it all again.'

Her words tumbled in the air. They made no sense.

'I don't understand what you're saying. You're talking as though I know stuff. What do you mean, "before"? What did he do?'

She looked at me. I saw Caitlin and yet not Caitlin. I saw the photographs all come to life; the children's faces dancing and cartwheeling in front of me. I saw their smiles. I heard their laughter.

'Paul did it.'

'Did what?' What was she saying? What did she mean?

'He killed them. All of them. Caitlin and the children are dead.'

Chapter Twelve

I listened to the creak of the floorboards across our bedroom and the squeal of a drawer shunting closed. I'd had three days. Three days of his endless oppressive kindness, his gentleness – his never leaving me alone for more than a minute, three days of me replaying and replaying what she had told me.

My fingers fumbled and stalled stupidly over the keyboard, my brain willing them to work faster as my eyes tracked the ceiling listening for his movements, making sure he wasn't on his way down. Why was I doing this? What was I thinking? None of it was right. She'd made it all up.

'Get out of here. Get out of here now!' I'd stared at her in horror. 'Or I'll call someone... Security... Someone...' My hand reached for the assistance button.

'You know you don't want to do that. All those questions you must have been asking yourself – I can give you the answers.'

'But murder? You're mad. You're talking gibberish... *Murder?* Seriously? Are you out of your mind?'

'She threatened to leave him. She was going to take the girls. He couldn't let that happen. He would rather kill them all than let them go—' Her words peppered the air. I couldn't take my eyes off her. 'He attacked her, physically... More than once... Then told her it hadn't happened, that she'd fallen... That she'd slipped somehow... That she was overreacting and had made it up. She began to question her own version of events. He was intelligent. He was highly educated. He was a psychiatrist for God's sake! Totally plausible. Who would've believed her? Where could she go?'

'Stop!' My hand came up, warning. I groped for the call button again but my fingers clutched at nothing. 'You know Paul could be here any minute, don't you?'

'But we both know he won't,' she smiled and looked at her watch. 'I've arranged to meet him in a pub, only I won't be there.' She smiled. 'I click my fingers and he has to come running. He daren't not.'

'So you're blackmailing him?'

'If you want to call it that.' She settled herself in the chair next to the bed and studied me for a few moments. 'I make sure he can never forget. You know he's spiralling again, don't you? I think it's because you remind him of her.'

I felt instantly queasy.

'I hadn't fully realised before, but now I see you up close—' she recoiled a little. 'You do.' A glimmer of grief flinched around her eyes. 'He can't forget, no matter how he tries. That's what this is about. Deep down inside I know he feels guilty.' She looked at me steadily. 'It will happen again, because you've triggered something—'

'I'm going to call one of the nurses—'

She didn't appear concerned. 'He'll have to control you. He's lovely and kind and then suddenly cruel. He switches from being completely reasonable to utterly bizarre. He's unpredictable. He got Cait to a point where she didn't know left from right. He'd argue black was white and then argue that it was black again.' Her hooded eyes were clear and passionate. 'You know what I'm saying is true. I can see it in your face.'

A warning creak overhead paused my fingers on the keyboard.

You should stop.

But you know you won't.

You won't stop because you know there's something in what she told you.

The page loaded in front of me and I compulsively scrolled down. I even tried different spellings of the name – Caitlin – Catelyn – Kaitlyn – but I couldn't find anything. *She was lying. She had to be lying.*

'You need me, Lucy. You need me more than you've ever needed anyone in your life.'

She dipped and reached into her bag. In her hand was a small mobile phone. 'This is the only phone you have that's safe. I've stored my contact on there already, but you'll need to keep it somewhere very, very secure. Memorise the number, yes? Just in case. You can ring me or text me whenever you like. But hide it, Lucy. Hide it really well.'

A strange wave of calm went through me and I stared down at her hand. 'You don't really expect me to take that, do you?'

She didn't answer the question. 'He won't let you leave and you definitely can't stay. The net's closing in. You know, you can feel it.'

'No!' Something furious rose up in me. 'Stop this.' I heard my own voice come out in a fierce whisper. 'Stop this – Stop telling me these things! None of what you've said can be true – he would have a criminal record wouldn't he?… Paul is a highly regarded psychiatrist –

He's well thought of – People would *know*… You can't cover up stuff like that!'

'Agree to meet me and I'll tell you everything.'

'What?… No! I'm not meeting you! I'm—'

'That's your fear talking Lucy. I can prove all of it.'

'Get out!' My voice was shrill and trembling. 'Get out! I don't want you here and I don't want to hear it!'

She stood, a towering figure, her maddened eyes never leaving mine.

'I'll go, but I'll say one thing before I leave,' she said quietly. 'I will always believe you, and I will always be there when you need me.' She walked swiftly to the door and opened it, but then paused 'Remember, I'm always watching.' And with that, she was gone.

I stared at the empty space that she'd left behind and I realised my palm had reached out and touched the small black rectangle of the phone. The danger of possessing that was more than I could even contemplate.

'You alright down there?'

Paul's voice shocked me back to the screen.

'I'll be there in a sec, just sorting out the washing!' He called down cheerfully.

My fingers flew to the browsing history and I immediately deleted it.

'See if you can find us a decent drama to watch, nothing too taxing or gruesome. We see enough of that in real life. Let's have a bit of escapism—'

'Sure! Yep!' I called back. 'I'll have a look and see what's on!'

My hands shook wildly as I closed everything down as the tread of his feet came slowly down the stairs.

We sat watching the television in our living room. Our living room. Everything was as it was before: sofa, table, chair, cushions. There was nothing abnormal about it or out of the ordinary. *Horror happens in TV dramas, not in real life*, my head told me. No death, no murder. That hadn't happened.

I had found an episode of *Maigret* to watch. A young woman had gone missing. All the signs pointed to it being the boyfriend or the father or the husband. It was always the boyfriend or the father or the husband, or the man next door, or the school caretaker: the one who should be taking care but does the very opposite.

Paul wasn't that kind of man. He was a lot of things but he wasn't *that*. How could I have sat and listened to that? Why didn't I call someone? *Because part of you wanted to hear it.*

'Look at what he did to you.' Moire's tortured face came back to me. 'Look at where you are. The net is closing in. You know. You can feel it.'

Dr McAndrew had turned up the morning of my discharge. I looked for Diane, but she was nowhere to be seen. I carried on packing my things as he sat on the edge of the bed, hooking one knee up and clasping it between linked fingers. The knuckles went white.

'So. You're leaving us today then Lucy! Congratulations! You've come a long way, haven't you?'

All the time I was folding and smoothing, my mind kept thinking exactly that: *I had come a long way... And a long way away was precisely where I was going. Once I was out of here, I'd be free of it: the madness, the chaos, the lies...*

'So we need to keep up that momentum.' McAndrew moved his arm like the piston on a train. 'We don't want you slipping back. So I'm discharging you on the condition that you'll stay under Paul's professional care. How about that for a bit of brilliant news?' he chuckled. 'Let's see if we can keep you out of hospitals from now on...' He smiled broadly. 'Of all kinds.'

The true impact of his words kept me dumbly standing there. It wasn't until he left that the absolute meaning sank in. Something like an earthquake shuddered through my arms and legs but I carried on mindlessly packing.

Moire's words came back to me over and over as my hands folded and refolded. My mind was on fire: I combed through every incident with Paul, all the accusations and threats. I thought about that moment in the shower, the pure and blinding fear of that snatched sudden memory. The pounding of water, his hands, the feel, the smell of his proximity – the fear, the revulsion, and now I was being handed to him like a piece of meat.

I pointlessly smoothed a T-shirt over and over. I wasn't going anywhere. The images formed again but I refused to let them grow. The word 'rape' hung nonsensically in my head alongside the word 'murder'. Despite everything that had happened, my brain wrestled and fought at the very idea. I couldn't put the man and those images together. They kept splicing off like reels of broken film. It had happened, it had happened to *me*, hadn't it? I tried to drag the images back and make proper sense of them, but they slipped through my fingers like grains of sand.

Is this how it started with Caitlin?

Is this *how it started with Caitlin?*

He's totally plausible, so who would ever believe her story?

Moire's words kept coming back to me. I'd been locked down, silenced, and out-manoeuvered. The truth was, whichever way I looked at it, I knew no one would believe me.

–

I became really good at being someone else.

Diane accepted the new version of me quite easily. By the second week we had a little pattern developing.

'Tell me about your week,' she'd ask, smiling. 'Anything. What you've done, or thought, or felt.' And I would dutifully oblige, never forgetting to mention Paul: how we'd laughed at something on TV or something we'd read and found interesting. I gave her some niggles too, some minor irritations, just to show that everything in my life was now on a perfectly even keel.

She nodded and made encouraging noises with her head tipped on one side. She was quite easy to con. But she wasn't the one who really knew me.

It was Emma who posed the real test. She was the one I had to convince.

'How do you like your new car?' She gazed out of the window at the gleaming thing on the drive.

'Oh I love it! What an amazing present! I'm dead lucky.'

'And you're sure you'll be okay?'

She meant driving, I knew.

'Absolutely fine. I've got Paul, how could I not be?' I laughed. It sounded false even to me. 'He's said he'll come with me the first few times and hold my hand.'

'So you're really feeling much better?' She sounded dubious.

'More than. Few aches and pains, but everything else is getting there… Can't you tell?' I grinned. I watched to gauge her reaction.

'It's just that I was supposed to be going to France for a couple of weeks, and I said—' she wrinkled her nose.

'You said you couldn't, because of me.' I looked at her levelly. 'Don't be daft. You can see I'm fine, can't you?' I held out my hands. 'Look, go on holiday Emma. Enjoy yourself. By the time you get back I'll be a whole new woman.'

–

'Louise says she hopes you're feeling better.' Paul walked into the kitchen and flicked the toaster on at the wall.

The name didn't compute for a second.

'Louise?' he tried again. 'Your sister Louise?' He glanced at me over his shoulder.

'I've left messages for her. I was waiting for her to ring me back,' I trailed off. 'Why was she phoning you?'

'Why shouldn't she phone me?' his shoulder blade twitched and my stomach jumped. 'I kept in contact with her all the time you were in hospital. Someone had to,' he said petulantly 'She was worried. Anyway,' he glanced round. 'You said you weren't interested in talking to her.'

I knew it was best to say nothing.

'Yeah. Don't you remember? You said she had enough on her plate with your mum... Mam...' he grinned. 'I've been giving her some advice about support services she can hook into if she needs them. She said she couldn't thank me enough. Nice woman. You must invite her down.'

He busied himself slicing the bread and slotting it into the toaster. A tiny piece of me went very still as though I'd heard another key turn in a lock.

'Did you see the weather forecast by the way?'

'No I didn't.'

'Today's going to be great before the weather packs in. We should go out for the day somewhere.' He turned and leaned against the work surface. 'A picnic maybe, what do you think? How about Kent? Do you know Whitstable or Broadstairs? Both are nice… Bloody hell, don't look so worried!' He laughed and reached out to stroke my hair. 'I'll be with you all the time. It's not too far. It'll be fun.'

-

The car journey was like purgatory. He chatted on and on all the way down, pointing out this and that, pausing only to ask me *if I was okay: too hot or too cold? Did I want to stop? Was I comfortable?* I tried to respond normally: reassuringly, with 'I'm fine', 'I'm great' and looking as though I was relaxed and happy.

Had he *known* I'd thought about going to Kent? Or was it just a coincidence?

'Let's stop in Whitstable. It's a bit more lively there.'

He found a parking space quite close to the beach and messed about in the back dragging out all the stuff he'd brought before pottering down onto the stones to look for exactly the right spot. He made a great show of spreading out the blanket and fussing with the stones underneath, arranging cushions and settling them around me, before opening up the basket with practised ceremony and bringing out a load of salads and cheeses and a bottle of wine. He was cheerful and over-talkative. We ate and drank and spoke about the view and watched a little dog chasing a ball into the sea. I accepted it all with a strange sense of pending anxiety. I had a blank, other-worldly feeling, as though I was watching him performing in a play in which I had a repeated walk-on part. I was exhausted; I couldn't talk anymore; I couldn't think anymore. I lay back in the warmth of the late autumn sunshine, shutting him out for a while. The cluck and hiss of the waves soothed me. The little dog barked excitedly and someone called its name.

I heard, rather than felt, him move as he shifted in beside me. I was suddenly awake, my whole body on high alert. I opened one eye and immediately stiffened.

He was lying propped on one elbow, gazing down at me, so close, his eyes crinkling in the sunlight. He was smiling curiously. I couldn't move. He raised a hand and tickled a long sea grass head down my cheek. I wanted to swipe it away.

'I've been thinking,' he sounded dreamy. 'When you're feeling better, when you're really feeling strong enough, we should talk about stuff – Stuff about the future.'

I stayed still.

'A family, maybe. Babies. That's something you'd like, isn't it?'

My skin crawled at the thought. I brought up one hand as though shielding my eyes from the sun so that he couldn't gauge my expression.

'I'm probably not quite there yet.' I said carefully. 'Diane and I have been talking—'

His finger came up and he touched my lip gently. I had to will myself not to flinch.

'Just when you're ready.' His fingers stank of sap. 'I think you're doing brilliantly with Diane. You've obviously connected with he*r* – she's really pleased with your progress.'

A gull's laughing waul kited overhead and a rush of sea air and tiredness washed over me. *She's spoken to him about me. Of course.*

'But how do *you* think you're doing? I mean, not just what you tell her. I mean deep down.'

I was aware of his lengthening shadow falling across my neck. I would've liked to have sat up, shifted away from him, faced him, but I knew instinctively I had to remain exactly where I was.

'I'm much better,' I said firmly. 'I feel more like my old self and I'm healing really well. Getting out of the house feels so good. Maybe I should consider going out on my own sometimes? What do you think? Not far… See how I get on.'

I smiled but watched his face cloud a little. The sun was behind him so he appeared a black cut-out silhouette with pits where his eyes should've been. 'I think it's a bit soon for all that,' I heard a little intake of breath. 'Let's just see how you go.'

'Yes,' I said slowly. 'You're right. Let's just see how I go.'

—

We got back late afternoon. Paul was his usual attentive self, helping me out of the car, insisting that I do nothing, even though it was clear I was perfectly capable of carrying a few bags and blankets. He dumped the basket onto the kitchen table and I began to sort out the dirty plates, loading the dishwasher and putting odd things back in the fridge.

'I don't know what you want to do about dinner later?' I had my back to him so I wasn't immediately aware of anything amiss. He didn't respond. I looked round.

He was staring at me with a look of incomprehension. 'What's that supposed to mean?'

'Sorry?' I stopped, with a cup in my hand.

'Is anything *ever* enough for you? Why do you always have to criticise?'

'Criticise?'

He mimicked the look on my face. 'You really are un-fucking-believable.'

'What did I say?' I bent to close the dishwasher door.

'Seriously? After all I've done.' He looked at me open-mouthed. 'If you really have no idea then there is no way I'm going to spell it out to you.' And he stomped off upstairs.

I stood listening to the creak of him walking back and forth overhead. Every inch of me was on high alert. This was the first time since I'd come out of hospital that I'd seen this side of him. I had no idea where it had come from. My nerves jangled and pricked the length of my spine. Was this a test to rattle me? Would he bring it up with Diane and use it against me? I took a deep breath and concentrated on putting stuff back in the fridge and packing the picnic things away. I would keep calm; I would hold it together. I would be aware: very, very aware. Putting the kettle on to boil, I started to make tea. I heard Paul's footsteps on the stairs. My gut froze in absolute panic.

'Are you making me one?' he called out.

'Can do,' I kept my tone light.

He walked into the kitchen and went to the cupboard.

'About earlier,' I said fishing a teabag from the cup. The surface of the liquid shimmered as though an earthquake was about to happen.

'What about earlier?' He reached a saucepan from the washing up rack and put it away.

'Whatever I said, I didn't mean to upset you.' I glanced at him. His head jerked round at me and he frowned.

'Upset me? You didn't upset me. What do you think you said?'

I gave a nervous laugh. 'I have absolutely no idea, something about dinner.'

He pulled a face and shook his head. 'Haven't got a clue what you're on about. I haven't even thought about starting dinner. Why, are you hungry?'

'Oh no. It's fine. Whenever.' I said guardedly.

'We said I was cooking pasta, didn't we?' He came over, kissed my cheek and then clocked the expression on my face. 'Go and put your feet up and watch some telly. I'll give you a shout when it's done.'

And the moment passed. I tried to let it go – breathe through it, stay focussed and not react, but the earthquake I had felt wasn't just inside me, it was inside Paul too. I could feel the deep rumbling within him, I could hear the hiss of building steam. The ground under me was splitting opening and I couldn't find any way to stop it.

Chapter Thirteen

I began not to know myself. I mean, really *not know*. I was functioning but empty. It was as though I was sitting in the centre of a room that was filled with doors, but each door was terrifying. I knew I should get up and walk through one, but I couldn't. I was stuck there, in that chair, in that house in front of that window, watching the world, but not connecting.

Moire, I knew, was trying to help me. That telephone was a link with the other side. I watched as the messages came through: one after another.

> Are u okay? How do u feel 2day? Do u feel safe?

Questions, questions, that I just didn't have the answers to. I never replied.

Days slipped by and I couldn't discern the time. Time slipped by and I don't think I moved. I needed Emma, or I needed someone like Emma, but I couldn't get hold of her. Was she still in France? I left messages, I sent texts, but nothing. And what would I say to her?

I knew I should be throwing Moire's phone away, but the thought of Paul finding it in the rubbish was terrifying.

It sat in the pocket of my dressing gown like a ticking bomb. In the end I zipped it into an old scatter cushion on the armchair. It would be close but somewhere he'd never find it. I also resolved to tell Moire that she had to stop. I couldn't help her. I was sorry but I just *couldn't*.

It was her grief talking. Her sister and children had died, it was a terrible thing and she blamed Paul – of course she did. People blamed people for things out of their control. I knew I had to say *something*.

> Moire I know you don't want to hear this
> but I think you should talk to someone.
> You've been through a terrible thing. There
> must be someone out there who can help
> you find some kind of peace. I do hope so.
> You deserve it. Lucy

I pressed 'Send' and waited. Nothing came back. I waited a bit more. There was silence. I prayed that would be enough.

–

'Heard from Emma recently?' Paul didn't take his eyes from the TV screen.

'No, actually I haven't.'

He flicked though channels, one after the other. 'Strange. I don't think she's back yet. Maybe she found some new bloke over there and sent the old one home. You know what she's like.'

'Probably.' I smiled and tried to read his face.

'By the way, I've arranged to go back into work – just a couple of hours to start with. Is that okay?' He turned to look at me.

'Of course. No problem.'

'Only if you're sure?' His gaze didn't drop. I swallowed.

'Good thing is, I'll get the TV remote all to myself, then. What a treat that'll be,' I teased. It was as though someone else was speaking the words.

He seemed convinced. 'I'll go in tomorrow then. Just half a day to start with then. Let's see how you get on?'

I smiled and then suddenly my smile froze as I felt the phone tucked behind me vibrate just once.

'You okay?' He looked concerned.

'Absolutely,' I reassured him, 'why?'

'Oh, that's good then,' he breathed. 'For a second there you looked like you were scared.'

–

That night I slipped out of bed while he was asleep. Each stair cracked like a gun going off and my heart went with it. At the bottom I paused and listened: all I could hear was the restless beat in my ears, but nothing moved. Not daring to put any lights on, I unzipped the phone from its hiding place and I read her reply.

> Meet me tomorrow.
> I know he'll be at work. I'll tell you
> everything and then you can judge for
> yourself.

She gave me a time and the address of a café not far away. My hand trembled as I pushed the phone back inside the padding and a creak overhead set my heart thudding. I walked quickly into the kitchen and ran the tap: 'Water' I'd say. 'Just getting a glass.' I rehearsed it in my head over and over so that it would sound natural. I stood for a few moments, listening, but I couldn't hear anything else. Creeping back up the stairs, I eased our bedroom door open, inch by inch. His back was a hump of duvet and his snores gargled gently. I slid back into bed and lay there, staring at the ceiling.

How the hell did she know where he'd be? See her again? The very thought of it shook me to my core. The idea of leaving the house on my own filled me with a terrible churning anxiety. I glanced across at Paul; the black sockets of his eyes stared back like a cadaver. What if he ever found out? What if he caught me? What if it was all a trap? What if…? What if…?

–

The next afternoon, I watched Paul pack his things together into his computer bag.

'Are you sure you'll be alright?'

He'd been monitoring my every move all morning.

'There's nothing you need or want? If you think of anything, ring me, and I'll pick it up for you on the way home.'

'There's nothing, I'll be fine, don't worry.' I grinned broadly, feeling my cheeks strain with the effort.

He came over and kissed me and I found myself holding my breath. 'Bye then!' I managed to sound cheery.

I watched as he walked down the path. I was counting the seconds until he got into the car. He began to back off the drive and I had a sudden surge of joy and took a great gulp of air. The whole atmosphere in the house had changed: it felt light and airy, as though a pressure had been lifted clean away. My ribcage expanded as I filled my lungs: my whole body feeling suddenly bright and aware and alive. I could do anything I wanted right now. I could run a hot bath and lie in it for hours, I could watch television, I could eat Nutella straight from the jar.

You could meet Moire.

No.

I glanced at the clock.

What are you afraid of?

His anger. His rage. His attack. I shrank at the idea. *It was much easier to stay indoors, be safe, do as I was told.*

My body was fearful but my spirit rebelled. I didn't allow myself to think. I put clothes on. I slipped on some shoes. The soles of my feet tingled with the press of the leather. My jacket was heavy and constricting; it wouldn't let me lift my arms properly to open the door. I stepped across the threshold. The world was sharp and in focus; the light felt too bright. There was a strange precarious sensation of not being guarded. What was I doing out here?

You've come this far. You can do it.

The driveway spanned away in front of me for what seemed like miles. I managed to put one foot in front of the other. The main road was another country, but I wasn't going back now. The new car sat there in all its insipid pale blueness. I could do this, I really could.

My knees nearly gave way as I tried to reverse, but I made it onto the road. Thankfully, my hands and feet remembered what to do and the streets slipped by easily. I pulled up at the café and shakily turned off the ignition.

I could see she was there. I was nervous and angry with myself, and nearly turned around and drove home. But somehow I made it across the road.

She didn't notice the door opening; her fingers were fiddling nervously with the cup handle as she agitatedly chewed at her lip.

'Lucy!' She rose and leaned forward to kiss me on the cheek. 'What can I get you?'

'No, no, I'll get it.' I flapped with my bag, searching for my purse. I was aware that she was watching me as I walked up to the counter. I brought my coffee to the table and sat.

'How's it going?' She searched my face.

'It's fine. I'm fine.' I took a sip.

'You got my messages?'

'Yes, yes, I did, but what I said, Moire, I did mean—'

'Wait… Before you say anything. You want proof—' She paused a moment and then reached down into her bag. '—So I thought you might like to see these.' She drew out a folder. It was battered and greasy-looking. She flipped it open and pulled out a wad of newspaper cuttings in a transparent wallet.

I saw the lettering '*Shropshire Herald*' on the first one. She slid it across the table towards me and I saw the date: Monday August 22nd, 2005.

House of Horrors, the headline said. Her name bounced out at me: *Caitlin Reece, 24, and her unborn child were found dead with Eloise, 3, and Roisin, 18 months, in the early hours of yesterday morning.*

A rollercoaster lurched through my stomach. The words swam blindly.

'Caitlin was pregnant.' Moire's face was a mask of pain. 'I knew. So did he, I think. I've always thought that was the trigger.'

No no no...

> Her partner, Paul Weberman, 24, was found with a life-threatening stab wound. Police suspect the attempted murder of Mr Weberman was part of a murder-suicide. Ms Reece had been suffering with depression after the birth of her youngest child. No one else is being questioned in connection with this incident.

'Paul Weberman?' I looked at her. 'Attempted murder?' None of this made any sense. 'This isn't what you said... You're saying Paul...? That Caitlin tried to...?'

'Paul Weberman is now Paul Webb. Here—' she pulled out a photograph of them all together: Paul, Caitlin, the children, one no more than a babe in arms. They were at some kind of event. 'See? Look at the name there—' My eyes scanned down.

> Caitlin Reece, author of The Dark Room, with her partner, Paul Weberman and their two children.

'She was interviewed by their local paper years ago.' Moire traced her finger down the picture, touching the baby. 'They used this photograph, after—' She couldn't finish the sentence.

'But—'

'He told them she was suffering from depression and that she'd tried to kill herself. Paul has plenty of psychiatrist friends to call on if he needs to.'

John McAndrew's face drifted through my mind.

'He said that one day she flipped and tried to harm the children. He tried to stop her and she stabbed him. When they found her, she was in the bath. Both of her wrists had been opened up... And the babies—' The words wouldn't come.

'The babies were in her arms, one on either side of her.'

Her eyes glistened with anger and grief. 'Paul was unconscious, minutes away from dying.' Her jaw contracted angrily. 'They looked at the evidence and they believed his version of events,' she said simply. 'A fine, upstanding, decent, highly respected middle-class white man,' she sneered. 'Of course he was telling the truth.'

I looked at the slew of articles and photographs in front of me. There was a photograph of Caitlin and the two children: one I'd not seen before. The three of them were sitting on a log in a wood, close together. Roisin was on Caitlin's lap, her baby hands extended to the camera. Caitlin was looking down at Eloise and laughing into her upturned face. I couldn't look. I pushed them away.

'I can't... I'm sorry,' my chair scraped back suddenly. The women on the next table looked round. 'I don't feel well. I'm sorry, I can't do this.'

'Paul Weberman!' she called after me. 'He said he changed it because he couldn't bear the memory of what happened. That's what he told the people he worked with, that's what he told his bosses. He said it compromised his position being in an attempted murder enquiry... But I know it was guilt...'

I reached the door and yanked it open. 'He's a devil and he's guilty as hell.'

I didn't look back as I barged my way out of the door. I was too scared that she might be behind me, that she might create a scene in the street. I walked quickly to the car, got in, and started the engine. I glanced into the mirror but the street was quiet.

She'd manufactured all that; I don't know how. *Caitlin murdered her children? Jesus... She tried to kill him? Madness... All madness...* I felt horror, pity, my heart grieved at the sight of those children's faces. I couldn't move. All those images tumbled together in front of my eyes, and then I had a sudden spring of absolute panic; the woman in the café... People might've heard all that... They might have seen me there... Somehow he'd find out... The muscles in my arms and legs wouldn't respond. I managed to start the engine and found first gear. With one glance back at the café, I pulled the wheel round, and then nearly stalled the engine.

She was standing there in front of the window watching. In her hand was the folder of cuttings. As I swung blindly out of the parking space, a car horn blared in warning and my heart pitched in terror. Frantically checking the mirror, I saw her raise the folder in a silent wave as I gunned the engine and sped away.

–

The drive home was terrifying. I kept checking the time. It had to be okay. I'd only been gone three quarters of an hour. There was no way he would be back this soon. I was safe, quite safe. Where would I say I'd been?

Caitlin. Murder. Caitlin. Babies. Paul Weberman... Paul Webb...

I was tired of being in the house, I'd say.

I'd grin all excitably. I wanted to see if I still had the confidence to drive. That would explain it all, wouldn't it? He couldn't be annoyed at that, surely?

My spirit argued loudly back; so what? I told myself. I am a grown woman, I can choose to be out; I can choose to stay in, why should he be angry?

But all the time I could feel a grinding panic in the base of my belly telling me that I had every reason to be afraid: there would be a scene, there'd be accusations, and threats. What if someone had seen me? What would I say?

When I turned the corner and saw his car, my guts turned to water.

I immediately felt for my phone, shaking it out of my bag with one hand and trying to steer with the other. No message, no call from him. My gut soured and churned a warning: he would have called me to check where I was, surely? He would have done that at the very least.

Pulling onto the drive, I tried to look confident and natural, but glanced surreptitiously at each of the windows. I couldn't see him but I suspected he had seen me. Blipping the car locked, I walked as casually as I could to the front door and slid my key into the lock.

The hallway was silent, but the oppression was back.

'Hello!' I called out tentatively.

There was no reply. Slipping off my shoes, I padded down the hallway and saw that the door to the kitchen was closed. I pushed at it gently and a soft wave of classical music flowed into the hallway.

Paul was at the sink with the water gushing, furiously scrubbing carrots.

'Oh! I didn't hear you come in!' He grinned over his shoulder. 'Too much racket going on in here.' He went over and turned the music down before going back to the sink. I couldn't take my eyes off the movement of his arms. His hands made fists.

'I've got dinner all sorted.' He briskly turned off the tap. 'There's a shepherd's pie in the oven.'

'Great.' My voice sounded weak and wavering.

'Well, come on then!' He dried his hands on a tea towel.

'Come on what?' The corners of my mouth tipped up but my eyes were frozen.

'Come and give us a kiss then! I haven't had one since you've been home!'

Stunned, I walked across the floor to where his arms enveloped me in a bear hug, squeezing hard, really hard. I tried to react in the way I knew I should, putting my arms around him too, but could feel my whole body shrink and crawl.

He kissed the side of my hair and nuzzled into my neck. The sensation stiffened my spine. He clocked it. I knew it.

'Do you fancy a glass of wine with dinner?' he said chirpily. 'I think there's some red open.'

All of my sensory antennae were on high alert. 'That would be really nice.'

I tried to sound off-hand and bright.

'Great.' He held me away from him, his hands heavy on my shoulders.

I could feel the weight of them pinning me there. He looked intently into my eyes.

I smiled. 'How was the office?'

He turned away and opened a cupboard to get the glasses. 'God, you know what it's like when you've been away – four hundred emails and a load of rubbish to wade through, most of which gets deleted.' He picked up a bottle of wine, unscrewing the top. 'No, you've obviously had a far more interesting day and I want to hear all about it.'

The whole floor cracked.

He had his back to me as he checked the glasses, squinting as he held them up to the light.

'Start from the beginning. You watched me drive away, and—?'

It felt as though I was observing myself from somewhere over by the door. I saw me tucking my hair behind my ears, then my hands dangling oddly, wavering in mid-air as I tried to explain. I heard the stammering and pausing, not knowing what I was saying or how I was saying it, feeling the heat in my face, cursing the complete lack of rehearsal and planning. I hesitated and lost the thread several times, even with such a simple story of taking a drive and looking in the shops.

Paul frowned, listening as he poured the wine. 'Parking is terrible round there. Where on earth did you manage to find a space?'

My mind went completely blank. He turned to looked at me as he waited, but then he only bit his lip and nodded.

'As long as you were okay and had a nice time. I'm sure getting out did you good.'

I didn't think I could speak. He moved on, prepping some cabbage and putting it in the steamer with the carrots, as he went over what had been happening at work.

I tried to concentrate on what he was saying but my mind was all over the place. I asked stupid questions, but he pretended to take them seriously. He served dinner, pouring more wine and ushering me to the table. I took my place, sipping at the wine awkwardly, and eating hardly anything.

'Leave all the washing up.' He aligned his knife and fork precisely on the plate. 'It's not going anywhere. Let's watch some TV shall we?'

I tried to look totally at ease as though I was settling on the sofa. He plonked himself into an armchair, flicking through until he found a comedy channel. 'Aww, great! Let's watch this!'

He laughed uproariously at all the right moments, turning to me so I would laugh right along with him. I tried to chuckle and make out that I was enjoying myself, but I couldn't take my eyes off the clock. It got to half ten, when normally he would suggest we turned in, but he didn't. He found a film that was just starting.

'This looks good,' he nodded at the screen. 'Do you want to finish this wine?' he proffered the bottle.

'No, no, it's okay, you finish it.' I clutched my wine glass to my chest.

'Don't be daft!' He got up and came over with the bottle. 'You've had such a good day, you should be celebrating!'

I couldn't detect anything. I let him fill my glass.

'Drink up,' he said, raising his own.

I drank, knowing he was watching. Moving my elbow against the cushion, I could feel the reassuring hard edges of the phone. Just knowing it was there, allowed me to breathe a little easier.

A sudden guffaw of laughter made me jump. 'Jeeze!… Oh Jeeze… Let me take that back… Just watch this…' He paused the film and began to rewind. 'I've been meaning to ask you…' he was still chuckling.

I looked at the screen.

'Those odd phone calls.' He settled back in the seat and scratched his neck. 'Do you still get them?' He rested his elbows on the arms of the chair, steepling his fingers under his chin.

The screen paused. He turned to face me. I couldn't speak.

'What's that?' My heart was scrambling.

He didn't move his eyes. 'You know, like you used to get. From Gould, that prisoner.'

My face was a mask. 'No. The guy was arrested.'

'Oh yeah, that's right.' He yawned widely and turned back to the programme.

'So they've all stopped then? No more weird messages.'

'No.' My mouth was filling with saliva and I had to keep swallowing.

'Actually, this film isn't your kind of thing, is it?' The remote was in his hand, his finger poised. He regarded me innocently.

I glanced at the screen, my mind whirling. I blinked. Stupid. 'Not really, no.'

'Fine. Feel free to go up to bed whenever you want. Don't wait for me.'

I sat there for a while nursing my wine and pretending to watch the screen but just couldn't take it in.

I kept sneaking a look at Paul's face. It was set hard and impassive. The reassuring rectangle of phone dug into my side. *You're not alone*, I told myself. *You're not alone, but you have to get out of here. Do something.*

I got up, sensing the danger in the air, but casually shaking out the cushion behind me so that he would have no need to, and sauntered over to him.

'Night, night.' I bent for a quick peck of a kiss. 'I might read for a while.'

'You do that.' He didn't attempt to meet my eyes.

I made my way quietly up the stairs, listening out the whole time, wondering what he was thinking, my brain going into overdrive.

I cleaned my teeth, got undressed and got into bed, hearing the muffled boom of the TV and wondering whether it was disguising any other noise. I tried reading but found I couldn't. In the end, I gave up and turned off the light, straining my ears into the darkness. He wasn't coming to bed. He was down there like a guard dog, guarding his territory. He'd hear if I walked across the floor. He'd hear if I moved.

I was trapped.

I lay there for what felt like hours. The booming of the TV changed to a thick silence. I shivered. Getting out of bed, I checked the time: 04:17. Pausing with one hand on the doorknob, I eased the catch and peered out. The landing lay bathed in silvery grey light. Softly, very softly, I tiptoed to the top of the stairs, craning carefully over the banister to listen. The moonlight had whitened each tread to dull bone. Nothing moved.

Slinking down the first three steps, I paused and listened again. I was terrified to go down there, scared of what he might read in my face, scared of what he might've found, but I had to know.

Padding down to the bottom, I stopped. There was no gleam of light from the living room, not a sound. The door sat open. It took several seconds for my eyes to adjust to the shapes and shadows but instinctively I knew he wasn't there. I patted for the light switch and everything sprang from monochrome to colour. I reached for the cushion; the reassuring weight of the phone was still there. *Thank God.* I checked the kitchen and the dining room, and then crept from room to silent room. No Paul. Looking out of the window, I realised his car had gone, and a huge wash of relief swept through me. I was alone. Whatever he was doing, wherever he was, I didn't care. He wasn't here, that was all that mattered.

Crawling back into bed I finally slept, dreamless and heavy for the next few hours, and then I was awake, my eyes flicking open with that sudden incomprehension that something wasn't right. I went to sit up. The gauzy rectangle of half-light from the window showed me nothing, and then I heard it: that steady draw and purr. I looked across. The bedcovers were hilly with his shape. I lay there, poised, not daring to move and then he opened an eye and looked at me.

'Morning, beautiful.'

My hand leapt to my chest.

He slid over onto his back, stretching and yawning noisily. 'You slept well, then.'

'Not really, no.'

He swivelled a look at me and laughed. 'God, I'd hate to see you sleeping badly then. I came up just after you and you were snoring your head off!' He chuckled. 'How are you feeling today?'

'I woke up…' I pulled the covers closer. 'You weren't there.'

'Eh? Well I don't know where I was, then.' He yawned again and smacked his lips.

'I went downstairs to check.'

'You must've been dreaming.'

'I don't think so.'

'Funny things, dreams.' He pushed the duvet back. 'Anyway, I've planned to see some clients this morning, and then I *must* attend a meeting I've been missing for the past few weeks. What will you be up to?' He pulled on a dressing gown and knotted it.

'Nothing. I've got to see Diane later on this afternoon but I'll cook dinner tonight if you like.'

'That'd be nice,' he smiled. 'I'll jump in the shower and get going.'

–

I waited until I could hear the patter and swoosh of water before I went downstairs and unzipped the phone from its hiding place. I rang Moire. She answered straight away.

'Lucy? You okay?' There was a note of panic in her voice.

'Look, I'm sorry for yesterday. I'm sorry for walking out on you like that, it's just that… Well, I totally understand how angry you must feel. Your sister. I can't imagine what—' I broke off.

There was a dull pause. 'You believe his version of events.'

'There's something not right with him. I know that. But what you're telling me is so… I mean—'

'Meet me again.'

'I'm sorry, Moire, I really don't see—'

'Just meet me once more. There are things I haven't told you. After that you never have to contact me again if you don't want to. I will leave you alone. If you want to tell the police about me, go ahead. I have nothing to lose. My whole life is lost anyway. Cait and the girls were the only things I had left and he's already taken them—' Her voice quivered but then she gathered herself. 'I know you have questions about Paul. Cait did, too. I know you want answers and you can't find them. You know there's something not right, but you don't know what it is.'

I stared at the ceiling, listening for the shower running. I heard the reassuring drumming, and then it stopped.

'I have to go.'

'The same café. Two o'clock. I will be there. If you don't want to come and listen to what I have to say, I understand.'

And then the phone went dead.

I heard Paul walking about upstairs. I went into the kitchen and clattered about, putting plates and knives and forks away and sorting out the breakfast things. My mind was in turmoil. He appeared in the doorway with a sheaf of papers in his hand, looking round as though he'd lost something.

'Have you seen my briefcase?' He cast about the room.

'In the hallway on the floor?' I said helpfully. Tutting, he went back into the hall and I followed him. 'Nope?... Umm, try the office.'

He disappeared up the stairs and I turned to go back into the kitchen, when something caught my eye. The cushion, which I'd left plumped on the chair, was lying flat on the seat. Eyes darting, I grabbed at it, patting it frantically, and then scrabbled to search the seat beneath.

'Is this yours, by the way?'

I whirled round. Paul was standing in the doorway. He smiled at my expression. 'I found it on the floor by your chair.' He dangled the phone between forefinger and thumb. 'It looks like one of your old ones... Is it?' He tossed it in the air and I caught it.

'We'll make a rugby player of you, yet,' he grinned. 'I'd best get going or I shall be really late for this meeting. See you later. I'll ring you.' He came over, kissed me briefly and then headed out of the door.

I stood, stunned, watching through the window as he strode down the path. There wasn't even a backward glance as he slid into the driver's seat, reversed easily around my car, and onto the main road. I looked down at the phone, so innocuous in my palm, and pressed the button to bring it to life. All Moire's texts were there, as were mine, on full display. My insides quailed at the thought. I imagined him standing in this room reading all the exchanges between us – and the dreadful realisation dawned: he'd known exactly where I was yesterday. He knew I was meeting Moire yet he kept up the pretence. Why? And now he'd openly declared his hand. And then something worse gripped me: if he'd looked at the phone, he'd also know that I'd made a phone call to Moire this morning.

Fear thrummed through me. The net had become a wire noose, and it was tightening.

I rang her.

'He knows,' I said.

'About the phone?' There was a pause. 'Does he know we're meeting today?'

'He can't know when, he just knows who... I'm so sorry Moire, I didn't—'

'Don't be sorry. Has he hurt you?'

'No, no. Nothing like that. He's being very calm, very ordinary.'

'If you're going to act, you need to do it now. You know that, don't you?'

I couldn't think straight.

'Do you know what his plans are?'

'Kind of. He's seeing clients this morning, then he has to be in the office for a meeting this afternoon.'

'Make sure that's the truth. Ring his office. Pretend that you're one of the people he's scheduled to see this morning. You'll be able to gauge what time the meeting is. Then ring again this afternoon to make sure he's attending. Once you're sure, we'll meet then. Okay?'

'Okay.'

'I'll see you later... And don't worry. You've got me on your side now.'

And then she was gone.

–

Don't worry? Jesus Christ. I was as scared as hell making the calls but I did as she said. A woman in the office said she was sorry but that Mr Webb was in a meeting and would be unavailable until at least three o'clock, but if I wanted to leave a message she would make sure he got it.

I rang Moire back. We were on.

I parked off the main road this time and slunk into the café although I knew there was no need: we were the only two people in there. She was waiting for me at the same table and had already bought the coffees. She looked self-assured and less nervous. Her hair was washed and tied back and her face was scrubbed into shiny paleness.

I sat down. I was the nervous one this time.

'I'm just going to tell you what Caitlin told me,' she began. 'Whether you believe what I'm going to tell you is up to you.' She folded her hands around her cup, hesitating. 'By the time she planned to leave him, she'd begun to hate him.' Her voice was soft and she kept her eyes lowered. 'She knew this last pregnancy would trap her there forever. She was exhausted by his continual demands for reassurance, the endless questioning over imaginary men he thought she was sleeping with. She couldn't stand the way he micro-managed her every move. She hated what he'd become: an obsessive, controlling, insecure toddler in the body of a dangerous, manipulative, violent and aggressive man.'

'So she never had an affair while they were together?' I suddenly found my voice.

'She never had an affair, full stop.'

I listened as she told me how they had met and Paul's immediate declarations of love: how her family – their mother – had counselled her to be cautious. Paul didn't like the implied criticism. He made her keep choosing between her family and him; she was constantly torn, there were endless arguments. She was exhausted by it all, which played right into his hands. Each child made the situation more difficult; the control became more subtle, more difficult to argue, and therefore more insidious.

'He came across as very reasonable,' Moire said. 'He kept telling her "We're a little team now... Our own special little unit. We're your new family. We're your priority".'

Roisin's birth, she explained, doubled his insecurity; his attention moved to personal attack. He didn't like Caitlin's hair, her make-up, her clothes, the way she spoke, the way she ate, her untidiness, the way she cared for the kids. Caitlin became very depressed and needed her family, Moire in particular. So Paul began to manufacture disagreements: insisting that Moire had insulted him, criticised him and tried to cause trouble.

'He would never have done any of this if my father had still been alive.' Moire's eyes glittered. 'He thought, as women, we were all fair game.'

I stayed silent the whole time she was talking, listening to the calm, quiet lilt of her voice, unemotional until the end when she described how things began to really unravel.

'Caitlin thought she was going mad, I mean, really, seriously. Totally weird things were happening in the house. Paul was telling people that her depression was returning, that she couldn't cope.'

'What kind of things?'

'He'd try to convince her that conversations happened that she said didn't happen. He played these little mind-games with her: inconsequential stuff. He'd tell her he liked something and then claim he hated it; he'd say they should visit someplace and then argue he had never wanted to go there. One Christmas he picked out an expensive scarf he wanted as a present, but when he unwrapped it, he laughed and told her to keep it for herself as they clearly had very different tastes. It was all so bizarre.'

'Was it a red scarf?' I stared at the table.

'Yes!' she looked surprised. 'How did you know?'

'He still carries it around. Go on.'

'So it started like that, with just the odd thing, but became more and more frequent. Cait constantly questioned herself. When she told me about these instances, I thought it was peculiar and privately, I questioned it too, who wouldn't?' She made a helpless gesture.

'It was anything and everything. She would never know where she was with him. It was unrelenting: day after day, like a dripping tap, sometimes nice, sometimes not, sometimes loving, sometimes cruel. Wearing her down bit by bit.'

'So how did she finally decide to leave?'

'She'd mentioned it to me loads of times, but I think it was after Roisin was born. He was obsessed that she wasn't his. Cait said he would stand over Rosie's cot staring down at her with a look of pure hatred on his face. He wouldn't let Cait nurse her – said that she had to be bottle fed. He barred the door to the nursery when Rosie cried at night. Then, one day, he told her he'd 'found out' who Rosie's real father was. Some guy in the village. He was obsessed that she was going to leave. What happened in the end was his last bid for absolute control. He'd told her that if he couldn't have her, then he would make sure that no one else could.'

She halted, the words clearly opening old wounds.

She closed her eyes momentarily. The lashes fluttered gently and then her gaze rested on mine.

'So he made it look as though she'd attacked him: he stabbed himself – here,' she put her hand on her side, 'but they found him just in time. Cait was naked. She was—'

'Yes, you told me—' I was aware of my breath sitting high in my chest. I saw the bath with the water running crimson. I saw her lifeless body, her hair floating out around her like Ophelia in her pool, the children folded like petals into her sides, and her face – white against the colour; the darkening lips, the mouth just paused and her lost eyes gazing past to somewhere very far away.

I began to feel light-headed. I drank my coffee quickly. I thought about McAndrew, about Diane, about the weight of the system that Paul had at his fingertips.

'That red scarf? That's his guilt. You know he's manipulated everything don't you? From the very beginning.' She picked up her own cup and paused. 'I was watching his flat the day he smashed it up.'

'What?'

'He smashed his own flat and moved into yours.'

An image of his jacket hanging on the chair and the little souvenir instantly came back.

'What do you want from me?' I blurted suddenly.

My heart was like an engine. I didn't know who I was more afraid of: her, Paul, or what I was hearing.

'I need a confession Lucy...' She looked down for a second. 'I need to hear it. It's a huge thing to ask, I know. But I'm asking you to do it – For me, for you... And for Caitlin and the children.'

'A confession?'

'And when he tells you what he did, that's your part done, you can walk away.' She sat back in the chair.

'I don't understand – how will I walk away? I don't get it.' That didn't make sense. 'You'll go to the police. I won't be walking away. I'll be the main witness. I won't be safe. What you're suggesting is madness!'

'I don't think you understand,' she said softly. 'I don't want him arrested, Lucy. I want him dead.'

I had stood up without realising.

'I'm sorry. I can't do this. I'm leaving.'

'Of course you are.' Her hands lay loosely linked on the table, still cradling her cup. 'I don't suppose I will ever see you again.'

She said it so matter-of-factly that, in some strange way, I felt as though I had let her down and betrayed her somehow.

'Goodbye, then,' she looked up briefly and smiled. 'Take very good care of yourself.'

'Thank you.' I said. 'But you must realise—'

But she held up a hand. 'Don't. The past isn't your drama. I just hope it never is.'

The barb hit hard. No more. I turned and walked to the door and went to yank it open but then stopped in horror. Paul's car was parked a way up the street. I stepped back.

'What's the matter?' I heard her get up behind me.

'It's him,' I stumbled away. 'It's Paul. That's his car. He must've followed me.'

'Oh Jesus.' I caught the look on her face. She'd frozen. 'He's coming over.'

He was attempting to cross the road, waiting for the traffic to pass.

'This way!' She hissed, beckoning. 'Quickly!'

I hurried after her to the rear of the café.

'Down past the toilets is a door. It's usually unlocked. I think it goes out into the yard,' she whispered. 'There's a back entrance onto the street. I'll keep the waitress talking. Make out you're going to the loo.'

I darted down the passageway and I heard Moire start up a conversation with the girl behind the counter. The passage descended into gloom. I could just make out a fridge and a mop and bucket. There was a thin plywood door to my right and on my left was a deeper blackness with a beading of white light. I quickly patted around to find the door handle, my fingers scrabbling but then suddenly I found it and wrenched it open. The gust of fresh air hit me and I stumbled blindly into the yard and ran to the gate, shunting the bolt back and slipping into the street where I spotted my car. I had never been so grateful to see it sitting there. It instantly sprang into life, my reflexes tuned and responsive. *I had to get home before Paul*, that's all I kept thinking. I had to get out of there. I wouldn't need much: a bag with a few things: papers, I.D.

documents, debit and credit cards – I made a mental list of what I needed and where in the house it was all located.

All the way I repeatedly checked my mirror, expecting to see Paul's car bearing down on me. I took the obvious and fastest route, terrified that I was going to see him rounding some corner and that he would beat me to it. Bumping the car onto the drive, I ran to the front door. The house was silent as I flew up the stairs to the bedroom, pulled a bag from the top of the wardrobe and began shoving things into it – then went into the office and straight to the safe. Punching in the code, I turned the key and the door swung open. My passport was there alongside a file full of documents. Grabbing both of them, I began to quickly leaf through the pile, flicking in desperation from one bit of paper to another. Then the realisation dawned. These weren't my documents, they were Caitlin's: her passport, her birth certificate... Her death—I stopped. Her death certificate. '*Exsanguination*,' leapt off the paper. She bled to death. I saw the children's names, but couldn't bring myself to look – letting the papers fall to the floor, pulling out all of Paul's stuff, hunting and rifling... But all the time knowing, *knowing* my documents weren't there.

The air rasped dryly at the back of my throat as I ran back down the stairs to my handbag, tugging it open and grappling for my purse. It felt weirdly light in my hands and I knew before I opened it – My bank cards were gone. There was a sudden gravelly scrape on the doorstep, a shadow bobbed for a moment and then the sound of a key in the door. I froze.

'Oh hello!' he said brightly. 'What are you doing? Just coming in or just going out?'

'You've taken my cards.'

'Eh?' he frowned. 'What cards?'

'My bank cards. You must've taken them. You've taken my passport and birth certificate. You've taken everything.'

Paul reached out to touch me but I snatched my hand away. 'Lucy,' he said gently. 'Lucy, Lucy. I haven't taken anything. Come on. Calm down.'

'They're not here. Where are they?' My voice shook with fear and fury.

'Please Luce, stop this. There's no need. They're all there, I'm sure. Let me help you find them.' He walked past me and up the stairs. I followed. He went into the office and knelt amongst the crackling papers on the floor, reaching into the safe and pulling out a folder I hadn't seen before.

'Here.' He half turned and held it out to me.

I took it, disbelieving, and gingerly opened the flap. Inside was my passport and all my papers.

'There,' he said, getting up stiffly. 'Happy now?' He walked quickly out of the room and went down the stairs. I checked the folder in my hands. A tiny residue of something sticky adhered to the back. I looked up and went after him. 'Where are you going?'

He was standing in the hallway with my purse in his hands. 'What are these then?' He had a fan of credit cards in his fingers. I looked at his face and back at the cards. He shook his head, shoving them back and into my handbag.

'Is it happening again, Lucy?'

Of course I hadn't opened my purse when I met Moire... *Had I?* I tried to think.

My phone began to ring. I let it. It trilled on and on from the depths of my bag, then stopped, as Paul's started. Without taking his eyes from me, he pulled it out.

'Hello?' He paused, still staring straight at me. 'Yes, yes she is.'

My heart contracted at the thought of Moire.

'What time was the appointment?'

I closed my eyes.

'It's okay Diane. I'll bring her now.'

—

This time he came in with me. Something passed between them as we walked in which made me think that he'd spoken to her very recently.

I scanned her face for clues.

'So how have you been feeling this last week?' She tipped her head on one side like a baby bird.

I tried to smile. 'Good.' I said. 'Fine. I even met a friend for coffee.' My gaze stayed pointedly with Diane. 'I enjoyed chatting to her.'

Paul shifted forward in his seat, resting his elbows on his knees. 'This friend she's referring to is the woman I've been telling you about.' He bit his lip. 'The one who's been in prison.'

Something inside me folded. I became aware that Diane was studying me.

'Were you aware of this, Lucy?'

'No. I wasn't. Are you sure?' I blurted. 'You know she's Caitlin's sister, don't you?' I turned to Diane. 'Caitlin is, *was*, Paul's partner and the mother of his children. She didn't leave him, like he told me. She died, she was—'

'I know,' said Diane. She looked at Paul. 'You haven't told her then?'

Paul looked down at the floor, hanging his head. I saw him swallow. 'No... No I haven't. I... I didn't tell her.'

He paused. 'Lucy, the truth is…' he began falteringly. His head snapped up suddenly and he looked straight at me. 'The truth is, Caitlin killed herself.'

I observed him, watching for some tic, some flinch. 'Did she?' I said coolly.

He nodded and swallowed again. 'She killed the children and then killed herself.'

I could hear my own breath shaking as it left my body. 'And why would she do such a thing?' I could feel Diane's eyes assessing my every movement.

'It was Moire.'

I stared at him.

'Cait had been seriously depressed after Rosie was born, agoraphobic, scared of everything, and she turned to her sister Moire.' He glanced at Diane who nodded for him to go on. 'Moire had always been jealous of Caitlin, ever since they were kids.' His eyes looked hollow. 'Moire wanted our kids and she wanted me. She wanted what Cait had…' He turned his gaze to me and then to Diane.

'You need to tell her the truth,' she said.

His eyes bored into mine. 'She and I had an affair.'

'What?'

'Yes, I know, I know…' His voice shook as he fought back the emotion.

'Moire saw Cait's death as a new beginning… *Christ!*' He turned his face away so no one could see the tears. 'I was weak, I was young and I was incredibly stupid. It only happened once, but in her head it was something else… Some kind of macabre romance I think. Letters, emails, phone calls. I was bombarded. You saw the rose she left—'

I recoiled.

'It became too bizarre for words. She was eventually convicted of stalking and harassment. I should've realised you would be a way to get to me. It hasn't stopped, even now. I'm building another case against her. She's repeatedly contravened the injunction. My life has not been my own.' His breath shuddered as he exhaled and he pressed his fingertips into his eye sockets. The blue, worm-like veins on the backs of his hands stood out.

'And you weren't aware Moire had been in prison, Lucy?' Diane turned to me.

The seconds dragged. 'No.'

'So what *has* she told you?' Paul peeped at me from between his fingers. All eyes were on me. What *had* she told me? What *was* the truth?

'She believes you murdered Caitlin and the children and she wanted me to get you to confess.'

Paul went very still. 'And what did you say to her?'

'I told her it was madness and I wouldn't do it.'

I saw his eyes narrow and widen as he weighed up whether to believe me.

'I left her sitting alone in the café the first time I met her,' I jabbered. 'And the second time I told her I was breaking off all contact.'

'So you've seen this woman on your own then?' Diane interjected.

I nodded.

'So you've been presented with a range of truth and delusional thinking and you've worked through what you believe to be true and come through the other side. Is that right?'

I nodded again.

'Well,' she said. 'That actually sounds very positive to me, Lucy. You have done all that without the active support of therapists or counsellors or indeed your husband, and yet you've come to a positive conclusion yourself. I think you should be congratulated for that.'

'So do I,' said Paul putting his hand on my knee. 'Thank you… Thank you for believing in me.' He leaned over and kissed me on the cheek. He left a trail of saliva.

'But you're still having problems trusting Paul?' said Diane.

I was very aware of the word 'still' even though I'd never discussed with her how I felt.

I made a little noise of assent.

'I think it's associated with the general anxiety,' Paul put in. 'Lucy misreads situations.' He squeezed my knee and slid me a gentle sideways look. 'She misunderstands conversations and even simple exchanges of information. She sees criticism where there isn't any: imagines that I'm slighting her. She misremembers things we've spoken about, believes that I'm out to get her, thinks I've hidden things from her, thinks I'm trying to control her.' He shook his head. 'Nothing could be further from the truth.'

'Is this right?' Diane looked concerned.

'Yes… Well, no. It is, but—' I saw their eyes meet.

Diane placed the flat of her hand on the notebook in her lap. 'Perhaps we should think about offering you these support sessions for a little while longer yet. Maybe discharging you now is a bit soon Lucy.' She made that slow, patronising nod that I hated so much.

'No!' I said, a little too sharply and they both looked at me. 'No… I mean I'm fine. I'm doing really well…' I broke off.

'No one's saying that you're not.' She attempted to be soothing. 'We're just saying you need a bit more support for a bit longer. Do you agree with that assessment, Paul?'

Paul nodded. 'That's exactly right. But of course, you're entitled to feel differently, Luce. This is about working out what's best for you. No one's trying to force you to do anything.'

I looked from one to the other and said nothing. I mimicked her slow nod. 'Of course,' I said. 'Of course.'

Diane began to speak. I don't know what about. It was as though some surreal whirlwind had taken over: everything around me was moving very fast. Their voices came to me loud and then soft. They couldn't touch me; it was keeping them out, but it was also keeping me in, locked in a place I didn't want to be.

–

'Emma's just sent me a message. She says you're not answering her calls.' Paul stood in front of me holding his phone. If this was another test, then I was adamant I was going to pass it.

'Talk to her for me, would you?' I blinked up at him. 'Explain I'm not feeling so well. I'll speak to her another time.'

It had been two weeks since I'd had any contact with her.

'Only if you're sure?'

'Perfectly sure.'

I could tell he was pleased and I felt a small shiver of victory.

He went to work every day and I was there when he left. He came back and I was there when he returned. I suggested that we went shopping together, cooked together, cleaned the house together. I began to behave as I knew he wanted me to. I was compliant, but not too compliant, I made jokes that weren't funnier than his, I chatted about things that I knew would interest him but I barely listened to his answers.

I was a nodding doll on the outside, but inside I was angry, raging. There was a force bubbling away in me that was difficult to contain, but I had to, for now. It had to stay all tucked away like a gift to myself: a present I'd wrapped up carefully and put away in a drawer. It was the fire that kept me going.

This time, *this* time, he had to believe he had total control. He didn't have to guard or monitor me anymore. I was his: absolutely, completely, mind and body. He had to believe he had me exactly where he wanted me – and for that to happen I would make the ultimate sacrifice.

One night in bed I, made the decision. I steeled myself, turning over to face him, and put my hand on his thigh. His eyes batted sleepily.

'Paul,' I whispered. His skin was alien under my hand. My fingers touched the coarseness of the hair and I felt a gag of nausea. Swallowing, I moved closer and put my lips to his. It was wrong, appallingly wrong: my throat rebelled, every inch of my body cried out with the abomination, but I moved my mouth in the way I knew I was supposed to move it, heaving as his tongue parted my teeth. He shifted his weight, using his knee to push me onto my back. My whole body was screaming but I held it in, the tension keeping my legs straight, my hands poised against his shoulders as if to push him off at any moment.

'Do you want this?' he said softly into my ear.

I didn't think I could speak. I nodded silently, feeling a tear leak down my temple and cluck gently into my ear. No, I didn't want this, but I wanted to escape from this more. I wanted freedom, and this was what I had to do to get it.

'I want this,' I said. 'More than anything.'

Afterwards, he lay on his back staring at the ceiling. He seemed relaxed and happy. He had his arm around me and I lay stiffly with my head on his chest, listening to the steady thrub of his heart. So strong. So powerful. It was never stopping; not unless someone stopped it. I tried not to think about what had just happened.

I pushed it out of my mind.

'Thank you for coming back to me.' He hugged me closer. I tucked my resting hand under my face, keeping my skin away from his. I pretended to stretch and turn over. He immediately turned with me, spooning himself around me. I curled into a ball, the violent urge to extricate myself almost unbearable.

He kissed the back of my neck and I felt the soft wetness turning cold. I shivered and he held me even closer. Every pore shrieked. I closed my eyes and listened to his breathing: the regularity of the tempo, until I heard its soft *tock-tock* and felt the weight of him slipping heavily against me. It was my moment.

Slowly, I moved his arm from around my waist and laid it on his thigh. His breath changed imperceptibly and I caught my own, letting it hang there until I could peel myself away, inching in tiny increments to the edge of the bed. He snorted and I jumped as, with a huge waft of the covers, he turned over and began to snore.

I almost fell off the mattress, half slipping onto my hands and knees, feeling the welcoming prickle of the carpet and crawling on all fours until I found my heap of clothes on the floor. Gathering them up, I winkled open the door and slipped quietly onto the landing. Keeping my bundle close, I half shuffled, half scooted down the stairs and paused at the bottom to pull on what I had: knickers, jeans, bra, but no jumper. *Shit!* It was freezing! I cast about, desperate, and then remembered that there was an old coat I'd used for gardening hanging in the back lobby. Finding my handbag, I scrabbled about in the bottom, looking for my car keys. They weren't there. Swishing around frantically, I saw Paul's lying on the table and grabbed them up, slipping out into the night.

The darkness was sharp with November cold. A slight dusting of frost sparkled prettily revealing the silver outline of his car. I slid quickly into the driver's seat and I took a glance up at the bedroom window. It stayed blank and still. Closing my eyes, I turned the key, praying that the car would start. The engine roared into life, sending a whole scatter of birds in the beech tree into a frightened squawking. I didn't have time to worry. Easing the car into reverse, I backed off the drive, and without another look, drove calmly away.

The streets and roads were empty. His car was bigger and more powerful than mine and I manoeuvred it easily, taking in all the signs that would lead me to the motorway and beyond. I didn't feel scared this time. This time I had done it. I had absolutely done it. A tickle of excitement shivered as the streetlights whizzed past. I glanced at my speed; there was no need to get stopped, not when I'd done so well; not now I'd got away. *I'd walked out of my life.*

I could finally breathe. The pressure had gone, the grinding weight had lifted. I wound the window down. *I've done it*, I said to the night. *I've actually done it.* The bitter air made me gasp with delight. I let it rummage through my hair, whipping strands across my face, pummeling my skin to a smarting, clean, freshness. I closed my eyes and then opened them. The black road tunnelled in front of me. I drove into it like a soothing blanket, watching the telegraph poles flashing by as they marked out the distance: the space I was putting between me and him. I had won. His darkness hadn't overwhelmed me... And then I thought of the children, of Caitlin. How he had taken their lives, piece by piece, suffocating them until his shadow had finally snuffed them out. I looked into the mirror. Caitlin's face loomed grey and quiet, sitting there somewhere in the back. I peered round: the children were there too, asleep, leaning across her lap, one either side. I watched the flickering shadows from the street lamps oscillating across her face, *on, off, on, off*, and then I became aware of another light: bright and maddening, joining in. Blue. Brilliant blue light. I jammed my foot down as hard as I could and the car obliged, boosting up to another level, skimming and flying, the violent thrumming drum of air from the open window battering my face.

My heart raced with the speed: *I'm not going back, I'm not going back, I'm not going back*. And then something began to fail, the car began to lose speed, no matter how much I stamped and begged the accelerator it wouldn't give me what I needed. The flashing lights got closer, filling the mirrors: the blue blinding roar of them, the wailing sound, filled the car as it began to roll and stall to a halt.

I sat silently, staring straight ahead, listening to the slam of the car doors, the twittering radios as the dark shapes came towards me. There was the gritty sound of feet on tarmac and I was forced to look round at the figure that was standing there.

'I can't stay,' I said craning up into the face that was peering down at me. 'I have to go. Please, don't keep me long. All I want to do is get away. I can't stay here.'

'We won't keep you any longer than we need to.' The policeman reached in and patted me on the wrist. 'Only until you're better.'

I blinked and when I looked back up at the face, it wasn't a policeman. I looked harder. It wasn't a policeman at all.

'What kind of officer are you?' I said.

'The nice sort,' said the face.

I looked back to the passenger side. I wasn't in Paul's car and it wasn't dark.

I looked at the hand on my wrist and then at the chair arm where my own hand was resting. There was no car, no streetlights, no children, no Caitlin. There was a nurse in a different sort of uniform than the kind I'd seen before.

'Who are you?' I said.

'I'm the charge nurse. Now you just sit there and relax.'

And then I remembered. I remembered what he'd done. My clothes, the car keys, his car. Why hadn't I realised there would be no petrol? It was all very clever. I knew no one would ever believe my story so I didn't try to tell it, there really was no point. I'd given Paul everything: my mind and my body but I'd never given him my spirit. Now he thought he had that too. I'd tried, I'd failed.

I sat in that chair and 'relaxed' as I was told to, and while I was sitting and watching, I realised something vital. All this time I'd been playing by his rules. I'd exhausted myself trying to out-think and out-manoeuvre him. And there, I knew, lay my mistake. The days of playing by someone else's rules were over. Now I was going to make up my own.

Chapter Fourteen

The days and weeks moved with the big black hands of the clock on the wall. The ward was bright with Christmas decorations put up far too early. Tinsel drifted lazily in the waft of sub-Sahara temperatures. There were curtains pinned with jolly Father Christmases that hid the open mouths of any distress behind them. I saw the mouths and bodies being wheeled off to somewhere that wasn't Santa's Grotto.

I wasn't going to be one of them.

Emma didn't visit. Paul didn't visit. I knew he'd spoken to them though; I knew the *'you need no distractions from outside'* were his words, not theirs. I didn't argue or ask why. Being a patient in a psychiatric hospital was really no different to being a prisoner in a prison. The clever ones not only didn't argue or ask questions, the clever ones went one step further. They were the ones that no one ever noticed. They were the ones no one really *saw*. Compliance, I realised, was only part of it. The key to it all was the one thing I'd been trying to avoid all this time.

You had to become invisible.

Every morning, including Saturdays and Sundays, we sat in our circles with our cod psychologist leaders and we listened to their quiet judgements as they encouraged us to 'find our true selves' as though we'd dropped them somewhere and not realised. But I knew the drill. This bit was easy.

'As I said, it's all a blank, really.' I looked away through the barred window at the slats of sky: a gauzy haze on a solid white nothingness – the way the drugs make you feel... Until you learn how not to swallow them.

The other women shuffled uneasily in the stifling, cranked-up central heating, designed to make us sleepy. The fluorescent overhead light buzzed. I noticed that the window glass reflected the institution clock face in reverse. Its black hands crept forward a little then dropped back.

'One detail.' I was aware that Trevor Jones, the one in charge, was staring intently at me. 'There must be something you remember?'

'Anyone else?' Geoff cut in. Geoff was the charge nurse. He sounded nervous. 'How about you, Melissa?'

'No,' said Trevor. 'Hang on. Let's stay with Lucy for a moment.'

My eyes slid from the window. His gaze shifted over me, the camera shutter lens snapping: *click*: face, *click*: breasts: *click:* legs. *He thinks he has me.*

Someone coughed and broke the spell.

'I— I lost my children.' Melissa said suddenly. The group attention wavered and Trevor frowned. 'The police had gone into my flat, I'd only been gone ten minutes, twenty at the most—' She stopped as her voice cracked.

'They took them.' Her bitten ochre fingers sawed relentlessly, desperate for a smoke. I heard the words but felt nothing. I was aware of Trevor's eyes briefly flitting from her to me and back again.

'I found blood in the cot – on the blankets. I don't know what happened.'

Her mouth was lined with practised pain. Her voice was becoming part of the walls and the floor, a noise trembling over the stacked chairs in the corner.

'My husband said… My husband told me…'

There was the bang of a door on the unit and someone shouted an obscenity. Trevor leaned in, nodding towards Melissa in the way he'd been taught to do. His job was to show he could connect, but without really connecting at all. He began to speak at length about how there are consequences for our actions, and how, if we applied some thought, we might achieve a different outcome. He showed he had no idea about Melissa, who she was, or what her life was like at all.

I looked down, noticing a stray hair clinging to the thigh of my tracksuit and I picked it off, letting it fall, watching it twist in the artificial light. Trevor couldn't keep his eyes off me. I knew what he wanted. I was vulnerable. He had all the power. I was a woman in an institution. I'm a woman, full-stop: that makes us all fair game, just like Moire said.

His eyes tracked over Melissa. *Tell us what you did*, I could feel his itching. *Every inch. Show me your vulnerability and I can use it against you.* In suits or out of them, his kind were all the same – wanting to get inside: push and force their way in. Oh yes, I knew all about men like Trevor didn't I?

Melissa closed her eyes briefly and nodded in acceptance. He wrote something on his notepad. I saw her take it in. *Tell us what to think and we'll think it. Tell us what to do and we'll do it.* Back-of-a-crisp-bag psychologists with the power to make your time easy or hard. Be grateful.

'I hadn't thought of it like that,' said Melissa. 'Thank you.'

Precisely.

Geoff smiled and glanced at the clock. 'Shall we leave it there, Trev?' It was Sunday, I could see he wanted to get off. He looked for confirmation.

Trevor pushed his chair back from the circle although there was no need. 'Good idea.' He looked at his watch. 'I've got to see someone on the unit before lunch anyway. I'll take the girls back.'

I stood, looking round at the women who couldn't look less like 'girls' if they tried: pale, shabby creatures with greasy hair and eyes like pack dogs. There were loud voices in the corridor outside that rose and fell. Melissa caught my eye but then looked away. Maybe she thought I was a plant. I knew I didn't look anything like the others. Paranoia was the one thing that bound us. We trusted no one, we didn't even trust ourselves: whatever that was. Whoever we had been in the past, we certainly weren't anymore. The drugs took care of that.

We walked like the prisoners we were, scuffing our way back to the unit. Trevor unlocked the door and that smell hit me again: it was in the walls and floors; it came out of our pores. We smelled of surrender.

–

Melissa walked by my side; she was prettier than average, blonde. In her old life she was the kind of woman who would have looked after herself. She was the kind of woman who appeared at any board meeting in any office in the country. She and I were from the same mould, and now look at us.

'Be careful, they all work for him,' she muttered, her eyes flitting nervously: left to right.

I glanced enquiringly at Trevor, who was locking the meeting room door.

'No, not him,' she hissed. 'Him. My husband. He pays them all. They can't go against anything he says, even if they want to. He talks through people on the TV and the radio. He makes things happen. He made things happen to the children. It wasn't me who did those things.'

I glanced down at the mottled marble lino and the flat roll of my plimsolls as they thrust the floor away beneath the soles of my feet. I was walking but going nowhere.

We reached Melissa's room and I took a look inside. It was neat and ordered. There were books on a bookshelf: Chagall and Monet, and art print postcards on a cork board.

'I went to university, you know.' She trailed a finger down the pictures. 'I had a job, I had a life, but it makes no difference.' Her hand dropped. 'Every avenue I take, every way I turn, every therapy programme or drug trial – whatever it is, I just keep coming back to places like this. Maybe this is where I'm supposed to be...' She tipped her head and regarded me. 'How about you?'

'The police picked me up. He'd reported the car stolen.' I was aware how deadpan my voice sounded, how matter-of-fact. 'He told them I'd tried to kill myself in a car once before, but that wasn't true.'

'And now you're here.'

'And now I'm here.'

She went and sat down abruptly on the bed and gazed out of the barred window into the grounds. The winter trees stood stark against the white sky. 'I was a mother, now I'm not even that anymore. I used to have people around me: work, friends, neighbours. They gave me an idea of who, and what, I was. At work I was a manager;

to my friends I was a nice person and a good cook; to my neighbours I was someone who would always help them out. Now they've all gone,' she said wistfully. 'Maybe I was always just a reflection of other people. When I met Charlie, it was easy for him to tell me who I was.' She turned and looked at me. 'I wasn't a whole person and he filled the gaps. I didn't have to think anymore.'

She knew. In all her madness, she knew her own reality.

'But *you're* not like that, are you?'

'Aren't I?' I was vaguely surprised.

'You're solid, you're yourself, and you're still fighting. I can see it.'

My eyes twitched warily. She got up and went to the notice board and pulled off a Chagall postcard of a floating bride. I could tell by the way it fell into her hand, this wasn't an ordinary postcard. She flipped it over. 'See?' she said. On the back was a very tiny, very thin phone.

'Oh my God!' I watched her peel it off and glance at the door before handing it to me. 'I've never seen one like that!'

'I know,' she smiled a little. 'Neither have the staff.'

Our fingers brushed briefly and she paused. 'Is there one person out there who believes in you? All you need is one. Get out of here, Lucy. I can't, but you can.'

I briefly thought about Emma. Who was Emma? She could have been someone I'd known a very long time ago.

'Come on ladies, dinner is served!' A voice behind made us both jump. We looked round. Geoff hung on the door frame before lurching off. 'Chop, chop,' he called to a group walking past.

I caught her eye and nodded briefly. 'Thank you,' I said.

'Thank yourself.'

She turned away to the window and I walked back down the corridor. There was a nauseating smell of burnt fat in the air. It might've been curry, you could never tell. Slipping the phone into my pocket, I walked into the dining room.

The tables were laid out in groups of six and eight, each with a pile of pale poppadoms balanced precariously in the middle. I chose an empty table in the centre of the room, knowing that the others preferred to be somewhere near the walls for safety. There were globules of yellow fat pooling onto the tablecloth.

I already had an idea of what I was going to do. It was the thing I'd learned very early on from dealing with prisoners. Know the staff. Watch their habits. Most staff are lazy: the easiest route, the least work. I knew the staff that were on today. They wouldn't have a clue.

Each table went up one at a time to the hotplate. I went up alone.

'This looks lovely.' I gave the caterer behind the counter a huge smile and the ladle dipped twice to give me my extra helping.

'You could do with feeding up,' he said with a grin.

I took my plate back to the table, and slowly began to work my way through it, one determined forkful after another, reaching across the table for a poppadom and pocketing the salt cellar on the way back.

'The last supper,' I murmured. No one heard me, no one was listening. None of the staff took any notice, and why would they? They never really listened. Their weakness was my strength.

Melissa's words were in my head as I felt for the press of the tiny phone in my pocket.

Sweeping a surreptitious glance around, I sauntered back to my room, opening the small plywood wardrobe behind my door as though I was looking for something amongst the sad limp clothes hanging there. I glanced back over my shoulder. I could see the goings-on through the glass observation pane but I knew from here, they couldn't see me.

I rang Moire. She answered straight away.

'Don't speak, just listen,' I said. 'I'm going into hospital tonight... I can't say when, but I'll be there. Can you help me?'

'What?' she panicked. 'What's happened? What hospital? Are you okay?'

'More than okay,' I took a breath. 'I just need your help.' I said. 'I'm getting out.'

–

I knew who would be on duty that evening. I'd taken a quick look at the Sunday rota in the office so I knew which charge nurse was on, plus today meant fewer agency staff – all paid next to nothing and barely supervised. The timing was perfect.

I waited until just gone six and poured the salt into a glass of water and drank it straight off. My stomach immediately objected. Quickly making my way to the main office, I tapped tentatively on the door.

'Yes?' the nurse was sitting at the desk writing. He didn't bother to look up.

'I don't feel very well. I've got terrible stomach pains and diarrhoea.' I bent over slightly and clutched at the door frame.

'Go and lie down, it'll get better by itself. It'll be just a bug or something.'

He waved his pen at me dismissively, and so I immediately began to retch, concentrating on the thought of
oozing fat and chicken curry all coming up, willing my
stomach to heave the whole lot out. He leapt from his seat
and backed away as a stream of vomit hit the floor.

'Sweet Jesus!!'

'I can't cope with the pain!' I groaned, almost sinking
to my knees.

'I'm scared for the baby!' I moaned breathlessly.

'Baby? What baby?' He pressed himself against the wall
in shock.

'I'm pregnant,' I whimpered. 'Don't let me lose it.'

I saw him reach for the phone, dialling frantically, as I
retched and retched again.

I was loaded into a wheelchair, a blanket tucked around
my knees, and wheeled backwards into the waiting ambulance. I grabbed at the nurse's hand. 'Would you ring my
husband for me?' I pleaded. 'Tell him what's happened
and ask him to come?'

'Of course, of course.' He extricated his hand from
mine. 'I'll ring him now.'

One of the agency nurses came with me. She was
young with a round face and scraped back hair. She sat
at my side, picking her nails constantly and looking past
me at the bored ambulance man who'd clearly seen all this
before. I closed my eyes and feigned sleep. Even when the
wheelchair was bumped up the ramp and into A & E, and
I was transferred to a trolley, I didn't open them. I listened
to the nurse consulting with the A & E staff at the desk,
the whole time praying they'd hurry up and get on with
whatever jobs they needed to do. I started to feel nervous.
The corridor was busy with people rushing about. This
would be a close-run thing; Paul would be on his way to

the hospital, but I couldn't make a move, not yet. My heart bumped behind my ribcage as I gingerly opened my eyes and peered through the lashes. The round-faced nurse was sitting nearby; she'd found herself some garish T.V. Choice mag. She kept checking the main nurse's station and then looking back to the clock. Sighing, she chucked the magazine onto the desk.

'I need the loo,' she said to a porter with a trolley full of bed linen who was passing. 'Can you watch her a minute?'

He nodded but I could see he hadn't understood a word of what she said.

I waited for him to wander off with his load, then peeled back the blankets and sat up, pulling my clothes straight and following the nurse into the Ladies'.

There was no one else in there, just the sound of someone urinating very loudly. I slipped into the end cubicle and stood with the tiny phone, fumbling to send the text as the nurse came out to wash her hands. I didn't have long. I heard the main door to the toilet open and close. There were moments that felt like hours of silence, and then the cubicle beside me squealed and shunted.

'Are you there?' Moire's voice whispered and I nearly collapsed with relief as I undid the door.

'I'm here.'

Her face appeared. She handed me a bag and I pulled it open.

Inside was a change of clothes, a woollen dress, a pair of leggings, a denim jacket, and a baseball cap. 'CCTV won't be looking for these,' she grinned but then stopped as we heard the nurse outside, all panicked and high pitched. Moire's attention snapped back.

'Give it a couple of minutes. I've got a hire car, I couldn't risk my own. I'll bring it around to the exit barrier. Be as quick as you can.'

She pulled open the door and I could hear the massive commotion outside.

The young nurse was on her phone. As the door slowly closed, I saw Moire walking head down past them all and disappearing into a huddle of people.

Terror grabbed me. I darted into the cubicle and frantically pulled on the clothes. Paul couldn't be too far away. He would work this whole thing out. Once he heard I'd been admitted to hospital, he'd know the chances of me escaping were high. I had to *move*, and move fast.

The corridor was frantic with activity. No one noticed as I slipped through the door.

'The husband's just rung,' I heard one of them say. 'They've told him which department. He's on his way.'

That galvanised me. I quickened my pace, keeping my face hidden as I hurried to the automatic doors which shunted open bringing with them cold air and the glorious scent of diesel and traffic dirt, birds, trees – and there was Moire, just as she said she would be, even though I couldn't quite believe it: she was really, really there.

I dropped into the passenger seat, not daring to look round, hardly able to bring myself to look at her as she pulled carefully through the barrier and out onto the road.

'Paul's already at the hospital,' I said.

'I know,' she smiled round at me. 'But you're not, are you?'

'Thank you.' I breathed. 'Thank you for doing this.'

'So where now?'

She caught the look on my face.

'I don't know.' The realisation paralysed me. 'All I have are the clothes that you brought me. I don't have anything else. Not a thing.'

'So, if I take you back to the house, do you think you can find your bank cards and passport?' She shot me a glance.

The memory of it sent a blast of fear into my guts.

'I can't see any other way. You'll only have minutes, though. You'll need to be a long way away before he gets back.'

'I know, I know,' I said. Then I paused. 'Thank you, Moire. You're doing all this for me and I've no right to ask you for anything.'

She shook her head quickly and stared at the road ahead. 'I couldn't do it for Caitlin. She wouldn't let me. So I'm doing it for you.'

I pulled off the baseball cap and looked out of the window. The outline of Moire's face was reflected there, like a ghost. Here was another person I didn't know. All those things they told me about her. Was any of it true?

Outside the window, life looked ordinary. Women and men in hats and coats, muffled up against the cold. Babies being carried, little children in mittens and anoraks shouting.

'You know what today is?' The sound of her voice made me jerk round. I noticed her knuckles tightening and loosening on the wheel.

'No.'

'It's the anniversary of Caitlin's death,'

I was aware of the anger coming off her. Waves of it.

'My mother and I laid a single rose on each of the graves. Three little roses, red against the black earth, can you imagine that?'

The image, the horror of it floated in front of me.

'It happened in the early hours of Sunday morning. So every Sunday I made sure there was a rose delivered to his doorstep, so he knew I was always out there, watching him. I saw him pick it up that day you were with him at his flat.'

I thought of Paul and Caitlin, Caitlin and Moire, Moire and Paul – all their stories, told and re-told. Truth. Fiction. Who would ever know?

'He threw it into a bin. The rage I felt when I saw him do that; the absolute rage. I knew then that roses weren't enough.'

I looked at the side of her face and saw her fixed gaze: blank and steady.

'He said you had an affair with him. He said you'd become obsessed and you went to prison for stalking.'

She stared hard out at the road. 'He got me arrested and charged but the judge threw it out. I was obsessed. I wanted to prove he was lying. He told Cait I'd come on to him. Nothing was right between me and Cait after that. He'd used the ultimate weapon and he won.' She shot a look across. 'You do believe that, don't you?'

I watched the white lines on the road trammelling away under the wheels. 'Of course I do.'

What happened, what didn't happen, lies, truth, all re-invented, re-told, re-packaged. Whoever knows, really? Black becomes white and then becomes black again.

'We're almost there.' Moire turned into the street, my street, and the excitement grabbed me as though I was seeing it for the first time. There was the copper beech tree in its magnificent glory, its russet leaves quivering, waiting, its pull drawing me in. I remembered how much I loved this place. This was my home.

She stopped at the bottom of the drive. 'Five minutes,' she warned, looking anxiously about. 'I'm being serious. You've got five minutes.'

''ll be quick,' I promised.

I walked quickly up the path and a whole raft of memories flooded back: that first summer, the bees mumbling amongst the flowers; I could smell the heat of warmed grass and brick, and with it came a massive wave of sadness. This time the house was in darkness. The solid bay windows stood unseeing on either side of the beautiful front door, the one I knew I would never walk through again.

I slipped down the side path, peering into the windows, and round to the back. I knew exactly what I was going to do. Bending to pick up a stone, I slipped off my jacket, wrapped it quickly and struck the glass twice, hard. The pane shattered, the shards tinkling inside. Carefully knocking through the splinters, I reached into the gap and unlocked the door. My feet crunched, scattering the broken glass in all directions as I hurried through the kitchen and up the stairs. He had no idea I was coming so everything was where it should have been. This time everything was easy.

I ran down the stairs, my fingers flying, my heart skittering, still not quite comprehending that in minutes I'd be gone: I'd become invisible and disappear into some other life.

I headed for the front door. My phone began to ring wildly and I clutched at it, thinking it was Moire as a long shadow lengthened like a weird marionette at my feet. I spun round.

'Aren't you going to answer that?' Paul walked through the shadows. 'It could be someone who really needs to speak to you.'

I couldn't move.

'Like your new friend, maybe?'

The terror surged in my chest, high and pounding.

'I have to say, you do look shocked to see me.' He raised his eyebrows in query. 'Why's that?' he shrugged. 'You didn't really think I'd go to the hospital, did you? There seemed little point, I knew she'd bring you here.'

I had turned to stone.

'I've rung them, in case you were wondering.' He waved his phone. 'Your doctors were very concerned. They're coming to get you – Both of you, probably.' He looked round. 'Where is she, by the way?' He glanced back into the garden. 'You really are two sad people together aren't you? *Folie à deux*. A shared psychosis… Is she wondering where you've got to?' He regarded me, coolly. 'Why don't you tell her I'm here?'

He saw the track of my eyes past his shoulder to the open doorway and he glanced to follow my gaze.

'Why don't you tell her I'm on my own? You should invite her in. Let's expose the madness.'

'Why don't you tell me yourself?'

He hadn't seen Moire appear behind him. He hadn't been aware of her bending quietly, the muted light moving around her silhouette, to pick up a shard of glass.

But I had.

He turned his eyes to her bloodless face, her arm held high as she sliced once, then twice, the puncture of the gash in his shoulder blooming red against a sudden glare of sunlight. He flailed round, grabbing her by the throat and I watched his hands, so large against the slimness of her neck.

They dipped and whirled together as my mouth formed her name, watching her feet rising in the air, paddling like a mis-strung puppet. The shard tumbled as her arms thrashed wildly.

He put his face close to hers. 'I loved her... I adored her... She was my whole life, don't you fucking understand that?'

I saw his teeth were stained with blood as Moire's eyes rolled and flickered in fear.

'There never could be, there never would be, anyone else—'

Run! Her voice shrieked and wailed. *Run! Get out of here, Lucy! Just get out!*

But I didn't.

I don't remember what was in my mind as I stooped to pick up the triangle of glass. My palm felt its bite, my eyes saw it lift and glint as it told its own story. His white shirt was made crimson, and his white skin turned scarlet. There was blood... More blood than I had ever seen before – down his neck, his arms, his back. Red, and more red. He wheeled blindly in the spray, reaching around for the thing that was wounding him, panting like an animal, wide-eyed and gasping, the black 'O' of his mouth no more than a hole in his face. He paused, his eyes hard and unseeing, gazing off into some past or future that I was never part of, and then toppled like a dying giant, his head cushioned amongst the shining splinters.

It all went suddenly quiet.

Moire wasn't there anymore. The traffic outside began its pleasant rumbling, the birds started twittering but the room was still, only the drip of the tap *plink-plinked* against the enamel. I looked down and I saw that my dress had torn. The blood was seeping into the gashes like wounds. Around me, the glass lay like jewels on a seashore, shifting a little and glittering in its ruby gore. I was strangely at peace.

'*Roisin! Eloise!*'

I looked round.

'*Where are you?*'

A little girl ran past the door, she was no more than three years old, I caught the blur of her as she passed.

'*Don't go too far!*'

I heard their excited giggling and I went to look. A tiny girl stood outside, chubby on her fat legs. She wobbled a little, with one finger in her mouth.

'Lucy?'

Moire was beside me, I was aware of the strength in her hands as she took my arm. 'My god, are you hurt? Come and sit.'

'No, I'm not hurting anymore at all,' I said.

My legs took me to the stone bench without my asking as we followed the sound of their laughter.

'*We're playing hiding,*' said a tiny voice beside me. I looked round. The other child was pretty, too; she had her mother's dark curls. She came forward shyly, and took Roisin's hand. '*We like it here.*'

I looked around me as though for the first time. It was madness: all crazily wild and tangled, not like the garden as I remembered it, nothing like it at all. A cold breeze rippled the wet wool of my dress, sending a quiet shiver of comfort down my spine.

'You can't hide in here forever you know.'

I heard the soft Irish lilt of her tone. Her hand covered mine. She sounded so much like Moire.

We both heard the soft crackle of tyres on the driveway.

'I think it's time we should be going, don't you? Come on.'

'Going?'

I don't think so. Once I'd told them, once I explained what really happened, I knew they would understand. They have to be stopped: the Paul Webb's in the world, the Simon Gould's, all those kinds of men. I did it because I had to. It was the only way.

I closed my eyes into the slipping sun and the world behind my lids burned purple and orange: the colours of dignity and fire.

'I think I'd rather stay,' I said. 'After all, this is my home.'

I opened my eyes. There was a sudden shattering brilliance: an explosion of white and gold radiating into an incandescence of dying sunlight, a family of us bound together: me and Moire, Caitlin and the children. And all I could see were stars.

A Letter From Elena

Thank you so much for choosing to read *The Man I Married*. If you have any thoughts, I would love to hear them via a review on the site where you purchased the book, or on Goodreads.

The Man I Married is a psychological thriller and essentially a piece of fiction, however at its core is a terrifying reality. I spent eighteen years working in H.M. Prisons. One of the prisoners I met there was serving a Life sentence for the murder of his wife and children. He was well-educated, friendly, and polite, with a good sense of humour. He was the kind of man you could have met in numerous social situations and thought he was a decent guy. Generally, life sentences don't mean whole life. One day this man would walk free. He would be at liberty to meet people: in bars, in clubs, in restaurants, and tell them whatever story he chose about his past.

So that begs the question: how much do we know about anyone really? Generally, we don't ask for proof of the things that people divulge about themselves. The stories we share are exactly that: created tales that are, for the most part, innocent enough – an exaggeration here and an embellishment there. But what of those people who take that one step further? These are the people who intrigue me and who I write about: the mad, the bad, and the dangerous to know. These are the people who walk amongst us. They appear ordinary, not very different from us at all, but when you scratch a little deeper, you discover they hold some very dark and dangerous secrets.

Get in touch with me via Twitter or Facebook:

www.facebook.com/elenawilkesthrillers
www.twitter.com/elenathrillers

Acknowledgments

Writers know how difficult the writing journey is. *The Man I Married* has been through a very turbulent and sometimes terrifying sea of evolution, but finally, *finally*, it has come out the other side. I am so grateful to the people who, directly or indirectly, have helped me get to publication.

It's a massive, massive thank you to Keshini Naidoo and Lindsey Mooney and the team at Hera Books. It's been a brilliant experience from beginning to end. I can't say enough good things about them. What a team!

In terms of my writing gang, the first person I have to thank is the amazing Amy Beashel – my friend and plotting partner for the last four years. Thank you, Amy, for all the breakfasts and brunches and the calm and considered critiques. You're truly a shining star.

Susie Basset. I know that somehow our paths were always destined to cross. Your friendship and support has meant the world to me. Karen Porteous, my partner in 'Crime' and co-conspirator. We're in this together, girl.

To the wonderful Janie and Mickey Wilson at Chez Castillon Writing retreat. It's impossible to define what you provide, but whatever it is, feels like pure magic. Thank you to Katie Fforde, Jo Thomas, Judy Astley, and Litty Williams. Your help, support, and guidance that fateful week at Chez Castillon changed the course of my writing life.

Thank you also to the people who have continued to encourage me through the years: my sisters, Julie and Tina, my oldest family friends Annie Smith, Rebecca Smith, and Joan Owen, and my lovely far-flung friends in New Zealand, Liz Hume and Christine Dickinson.

Most of all, I have to say thank you to my husband Ian for all the support and inspiration, and without whom this book really wouldn't have been possible.